THE FERRYMAN & THE FLAME
SURRENDER
BOOK ONE

THE FERRYMAN & THE FLAME
SURRENDER

BOOK ONE

RHIANNON PAILLE

To Mitch,
And so it begins!
Remember — I
will BETA read
for you!
RM Paille

WordFire Press
Colorado Springs, Colorado

ISBN: 978-1-61475-181-6

Cover Design by Mae I Design

Interior Art by Linn Borsheim

Map by Christopher Boll

Book Design by RuneWright, LLC
www.RuneWright.com

Published by
WordFire Press, an imprint of
WordFire, Inc.
PO Box 1840
Monument, CO 80132

Kevin J. Anderson & Rebecca Moesta, Publishers

WordFire Press Trade Paperback Edition May 2014
Printed in the USA
www.wordfirepress.com

ACKNOWLEDGMENTS

WordFire Press is pleased to be the new publisher of The Ferryman & The Flame series, but would like to include the author's original acknowledgments to recognize all those who helped build this series from scratch.

Kevin J. Anderson
Publisher

I thought publishing a book was easy—until I did it. What I've learned about myself from publishing is that I'm a spazz case, control freak and perfectionist. I feel like most of the people I need to thank on this list I also need to apologize to, for all my author craziness.

A.P. Fuchs, Jennifer Laughran, and Natasha Heck, I have no idea how you put up with all my incessant e-mails or how you managed to encourage me to stick with it even when my whole world was a boatload of no.

Sue Dawe, I don't know how to thank you enough for being honest with me and telling me not to Tolkienshire it up. It's because of you that I have avoided many lawsuits.

Marc Wolfe, I don't know what it is about your artistic vision but without it, I don't think anyone would have gotten Kaliel and Krishani's likeness. It's like you took them directly out of my head and put them on paper and they look like real people, real non human people.

Primo Cardinalli and Hugh Rookwood, your illustrations were incredibly on point and accurate to the characters. I seemed to give you an idea and you ran with it, again, taking what was in my head and putting it on paper in ways I never could.

Tommy Castillo, for the painting that looked like it was something Michaelangelo painted five hundred years ago. That will always be my classic version of the Ferryman + the Flame and I don't know how to tell you how much I will always love it.

Christopher Boll, I know you're not a map maker anymore, but you certainly did a fantastic job on my map.

Regina Wamba, you fantastic lady you! We had a short deadline, not a lot of options, a whole lot of stubbornness on my side, and you managed to make me a cover that I can't stop staring at, it's sooo pretty!

Cory Putman Oakes, Evie Seo, Lucy D'Andrea, Molli Moran, Kathy Habel, Rachel Rivera, Sammie Spencer, Susan Haugland, Laura Kreitzer, Marie De La Rosa, and well the endless list of bloggers I'm forgetting to mention personally, thank you so much for your constant support and encouragement. I would have given up if it weren't for people like you.

Rae Smith and Sabina Grosse, you two have been my little secret weapons, BETA reading well into the night and finishing my books in record time. I'm so glad I have written books that you ladies cannot put down. Thank you both for being there for me.

Lastly, you may have noticed I dedicated this book to Michael, because without him I wouldn't be writing.

Rhiannon Paille

Contents

LANDS ACROSS THE STARS

ZAN - ZANANDIR
NAZ - NAZOLE
TAL - TALANISDIR
CAM - CAM'WETHRIN
ANG - ANGRENOTH
TER - TERRA/EARTH
NIM - NIMPHALLS

AVRISTAR
LANDS OF MEN

NIM
TER

THE GREAT HALL

CAM
ANG

ZAN
NAZ
TAL

AVRIGOST
LAND OF THE DEAD

AVRISTYR
LANDS OF BEASTS

AVRIGARD
LANDS OF IMMORTALS

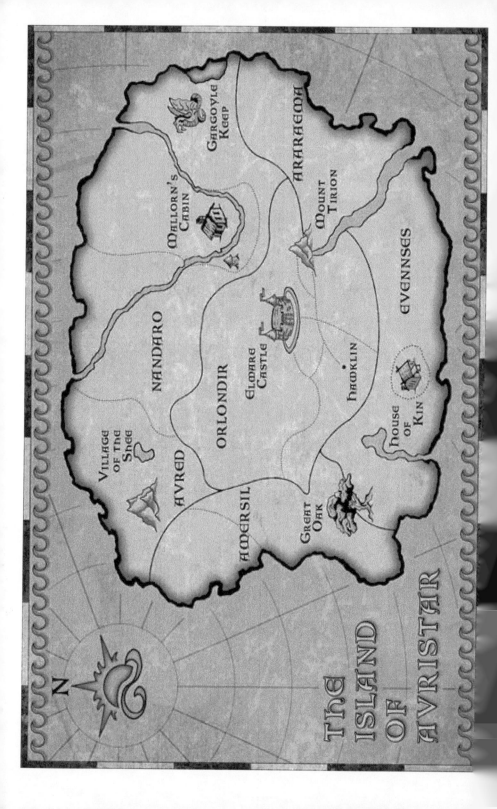

N

The ISLAND OF AVRISTAR

0–THE GREAT LIBRARY

Secrets never stay hidden forever.

Kemplan sat in front of the fireplace watching salamanders dance among the flames. His eyelids were droopy, and he needed sleep. He drifted, then shot up, realizing he needed to add another log to the fire. He pushed off the old leather chair with the high back and waddled over to the stack of logs. He picked one up with his chubby hands, removed the gold fence surrounding the fire, and threw it on top of the other logs. The new log was instantly devoured by the flames. He smiled and turned towards his chair.

There, perched on the bottom cushion was a piece of parchment. Kemplan glanced into the skies of the library, the ceiling too high to see due to the shadows collecting above him. Kemplan gawked at the parchment. Never in all his time had a page appeared like that. He waddled over to the chair and delicately grasped the parchment.

He turned it over and inspected at the images before him. A Ferryman perched on a throne, wearing the royal colors of black and gold—across from him—a Flame. They gazed upon each other with a look that meant one thing—soul mates. Kemplan blinked and shook his head. He wanted to shove the parchment back into the high shelf it had come from. Memories clouded his mind as he revisited the past he barely survived. He nervously cleared his throat, clenched his fist. There weren't many things in the Great Library that were forbidden, but this was one of them.

Kemplan dared a peek at it in the hopes he had been hallucinating, but the parchment was unchanged. The sun showered them in golden beams of light. Two ankhs, shaped like crosses with hoops at the top, hung at the edges of the beams of light, a symbol of their importance to the Lands Across the Stars. Kemplan knew which Ferryman and which Flame these were, the only two that had ever met, Krishani Mekallow Mekelle of Terra, and Kaliel, The Amethyst Flame, her name burned into her very soul by the enemies she defeated.

Kemplan scoffed and threw the parchment on the chair. He paced the small embroidered rug, wringing his hands out. He was afraid to look at it anymore, afraid of what horrendous things would prick his mind. He balled up his fists; glancing at the parchment each time he turned.

After a few paces stared the parchment down, crossed the floor, seized it, and tossed it into the fire. He tried not to watch as the flames licked away the edges of it. He knew it wouldn't burn easily.

Kemplan expected to find it devoured, but instead he was met with staggering symbols that appeared overtop of the images. His stomach lurched, the message too blatant to mistake—infinity. He fell on his back and mouthed the word 'no'. Scrambling backwards, he tried to put as much distance between himself and that vile thing defying the fire.

A deafening screech erupted from the fireplace and Kemplan instinctively brought his hands to his ears, trying to dull the sound. He closed his eyes seeing nothing but fire. He wanted to escape the past but memories came on hot and strong. As he blinked he saw a flash of his wife, charred. He begged not to see the images of his children, his house, his life, but whether he recalled them or not, they were emblazoned on his mind.

He would never forget.

He let out a gasp and looked at the fireplace. It crackled like it was about to explode. He rolled over and squeezed his eyes shut. Chaos. His life had become nothing but chaos. He let out a whimper as crippling sadness rippled through him. He could never have that life back. He would always be trapped in the Great Library, and it would always be their fault.

He closed his eyes, trying to force the images away. He remembered the words of High King Tor, 'It was said long ago that one of the Flames would fulfill a great prophecy.'

Kemplan snarled. Precious but dangerous, the Flames were never to be trusted. Life was better when they were hidden. He couldn't believe High King Tor would return them to the Lands Across the Stars—especially not her, The Amethyst Flame. And yet the parchment was clear, Kaliel would return, as would the Ferryman, and no doubt by some grand accident they would meet.

He gritted his teeth and waited for the fire to explode, hoping it would erase him from existence for good. A dead calm washed through the Great Library as darkness covered him. Smoke rose from the fireplace and Kemplan sat up. He pawed through the smoke to where the parchment was, glowing, unburned. He stifled his disgust but his heart dropped, the symbol for the Isle of Avristar appearing overtop of the infinity symbol.

And so it begins, he thought bitterly.

This is the legend of The Ferryman and the Flame.

1-SAMHAIN

The merfolk were dangerous. Everyone on Avristar knew that. The kinfolk stayed away from the lake and the mists that curled around them, concealing the island from the Lands of Men. Avristar was safely tucked away from the humans and their wars, but the merfolk gravitated to the shores, living in an underwater paradise below the island. They slid their slick black bodies through the cracks in the rocks and pooled forth into the chasm underneath the mountain. There were stories about them finding their way to the surface, but the stories were centuries old. Fear flooded the kinfolk and forced them away.

Krishani shifted his weight on the stone platform behind the forbidden falls and peered out from sheets of water blocking the entrance to the cave. The falls were on the south side of Mount Tirion, and they were off limits. Krishani narrowed his gaze at the banks of the pond, his heart thudding. A girl kneeled on the edge, her white hair cascading down her back in curls and waves, her pasty hands pressed against the ledge. She peered into the depths of the pond. He never saw anyone do that before and it made him nervous. He was brave enough to ignore the elders when they said not to travel to the waterfall. When he was forced to be in the royal city of Orlondir for the Fire Festivals he preferred the cave behind the falls over the dancing girls, the hairy feorns and the sparring matches.

He slid a fraction of an inch down the stone as the girl backed away from the ledge and a fin on top of a smooth black head bobbed along the surface. The girl ran her hands through her hair, trying to push it away from her face, and for a second Krishani thought she might be scared. He was. He pressed his back against the stone behind him, and let out a deep breath. The merfolk pushed its head through the white tufts of foam forming on the surface. And then everything moved too quickly. Krishani blinked and heard a loud splash. When he looked, the girl who had been clothed in an ivory maiden's gown was naked. He tore his gaze away, but the image was already imprinted on his mind. It made warm tingles run down his torso and he clenched his stomach muscles in response, trying to control himself. He never cared about the girls from Araraema or Evennses, and he especially felt nothing for the feorns. He heard another splash and when he dared a glance back at the banks she was gone.

His pulse quickened as he thought about removing his cloak and diving into the pond after her. Nervousness washed over him, his pulse pounding in his ears. To grasp her, pull her out, touch her skin, it made him crazy.

He slid further down the stone stairway in an attempt to get a better look. There was nothing floating along the surface of the water. He needed to know if she was going to be okay. He also needed to know why she was being so stupid, but that was something he wasn't brave enough to ask. He wasn't even supposed to talk to her or watch her or near her. He was supposed to be at the Elmare Castle eating pheasant and apple pie while keeping to his own with the Brotherhood.

Still, he kept staring at the pond, waiting for her strands of white hair to graze the surface. It took too long. He frowned at the waters, and took a deep breath. Flashes of nightmares raced behind his eyes. He promised himself he would forget about those. He had suffered from nightmares for as long as he could remember. Nobody knew about them, not even his elder, Adoron of Amersil. He was too afraid to admit he dreamt of death all the time.

Krishani sucked in a breath as he caught sight of white hair on the surface. He realized that if he didn't move quickly she would see him, and he would see her—again. He clambered up the stony incline and peered over his shoulder as he reached the platform behind the falls. She had her dress on and was wringing her hair out over the falls. He smirked; she would be in a lot of trouble if the elders knew what she was doing. Then again, he would be in trouble too if they knew he was planning on spending the night in the cave. He barely got away with it last time.

Being rebellious didn't come naturally to Krishani; it was something that seemed to follow him around. He envied his brothers with their sharp combat skills, elemental manipulation and pure knowledge. They were probably the smartest kinfolk on Avristar. All of them destined for greatness, all of them expected to go to the Lands of Men across the lake.

Krishani was unsure about his own greatness. Even though the Great Oak had given him a promising parable, he wasn't sure he'd live up to it. The Great Oak was the oldest tree on Avristar, its wisdom beyond measure.

Adoron seemed to believe Krishani was a warrior, but Krishani didn't really feel like one. Keeping up with the brotherhood had proven difficult at best.

The girl ran her fingers through her knots of hair. He leaned forward to get a better look at her. She was petite, the ivory dress hugging her body in a very flattering way. Her skin was a soft pasty white. He desperately wanted to know more about her. She was the first thing that left him stunned and mesmerized, heart thumping and palms sweaty. His mouth dropped open involuntarily as he stared at her, watching her thin fingers caress her hair like a harp. He wanted to spend all day speculating about who she might be, where she might be from, and what she might be destined for. She looked old enough to have been to the Great Oak, to know her parable and station in life. It had to be better than his. He didn't really understand the armies of Avristar and their battles in the Lands of Men. He didn't like the idea of being a pawn. He was barely good with a sword, let alone hand to hand combat. No, he wanted to forget all about the brotherhood, his destiny and his nightmares.

All he really wanted to do was talk to her.

Before he had a chance to back away and hide, fall into the ranks of duty and push the thought aside, she looked at him. Bright emerald green eyes caught his and widened. Her hands dropped from her hair and nervously ran along the hem of her dress. She chewed on her lip and dug her toe into the ground.

Krishani gulped and forced himself away from the girl, retreating into the cave. His breathing heavy and ragged, he tried to calm down

7

enough to believe this wasn't happening. She wouldn't come looking for him, she wouldn't confront him. He didn't know how to talk to a girl; he had never done it before. He held his breath as he crouched in the shadows and waited for her to leave.

• • •

It was the pressure and the lack of air that made swimming in the pond scary, not the stories about the merfolk dragging unsuspecting kinfolk to the bottom. The merfolk were actually gentle creatures, cooing and floating around her, pulling at Kaliel's hands and wondering at her differences. She wasn't sure what to expect from Orlondir, the royal city of Avristar. In Evennses the lake was an hour walk from the House of Kin and the beach was blocked by trees. The trees never let the kinfolk see the lake, let alone swim in the waters. They had the creek for that.

She shook her head, disappointed she hadn't been able to touch the bottom of the pond. It made her curious, the lake, the pond, the waterfall. She knew all the familiar stories, the ones about the dangerous merfolk, the ones about the tarnished Lands of Men across the lake. She heard stories of the mists, the protective shield that turned the lake into an endless sea. There was no coming or going from Avristar without an ancient incantation. At fourteen, Kaliel was nowhere near old enough to know it; the most she knew was land magic. And she was bad at it.

Without the threat of danger in Avristar it was hard to imagine anything lethal in the waters, across the waters, in the pond. Still, her elders seemed vexed by the merfolk. It might have been beginner's luck, but she found them tame and playful.

She worked her fingers through her hair and a prickly feeling washed over her. She glanced at the falls and saw them—eyes watching her, one blue and one green. The rest of their form was masked by a black cloak, and it disappeared behind the falls as quickly as it had appeared. Self-consciousness made her cheeks turn pink as she left her wet hair and went to climb the stony stairway.

Her slippers fought to grip the rocks and she had to use her hands to pull herself up and across the platform behind the falls. Nobody was there. She frowned and crossed to the cliff on the other edge. She glanced down, seeing sand and the outlines of vegetation.

"Pux?" she called. He was the feorn friend that had told her about the waterfall. She thought he went back to the castle already. She also thought she was alone when she decided to strip naked and swim with the merfolk. Her knuckles turned white against the stone as she gripped it hard, fear ripping through her at the thought of the eyes. She scanned the ground one more time and decided she imagined it. As she rose to her feet and turned, a scream erupted from her lips. She grabbed the clammy stone wall beside her and cursed her luck.

Whoever it was stood on the opposite edge of the platform, blocking her only escape.

"You shouldn't be here," he said, his voice deep and full of alarm.

She tried to find her feet as her head swelled with dizziness, her cheeks flushing. Mist drenched her, creating water spots across her ivory dress. She tried to find her confidence, but the bravery she had earlier drained away. Her knees felt weak.

"Was it you?" she asked, her voice ripping through the air like a ghost.

He froze, didn't say anything for a long time, which made her heart hammer even harder in her chest. "I saw you in the pond."

She gripped the stone harder. "How much did you see?" She thought nobody ever came to the waterfall, that she could keep her curiosity to herself. She thought she could avoid the hard stares of the elders, but this made her fainter by the second. Not knowing who he was, not knowing what he wanted, it left her trapped in limbo.

"I saw you wring your hair out," he said.

She exhaled loudly and pushed herself off the stone. She found her balance even if she had to keep her hand planted against the wall to do it. She waited for him to move, but he stood there like a statue. Nervousness flitted through her.

"I should return, Elder." She stammered on the last word, knowing that saying it would make it true, but she had no choice. He probably *was* an elder and she was probably in a lot of trouble.

He didn't move.

She felt worse. "Do you want to take me back to the castle?" There was something belittling about being carted around red-handed. "I thought I was alone." Her shoulders shook.

9

He buried his face in the rocks and pressed himself against the smooth stone. "You weren't alone." His voice was thick and almost rude.

She frowned as she neared him. "I know."

"And I'm not an elder," he added.

"Oh." The guilt waned a little. It was really hard to tell with his height and the cloak concealing every part of him. "Then who are you?" She stood behind him, feeling the heat radiating off his features.

"Does it matter? It's not like I'm going to tell anyone," he snapped.

His words stung. She opened her mouth ready to fire something vile back at him, but closed it, her thoughts circling around nothing that would hurt as much.

"Goodnight," she forced, trying to make the pleasant sound of her voice as unpleasant as possible. She went to descend the stone incline and forgot it was slippery.

"Wait," he said.

She turned and her foot slid on the frictionless rock; she careened towards the pond. Her heart wildly pounded in her chest as her arms flailed, trying to find something to hold onto. She couldn't believe she was having a clumsy moment right then and there. Her cheeks turned bright red as she thought of tumbling down the rocks and splashing into the pond. And then there were arms circling her waist and warm fabric against her smooth skin; her body pressed against something hard. She felt disoriented and elated all at once. A hand slid into hers and warmth was replaced by cold. Her stomach did flip-flops as she thought of pressing herself against the warmth again.

"Maybe I should take you back to the castle," he grumbled, his voice gruff.

She opened her eyes and found herself perched on the stone incline, mismatched eyes knifing into hers, his hand still curled around her fingers. He squeezed them hard, trying to keep her in place. He sounded annoyed with her, but his expression said it was all concern. Her eyes hardened as his words sunk in.

"Who are you?" she demanded.

He let go and retreated behind the falls. She almost fell on her knees, but found the wall and scaled across the stone incline. She paused at the edge of the platform and peered into the cave; it was something she hadn't noticed before. She crossed her arms and glowered at him. "I'm not leaving until you tell me who you are."

He pushed the hood off his face, revealing long locks of jet-black hair, a sharp narrow face, high cheekbones and ghostly white skin. Her knees trembled as he stared at her, clearly mesmerized.

"Stop looking at me like that," she said quietly as her eyes hit the ground.

"You first. Who are you and why haven't I seen you before?" He pushed his hands into his sleeves and gripped his elbows.

She shook her head in disbelief, looking for some excuse to avoid the question. Defeated, she gulped, digging her toe into the stone. "Kaliel of Evennses," she muttered, curling a strand of hair behind an elongated ear.

He continued staring at her. "Aren't you old enough to come to the Fire Festivals?"

She raised an eyebrow and thought back to her home, an exasperated sigh escaping her lips. "Old enough ... but um ..." She cast around for a way to explain that she was always tardy for her lessons, always botched assignments and was never where she was supposed to be. Pux was worse; the elders spent more time chasing after him, but she wasn't any better.

He folded his arms against his chest. "Don't tell me you're always like that."

She furrowed her brow and shot him a look. "Always like what?"

"Endangering yourself?" He almost smirked, but his lips spread into a straight line and he nodded towards the waterfall.

She looked at the ground, her cheeks turning pink even though she didn't want them to. She was about to answer him when she realized all of this was avoidance. She pulled her arms tighter across her chest and stood up straight, making direct eye contact with him. It made the butterflies return, but she tried to shush them with her will power. "You still haven't told me who you are."

He shifted away from her. For a second she thought he was going to dive into the waterfall, but he stopped and dropped his arms to his sides. "Krishani of Amersil."

That wasn't something she expected. It made her lips twitch into a frown as he put more distance between them, another step back, and what seemed like the length of a field. If there was anything she knew about Avristar it was that Amersil was full of the handpicked apprentices of the land. They were able to command the elements, move mountains with their mind, make rain, manipulate fire. Most of the other kinfolk listened intently to stories of their greatness. They were private, and aloof. The worst part of it was they knew they were better than everyone else, and they constantly reminded everyone about it with their ignorance.

"Oh," she said.

His expression changed. It was like he was testing her reaction, his eyes bashful and embarrassed. She didn't have anything else to say so she just stared at him, curiosity and intrigue crossing her face. Moments passed, their eyes lost in a lock, and then he let out a sigh and turned towards the falls.

"You haven't heard of Amersil have you?"

She frowned. "Yes I have." She dropped her hands to her side and began rolling up the hem of her dress.

"Then you should know the stories." There was something tortured behind his words. She uncrossed her arms and pushed off the stone.

She shrugged. "You're not like the stories."

He turned back, a smile creeping across his lips. "Is that what you told yourself about the merfolk?"

She shrugged again. "They're not like the stories, either."

He moved closer. "You're lucky to be alive."

She twisted her hands together, pressing them against her knees. She felt nauseous, something gnawing at her gut. The words struck a chord with her, but she couldn't figure out why. She tucked a strand of hair behind her ear. "Is that why you were watching me?"

He turned green. "Um ..." His cheeks flared a pinkish color and he ran a hand through his hair. His eyes couldn't lie: they were full of concern. "Morbid curiosity," he muttered, trying to force a smirk, but he looked like he wanted to vomit. "At least someone could tell the elders what happened if ..."

She put a hand around her neck and let out a short breath. "You mean if I turned up dead?" That was more unheard of on Avristar than war. She regretted it the moment she said it.

He shook his head and passed her, clambering down the incline. "Yeah, that." He reached the bottom and went for the break in the trees. She slid down the rock as quickly as she could and grabbed his shoulders, pulling him away from the path.

"I'm sorry," she squeaked, silently begging him to stay. "I won't go back in the water if you don't want me to." Her voice cracked as urgency fled through her. She felt hot, like her entire body was pulsating with fire.

He turned, his fingers entwining with hers, his eyes working their way over her body, making her feel naked again. Tingles spread through her chest and for a second she thought she would pass out

He glanced at the waterfall and slid away from her. She let out a breath as he passed.

"Can I show you something?" He climbed the stone behind her and moved towards the falls.

She frowned, but followed him back to the platform. She pressed her shoulder against the rock as she watched him push his hands together, take deep breaths and plant his feet on the stone. She cocked her head to the side as his cloak fluttered open, revealing a cream-colored tunic, leather belt and black breeches. She hadn't noticed how lean he was with the bulky cloak in the way. She choked on her breath and coughed.

He glanced at her and worry streaked his face. "You need to close your eyes."

She raised an eyebrow, but did as she was told, the magnitude of his presence only stronger when she couldn't see him. She could feel him better, his unstable energy, his mismatched eyes, his strong hands and lanky frame. It was hard not to think about the warmth he emitted when he touched her.

Moments passed with her eyes closed, her thoughts drifting to the Elmare Castle, to Pux and Luenelle and her elder Desaunius. She would be in a lot of trouble if she got caught. She twisted her toe in the ground, uncertainty coursing through her. She knew the merfolk were dangerous, but she swam with them anyway and someone had seen her. Part of her wondered if he would tell the elders. There was the gnawing feeling in her gut that what she did now would color what the Great Oak would say to her when she went back to Evennses. She was nearly old enough to hear the words of the ancient tree.

"Kaliel?" Krishani asked.

Her eyes snapped open and she was met with a handful of ice, a smooth round ball attached to his hand. Her mouth hung open. It stung as she ran her fingers along it, breathing over it, causing the top layer to turn to water. She drew her fingers underneath it, separating it from his frozen hand, and tremors moved through her. It was the most amazing thing she had ever seen anyone do in her life.

"It's so cold," she whispered, her eyes meeting his. They seemed far away, dull and exhausted. He dropped onto one knee and winced.

It was her turn to feel concerned. "Are you okay?" She cradled the orb in one hand and put her hand on his shoulder. He shook his head while gasping for breath.

"I've never … tried something like that." His hands fell to his lap, his head drooping towards the stone.

"Why would you try now?" she blurted, and regretted it. She tried to withstand the coldness of the ice, but she put the orb on the ground, her hand numb.

He shook his head and tried to stand. "It's you, you're …" He moved to his feet and pulled his hands into his cloak. He looked away as she let her hand linger on his cloaked forearm.

She didn't know what to say. The ice continued to melt away at her feet and he was the most confusing person she had ever met. "Is that why you were so harsh?"

"We're not allowed to speak to outsiders."

Nervous attraction raced through her as she pulled her hand away and dropped her gaze to the stony ground. "Then, why me?"

He looked at her briefly, his expression unreadable. He pushed past her, descending the incline. "I'm only an apprentice." He turned the corner and disappeared through the trees.

She picked up the orb and ran after him. "Wait!"

He stopped, his expression mangled.

"Will I ever see you again?" she asked.

"Probably not." He turned, the cloak billowing around him as he stalked away. She watched him until he was nothing but a shadow amidst the trees and sunk into the dirt, burying her face in her hands. A hollow feeling spread through her as the orb slid into the mud, melting at her side.

"Farewell," she whispered as the first signs of dawn erupted over the horizon. She glanced up and a sticky feeling raced through her.

They had been there all night. She sighed and picked up what was left of the orb, trudging along the path, loathing the punishment she would endure for her mischief.

2-Mischief

Thick forest vegetation surrounded the trees as Kaliel traipsed along the thin, winding path. There wasn't a lot of space between the trees and shrubs that dotted the south side of the mountain, but it provided a sense of comfort. She was well-covered; not many of the kinfolk were brave enough to trespass for all sorts of reasons. Maybe nobody would catch her after all. She smiled to herself as the path curved around a patch of ferns and trees dropped away, giving more room for shrubbery. She neared hedges on the side of the main road into Orlondir. They didn't have a lot of roads; the only ones thick enough for carts were the ones from the three provinces of Avristar—Evennses in the south, Amersil in the west and Araraema in the east.

Kaliel ducked behind the pristinely trimmed hedges. She peered over them on her tiptoes and breathed a sigh of relief. No one was stalking the grounds. Desaunius wasn't standing on the moat with her arms crossed, pacing back and forth like Kaliel had imagined. All she had to do was cross the bridge and push open the big heavy doors and she'd be inside the courtyard.

She pushed through the hedge, careful to conceal the orb. She quickened her pace and skipped over the bridge, glancing over the railing at the fishes and swans. Her frail hands pushed against the big doors and even though it took a lot of force, she managed to get them open wide enough so she could slide her body through. The courtyard was empty. Trellises crawled along the walls and statues adorned the walkways. Kaliel moved to the archway leading into the Grand Hall.

Beyond the archway were two wide staircases, one leading to the west, the other to the east. Ahead of her was the continuous creamy marble floor that stretched across the hall and curled around a fountain in the center. A glamorous chandelier of glowing crystals hung above the fountain, while water trickled off of lily pad-shaped sheaths into the pool below. It always made her breath catch, being the most sophisticated room in all of Avristar. In the dawn light the hall was empty. She crept up the staircase to the west and passed the large double doors to the library. About halfway down the corridor she reached the tiny hallway that led to the individual rooms for the kinfolk.

She almost jumped out of her skin as she turned the corner and saw a figure standing in the shadows. A hand flew to her mouth to stifle a scream and the figure moved, showing themselves. She almost let out a growl.

"What are you doing there?" she whispered.

Pux—with his hairy face, vest, and animal legs clad in knee length breeches—frowned at her. "Where have you been all night?"

Kaliel glanced at the floor and took a deep breath. "At the waterfall."

Pux seemed frightened. "Why would you stay there?"

Kaliel sighed. He showed her where the waterfall was, but he never expected her to like it. He was so afraid of water he wanted her to go there and draw it for him in her journal. She could see from his expression he had stayed up all night waiting for her to return. "Sorry," she muttered.

Pux smiled. "Never mind it." He looped his arm through hers. "Come on, you can sit on my cot and tell me all about it." He pulled her down the hallway, but Kaliel froze, remembering what had happened.

"I'm really tired. Can we talk about it later?"

Pux sighed. "Okay," he said. "Besides, you do look terrible."

Kaliel self-consciously lifted a hand to her cheek and shook her head. "Does it look like I've been anywhere?" She feared Desaunius noticing all the subtle differences in her appearance: splotchy cheeks, bags under her eyes, disheveled hair.

Pux inspected her, brushing a leaf out of her hair. "Try to sleep late then. They'll be awake soon and I'll distract them while you try not to look like you've spent the night in the bush."

She gave him a half-smile. "Gee thanks." He looped his arm through hers again and pulled her down the hallway to one of the six doors along it.

"Goodnight, milady," Pux said. He tipped an imaginary hat as he opened the door for her and ushered her into the empty room. Kaliel half expected Desaunius to be sitting on the stool in front of the bureau, but it was empty. She let out a breath as she passed Pux and moved towards the cot. He swept around her and pulled back the quilt. Kaliel gave him a wistful look as she slid onto the cot and let him cover her with the blanket.

"Sleep well." He winked as he bounded towards the door.

She laughed; it was always like that with Pux—playful and carefree. He paused at the doorway to look at her and she slumped into the pillow and squeezed her eyes shut.

"Goodnight!" she whispered loudly as she heard the door close.

Once he was gone, she let out a sigh and opened her eyes only to trace the patterns in the wooden beams above her. It was really hard not to think about what Krishani had said to her, and worse than that was the way he made her feel. She winced as she shifted and pulled out what was left of the orb of ice.

She rotated it in her hands, over and over again, repeating the conversation in her head. Krishani really wasn't like the rest of them and that made her feel warm and tingly. She put the orb of ice on the blanket and let it soak into the quilt while she folded her hands across her lap. The Fire Festival was over; this was their last night in Orlondir. In the morning she would be going back to Evennses. She wasn't even sure if she would be back for Beltane. With so many other kinfolk it was more likely someone else would go. She sighed as she realized he was right.

She probably wouldn't see him again.

Not even if she wanted to.

• • •

Krishani glanced back at the Elmare Castle in the distance, its turrets glimmering against the sunset. The Brotherhood was on their way back to Amersil, already past the apple orchards. It was customary for the Brotherhood to stay after the Fire Festival; being part of the winner's circle entitled them to a final feast with Lord Istar and Lady Atara, the appointed sovereigns of Avristar. Krishani had slogged through the meal, not really enjoying the sparkling water and honey-crusted quail. He had pushed a lump of bread through the sauce as he tried to make it look like he was eating. It wasn't like he wasn't used to seeing girls. He saw them all the time at the festivals—elvens with fiery or chestnut hair, feorns with trimmed facial hair, even fae folk with shimmering skin and glass-like faces. The problem was he never met anyone like Kaliel. It wasn't about her beauty; everyone on Avristar was beautiful. Well, maybe not the feorns, but the elvens and fae were breathtaking. It was more about her disposition. She was curious and naïve and it made him worry about her. He never worried about anyone he lived with; all of the brothers were independent, even scary at times considering the things they could do.

She didn't have an air of arrogance about her, not at all. It was refreshing compared to the way he was ogled by the girls from Evennses and Araraema—not in a romantic sense; they were just awed by his very presence and often tripped over their words when talking at him. He never said anything, never even bothered to make eye contact with them.

But he saw Kaliel, in a way he'd never really seen anyone else in his life.

"What has you deep in thought?" Benir asked as he stepped into line with Krishani. The forests were drab, trees thickening around them as the path narrowed towards Amersil. Adoron led the brotherhood at the head of the pack with his staff in hand. It was carved with symbols that signified his triumphs. He had too many of them to count. Krishani glanced at Benir; the elven had blue eyes and tousled dirty blonde hair that he kept pushing out of his eyes. Benir might have been a couple of summers younger than Krishani, but he had more skill.

Krishani shook his head. "It's nothing."

Benir sighed. "Another year over."

Krishani grimaced and then smiled at Benir. "Another year of triumphs." He tried not to sound disgruntled. It was more triumphs for the rest of the brotherhood, but sometimes they didn't notice that Krishani never won.

Benir beamed. "And more tales to tell in the Lands of Men!"

Knots formed in Krishani's stomach as he thought of the nightmares, the endless sea of deaths that plagued his dreams. "Aye, the Lands of Men." He pushed his hands into the wide sleeves of his cloak.

"Zulnas will take his last rite soon," Benir continued.

Krishani didn't like Zulnas. He was the oldest of the brothers, and the most boastful. Adoron and Sigurd wanted him to stay in Avristar and become an elder, but Zulnas was in pursuit of adventure. Krishani thought the Lands of Men were dangerous, but for Zulnas it seemed the other way around. The Lands of Men would fear him, and as a Judge, they would have full reason to.

"When will he marry the land?"

"Beltane as always," Benir said. He seemed distracted as they trudged through the forest passing over the well-worn dirt path, their cloaks brushing along ferns at the feet of the trees. He looked at Krishani, his eyes full of concern. "What about you?"

"What about me?"

"I heard about Tolemny. Talnas asked me to come with them to repair the damage."

Krishani looked at the canopy and sighed. That was the first time he tried to pass the second rite, the one he was supposed to have passed almost four summers ago. He glanced at the trees, trying to see through them as far as his sight would allow. Rays of sunlight speckled throughout the shadows, making it difficult to see all that far.

"It was an accident," he said as he quickened his pace, trying to put distance between himself and Benir. He was going to ask Adoron a random question, but Benir kept up with him.

"We never make mistakes, precision—"

"I know," Krishani snapped. He tried to continue walking at a normal pace so the others didn't notice, but he didn't like where Benir was going with this. He didn't have the courage to tell his brothers that even with all the training, when he tried to manipulate the elements, they lashed back at him and caused mass destruction to the land. Benir went quiet and Krishani wondered if he actually saw what had happened to Tolemny. "Did you go with them?"

Benir shook his head. "I was too busy with chores."

Krishani stiffened and nodded. "It wasn't that bad."

"You didn't pass the rite though," Benir pointed out.

"Nay."

"They're going to make you do it again, soon probably."

Krishani sighed and closed his eyes. He knew they would push him as much as they could, make him repeat the rite again and again until he passed it. It almost felt like his nightmares; how they came again and again without relent, as though if he saw enough bloodshed he would pass some other rite. The thought made him shudder as a swift cold wind blew through the trees.

Benir sniffed the air. "Almost home."

Krishani smelled burnt hazelnuts and it reminded him of simpler times, summers long before the Great Oak's parable and the Brotherhood, long before the rite, but never before the nightmares. No, there wasn't a time he could remember before them.

He pulled his hood over his face and kept his eyes down as they passed the last stretches of forest into their village.

3-HARD LESSONS

The trees whipped by Kaliel as she raced through the forests of Evennses. The path curled around the thick trees, their roots littering the ground like giant unmoving snakes. Her heart thumped fast as she skipped over another root. Then, without warning, her foot snagged and she slammed face first on the ground. She lay there for a moment stunned by the blow. She moved slowly, pushing herself onto her back and staring at the canopy of leaves that blotted out the night sky. She couldn't see a single star yet. Breathing heavily she sat up, her body aching from the fall; she rubbed her torso with her delicate hands.

"You moved it," she whispered.

"That I did not, Little Flame. You did not remember where it was." The tree creaked at her in a deep voice. She was used to the familiar nickname the trees had given her, even if she had no idea what it meant.

"Nay." She dusted off her ivory dress and smiled at the tall red cedar, placing her hand on its bark. "There's nothing to light my way." That was true; it was pitch black under the cover of the forest canopy. The tree remained silent as she continued down the path. Her fingertips brushed along the trunks of the trees. They grew so close together and their trunks were so thick they created what seemed like stone walls. As her fingers brushed along the bark of another, the wind rustled the leaves and she knew the lake was near. She needed the comfort of the waters, the heat inside of her burning to a point it was hard to think about anything but Krishani's blue and green eyes.

Five moons had passed since the Fire Festival in Orlondir, and her frequent trips to the lake were the only thing that helped her escape her own dreams. These ones were of fire, startling her awake in the middle of the night, indigo-colored flames piercing her memory. They made her feel warm and restless inside.

The trees moved closer together and a dead end blocked her way. She sighed and slunk into the mud, her back against the bark. "I must see them," she said.

"You can see them in the meadow." The tree was not comforting.

"Not the stars."

The tree didn't speak. It creaked and groaned and revealed a small crevasse between itself and its neighboring tree. Kaliel placed her hand on the tree in thanks, sharing her magic with its roots. As she stepped through the small hole between them a tiny purple flower sprouted from the earth at the tree's feet, something she was used to.

On the beach, the forest faded, her feet sunk into the sand. She wiggled her toes around the grains and padded towards the water. Her eyes beheld the brilliance of a million stars above her. They painted pretty pictures in the night sky, a slight reddish color streaked along with bright whites and all sorts of hues of blue. A sense of calm overwhelmed her as she moved her focus to the thin line of the horizon. It was a faint gray, the midnight blue of the sky melting with the deep dark purple of the water.

She unbuttoned her dress and left it on the beach. Her feet hit the water, it was warm. She walked a few paces and felt for the drop with her toes. The lake was known for being mysteriously deep. The water reached her waist when her toes curled around the ledge of underwater sand. She glanced back at the shore, her eyes burning with mischief before she dove into the water.

It was cold as she paddled through the murkiness, certain there was nothing to fear. She let her thoughts drift to the waterfall and Orlondir and shivered as the cold intensified.

Something curled itself around her ankle and she tensed. Its webbed hand stretched out on her leg and she heard a *coo* from the merfolk. She tried to relax; these merfolk were wild like the ones in Orlondir, but their home was bigger and deeper. More hands grabbed at her thighs and her forearms and she realized there was a swarm of them. They cooed at her in gentle tones, trying to make her relax, trying to make her trust them. She let her body go limp, knowing that fighting against so many would only force them to drag her deeper. She floated towards the surface and they took turns experimenting with the buoyancy of her body. It was hard to explain the feeling: like flying, but slower. She wasn't brave like Pux. He climbed trees and jumped out of them and tackled her to the ground all the time. He was mischievous and naïve and she loved him for it. It made all the seriousness of lessons and rules that much easier.

After what seemed like forever they decided to drag her deeper, the surface draining away. The pastels of the stars blurred, fading to black as fear crept into her heart. She gulped as the merfolk pulled and pulled; their webbed hands like shackles on her limbs. It got colder, and it got darker. The air in her lungs bubbled out, making her starved for air. Pressure built up in her elongated ears and they popped. She hadn't intended to fight them, but with the ache mushrooming across her temples she had no choice but to kick them until their hands left her legs. She peddled upwards, longing for the safety of the shore.

Her head breeched the surface. She gasped, taking in a breath of the mists settling around the lake. She swam to the ledge and placed her foot on it. She stood, water receding to her waist. The wind made her shiver as she walked towards the shore. She smiled to herself feeling tired enough to fall into a deep sleep. It was worth walking the fine line of danger.

"Kaliel," a woman snapped.

She stopped in her tracks, water circling her ankles. Her stomach clenched as she glanced at the treeline on the edge of the beach. In the moonlight she could only make out the form, but she knew it was her elder. Tension built as she carried her naked body across the grass, and without giving it time to dry, threw on her ivory dress.

"Forbidden means forbidden," Desaunius said firmly. She turned and slipped her tiny body through the crack provided by the tree. Kaliel followed silently, feeling disappointed at being caught. The woman walked skillfully through the dark, avoiding every root and overgrowth the path provided them. "What fascinates you so?" she asked as they stumbled through the forest.

Kaliel's insides ached as the effects of the fall earlier took their course. She rubbed her ribs as she contemplated her answer. "Beauty."

25

The woman paused for a moment and stepped over the root Kaliel had tripped on earlier that night. "The forests are beautiful."

"Aye." However, she was thinking about the scene that stretched out before her on the shore. She was still curious about the merfolk; there was something about them she would never know since her freedom had been compromised. A sticky feeling entered her as she thought of Krishani. How would she distract herself from thinking about him now?

"What is so beautiful about the lake?" the old woman asked.

Kaliel paused as she ran her hand along the trunk of a tree. *Shh*, she thought to herself as though the tree might decide to speak out loud in the presence of her elder. The tree remained still as they passed. "It's the horizon. The way it meets with the sky is ..."

The old woman crossed into the meadow and shuffled through the knee-high grass in the clearing. Kaliel followed, knowing the answer displeased her. They reached the porch at the House of Kin, the wide wooden platform stretched to either side of the house. A rocking chair and various carved wooden toys were strewn across it. Kaliel ascended the stairs as the old woman held the door open for her. The hearth fire was burning; light reflecting off the old woman's face, revealing her pasty white skin and green eyes, identical features to Kaliel.

"You mustn't return to the lake," Desaunius said. "It is forbidden."

Kaliel hung her head and looked at the winding staircase in the middle of the common room. "Aye."

"And you will not be tardy for our lesson at dawn."

Kaliel nodded as she retreated to her room.

• • •

"Kaliel!" Luenelle, the House Master, called.

Kaliel hastily pulled on her dress and slippers. She loathed the thought of seeing her elder disappointed, but she was already late. She wiped her face with her hands and combed her fingers quickly through her long white hair. She took a deep breath and left, descending the staircase that led to the common room. She glanced at the House Master.

"Good morning, Luenelle." She smiled.

"Desaunius is waiting for you," Luenelle said.

She nodded as she left the House of Kin, and broke into a run through the meadow. She spotted the thin path at the break of trees that led eastward to her elder's cottage. The forest was no different than the one leading to the south—tall cedars lined the path, their thick trunks providing an obstacle course for the kinfolk. Kaliel thought about the night before. No doubt she would be lectured about the dangers of the merfolk and the establishment of peace between their world and Avristar.

The light of the sun barely reached the moist soil as she stepped lightly through the shadowy forest, taking care not to arrive covered in mud. The past fifteen summers on Avristar had been filled with awkwardness and peculiarity. She was a Child of Avristar, like Luenelle and the rest of the children living at the House of Kin, which meant she was born of the land *itself*. The only difference was her disposition. She was clumsy where they were precise; she was quiet where they were boisterous; and she was curious where they were cautious. She often felt separated from them despite their attempts to include her.

She saw the cottage through a break in the trees, a bed of flowers stretching out in the meadow that surrounded the small hollowed-out mound. Desaunius preferred to live in the most beautiful place in Evennses.

Kaliel exhaled as she took in the sweet scents in the air. She picked a purple flower from the field and walked towards the door. It was stained cherry red with natural dyes and made of naturally-formed woods. Her eyes traced the deep gouges between the thick branches. She knocked once and waited. There was a shuffle inside followed by footsteps. The door opened and the old woman retreated towards the kitchen.

Kaliel entered the mound and smelled something brewing. She scrunched up her nose and closed the door. To her left was a small common room with logs and a thin slab of flat wood balanced on top of two smaller logs. To the right of the hallway was a closed door that led to her elder's private quarters. To the back of the cottage was the kitchen.

Kaliel followed the footsteps and found Desaunius bustling around a cauldron that hung over a fire pit in the hollowed-out shell of the wall. She wore a flowing royal blue gown to her ankles, silver embroidery circling her elbow, the sleeves fanning outwards. Kaliel set the flower on the wooden counter to her left. "Good morrow."

Desaunius looked at her for a moment and then at the brew. She sniffed the bitter aroma and frowned. "It's missing hawthorn."

Kaliel sighed as she looked at the wall of herbs and spices extending to the ceiling. Her eyes followed the symbols of their native tongue until she found the one that signified hawthorn. The jar was empty.

"I told you not to be tardy. Hawthorn is best harvested at dawn. Without it this tea will be tart." Desaunius glared at her.

"I'm sorry." She wanted to avoid the topic of the lake.

"Never mind it." Desaunius turned towards the wall, reaching for an herb that was too high.

"Can I help?" Kaliel asked meekly as she crossed the floor. She rose on her tiptoes and grabbed the bottle, handing it to her elder. Desaunius opened it and threw a pinch of green flowery herb into the brew.

"Thank you. I could reach that shelf yesterday," Desaunius mused. The brew began to bubble and she grabbed a linen cloth and removed the small cauldron from the hook. She placed it on the counter and turned towards the fire and placed a hand over top of it. The fire extinguished itself, smoke rising up to the hole in the ceiling.

"Follow me." She moved towards a door at the back of the cottage, leading to the most miraculous magical garden in all of Avristar. The trees thinned out to allow for every herb, flower and plant to grow. Kaliel knew it was no stroke of luck; Desaunius was an elder from the First Era, her magic was beyond comprehension. The small old woman treaded along a thin winding path between the plants. Kaliel followed, being careful not to lose her balance and fall on a bed of herbs. Desaunius stopped abruptly and turned to her apprentice.

"What do you recognize?"

Kaliel looked at the ground and saw many different plants growing with one another. There was one with a single white flower, and another with pods that dangled from the leaves. Another had yellowish flowers and there was one underneath a tree to her right that grew a few feet high, with purple flowers that alternated along the bruised stem of the plant. She recognized it almost immediately and smiled to herself. "Nightshade."

"Aye, that is easily spotted. What about this one?" Desaunius gestured towards the single white flowered plant that grew only a few feet away from the nightshade.

Kaliel thought for a moment and drew a blank. "Saffron?"

Desaunius sighed and took a few steps away from the plant. "Sanguinaria," she said. "It has only one flower, and one leaflet, and it grows to be a quad tall. We have been over this, Kaliel. You do not retain what I teach."

"I'm sorry."

"Had you used this as saffron you could have made yourself very ill." Desaunius stepped around her and headed back towards the mound.

Kaliel frowned, following her. "How would it make *me* ill?" she asked as she entered the kitchen.

Desaunius moved towards the cauldron and steeped the tea into a clay pitcher. The elder sighed. "I doubt it would make *you* ill. Elvens rarely are. Do you remember anything about how the herb works?" She handed Kaliel a cup of tea.

Kaliel thought for a moment. "It's an emetic."

Desaunius raised her eyebrows as she poured another cup and sat beside Kaliel on the log. "Do you know what that word means?"

Kaliel cringed again. "Nay."

"Let me explain. The Sanguinaria is helpful when one experiences shortness of breath. However, used in excess it will cause vertigo and in severe cases, death. When an overdose has occurred, one can only wait for the emetic effects of the herb to take place." She paused, looking like she wanted Kaliel to understand. "Emetic means vomiting," Desaunius finished with a disappointed glare.

Kaliel scrunched up her nose and took a sip of her tea. It tasted bitter. She winced at the aftertaste and paused before taking another sip. "When will I ever use this knowledge?" In her opinion each herb had qualities that sounded the same, and without the threat of sickness she felt odd learning what she couldn't apply.

Desaunius stared at the dormant fire pit. "We won't know until the Great Oak speaks."

Kaliel's heart dropped as she followed her elder's gaze. The Great Oak stood between the boundaries of Evennses and Amersil. It was the only tree the elders took guidance from. She nervously tapped her foot on the ground and shifted her weight. Luenelle had seen the Great Oak years ago and was to follow the path of a Lorekeeper in the Lands of Men. Others had been given parables that took them to various ends, healers, seers, landkeepers, weavers, judges, messengers, warriors, and elders. All Kaliel could think about was how life changed after hearing those words. Every apprentice she had admired since childhood had become a new person. Now that her turn was up she felt increasingly agitated at what those words would be. "Will you tell me more about the journey?"

"I cannot. You must seek the path for yourself."

"Aye." Kaliel stared at the tea, dark and strong.

Desaunius stood and took her cup to the counter. "How did you arrive at the lake?"

She grimaced at the mention of the previous night and rolled up the bottom of her dress with her fingertips. She gulped, unable to lie to her elder and unable to reveal the entirety of the truth. Desaunius was unaware of the fact the trees spoke to her. "I—I ... don't know."

"Wretch! The trees do not move on their own!"

Kaliel was taken aback by the vibrancy of her elder. "I'm aware, the crack ... it appeared, and I was curious."

"Curious enough to strip naked and swim in the lake?"

"There's nothing to fear, and there's no shore on the other side." Kaliel tried to avoid the piercing eyes of her elder but it was hard not to notice the tension in the room.

"We do not cross to the other side." Desaunius wildly paced as the conversation gained more agitation. "You ... cannot and must not leave Avristar. Do you understand?"

Kaliel bit her lip and nervously crossed her legs. Desaunius sounded vexed by something deeper than the lake. Kaliel rubbed the bruise on her midsection again in hopes that it would feel better soon. She nodded, feeling the weight of the transgression falling on her. "I wasn't trying to leave Avristar."

Desaunius paused, the truth seeming to dawn on her. "They were in the water with you."

"Aye," she said as her heart pained her.

"I will not caution you again. The merfolk do not belong to Avristar. They are free spirits and they do not live by our laws."

"I understand."

"What makes you so fascinated with them?"

Kaliel groaned inwardly and gritted her teeth. *They are all I have left of him*, she thought as she tried to avoid the question.

"Well?"

"They're beautiful."

"You will not go there again."

"Aye."

Desaunius crossed the floor and pulled a tincture off the wall. She folded it gently into Kaliel's hand and looked her in the eye. "Calm yourself. Nothing the Great Oak says will change who you are. No matter how many stunts you pull, you will still hear its wisdom in seven moons." She stood. "You may go. Our lesson is done."

4-THE LANDS OF MEN

K aliel plodded along the path away from her elder's quarters. She thought back to the lake, her solitude and her comfort. She hadn't revealed to Desaunius the real reason for her desperation. The boy in Orlondir—Krishani, he pressed on her thoughts constantly. She couldn't shake him, he made her feel warm in a way that made her cheeks flush. There was something unusual about him, something tortured and dark that made him different than the others, more compassionate, less arrogant, and a lot more observant.

She picked up another purple flower that strayed a bit from the path. She couldn't explain why they bloomed so frequently at her feet. Her touch seemed to invoke the land and they sprouted forth wherever she went. She sighed and nestled the flower into her hair and continued walking towards the House of Kin.

Orlondir drifted into her thoughts. It was a magnificent city that created the central hub of Avristar. Desaunius had told her a lot about Lord Istar and Lady Atara, the appointed sovereigns of the land. They lived at the Elmare Castle of Orlondir. Smaller villages scattered the lands, hiding within their bounds magical secrets and sacred spaces only known to the villagers. Compared to the routine lifestyle in Evennses, Orlondir seemed like an exciting labyrinth of wonder to Kaliel. Evennses was tedious. Nothing of importance happened aside from the journey to the Great Oak, and Kaliel feared the ancient tree.

She paused on the path and heaved a sigh. There was a place off the trail that led to a closed chamber next to a tree she enjoyed speaking with. Instead of returning to the House of Kin, she crossed through the tall trees and stumbled over the forest brush littering the path. She crawled under a thick root and when she came up she saw the tree. The sunlight hit the grass perfectly through the canopy of leaves. She smiled and sat next to the tree. She said nothing at first, closing her eyes to feel the sun on her face.

"I went back."

Leaves rustled as a wind blew through the confined space. "What did you find, Little Flame?"

Kaliel sighed. "Comfort."

"Then you are satisfied."

"No."

"Why?"

"I miss him."

The tree creaked and shifted its roots. "You still remember him?" A root presented itself to her right and she fell to her side, resting her head on it.

"I remember everything about him." She smiled; this wasn't the first time she had talked to the trees about Krishani. She gulped, stifling the urge to say more, explain the longing for his touch.

"You weren't meant to meet."

Her heart thumped, nervous. The tree had told her that too many times to count, but her answer was always the same. "Aye, but we did."

"And now it is no more."

"I can't forget him." She sighed and closed her eyes, letting the image of his mismatched eyes and shoulder-length black hair invade her mind. It didn't matter how many moons or days had passed, she would always remember exactly what he looked like, exactly what he said, and exactly what she felt when his eyes had combed over her.

"He will marry the land." The tree grunted.

Kaliel hummed and tried to push that thought away along with all the other truths about Krishani's Brotherhood, the oath of silence, and his chances of going to the Lands of Men.

"Maybe Avristar will let us be together," she whispered.

"You will marry the land, too."

Kaliel piled her hands in her lap and grew silent. Krishani had already worked his way into her heart; it was a feeling that would never leave her. The thought of marrying the land made her sad and angry at the same time, worse than betrayal. "I hope that isn't true," she said, fighting off the urge to let the heavy thoughts cloud her mind. She pushed herself to her feet and glared at the tree. "And now I must go find Pux. I promised to pick flowers with him this afternoon." She didn't let the tree respond as she darted through the brush towards the main path.

• • •

"What do you think the Great Oak will say to me?" Kaliel asked as she paced through the forests with Pux. He was busy chasing a squirrel around a tree. She watched as it curled around the trunk, climbing higher than his reach.

"Wretch!" He scrunched up his nose as the squirrel escaped into the branches. He turned to Kaliel. "What do you mean?"

She shifted in the grass uncomfortably. "I don't want to go to the Lands of Men."

Pux laughed. "I didn't, did I?"

She frowned. "I still don't understand why."

"How did it put it? One step, two step, three step, four, you take three steps and you never learn more!" He recited it gleefully as he looked at the glimmers of sunlight through the canopy. A canary chirped and fluttered around the treetops. He watched it precariously.

"You act invalid," she said.

Pux smiled. "I am invalid. No, I'm happy to live blissfully. Besides, nobody knows what I can do and I prefer it that way." He listened for the bird. It flew around in circles awhile longer before landing on a branch. When he spotted it he focused and blinked.

Kaliel watched as the bird's feathers turned from yellow to blue. She shook her head. "You should show that trick to Grimand."

"Why? He would tell me not to do it." Then, mimicking the Elder's deep voice: "Disrupting the natural flow of nature."

Kaliel sat on a root and watched him as he used his unique gift to turn another bird purple, and a squirrel orange. "You don't think they'll notice it if you keep doing that?"

"Why would it matter?" He ran down the path towards the next bend in the forest. Kaliel followed him slowly and he turned back holding a single white flower.

She inspected it. "Sanguinaria." She recognized it from the morning's lesson and put it in the basket. It was the first flower they had found all afternoon. "Will you really stay in Evennses forever?"

Pux was a few feet down the path scouring between trees. "No."

She sighed and idly looked through a space between trees. There was a small yellow daffodil on the other side of the trunk. She reached around and pulled it out. Her thoughts were still on Krishani and Amersil. Part of the journey to the Great Oak meant reaching the boundary between her province and his, and the thought of being closer to him made her warm and nervous at the same time.

Pux backtracked to where she lingered. "Come on Kaliel, what has you so glum?"

Kaliel gritted her teeth and looked at the soil. "I can't tell you."

"You always say that." His expression turned serious. "We're not like them. You can hear the trees and I can change things. I can't explain it, but I'm not interested in unraveling the mysteries of the land. Why can't you accept what is and stop being such a worry wart?"

She grinned. "I'm not *that* different." She raced towards the tiny bridge that crossed the skinny creek. Frogs swam underneath its murky surface amidst the lily pads and moss. She paused. "I worry because Evennses is too small for me, and the Lands of Men are too big. I want more than this, but I don't want to lose all that I have."

Pux came to stand with her on the bridge. He had two more flowers in his hand. He dropped them into the basket at her feet and rested his hairy elbows on the wooden rails. "You won't lose me."

She rolled her eyes. "Nay, you are never changing."

"Never ending!"

She giggled and turned her back to the ledge, resting her elbows on the wood and staring into the trees. "I went back to the lake last night."

Pux stopped poking fun. All the joy within him seemed to drain away with those words. Without a word he haughtily stormed back through the forest the way they came. Kaliel followed him, unsure what she had done to make him so upset. He stopped a few minutes later and turned to her. "You promised me you would be here today."

"And I kept that promise."

"No! You went to the lake again! I thought you were my friend." He turned and continued storming towards the House of Kin.

Kaliel's heart dropped. "Desaunius caught me," she called after him.

He spun around, an astonished look on his face. "Good." He continued walking.

She ran and caught up to him, stepping in line as he quickened his pace. "I had to try again."

"Why? Why do you always avoid that question?"

"I like watching the mists."

Pux stopped and shook his head. "No, that isn't why." They reached the fork in the road. The path to the right led back to the House of Kin and the other led further into the forests. Pux took off down the path to the left.

She followed with frustration, self-conscious. "Fine." He continued walking as though she hadn't said a thing. "The lake calms me," she admitted.

Pux turned, bewildered. "You need calming from this place?" His brow furrowed in confusion.

"I can't sleep until I've seen them."

"I'm lost."

"Never mind it, then. I told you before I couldn't tell you why."

He stopped and sat in the grass beside one of the trees. "You've been different since we returned from Orlondir."

She sat down beside him. "I know."

"Why didn't you come back?"

She had avoided this topic as well since their return. She fidgeted in the grass and rolled the edges of her dress. "I saw something."

Pux waited for her to continue, his brown eyes and hairy face full of questions.

Kaliel sighed and leaned against the tree. She tilted her head towards the sky. She contemplated telling him the whole truth, but settled for a half-truth. "There were creatures in the pond, merfolk I think, like the ones in the lake. I swam with them."

Pux stood. She knew he was comfortable with the safety of Evennses; he liked knowing the lay of the land. For him, mapping a forest was much more rewarding than gallivanting off into uncharted waters. "That frightens me."

Kaliel sighed and piled her hands in her lap. "I ... I can talk to them."

He chortled. "You talk to everything!"

She shot him a warning glance. "I do."

"How did Desaunius react?"

"I've never seen her more disappointed."

"So you won't go back then?"

Kaliel took a deep breath though her heart was breaking. "No."

• • •

Kaliel stared at the ceiling for what seemed like forever. The rest of the day had passed quickly. She saw Desaunius for another lesson and ate dinner in the mess hall with the other kinfolk. When the sun slipped over the horizon she sat outside in the meadow staring at the stars until Luenelle motioned for her to take to her quarters. Her heart was heavy as she tried to resist the urge to see the merfolk again. They were the only reminders that what had happened in Orlondir was real.

She rolled onto her stomach and stuffed her head into her feather pillow. She took a deep breath and exhaled slowly, trying to calm herself enough to sleep. Time dragged on for what seemed like an hour but was probably only a couple of minutes. She opened her eyes. Sleep wasn't possible; her mind was clouded with thoughts of Krishani. She sat up and put on her slippers. Maybe she would sit outside under the stars and listen to the crickets and play with the fireflies in the clearing. She opened her door and shuffled quietly across the floor. When she reached the top of the stairs she saw light from the hearth fire still burning. Carefully, she placed her foot on the step in front of her. It creaked, she winced.

"She told me you wouldn't listen to her tenet," Luenelle said from the rocking chair in the common room.

Kaliel's heart sank. "Did she also mention that I can't sleep?"

"No, but I knew it was so."

Kaliel descended the remainder of the stairs. Luenelle had a manuscript across her lap and she was situated right between the door and the hearth fire. She was a few years older than Kaliel, her elongated ears awkwardly poking out amidst her long brown hair. Her blue eyes didn't move towards the girl as she came and took a seat on a log near the fire.

"What's on the other side of the lake?" Kaliel asked.

Luenelle took a deep breath and let it out, obviously impatient. "The Lands of Men." She put the manuscript on the log beside her.

Kaliel sighed. "I mean, what are the Lands of Men like?"

The House Master grimaced and shifted her eyes to the fire. "They're full of dangerous things."

"Like what?"

"Left over chaos caused by the Valtanyana," Luenelle whispered.

Kaliel shuddered. She had heard of them before, always in the cautionary tales, but they were locked away in Avrigost, they were never coming back. High King Tor and the Flames had defeated them, she had nothing to fear. She noticed the embers in the fire dying down. She picked up the poker and opened the gate to the wood. She poked it gently, moving around the ashen pieces. The fire blazed at the motion. She wasn't satisfied with Luenelle's answer. If the Lands of Men were so dangerous, why were they expected to go there? The prospects of seeing Krishani again grew bleak and all that settled her soul was the adventurous pursuit of beauty, of wonder. She paused and held the poker in the fire, staring absentmindedly into the flames. They reminded her of her dreams. She shuddered.

"What troubles you, Kaliel?" Luenelle whispered.

The other girl was pulled out of her stupor, turning and looking at Luenelle's blue dress and the beige quilt on her lap. It fell to the side and landed on the floor. "I want something I can't have."

"The merfolk aren't something you can possess."

Kaliel shook her head. "Not them. The Lands of Men. I don't want to go."

"Relax, the Great Oak will give you clarity."

"Aren't you afraid?"

She smiled wistfully. "I'm in no rush to find adventure. When I go, I'll be prepared for my journey. Nothing will scare me."

Kaliel put the poker away and sat on the log again. "I can't imagine life outside of Avristar."

"You won't need to for a long time."

Knots formed in her stomach. She knew no matter what she wanted in her heart, the land would decide her path, its will was something she couldn't alter. Up to this point in her life she thought the land wanted very peculiar things from her: to listen, to heal, and to hurt. It wasn't just the bruises that speckled her body—it was the aching in her heart that hurt the most.

"Maybe you should try again," Luenelle said.

Kaliel's eyes lit up. Adrenaline rushed through her veins as she envisioned her body gliding through the waters. "Really?" she asked, unable to hide the excitement.

Luenelle shot her a glare. "To sleep."

Kaliel's face dropped. She nodded and trudged back up the stairs to her room.

5-NIGHTMARES

K rishani followed the elders through the over-trodden paths, his head hung in defeat, his cloak soaked with the memories of his failure. They passed a familiar fork in the trees, cold wind whipping their robes with unusual force. He caused the rain that drenched them in buckets of water, and topped it off with stinging wind. Both were unintentional, but after sixteen summers and countless moons of folly he should have known better.

At least he avoided the lightning this time.

They broke into the clearing and the eight of them, one by one, came around the center of the hearth, singing songs under their breath as the rain slowed and ceased. Logs sat around the hearth in an octagon pattern, the ground dry with remnants of sand, dirt and pebbles, reminding Krishani how close the lake was.

He waited as one of them removed their hood and long brown hair fell around aged features, sallow skin and a narrow face. Adoron's eyes were dark with power as he rubbed his hands together and sparked a fire. Flames came to life as the others took off their cloaks and sat.

"Step forward, boy," Adoron said, his dark eyes on Krishani. He gulped and removed the soaked cloak. A sea of agony festered in his gut, but he forced himself to step over the log. He went to sit, but Adoron shook his head. "You have failed the second rite of passage," the elder said. "Again."

Krishani gritted his teeth and clenched his fist. His eyes bore into the orange-white flames of the fire. Their tentacles twisted into the sky, smoke painting the canopy above him.

"Apologies," Krishani muttered.

The others grunted in response, all of them agitated beyond normal recollection. Adoron raised his hand to silence them, his gazed fixed on Krishani. "Tolemny was a sacred site. You destroyed it."

Krishani was unsure if he wanted to hear more. That was the first time he had tried to pass the second rite; the destruction was catastrophic. "Apologies."

Adoron kept his eyes hot on him. "Beonwyn was a place for reflection. It too is destroyed." The others grunted in contempt.

Krishani liked the Beonwyn tree. It was bigger than the others, but not as large as the Great Oak. He often sat by it, brainstorming recipes. As an apprentice, he was responsible for kitchen duties, and most of the other adepts yielded to his cooking skills.

"Larna was a place we assumed you could not destroy, but the meadow lies in ashes," Adoron said.

Krishani disliked the third attempt the most. It was the middle of summer, there was barely any moisture in the air. The moment he began to engage his senses, a spark hit the grass and flew through the meadow. The elders had narrowly escaped.

"Yerbia was the final chance you had to pass the second rite, and you have failed."

Krishani hung his head. Yerbia flooded, and the elders spent the evening wading through knee-deep water. His heart sank. There was no reason for him to be there, pretending to be a prodigy when he had only shown potential twice in his life. The first time was at the palace in the royal city of Orlondir. The second time was at the waterfall. He tried to hide his smile as the elders exchanged wary looks between them.

Krishani focused on the fire and let his senses dig into it. There was fire in Kaliel's eyes and sweetness in her smile, and something he couldn't place about her. Something different.

She was all he ever thought about.

"I hereby denounce my title as mentor of Krishani of Amersil. Will any other accept the challenge?"

The other seven elders whispered among themselves, but all of them shook their heads, their eyes too wild with bewilderment and fear. Krishani was nothing but a boy with uncontrollable power. None of them were willing to risk the wellbeing of the land for his training.

Adoron began to look sick as his comrades each declined the invitation.

Krishani waited in silence, his eyes fixed on the flames, thinking of trees, floods, skies and eyes. Her eyes, the eyes of the girl he met in Orlondir. He longed to see the green in her eyes again. He felt energy building up in him, power racing through him. The wisps of fire went bright white and began settling into greens. There were deep greens like the evergreens, and brilliant emerald greens like her eyes. One of the elders gasped while the others smirked and Adoron let out a laugh. It was an unpleasant sound.

"Fire manipulation is for the twelve-year-olds, Krishani," he snapped. He glanced around the grove and narrowed his eyes. "Will none accept the challenge?"

"I will," a voice said, but the voice didn't come from one of the seven, it came from behind Krishani, in the trees. All of them gasped and Adoron stumbled backwards, his feet finding the log and his body sitting with a thud.

Krishani had no idea who they were staring at until his gray robes came into view. His white beard hung to his torso, his silvery-white hair falling in waves over the folded hood of his cloak. He held a staff in his left hand; half the size of his body and made from an oak branch. It was covered in symbols. Krishani felt words catch in his throat as Istar, the Lord of Avristar, approached Adoron with a strong look in his stone blue eyes.

"I think the time for forests is over," Istar stated, glancing briefly at the boy.

Krishani hung his head and waited for Adoron—for anyone—to speak. There was nothing but silence. He let out a breath and wrung his hands out along his sides. Istar smirked at Adoron and turned to face Krishani. "You have until Beltane to prepare him for my trials," he said, inspecting the boy.

Krishani looked down at his plain garments: a cream-colored tunic over black breeches and shin-high boots. Istar looked into his mismatched eyes, and Krishani knew that despite his failure, Istar planned to turn him into a champion.

"Your trials?" Adoron stuttered, still gaining his wits about himself.

Istar glared at him. "Yes. He will come to Orlondir at Beltane, and I will train him."

The elders gasped and Krishani felt sicker inside. Being chosen to train with Adoron in Amersil was an honor he could accept. After countless summers of nothing but small triumphs he was unprepared to face something as big as Orlondir and Istar, the Lord of Avristar himself.

"This gathering is over," Istar said. He tapped his staff on the ground three times and the green fire turned to smoke, showering the elders and Krishani in nothing but the eerie glow of stars.

• • •

The river bank was sloppy and full of muck. Krishani watched as clumps of mud eventually fell into the river, washed downstream. He never knew where he was when he dreamed, but they always began like this, in the dead silence, or in the din of places he had never been before. The only place he had ever seen rivers were in his dreams, and the only time he heard about rivers was when the brothers talked about the Lands of Men. This river was no exception. He waited for the other thing he would see, the things he had seen since he woke up a child in a forest, abandoned by the men. They had smelled like sweat and firewood. It was a musky male smell that the elders on Avristar never possessed no matter how blistering hot it became in summer.

Water babbled as it rushed over the rock bed, little pools of ripples fluttering across the surface. Krishani grew anxious. He hung there, seeing nothing but clumps of mud let go of the banks and follow the ride of the winding river. He peered downstream and saw it curve and curl as it cut through tall spruce trees on either side. Part of him wanted to wake up, but part of him hated the reality he would wake up to. Days of careful planning, of menial tasks, nothing like what he endured during the rites; this was much more intense.

He was always aware during his dreams, as though he was really there, watching from the shadows. He turned his attention upstream. There was a body floating face down, moving towards him. A white shirt swished around the body and clung to tanned skin underneath. Sandy blond hair covered its head and bared ankles floated up out of the water. Krishani moved instinctively, throwing off his cloak, planning on diving in after the body, but a hand on his shoulder stopped him.

Krishani looked to his right and a tall man with his back turned came into view, plodding along the banks with body language that said he was equally disappointed. The floating body belonged to a child, maybe nine or ten.

Krishani hung his head and watched the body float downstream, knowing there was nothing he could do to help. The boy was already dead.

• • •

Krishani wrestled with the quilt as he tossed and turned in the hammock. He pushed it out of the way, his heart thudding, his senses making him crazy. He smelled river water, and it reminded him of the boy. He pushed the quilt off his legs and lay back in the hammock. He threw an arm over his eyes and tried to blot out the images of death cluttering his mind with unnatural abhorrence. That was the secret he never told Adoron or any of the elders in Amersil. He bottled up the dreams and made them seem far away because the man that appeared in them reminded him of a place he could barely remember. He had no idea where he had spent the first six years of his life. The dreams were like memories, or at least they seemed to be. The smell reminded him of a home he never knew he had.

The ability to sleep evaded him. He grumbled to himself and slipped off the hammock. His was one of the highest in the cabin; he slept with eleven others, all chosen for the Brotherhood, all showcasing their potential in ways he never could. His feet landed hard on the floor, but everyone remained asleep. He quickened his steps to the front of the cabin, descended the stairway and followed the trails through the trees to the hearth fire in the woods.

It might have been forbidden, but the way the flames turned the green in Kaliel's eyes made him anxious to distract himself. He knew it was wrong to think about her. His life was so full of incoherence and secrecy and mishap he could never imagine someone liking him for those qualities. And there were always the dreams of death. Somehow it seemed too morbid and out of place for him to live in a land that was impervious to war and death. Avristar was a land of thoughtfulness and bliss.

He broke through the trees and came upon the hearth. Krishani rubbed his hands together and let them loose, a spark igniting the flames and bringing them to life. He smiled. That trick wasn't part of the rite. Fire was much easier to manipulate than land. The flames built up, their whites and oranges shooting up past the height of the trees.

All he wanted was another glimpse of those eyes—those wide, green sparkling eyes that ignited an immense desire within him. Krishani felt his entire body shake with tremors the first time he touched her, and that had been an accident. He knew he was too close, it was too much. He was taking liberties with his limitations, both personal and bound. The brethren forbid him to speak with others, most of the time it didn't matter because he wasn't interested in knowing the kinfolk from other parts of Avristar.

She was hard to forget.

The fire continued shifting colors, slower now, first moving to yellow then a yellowish green and finally settling into the emerald green he found mesmerizing. He watched the fire as he let the coils of death unravel and break off, the chains of his existence allowing him freedom for a few moments. He closed his eyes and focused on her— soft white hair, elongated ears, heart-shaped face and pink lips.

Krishani blinked and stared at the fire. It was blazing a vibrant whitish violet hue, streaks of blue and purple mixing with the hot whites. There was something familiar about the color of amethyst. He shook his head and his concentration on the flames broke. It was as though they were sucked out of the sky as smoke rose and wisps of it drifted to the stars.

Krishani heaved a sigh and stood, willing himself to go back to the cabin. He would have to go to Orlondir soon, and this time he wouldn't be leaving.

Leaves crunched under Krishani's feet as he moved towards the path through the trees. He paused. There were other footsteps. He backed up and casually sat on a log, tense, waiting for whomever it was.

Benir emerged moments later and Krishani relaxed. Benir stretched. He didn't have his cloak, only a loose-fitting pair of brown pants and a tunic. He had sandals on his feet and looked uncomfortable and tired.

"You seem to think I don't hear it when you wake," Benir began, sitting on the log across from Krishani and rubbing his hands together. He let them loose and the fire sparked up again, orange.

Krishani grimaced. Benir held the cot under him, but never bothered to follow him in the past. "I assumed you were a deep sleeper."

Benir shook his head. "Not lately."

Krishani frowned and went to ask why but shut his mouth. He knew why. Benir had seen fourteen summers. It was almost time for him to go to the Great Oak and learn his parable. "The Great Oak isn't scary."

Benir traced patterns on his pale hands, shadows dancing across his face. "Its words are scary."

Krishani shook his head, unsure what to tell him. He had been to the Great Oak moons ago, and his parable was confusing. Being a warrior still seemed wrong, especially when he was such a failure to his elders.

"Stop worrying about it." He wanted to forget about his parable and the fact he was expected to join the armies of Avristar in some distant and unforeseeable future. He went to leave Benir to his thoughts when the younger elven glanced at him, his blue eyes full of concern.

"You were having nightmares again." It wasn't a question.

Krishani shrugged. "They were just dreams."

Benir glared. "I know when they're nightmares. You twist in the hammock all night and make a lot of noise."

Krishani let a sly smile creep across his lips, more out of embarrassment than joy. He really wanted to keep the nightmares to himself. "I'll try not to disturb you in future," he said coolly as he moved to the path.

"Just tell me what they're about." Benir seemed out of control and when Krishani looked back at him he noticed the bags under his eyes and the pale skin on his cheeks. He looked desperate and awkward. "I have bad dreams, too."

Krishani walked back to the hearth. "What are yours about?"

"Sigurd booming at me," Benir said quietly, his eyes cast to the ground, his cheeks flushed with redness.

Krishani laughed and shook his head. "Those are nothing."

"Are yours ... worse?"

He shot Benir a cold stare. "Much worse. So much worse." He pulled his fingers into a fist and fled from the hearth.

6-THE GREAT OAK

K aliel stood in the clearing of the forest, the path to the Great Oak looming ahead of her. She took a step and began wading down the winding trail, knowing the border to Amersil was closer with each step. Her stomach was a muddle of knots, fear of what the Great Oak would say pressing against the nerves that racked her frame at the thought of Amersil and Krishani.

The path took forever to walk. The sun sunk to midafternoon and then to late afternoon and she feared she would never find the tree. She smelled the moisture in the air and knew the lake was somewhere near. She thought about darting through the thin trees with the pretty light green leaves and racing towards the smell of the waters, but stopped herself. She couldn't get in trouble again. She ran her hand along the bark of a red cedar and smiled at it in hopes it would tell her where to go.

"Please," she whispered.

The tree stood still, unwavering in its strength. She sighed. They protected the Great Oak and none of them would betray the ancient tree.

She stopped looking ahead and followed the pattern of the ground, watching her slippered feet slide across the mud. Ferns littered the sides of the path and birds chirped and flitted from tree to tree. Her eyelids became droopy and she let her head sink towards the mud, her shoulders hunched over, her body heavy with fatigue.

"Stop!" the trees called to her.

Kaliel jerked up and noticed three paths in front of her. "Which do I choose?" she asked, glancing at the trees.

"That is up to you."

She grimaced and crossed her arms across her chest. The three paths all had distinctive features about them. The one on the left was full of ferns and forest brush. The trees were thinner and rays of sunlight trickled through the canopy. The path on the right was darker, thicker with trees, and it reminded her of the path to the lake. The one in the middle was a mix of the two and she carefully chose it, hoping the trees wouldn't yell at her again. They didn't say anything and soon she was lost in the forest once more.

Her feet followed the trail as it grew darker and darker. Her shin crashed into a log blocking the path. She frowned and stepped on it, swaying to the right. She slipped and crashed down, her shoulder hitting the soft soil beneath the leaves. She muttered to herself as she sat up and rubbed her shoulder, trying to figure out where she was.

"Kaliel."

The deep baritones of the Great Oak made her jump. She moved to her feet and noticed the thick roots snaking out of the ground towards the capacious tree. It was huge and wide, its branches creating its own umbrella. She stared at it, both mesmerized and afraid.

"Come forward, Little Flame."

Kaliel carried herself over the roots to the tree and didn't trip once. Amersil was on the other side but with the expanse of the tree blocking the path she knew she wouldn't dare to cross the boundary. She stopped when she was in front of the tree, and realized how tall it really was. She let out a slow breath, taking in the magnificence of the ancient tree. Her eyes closed as she waited for it to speak again, but then remembered something Desaunius had said. Sheepishly she pressed her palm to its bark and looked up at it again. It was such a common gesture for her; she did it all the time with the cedars in the rest of Evennses. They talked when she pressed her hand against their trunks. She should have instinctively known to do that with the Great Oak.

"Your purpose," it said, its words making the ground vibrate. She tried to hold herself up but the anxiety made her feel weak and hollow inside.

"A seed to bloom knows not if it will be, a flower or a weed, and cannot change its form once matured. Bloom the weed of temptation and expire the great garden of life. Bloom the flower of sacrifice and sustain the great garden in strife," the tree said.

She let the words sink in, repeated them in her mind slow and steady. Her hand slid down the trunk as she fell on her knees. The words pierced her, like venom through her veins as their meaning sunk in. Understanding didn't come right away but there was something sinister about the words that made her sense darkness. Tears pricked at her eyes as she tried to find the will to stand. She gulped.

"You must go," the tree hissed.

She looked at it with curious eyes and nodded, her hands finding the roots as she stumbled over them. Her mind whirred with thoughts of danger in the Lands of Men, hoping it wouldn't come to that. Her palm pressed on a root as her energy mixed with the Great Oak, a trail of violet flowers sprouting up along the path as she retreated to the House of Kin.

$$\bullet \quad \bullet \quad \bullet$$

Desaunius waited for Kaliel in the clearing. The sun was setting over the horizon, and Kaliel's cheeks were pink with exhaustion. The girl hastily walked passed her elder without a word. The woman frowned and followed as she pressed on through the forests not bothering to slow down. Kaliel had no idea where she was going or which path would lead her back to the House of Kin, but she wanted to return. She needed to write in her journal and no matter how late Luenelle stayed up she was determined to visit the merfolk again.

"Slow down," Desaunius said, panting.

Kaliel automatically obeyed the command and kicked herself for it. She wasn't ready to tell her what happened on her journey. Desaunius stepped into stride with her and laced her arm through Kaliel's, tightly holding the girl's hand. They walked a few more steps in sync with each other.

"Will you tell me?" she asked gently.

Kaliel felt the hairs on her neck stand on end. She longed for the comfort only the lake could provide. She hung her head. If she didn't tell, Desaunius could send her to Orlondir, and she couldn't deny the Lady of Avristar. She took a deep breath, and recited the parable. Desaunius didn't respond. She became rigid, her body as still as a statue.

51

"That was it," Kaliel said, as though her elder's silence had to do with belief. She couldn't lie even if she wanted to. She slid out of Desaunius's arm and walked ahead. She saw an acorn on the ground and kicked it away with her toe. Desaunius wasn't usually this quiet and it worried her. She stared expectantly at the elder who seemed lost in thought. Their green eyes met and the old woman was pulled out of her trance.

"Aye, puzzling indeed." Desaunius sounded distant and uncertain. That didn't calm Kaliel at all.

They continued the rest of the walk in silence and reached the meadow from a new entrance she hadn't seen before. From this angle the left side of the house extended about a hundred feet towards the tree line. There were circular windows all along the three levels of the house, something she was used to looking out from but not the other way around. She looked at the sky as Desaunius crossed the meadow.

The stars swirled above her. She soundlessly collapsed in the tall grass and blinked. When she opened her eyes the sky looked different somehow and seemed to sing like a symphony. She never heard a sound so beautiful in all her life. She closed her eyes again and let the sounds take her away. The wind rustled through the grass and she heard Desaunius walking back towards her. She blinked and everything was the same as it had been.

Desaunius stood over her. "You must be hungry."

Kaliel smiled. That was more like the elder she knew. "I need to rest a moment."

Desaunius sat down in the grass beside her and patted her knee. Kaliel sat and gazed at the tops of the trees against the midnight of the sky. "Do you feel different?"

I feel more awkward, she thought. "A little, I suppose." Kaliel pressed her back into the grass and looked at the sky again. *Did it really sing?* The moment came and went so fast she wasn't sure if she had truly heard anything at all. She eyed the unmoving constellations in the sky and spotted the phoenix. Ever since she was a child the phoenix was her favourite. She traced the outline of the star pattern with the tips of her fingers whenever she could. The stars had been something she longed to be closer to before Orlondir, Krishani, and the merfolk. She sighed as she traced the dotted lines. She was very tired; the day wore on and night fell too quickly. She contemplated her fervent need for the merfolk. Tonight she wouldn't go.

"Come, we will eat," Desaunius said. She stood and gave Kaliel her hand. The girl took it and allowed her elder to pull her to her feet. Together they continued through the meadow to the House of Kin.

• • •

Dawn came too early and Kaliel ignored first call. By the time the third call came she was still hazing in and out of dreams. The night provided a heavy revelation for her: the Great Oak was more terrifying than wondrous and its words made little sense to her. She wondered what insights Desaunius would have. The thought of her elder only made her stomach grumble with hunger. She had picked at her food like a bird due to the nausea that came and went and slept without a full helping.

As the morning drew on she spent time on personal grooming. Her stomach was still growling by the time she had finished bathing.

She peered down the stairs to the common room and decided it was as good a time as any to go to the kitchen to find leftovers. The mess hall would be empty, most of the kinfolk attending lessons. The staircase creaked as she crept across the common room and found the hallway on the left side of the house that led to the kitchen. As she turned the corner she spotted someone in the hall.

"Good day," Luenelle said.

"Morning, Luenelle," she said, her eyes cast to the floor. She waited for Luenelle to tell her how late she was.

"Afternoon, actually," Luenelle chirped. She was in an unusually cheery mood for a House Master that looked after seventy-odd kinfolk.

Kaliel smiled. "I know I'm tardy again."

"In fact you're not. Desaunius left this morning on business. Your lessons have been canceled." Luenelle began to walk down the hallway towards the mess hall.

She followed the House Master, uncertainty filling her. Desaunius only left Evennses for two reasons: new children born to the land, or the fire festivals. Children of Avristar were usually found in the spring during Beltane or the summer during Lammas. They sprouted from the hollows in trees or thickets of grass. It was something the elders handled, with new children being brought to Orlondir immediately.

Once they could walk they'd be given to an elder in one of the three provinces, Evennses, Amersil or Araraema. Kaliel had been found nestled in a bed of violet flowers, the same ones that bloomed at her feet when she touched the land. She doubted her elder had left for either of those reasons.

"What for?"

"She wouldn't say. She's on her way to Orlondir to speak with Lady Atara."

Kaliel gasped. The room spun around her and everything went dark as she bumped against the wall, threatening to fall to the floor.

Luenelle caught her by the arm and pulled her up, staring into her eyes with alarm. "Kaliel? Are you ill?"

She shook her head; but it made it worse. She waited a moment, trying to compose herself. "I haven't eaten," she said between heavy breaths.

Luenelle kept hold of her and stiffened up. "Then we shall get you some food." She pulled Kaliel down the corridor and passed the doors leading to the kitchen. She entered through the mess hall and sat her down on one of the wooden logs at the front, ducking into the kitchen.

Kaliel stretched out along the table top's wooden slab and closed her eyes. Before she had a chance to think, Luenelle came bustling through the doors with a bowl of porridge and a spoon. Kaliel began to devour the food. Luenelle remained quiet while she ate. The last few moons had made them grow closer as friends.

"How was your journey?" Luenelle asked.

Intimidating, Kaliel thought. "It was fine," she answered.

Luenelle beamed. "And, you're not invalid."

Kaliel smiled as she was expected to at the joke. It was clearly aimed at Pux. *I would have preferred that,* she thought as her mind drifted to him. "No, I'm unchanged …" … *except the stars sang.*

"Desaunius will return with good news. I'm certain her business has nothing to do with you." She stood and spied the empty bowl, raising an eyebrow. "Another helping?"

Kaliel shyly withdrew. "No, thank you. I think I'll take a walk this afternoon."

Luenelle said nothing as she disappeared into the kitchen again. When she reappeared she pulled a piece of parchment out of her pocket and handed it to her. "Your elder left you homework. You have some herbs to collect, and a tea to brew," she said, then laughed. "I'm so happy you've taken your journey to the Great Oak!" She sat down at the table across from Kaliel and took her hands in her own. "Nobody understands. I'm the only one who hasn't been called to duty. Everyone else ..." she trailed off as Kaliel began to feel seasick. She shook her head. "You know ... we all leave eventually."

Kaliel faked a smile and took a look at the list. "Chamomile tea."

"That's an easy one."

"Right, well, I suppose I will go for a walk then. Maybe Pux can help me with the herb list?"

Luenelle snorted obnoxiously. "Pux can't even help with the chores, let alone anything that requires real intelligence."

Kaliel only gave her another fake smile as she rose and left the mess hall. When she was in the hallway she grimaced at what Luenelle had said about her best friend. Pux wasn't invalid, but he wanted to keep his secret. She scurried down the corridor, grabbed a wicker basket from the porch, and raced off through the meadow to find out where Pux was frolicking in the forests.

7-THE FLAMES

D esaunius pulled the horse into the courtyard in Orlondir and slipped off its chestnut back. She moved her hands through her ankle-length hair and wound it in a tradetional bun, pinning it into place. She grabbed the reins, looking for someone from the Grand Hall. It was dismally quiet in Orlondir when the Fire Festivals weren't happening. Hearing nothing, she began circling the courtyard, pulling the horse across the cobblestone walkways and weaving around the crystal statues and perfectly trimmed grass. When she glanced back at the archway to the Grand Hall, she noticed a woman standing there in a long white gown, beaded necklaces hanging to her waist, locks of summery brown hair down to the small of her back. Her face was like glass, her piercing brown eyes glaring at Desaunius.

She eyed the woman scrupulously as she brought the horse round to the pavilion in the center of the courtyard.

"Ahdunie," the woman said with a sly smile. She sounded almost mocking.

Desaunius recognized the familiar sound of the ancient tongue of Avristar. "Ahdunie," she replied. She pulled her eyebrows down and let her hand slip off the reins. Even in the blue and silver embroidered gown anyone should have recognized her. Desaunius thought she knew everyone residing at the Elmare castle. There weren't many of them.

"Oh bother!" the woman shrieked, throwing her hands up in disgust. She crossed her arms and remained leaning against the arch to the Grand Hall. "I assume you expect me to take that infernal thing to the stables?"

"Where is Melianna?" Desaunius snapped, offended. Melianna was Lady Atara's servant, studious and prompt. Desaunius was perturbed by whoever the woman was and why she was trespassing in Orlondir. She didn't have a chance to ask as the woman retreated across the marble of the Grand Hall and disappeared. Several moments later, someone appeared behind Desaunius and almost made her jump.

"I'll take the horse now," Melianna said as her hands slid over the reins. "You came to see Lady Atara?"

Desaunius glanced at her as she rounded the horse, mousy brown hair blowing in the breeze. "Yes, I have something to discuss with her." She sucked in a breath as she recalled the words of the Great Oak. Memories of the First Era flitted through her mind, but she quelled them. It had been centuries since the wrath of Valtanyana; war wasn't something to fear. She coughed as a means of clearing her mind. Melianna held out her hand towards the Grand Hall.

"She's in the study in the lower west wing. Do you wish me to escort you?"

Desaunius shook her head. She had been to the lady's study enough times to know where it was, and the lay of the castle was rather easy to remember. Melianna softly clucked as she led the horse across the courtyard towards the stables. Desaunius didn't waste time as she glided across the marble and ducked under the archway to the lower west wing. She passed the lavatory and took a left when the corridor reached a dead end. At the end of the hall, with its burgundy carpets and crystal torches along the glowing stone walls, was Lady Atara's study. She knocked on the polished wood and waited.

It slid open a crack and Desaunius pushed herself into the room. The door closed behind her. There was an atrium behind the door, then an arch, and then the room opened into a large cavern with a high ceiling. There was a window that looked out to the courtyard on the far side, a bureau to the right with a mirror, and on the left was a fireplace. The logs snapped and crackled within. There was an altar along the back wall and colorful pillows arranged in various areas for sitting.

Atara sat on the wide windowsill, an ivory knitted shawl pulled across her shoulders, her hazel eyes focused on the courtyard. Auburn hair flowed down her back, so shiny it glimmered in the pale light of the room. She wore a rose-colored dress that fell to her ankles, her feet bare. Desaunius cleared her throat and Atara glanced at her, a lazy expression on her face.

"You came without a messenger," she said as she dropped her knees off the windowsill and pushed herself gingerly to her feet. She was much taller than Desaunius, at least by a head, if not more. She wandered over to the bureau and pulled out a drawer, lighting a stick of incense with her fingers and placing it in a holder in front of the mirror.

Desaunius glared at her. "I had no time to send a messenger. And you don't look busy."

Atara hummed thoughtfully and put her hands together. "No, I'm not occupied."

"Then you have time to listen to my dilemma," Desaunius said.

Atara stretched her hand towards a cluster of pillows. "Come sit. I'll have Melianna bring some tea." She went to gesture to her servant, who was nowhere near them, but Desaunius held up a hand.

"I won't sit," she said, her voice so thin and papery it almost cracked. "And you will understand me." Despite Atara's station on Avristar, Desaunius was older and wiser. She was vexed by Atara's dreamy presence. Atara was smarter than she acted; her lack of seriousness bothered her.

Atara grasped her elbow with one hand and narrowed her eyes. "Speak, and I will tell you what I see." On top of her sovereignty, Atara had always been a gifted seer and healer. Her adepts in the Lands of Men always benefited from her guidance and foresight.

Desaunius took in a breath and closed her eyes for a moment, the heady scent of dragon's blood wafting through the room. "My apprentice Kaliel has recently been to the Great Oak."

Atara let her arms drop to her sides. "And this is why you did not send a messenger?"

Desaunius pulled her jaw taut. She squeezed her fist, and lifted her chin so she could see Atara better. She was finished with toying with the Lady of the Land. If she needed to be startled then she would be. "A seed to bloom knows not if it will be, a flower or a weed, and cannot change its form once matured. Bloom the weed of temptation and expire the great garden of life. Bloom the flower of sacrifice and

59

sustain the great garden in strife." Her words bounced off the walls in the vast chamber.

Atara's eyes widened. She backed up and slumped into a heap of pillows, her lips mouthing words, but no sound came out.

"You tell me what you think it means," Desaunius said evenly as she crossed her arms.

"A catalyst," Atara replied, her voice low. She glanced at Desaunius, her eyes full of sorrow. "Your apprentice will play a great part in a war." She whispered the last word, as though she was afraid to say it.

"My apprentice is only a child."

"She won't be one forever. We can't be sure where—"

"Obviously in the Lands of Men." She didn't want to entertain the thought of Avristar under attack.

Atara dully nodded. She pushed herself out of the pillows and began pacing the floor. "Yes, of course, the Lands of Men, but the parable, it means a great deal more." Her lips curled around her fist as she closed her eyes, appearing deep in thought.

Desaunius frowned then smiled with amusement. "You would revel in the glory, wouldn't you?" She snorted and crossed her arms. "This isn't about glory or champions of Avristar. Kaliel is …" She was unsure how to explain it. The girl was shy, clumsy and mischievous. She didn't have any of the qualities of a warrior much less a champion. It was hard to see her as anything but fragile and naïve.

"It doesn't matter. The Great Oak is never wrong," Atara said.

"Do you think it believes what you do about the girl?"

Atara's eyes widened then settled into apparent denial. "That she's a Flame? No, and it's nearly impossible."

Desaunius gulped. "Yes, with there being only nine of them in all the lands."

Atara let out a breath. "I didn't mean that. Yes, the odds are slim, but why would we need one? We have the armies, the Valtanyana are locked away."

Desaunius glanced at the incense on the bureau, the chalky ash tumbling onto polished mahogany. She didn't want to follow Atara's train of thought at all. "The Flames have only been used in great wars."

"And Avristar has not seen war in thousands of years. Which is why she couldn't possibly be a Flame," Desaunius said. "The idea is ridiculous."

Atara straightened her back and stopped pacing; she made eye contact with Desaunius, her mouth set in a straight line. "Either way, she is a catalyst, someone who will make a difference. I think it best that she comes to me, trains here in Orlondir. Evennses is a place for children and she won't be a child when she leaves Avristar."

Desaunius hardened her gaze. "I always hoped she would never leave."

Atara smiled faintly. "She'll be strong when she does. Come, will you stay for tea in the courtyard?"

"Nay, I should return and deliver the news," Desaunius said as Atara drifted out of the room, entering into her dreamy façade again. She grimaced to herself: there was no way Kaliel would ever survive the Lands of Men the way she was now, and the way the Great Oak made it sound, she wouldn't have a choice. She followed the Lady of Avristar through the corridors towards the courtyard.

• • •

Kaliel got tired of searching. She hadn't found any of the ingredients for the tea and she was becoming irritated that Pux wasn't in his usual spot.

"Pux!" she called into the forests.

No answer.

The birds chirped back at her and a rabbit darted through the trees. She sighed and threw her hands up in the air. She turned around in circles and then planted her back firmly against a tree trunk. Just as she was sinking down to the ground a hand reached for her shoulder and tapped it hard. Her head whipped in the direction of the tap, but no one was there.

"Boo!" Pux jumped out from the other side of the tree and startled her. She screamed and snapped her head in the opposite direction.

"You! I've been looking everywhere!"

Pux grinned arrogantly while she glowered at him. "The master of disguise."

"How about I chase you back to Luenelle?" she shrieked.

Pux shuddered. "She doesn't like me."

"I know." Kaliel frowned. She pushed her back off the tree. "I have to find herbs to make a tea. Would you like to help?" Her rotten

61

mood from earlier faded away. When she was with Pux life was uncomplicated. She wished she could feel that way all the time.

"Sure, but I don't know the names of any herbs."

"All you need to do is tell me if you see any flowers or plants growing anywhere on the trail."

Pux raised an eyebrow. "Is that all?"

"I'll decide if I need them or not."

He seemed to contemplate it. "Okay, I'm in. Where do we begin?"

She thought for a moment. "Was there anything behind that tree you jumped out from?"

"Mushrooms."

"No, don't need those."

"Good because they were yummy."

Her jaw dropped. "You ate them?"

He grinned from ear to ear. "I turned them green first."

Kaliel turned, disgusted by the childishness of her friend. A day ago she would have thought it was funny, but today it just made her frustrated. She peered between two trees, trying to look for chamomile flowers, but there was only grass and brush behind them. Pux skipped along behind her, using his magic to turn leaves different colors.

"That's odd," he said.

"What is?"

"Leaves."

Kaliel cocked her head to one side in confusion.

"They only turn yellow, brown, red, orange and green."

She poked her head through another break in the trees and looked around. She was almost certain there was nothing there until her eyes caught sight of them. There was a perfect batch of chamomile flowers growing just out of her peripheral vision. She turned back to Pux. "What color were you trying for?"

"Blue." He caught up to her and watched while she struggled awkwardly to fit her leg around the overgrown stump that forced the two trees together. Once she was on the other side she looked back at him.

"What happened?" She rummaged around on the ground, picking up the flowers. She held them like a bouquet as she tried to climb back over the stump.

He scrunched up his nose. "It turned to a puke color."

62

She hopped down and made eye contact with him as she put the bouquet of flowers in the basket he held out for her. "Maybe the land is telling you not to mess with it."

Pux frowned. "Maybe I'll turn the sky pink."

"Not that you could!" Kaliel laughed. Normally she would have encouraged him to try it and she would have warned him about getting caught for doing so, but today she found him more impish than naïve.

"How many days are left on the countdown?" he asked, changing the subject.

Kaliel shot him a glance. "I went yesterday."

"Oh."

She noticed the bitterness in his tone as she continued to scour the lands for herbs. Luenelle was right: he wasn't better for more than holding the basket. She plodded up the path without answering him and he came shuffling after her like a forlorn animal. "Nothing is different," she reassured him. She found a patch of lemongrass growing near a tree and carefully ripped up a few strands.

"What did the Great Oak say to you?" He sounded wary.

Kaliel brushed him off. "I can't tell you." She spotted a hibiscus flower on the south side of a tree.

"I told you mine."

"Yours was different. Mine was ..." Her face burned with embarrassment and fear.

"It was bad?"

She sighed. "Desaunius went to Orlondir."

Pux's eyes widened like someone had punched him in the ribs. Stumbling back, he tripped on his own feet and landed on his back, his elbows digging into the mud. "You'll leave me," he squeaked.

Kaliel couldn't help the knots forming in her stomach. He was older than she was, but he acted much younger. She knelt down beside him and threw her arms around him, squeezing like she needed him to breathe. "Not right away. Luenelle hasn't been called. She'll leave long before me."

Pux seemed unusually disturbed by this. "You aren't a child anymore."

She giggled. "I haven't grown up in one day." She was trying her best to calm his nerves so she could forget all about the Great Oak and concentrate on making chamomile tea. On the inside her emotions were crashing within her and she hoped he wouldn't speak the words she was thinking.

"But something *is* different."

"Aye," she whispered. "I can't be afraid."

She crumpled onto her knees and crawled over to the tree. She turned around and sat with her back against the trunk, taking deep breaths. She became very quiet and all Pux did was stare at her. "All will be well," she said. She stood and stuck out her hand to help him to his feet.

Pux avoided her touch and got to his feet on his own. They slowly walked through the forest back to the House of Kin.

8-The Valtanyana

There was a bustle of kinfolk around her, trying to cook dinner. Kaliel took a spot away from the commotion and began cutting up the herbs she had collected.

"How did you manage to take so long finding these?" Luenelle asked.

Kaliel looked at the chamomile flowers and winced. "To be honest, I don't even know if I have the right ones."

Luenelle cringed and went to work sorting the herbs. She helped Kaliel add the ingredients to the pot. When they were finished they hung the pot over top of the flames. "I'm sure it'll be fine."

"I hope so."

The water boiled and Luenelle took it off the hook with a rag. She set it on the counter and took out a clay pitcher and two cups from one of the cupboards. "You can steep it now."

Kaliel took the pot and steeped the tea into the pitcher, then poured herself and Luenelle a cup. She took a deep breath. "Do you want to try it first?"

"Together," Luenelle said. Both girls held the cups to their lips, blowing the steam off the hot liquid before taking a sip.

"Blech!" Kaliel exclaimed as she swallowed a mouthful of rotten tea.

"Blech!"

Kaliel sighed and looked at her friend. "I didn't get the right herbs."

"Gah ... it tastes like bindweed!" Luenelle exclaimed. She took the cups to the door and dumped the liquid back into the land at the tree line.

"I'll never get it right," Kaliel said as she fled from the kitchen. She ran down the corridor towards the common room. All she wanted was to escape to the depths of the lake, to swim with the merfolk and to feel the way she had when Krishani's eyes were on her as they had been that night in Orlondir. However, as she turned the corner she noticed a small old woman in the common room. Desaunius had returned. She gasped and doubled over in shock. "Elder!"

Desaunius had a forlorn expression on her face. "I must speak with you, Kaliel." Her eyes darted towards the kinfolk that trickled through the room, playing with toys. "Can we go to your quarters, please?"

Kaliel nodded. She followed Desaunius up the stairs to her room and tried to avoid the curious expressions of the kinfolk around her. When they were upstairs, Desaunius sat on the bed and motioned for her to sit as well. She reluctantly obeyed.

"There comes a time, Kaliel," Desaunius began. She looked afraid; faint redness circling her eyes as though she had been weeping. She took Kaliel's hand in her own; it was trembling. "There comes a time when a glorious opportunity comes to us."

Kaliel only gave her a hard stare, allowing the words to sink in. Desaunius wasn't allowed a chance to continue when the anger within Kaliel crashed against the fear and sadness she had been feeling all day. "You're sending me away," she shouted at the top of her lungs. She sprang to her feet. "I knew it would change everything, that wretched tree, it's vile!" She looked at Desaunius, who was taken aback. Before her elder could speak another word she dashed out of her room and clambered down the stairs.

She couldn't even think except how much she needed Krishani. It wouldn't be so hard if she knew she would see him again. But being sent away meant the Lands of Men, and that scared her most. She broke into a sprint when she reached the meadow and continued until she hit the forbidden path. She skillfully skipped over roots and crevasses, as fast as her feet could carry her she wound her way down the path until she found the dead end.

"Let me through," she commanded.

"Such anger, child," the tree said.

Kaliel's heart ached. She wanted to pound her fists against the tree, but she knew it would do nothing. She sunk to her knees. "Please, I beg you. I want to see them one last time." She touched the tree to share her torment and it received the message. The hole appeared between the trunks and she disappeared through it.

Kaliel stared briefly at the magnificence of the late-afternoon sky as she ripped off her green dress and stumbled into the water. Anger bubbled in her veins as she felt for the ledge of the sandbar. Her toes curled around it as she plunged herself into the depths. She called out to the merfolk with her thoughts, but they were muddled and instead of the usual cooing it came out scrambled. She peddled on like a frog, using her legs to force herself deeper. Even when the pressure in her ears built up she continued on. They burst and her head swelled with pain. None of it mattered if they were to send her away to the Lands of Men, if everything she had ever known was going to change.

Her mind drifted to Pux. He would be so angry when he found out. What was so important about the Great Oak's message? Why did she need to go anywhere?

She fought to control herself as the water became unnaturally cold. Almost at the bottom, she pushed further, wondering why the merfolk hadn't come yet. She was sure they would notice her presence. Her hand curled around something at the bottom of the lake—packed mud. She smiled to herself—reaching the bottom was something she had always wanted to do. It reminded her of the shimmering rocks underneath the waterfall in Orlondir. Kaliel smiled as she turned around and prepared to swim to the surface.

Something crept around her foot. She pulled away, wondering if it was her merfolk friends, but it wrapped her leg tighter and something slimy pressed against her skin. She panicked. The mysteries of the deep weren't something she had considered before this. She paused, allowing her body to go limp. She thought about the language of the merfolk, hoping they would arrive soon.

Kaliel contemplated her options: wait longer or do something to free herself. She cringed at her decision and opened her mouth, letting a loud *coo* roll off her tongue. She knew she would lose almost all her air in doing so, but she had no other choice. Unfortunately, her idea didn't pan out the way she had planned. Her call must have frightened the beast that shackled her leg because instead of loosening its grip on her, it tightened. She tried to scream, but her lungs filled with water. She began to kick and bat at the creature frantically trying to free herself. It only gripped her leg harder in response. Kaliel felt faint. She fought until she had no will, and then passed out.

The blackness was like the thick mist that surrounded the island. It made her feel weightless and free. The pressure in her ears subsided, and everything grew quiet. All she could think about were the warnings she had been given, and how she hadn't listened. There was a roaring sound from far away and something warm hit her cheeks followed by something cold. Kaliel gasped, coughed and sputtered as she splashed around in the lake, her head above water. There was a hand clamped to her forearm, holding her in place. She shook it off, and the slick black merfolk dove back into the lake, leaving her to find the shore on her own.

She paddled clumsily to the ledge and fell on her knees. She took deep breaths in the waist-deep water, trying to catch her breath. Shaking her head in disbelief, reality crashed down on her. There *was* something to fear in the lake. She turned towards the shore and saw a parade of kinfolk from the House of Kin staring at her with mixed looks of disbelief and disappointment. Her stomach churned; she was in more trouble than ever this time.

● ● ●

Desaunius waited for Kaliel in the morning. She wouldn't allow her to walk through the forests unaccompanied any longer. They made good progress on the way to the cottage, both of them remaining silent while they walked. Kaliel hadn't said a word on the way back to the House of Kin the night before, and she was ready by the time her elder had arrived to pick her up.

"There is no lesson this morning," Desaunius said. Kaliel hung her head. They entered the cottage and Desaunius led her into the common room, two cups of tea already waiting for them on the small wooden table. Kaliel sat and looked at the floor.

Desaunius sighed as she inspected the girl. She looked too proper—her dress unwrinkled, her hair combed at its sides, and her face clean. "You have been summoned by Lady Atara of Orlondir. She wants you as her apprentice."

Kaliel turned green. "Is that because of my trespassing?"

Desaunius frowned. She didn't want to talk about the merfolk. Why Kaliel risked her life was beyond her. "Nay, it is due to the Great Oak." Her voice was low.

Kaliel seemed scared as she took a sip of tea. Desaunius figured she was trying to avoid another outburst, drifting in and out of the conversation. She couldn't blame the girl for barely listening.

"How long until I must …?" Kaliel choked.

Desaunius looked at the girl with compassion. "We have until Beltane to prepare you." She reached for the tea and took a sip. No matter what Kaliel had done in the past, she was still saddened by this turn of events.

"That isn't long at all." She looked at the solid wooden slab of the tabletop. She put her tea on the table and twisted her hands in her lap. Desaunius followed, turning towards the circular window behind her. Strips of sunlight dimly lit the room, casting Kaliel in shadows.

"I will still see you at the Fire Festivals," Desaunius said.

"Twice a year," Kaliel mumbled.

Desaunius let out an exasperated sigh. "This shouldn't be this hard," she began but wasn't sure who she was talking about—herself or Kaliel? It was hard to let such a fragile girl go to Orlondir to train with an elder like Atara. She feared what would happen to Kaliel, the girl had become like a daughter to her.

"But it is," Kaliel said, her voice choked.

Desaunius resisted the urge to pull her into her arms and instead smoothed out her royal blue dress. "What have you learned about the parable?"

Kaliel made a noise that was somewhere between a burp and a hiccup. She glanced at the floor and shifted her weight. "I don't know why me."

"Why you?"

"Why would it tell me that?"

Desaunius shook her head. "I don't understand what you mean. The parable is yours; I cannot tell you what it means. That is for you to discover."

Kaliel let out a frustrated breath and dropped her hands at her side. She pushed a lock of snow-white hair out of her face and let her green eyes fall on Desaunius. "It scares everyone, including me. Why would the Great Oak do that?"

She tore her eyes away from her apprentice and glanced at the floor. "Do you remember the stories about Avred?"

Kaliel pulled her eyebrows together and shook her head. "Who is Avred?"

Desaunius kept her eyes on the floor, shuffling her slippers back and forth against the dirt. "He was—*is*—the male spirit of the land. When Avristar was under attack by the Valtanyana, he became the difference between salvation and destruction."

Kaliel went rigid. "Why are you telling me this?"

"Because some of us have a great purpose in life, Kaliel, and whether you choose to see it or not, the Great Oak was only telling you the truth." She opened her mouth to continue, but closed it and shook her head. "I cannot tell you more. You know how it used to be."

"The Valtanyana ruined everything," she whispered.

"Yes, they did. They began in Avristyr and its sister realms and spread to Avrigard, and eventually to Avristar and its seven Lands of Men. There was no stopping their unnatural destruction."

"But Avristar won. They beat the Valtanyana," Kaliel said, her eyes shining with a false sense of pride.

Desaunius nodded. She had told stories of the First Era to every apprentice she had counseled since those tarnished times. Many of them had gone to the Lands of Men, others had stayed in Avristar, escaping to Nandaro in the north and living with the secluded tribes. She wanted a simple life for Kaliel because there was something about her that made Desaunius feel overprotective. Kaliel wasn't like the other apprentices. Sometimes she was too naïve and other times too curious for her own good. She was as delicate as the bed of flowers they had found her nestled in. She eyed the girl's appearance, a thick red bruise on her left shin just under her knee cap. Kaliel was obviously trying to conceal it by crossing that leg behind the other one, but part of it still peeked out.

"Avristar needed Avred to win that war. She also needed High King Tor and the Flames. He trapped them in Avrigost," Desaunius said.

"The place nobody speaks of," Kaliel said, her eyes meeting with her elder's.

"Yes, because that is an ugly fate. Nobody ever comes back from Avrigost. It is a wasteland."

"You told me the Lands of Men were a wasteland," Kaliel pointed out, with an uncomfortable expression on her face.

Desaunius softened. "The Lands of Men aren't like Avrigost. The Lands of Men are simply in need of our help. After what the Valtanyana brought ..." She looked troubled. "The kinfolk of Avristar have been charged with the task of restoring the Lands of Men to their former glory."

"You mean bring peace to them?"

"Yes, I've told you this many times, Kaliel. You don't have anything to be afraid of. You won't go until you reach the age of maturity and marry the land."

Kaliel quickly grabbed her tea and took a long sip, followed by a deep breath. She seemed put off by the entire conversation, but was handling herself rather well. Desaunius noticed her knee was shaking, and her fingers trembled against the cup. At least the girl hadn't run off to the lake again. It was a start.

"How did you end up on Avristar?" Kaliel asked. She put the cup on the wooden slab and wrung her hands out along her sides, pressing them under her thighs to avoid the trembling.

Desaunius shook her head. "Maybe I will tell you another time."

"We don't have that much time."

Desaunius let out a haughty laugh and glared at her. "I escaped from Tempia and came here for refuge. I hid in the rainforests of Nandaro in the Village of the Shee until the war was over. Then I came to Orlondir and asked Lady Atara if I could stay."

"What about your other life?" Kaliel asked. It was a bold move.

Desaunius sucked in a breath; the glare not leaving her face. "Tor ... he was mine until the Valtanyana came for him. They wanted him to join them."

Kaliel's eyes widened. Desaunius never told her that before. "He was what?"

"My betrothed."

Kaliel gulped. "You mean the land let you be together?"

Desaunius let out a sigh. "It wasn't like that on Tempia. Traditions were different."

"Did you love him?"

"And what do you know of love Kaliel?"

"Nothing ... I just ... I wanted to know why you couldn't be with him anymore."

Desaunius bit her lip and stared out the window. She didn't want to explain this to Kaliel. Elvens on Avristar married the land and went to the Lands of Men to serve. They weren't like the feorns, the fae, the shee, or the centaurs, frivolously falling in love and settling down in villages throughout Orlondir and Nandaro. Love wasn't something Kaliel would ever know. It seemed so awkward for her to want to know anything about it. She glanced at her apprentice. "High King Tor lives in the Great Hall and keeps the peace between all the lands. I stay on Avristar and train apprentices that will do the same." She pursed her lips. "Chores. You need to be off to do yours." Desaunius stood and led Kaliel to the door. The girl stepped into the hallway and turned. Her green eyes seemed dull, even sad.

"Do you think you'll ever see him again?" she asked.

Desaunius looked stricken; she flinched and narrowed her eyes. "That's quite enough, Kaliel. We are finished for today."

Kaliel gulped and pulled the door open. She darted through the garden without another word and raced across the path away from the hollow mound. Desaunius watched her go, knowing she had made the girl upset. She sank onto the log and stared out the window. She *did* miss him, but there were more important things in the lands than love.

• • •

Nightfall came. Kaliel shot up in her cot, pressing her hands to her chest. She tried to catch her breath as the nightmare drained away. Instinctively, she pushed the blankets aside and stood up. Her head swirled with dizziness and she fell back onto the bed. Closing her eyes, indigo flames danced behind them. She didn't know what to think of the flames, but ever since she had gone to the Great Oak she had dreams of them. She pushed away the images and sat up again, her eyes scanning the room. She rolled over and pulled out her birthstone from the nightstand. It was something she had been given in Orlondir. Hers was shaped like an egg with a milky white translucency. She held it in her hands and closed her eyes again. The lake, she thought of the lake. The pounding subsided, and she relaxed. She opened her eyes and looked at the ceiling.

She tried to stand and everything seemed normal. She padded down the hallway and reached the stairs. She glanced over the railing into the common room, Luenelle sitting on the rocking chair, knitting a beige quilt.

"Kaliel?" Luenelle asked as the girl turned away from the rails.

She hung her head and trudged down the steps, running her hands along her nightgown. She reached the last stair and gave Luenelle a crooked smile. "I can't sleep."

Luenelle sighed. "Would you like to sit with me? I still have a fire going."

Kaliel felt a shock hit her chest at the thought of the fire. She shook her head and backed onto the second step. "No."

Luenelle put the knitting needles in her lap and narrowed her eyes. "You won't go to the lake again."

"I know," she whispered, moving to the next stair.

"Morning will come sooner than you think," Luenelle said gently.

Kaliel nodded, hiding the fear that was circling her senses. It was only a dream; the girl with the indigo eyes, the flames, it was her imagination. Still, she had no desire to watch the hearth fire. She eased up the winding staircase and found her room. She pushed her face into the pillow and tried to convince herself it wasn't real.

9-THE ROYAL CITY

K aliel darted inside the House of Kin after her lesson. Moons had passed since the call to Orlondir, and the time to leave drew near. She dragged her feet up the stairs and glanced at the bags that had been there for days. She sighed. There wasn't much for her to take: the dresses in the drawers, her hair brush and ribbons for tying it back, her slippers, journal, and the birthstone. It was sitting in the middle of her dresser in a small box Luenelle had lent to her. She took the stone in her hands, turning it back and forth, staring at its milky white translucency.

Someone passed by her room without stopping. Kaliel blinked and put the stone on the bed. She smiled, hoping it wasn't Luenelle checking on her progress with packing. She opened one of the drawers and took out a stack of dresses and placed them in the bag. Silence ensued, and she realized that nobody was interested in speaking with her. She closed the door for security and turned back to the bed. Picking up the stone, she closed her eyes and tried to invoke its energy.

Please, she thought.

She hadn't thanked the merfolk for saving her, and wasn't sure how they would react if she tried to visit them again. She shuddered at the thought of the beast that had kept her prisoner to their depths. Desaunius might not have been right about the merfolk, but there was something to fear in the waters.

Kaliel sighed as she held the birthstone. She felt the currents of the lake swishing back and forth over the crystal as it remained embedded in the soil. Luenelle said that was where the birthstones formed, at the bottom of the lake. Kaliel felt as though she were surrounded by the sounds of the lake as the currents pushed and pulled at her.

A rush of violet-colored light struck her. She gasped and dropped the stone. The violet light faded as she gawked at it. Underneath the milky white cover the birthstone shone a faint violet hue. She took a deep breath and as she exhaled the violet intensified, encompassing the aura of the stone. Her jaw fell open as she passed the stone from hand to hand, staring at it in wonder.

There was a knock on the door, and she quickly placed the stone in its box.

"Kaliel?" It was Pux.

She sighed, anxiety building. Pux had been upset when she told him she was leaving. He hadn't spoken to her in weeks. She cautiously opened the door and he came flooding into the room.

"I came to say—I mean—you didn't think I was going to ..." He paced, then stopped and hugged her sheepishly. "I'll miss you," he said as he left.

Kaliel fell back against the dresser. "I'll miss you, too." She shook her head and sunk to the floor and began to fill the bag with more clothing.

• • •

Kaliel lay awake in her bed in the middle of the night. She hadn't paid much attention to the Beltane festival this year because there was too much on her mind. Desaunius came at sunset, along with the rest of the elders from the forest, nineteen of them in total. Food was served and music was played and blessings were given. Kaliel watched the others enjoy the celebration; there was nothing for her to celebrate.

She rolled onto her side and closed her eyes hoping sleep would come. It had been a dreary day and all she longed for was its end. She turned onto her other side and hugged her pillow tighter, then she rolled onto her back and stared at the ceiling.

One last time, she thought as she threw off the blanket and pulled on her slippers. She padded down the hallway to the staircase. Luenelle was passed out in the rocking chair across from the hearth fire. Kaliel thanked the stars for her last endeavor to see the merfolk. She slipped out the front door, past the porch and broke into a run through the meadow. Her heart soared with passion and exhilaration as she hit the break in the trees and began winding down the path towards the lake. This time she didn't trip. When she ran her hands along the trees they whispered to her in a voice she missed hearing. She smiled. It was gibberish, they were speaking all at once, and she had no time to sit and listen to them. Still, it was wonderful to hear. The path narrowed. She pawed around in the dark, looking for the dead end and then her hand touched the bark, and she let it sink into the tree.

"I have returned," she whispered with a smile. She slunk to the ground and sat against the tree.

"I cannot allow it," the tree boomed.

Her heart dropped. "You won't let me pass?"

"Nay, you may not pass."

She thought for a moment, the comfort and freedom dissipating. "Why?"

"They have forbidden it."

"Who?"

"The elders of the merfolk."

Kaliel gasped. Suddenly she realized how much her treachery had cost her. They didn't follow the laws of Avristar; it wasn't their place to save her life. "Will they be reasonable?"

"They will withdraw."

Kaliel nodded. She understood. They would leave the shores of Avristar and find a new home. There was no point in facing them; their elders would force her to suffer the consequences of her wrongdoing. There was no way to fix it. She pressed her hand to the tree in apology and hoped for a flower to sprout at the base of it. When her hand brushed across the grass in front of the tree she felt the prickly sting of a leaf. She gasped.

Bloom the weed of temptation.

Pangs of guilt hit her as she stumbled away from the dead end and headed towards the House of Kin.

• • •

The ride to Orlondir was dreary and slow. As they passed the wide path between the trees, Kaliel heard their whispers of goodbye, and it broke her heart to think she might never return. Long silences ensued and once Evennses was a memory behind them, Kaliel inched up to the front of the carriage, poking her head through the canvas.

"Do you know what the lady thinks of my parable?" she asked. Some conversation was better than the bitter silence. Apprehension of meeting the Lady of the Land pressed on her temples.

"I cannot tell you, Kaliel," Desaunius replied as she kept her gaze on the path.

Kaliel sat back with a huff and then leaned forward again. "Why?"

"Because I don't know," Desaunius said.

The carriage pulled into Orlondir and the smell of apples hit Kaliel full on. Her lips spread into a smile at the sweetness of it, and she sighed. Everything about Orlondir reminded her of Krishani. Being in the place they met a year and a half ago only made her more nervous. She wondered how she could distract herself from the pull of the waterfall, the longing to see the merfolk in the pond. It would be impossible. All she could hope for was benevolence or ignorance from her new elder.

Orlondir stretched on for acres. The trees weren't as tall as the ones in Evennses; they thinned out to allow for grass, small ponds and springs to sprout from the land. They passed a break in the trees where a smaller path led to one of the many villages in Orlondir. Kaliel could smell the smoke from the hearth fire and let the scent comfort her.

She poked her head through the canvas again. "Does Lady Atara have any other apprentices in Orlondir?"

"No," Desaunius answered, her shoulders tightening.

Kaliel frowned. The prospect of friends was out of the question. "Has she ever had apprentices?"

"Yes, many of them."

"Where are they now?"

"The Lands of Men," Desaunius said.

Kaliel twisted in her hands in her lap, unsure what to think. She was curious about the affairs in the Lands of Men, but not curious enough to leave Avristar. "Do they ever return?"

"Sometimes."

Kaliel stared at the roof of the carriage. Orlondir was so vibrant during the festival season; it seemed so cold in between. The Beltane Festival had just ended, and so it would be many moons before Samhain. A pang of nerves hit her as she realized if she was patient, she might see Krishani again. She peered out the front of the caravan. The horse's tails swished back and forth as they pulled towards the bridge and the moat. She caught them out of the corner of her eye and her senses perked up, the sadness draining away.

"Is that—?" she asked, pointing at the stone walls around the castle.

"Aye, we have arrived," Desaunius said.

The horses pulled through the wide, heavy gates and trotted into the courtyard. Desaunius yanked on the reins and pulled them to a stop.

Kaliel paused in the back of the carriage, and waited for Desaunius to come around back and assist her. The girl who showed herself a moment later wasn't Desaunius. She had long brown hair and eyes, pointed ears and a bland linen gown.

"Greetings," the girl said with bright eyes.

"Greetings," Kaliel said.

The girl held out her hand and Kaliel hopped off the back of the carriage, landing on the cobble-stone walkway. She winced at the hard stone against her slippers, but shook away the discomfort. She went to get her bag, but the girl already had it on the ground. Kaliel quickened her pace and reached for the little box with the birthstone. It was the only memory of home she had.

Desaunius rounded the carriage and pulled Kaliel into her embrace. "Be well, child," she whispered into her hair.

Kaliel was unsure how she would feel when the moment came, but now that it was here she was sad. "I want to go home."

Desaunius laughed. "Be strong," she said, then whispered, "And wild."

Kaliel pulled her into an embrace. "Thank you," she whispered. She glanced at the servant girl for a moment, hoping she would say something, but she stayed silent.

"Give Atara my regards," Desaunius said.

The servant bowed her head and struggled to sling the bag over her shoulder. "This way, Kaliel."

Kaliel followed her, but turned, watching Desaunius pull the carriage out of the courtyard and over the bridge. She felt a hand on her shoulder.

"It gets easier," the servant girl said.

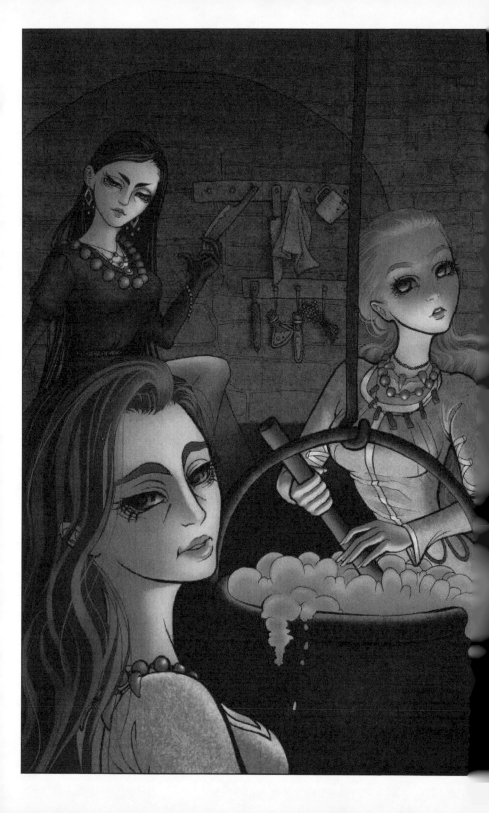

10-THE WITCHES

The servant girl, who had introduced herself as Melianna, returned hours later when Kaliel had settled into her quarters. It was a tower room in the west wing, circular, a green embroidered rug stretching to the edges of the room, leaving a thin strip of stone bare. To the left was a chest that opened to reveal various compartments. Kaliel put the birthstone in one of the hidden drawers for safekeeping. The rest of the room was typical: a bureau sat to the right side, the wide bed in the center, the nightstand beside it. There was nothing else but a cloak stand.

"Lady Atara is ready to see you," Melianna said with a knock at the door. She never crossed the threshold, patiently waiting in the hallway.

Kaliel emerged, her hair tied up in a ribbon for a change, her ivory dress traded for the green flowing one she had worn the day after she saw the Great Oak.

"You look pretty," she said as she led Kaliel to the lower west wing. Even when Kaliel lived in Evennses she knew the joined quarters of the Lord and Lady were across from the balcony that hung over the Grand Hall. When they reached the door Kaliel noticed a shimmer-like glow to it that made her nervous. "Lady Atara is very kind. You shouldn't be afraid," Melianna said. She knocked on the door and waited while it swung inwards. "Farewell," she chirped as she left Kaliel to her own devices.

Kaliel gulped as she crossed the threshold into the room. A soft scent tickled her senses and she breathed it in. *Lavender,* she thought with triumph. If Lady Atara had plans to resume her study of herbs, she was confident she could impress. She passed the small atrium and followed the soft glow of the candles. Burgundy throw pillows were arranged around the room in various patterns for sitting. On the left was a fireplace, to the back was an altar, and on the right was a bureau.

Kaliel noticed immediately the room was bereft of a bed, but she assumed the lady didn't sleep there. She felt an odd sense of calm wash over her as Lady Atara turned from the bureau and looked her over.

"Brilliant," Atara whispered.

Kaliel found herself speechless, her tongue caught somewhere in her throat. She shook her head and stammered on her words. "Greetings."

Atara raised an eyebrow. "Desaunius warned me of this. Day-dreaming again?"

Kaliel flushed as she dropped her eyes to the ground. She shook her head, unsure what to say.

"Come, please have a seat." Atara gestured to a cluster of pillows in the far corner and Kaliel reluctantly sat. She bit her lip as her eyes met Atara's. They were a beautiful hazel.

"Do you know why you're here?" Atara asked.

Kaliel nodded. "It's what the Great Oak said."

"Yes, exactly. Do you understand the parable?" Her eyes filled with compassion and curiosity.

Kaliel hugged her knees to her chest. "It had to be wrong," she mumbled, thinking of the weed that sprouted at the tree's feet in Evennses. It was easier to believe there was a mistake than believe she would bloom into anything, much less a flower or a weed, than take the Great Oak's words as truth.

"Excuse me?" Atara asked. She sounded offended.

Kaliel gulped. "I mean, I'm not special. I'm not destined for greatness, or a chosen one, or anything. I've always been shy."

Atara let out a short laugh. "You do not see what the Great Oak sees in you."

Kaliel shook her head.

"Do you distrust its wisdom?"

Kaliel continued to shake her head. She didn't know what to think being in the presence of Lady Atara. The woman was so different than Desaunius it was unnerving. Her direct questions and piercing gaze caught Kaliel off guard. Atara wasn't scrutinizing her, she was wondering at her. That didn't calm Kaliel at all. "No," she said immediately. "I distrust … myself."

"We will work on that. You can trust me, Kaliel. I'm only here to help you with your abilities."

Kaliel looked up from her knees, panic triturating through her. "Abilities?"

"Things you can do that the other kinfolk cannot. Have you had any experiences like that?"

Kaliel sighed, thinking back to her childhood. Every occurrence was something no other kinfolk had experienced. Her mind traced over the flowers and the conversations with the trees, and the merfolk. She scowled. Why was Pux still in Evennses if he could manipulate nature? That was unique. Atara continued to eye her and Kaliel knew she had to answer.

"Yes, I have experienced things like that."

"It will help me more if you would explain."

Kaliel straightened and smoothed out her dress and avoided eye contact. She wanted to answer truthfully, but she also wanted to keep her secrets, like her best friend and his abilities. "I have trouble remembering things," she said, hoping she had expertly diverted her elder's attention.

Atara narrowed her eyes and shifted her position on the pillow. "What do the trees think?"

Kaliel scoffed without realizing it. "They are too cheeky sometimes, they call me names and they think I'm a fool." She glanced at Atara, who wore a knowing grin, and clapped her hands over her mouth. She wanted to stuff the words back into her mouth.

"And do you not think that makes you special?"

"It makes me different, and swimming with the merfolk gets me in trouble." The words just came out. She covered her mouth again, willing herself to stay strong, to keep something to herself. Being kinfolk made it impossible to lie but there were always ways around telling the whole truth.

"The merfolk?" Atara repeated; her voice pitchy and uneven.

Kaliel shot her a sideways glance. "Yes …" she said slowly, carefully monitoring her words.

"How did you—?"

"With my thoughts?" Kaliel tried, tension coiling her muscles. She hoped the merfolk at the waterfall hadn't left, too. She wished Atara wouldn't ask her more about them.

Astonishment crossed Atara's face. She nodded and stood. "Right. We will begin our study of meditation tomorrow." She seemed to force a smile on her face.

Kaliel felt the tension thicken as the meeting came to an end. She followed Lady Atara to the door. "Did I do something wrong?"

Atara's expression warmed. "No, not at all. You are very special, Kaliel, remember that."

"Thank you," she mumbled as she exited the room.

• • •

Kaliel found herself alone in the corridor, crystal torches illuminating the burgundy carpet. She tried to find her way back to her quarters. Melianna had given her a full tour, but it wasn't as simple in practice as it was in theory. She passed the lavatory and saw the continuous marble floor stretch across the Grand Hall. The fountain loomed in the distance and she realized where she was.

As she passed the archway into the room she heard a whisper. Her heart raced, startled by the subtle noise. She treaded across the floor towards the staircase and heard it again. She paused; it was coming from the lower east wing. She furrowed her brow and crossed the floor, passing another archway and went down a long corridor towards an unknown part of the castle. Melianna hadn't toured there.

The whispers grew as she neared the door. A thin strip of light cascaded across the floor, showing off the cream-colored carpet. She stopped and listened for the whisper again.

"You are still missing something for the brew."

"We can do without it."

"Begin the incantation."

Kaliel's breath caught in her throat as the whispers formed words. Fear pricked at her insides as she tried to pull herself away, but the door swung open.

She froze as she took in the three women inside. They all had long hair, black, brown and blonde. The blonde one wore a blue dress, the one with black hair had a black dress, and the one with brown hair had a white dress. There were strings and strings of beads hanging from their necks, and each one of them had wrinkles around their eyes. They turned to stare at her, their sharp gazes digging into her.

"Look at what we have here," the one in black said.

"A trespasser," the one in blue replied.

Kaliel took a step away from the door. "I …"

"Don't be rude, standing in doorways. Come in," the one in black said.

Kaliel felt her feet move without her permission as she entered the room. The door shut behind her and she suddenly felt claustrophobic. She ran her hands along the folds of her dress, trying to calm her nerves.

"Are you sure you want to play this game?" the one in blue said as she inspected the girl.

"What game?" Kaliel asked.

She smiled. "None of your concern, child."

Kaliel looked at the floor, unsure what to say next. She desperately wanted to retrace her steps, choose to go to her quarters and stay away from the east wing. She understood all too well why Melianna had avoided it.

The women exchanged wary looks between themselves. "Why did you come here?" the one in black asked; her eyes hard.

Kaliel shuffled back and forth. "I heard your whispers," she muttered.

The one in black let out a squeal and clapped. The one in white continued to stir the brew and Kaliel inhaled the heady scent. It made her dizzy. The one in black composed herself as the one in blue moved towards the witching wall on the opposite end of the room. "You could be very useful to us," she said.

Kaliel glanced behind her at the door. "I could?" Her insides felt like sand, her mouth dry.

The one in blue turned back from the witching wall, carrying something in her hands. She shot a warning glance at the one in black. "Pardon our manners," she said coolly. "I'm Shimma, and this is Kuruny and Kazza." She indicated the woman in black as Kuruny.

Kaliel let out a sigh as she stared into the oceans that created Shimma's eyes. Even with the wrinkles that circled them, she was beautiful.

Surrender

"Come now, where are your manners, trespasser? Who are you?" Kuruny said.

"I'm Kaliel of Evennses," she mumbled, her hands clasped behind her back.

Kuruny smiled. "You're Atara's new apprentice." She spat out the word "apprentice" like it was a bad thing.

"Aye."

Shimma glanced at Kuruny, and without another word grabbed Kaliel's arm and pushed up the sleeve of her green dress. She whipped out a needle and began inspecting the area she would puncture. Kaliel's eyes went wide as she tried to pull her arm away, but Shimma was stronger than her.

"It's better not to struggle while she takes your blood," Kazza said, her voice full of disdain.

Kaliel felt like a sheet of ice. Her pulse quickened as she struggled against Shimma. "Why do you want that?" she asked; her voice thin and airy.

Kuruny shrugged. "For the brew. You're a virgin."

Kaliel had never heard of magic like this; it was foreign and frightening to her. She watched helplessly as Shimma turned her arm over and inspected it closely, holding the needle above her.

"Her veins are so faint," Shimma said with a scowl.

Kazza shook her head. "Use an athame. Must you always be so sterile?"

Kaliel let out a scream as Shimma poked her here and there, but no blood oozed out of the wounds. It pinched and made Kaliel feel like she could melt into a puddle.

Kuruny shot a warning glance at Kazza and the older sister turned from the cauldron and grabbed the athame. Before she returned there was a loud bang and the door swung open with a gust of wind, Lord Istar filling the doorway.

"You will stay out of the affairs of Avristar, so help me!" he roared at Kuruny as she shrunk away.

Shimma dropped the needle and apparatus on the floor and scurried into the corner.

Kaliel's arm dropped to her side and she rubbed it, trying to sooth the pain. She darted behind Lord Istar and waited.

"We caused the girl no harm," Kazza said as she approached with the knife in hand.

Istar glowered at her. "And what is the knife for?"

Kazza smirked at him and cut her own hand, holding it over the cauldron and letting her blood drip into the brew. She smirked. "Blood."

Istar's cold blue eyes blazed at her. "You will leave Kaliel alone. She is not your business." He put a hand out and the liquid inside the cauldron evaporated, causing both Kazza and Kuruny to let out a protested cry. He slammed the door shut and turned to Kaliel.

"Are you well?" he asked, his voice only slightly gentler.

Kaliel nodded, and stood straight. Istar stalked towards the west wing. She followed, his long strides making it hard to keep up.

"Who were those women?" she asked when they were far enough away.

"My daughters. They returned from the Lands of Men, and they no longer follow the traditions of Avristar. They call themselves 'witches.'"

"Oh," Kaliel said quietly as they passed the crystal fountain and found the staircase to the west.

Istar looked her in the eyes. "I advise you not to speak with them again."

"Will they hurt me?"

Istar nodded, and she shuddered. "They know no difference between sacred and profane."

Kaliel nodded. "I understand." In truth, she was more afraid than ever. Orlondir wasn't providing any comfort; it was becoming a dangerous land to her, laced in mystery.

"Well, goodnight then," Istar said. He took off towards the lower east wing and Kaliel slumped on the stairs.

11-THE WATERFALL

P art of her wanted to crawl under the covers and attempt to sleep, but she was afraid of nightmares. She was also afraid the witches would come into her room and try again.

She closed her eyes and let out a deep breath. She felt the familiar restlessness in her bones. The waters—they were the only thing that calmed her. The stone castle was so unfeeling compared to the forests she had lived in her entire life. Her heartbeat thrummed as she closed her eyes and remembered the waterfall. As much as she fought to avoid it, there was no use. She had to see if the merfolk were there. A muddle of knots rested in her as she thought of Krishani. The wait to Samhain was too long, especially if there was only a slim chance he would come.

She ducked through the archway and into the courtyard. It was breathtaking with the moon casting light on the ivy plants crawling over the stone and statues. She quickened her pace and pushed open the gate. Closing it behind her, she hopped over the moat, smiling to herself as she breathed in the night air.

The path was longer than she remembered, winding and twisting through the forest. Her insides shook as she took careful steps. *It's just a waterfall,* she told herself as she heard the rush in the distance. Butterflies crawled in her stomach as she turned the final corner.

It was better than the first time she had seen it. She drifted towards the pond, its surface littered with ripples and foam. She knelt and squinted. She never questioned the light illuminating the pond, but in the darkness, it was mystifying. She watched as one of the creatures swam along the stony floor, its finned head and webbed hands pushing water out of its way. She breathed a sigh of relief. Not all of them had left. She reached up to untie the ribbon in her hair. Even if she couldn't see Krishani again she wanted to swim with them.

"What are you doing here?" someone snapped, their voice deep and uncomforting.

Kaliel shrieked as she turned to face whoever it was, her eyes wide and her heart faltering. She lost her balance as she came to her feet and felt herself careening into the pond. Her eyes found the bushes and the mountain; they seemed to find everything but the person confronting her. Her arms flailed as she braced herself for the ungraceful splash.

Arms surround her waist and pulled her away from the pond, her feet gliding several inches above the stone. She closed her eyes as her feet hit the ground and the arms relaxed around her. Her face flushed with heat and she felt like an idiot for being so foolish. Really, she was going to swim in the pond anyway. This just interrupted everything. The arms left her entirely and she opened her eyes only to find herself confused.

"I'm sorry, Elder, I couldn't sleep," she said, staring at the cloaked being.

He chortled softly, his back turned, his breathing heavy. "I'm still not an elder, not quite."

Kaliel froze. That voice was familiar, melancholy and smooth with confidence at the same time. It was her turn to whip around and bury her face in her hands. Her stomach did a flip-flop, making her pulse reverberate in her ears. She wanted to run, but she felt paralyzed.

"Krishani?" she scarcely whispered, hoping she was wrong, hoping this was someone else.

Anyone but him.

"Kaliel," he said. It was Krishani.

She heard him slide the hood off his cloak and as she turned to face him, she caught his eyes on her, raking over her green dress.

Kaliel stared at him, her heart pounding so hard her ribs ached, her cheeks warm. She tried to hide her blush, but it was impossible. She glanced at the ground to avoid staring into his mismatched eyes.

"I'm such a fool," she muttered to herself, unable to control how she felt around him. Why was he there, anyway? She wanted the ground to swallow her whole, but she also wanted him to run his fingers along her skin. She covered her face, fighting so many urges to touch him it was impossible to think.

"Sorry I scared you," he said, awkwardly running a hand through his hair. He looked at the waterfall and she followed his gaze. Kaliel dared a glance at his profile and died inside, remembering the last time they were at the waterfall, the last thing he said to her. She crossed her arms and tried to find her strength. When he looked back at her she dropped her arms and gritted her teeth.

"I had a bad day," she said, trying to justify herself.

Krishani scowled. "What happened?"

"I met the witches." She tried not to think about what they had done.

"They didn't hurt you, did they?" Krishani's expression softened into concern. He took a step towards her, his frame towering over her. He looked down and she tilted her head up to meet his eyes. It made her melt. "I mean, if they did something, I would ..."

Kaliel wrapped her arms around herself, unable to be that close to him without wanting something more. She moved towards the stone incline, silently begging him to follow. "They scared me." She glanced back at him, curious. "What are you doing here?"

Krishani looked at the ground and shuffled his feet. "I've been here for awhile now."

"Oh." Awkward silence hung between them.

"Lord Istar thought it would be better if I trained with him here."

Kaliel sighed and avoided his gaze. It made her feel transparent. She wanted to sink into the pond and forget everything. She blinked. "Lady Atara summoned me, because of the Great Oak." She looked at him, but his expression was unreadable. "Because of what the Great Oak said."

Krishani moved towards her and brushed the loose hairs off her face. "So you're here to stay?"

Kaliel nodded, stifling the moan in her throat. A single touch and she was undone. He caught her hand and squeezed it as he pulled her up the stone incline and stopped behind the falls. She untangled her sweaty palm from his and faced him, her heart thudding. His closeness was everything she had wanted when she was in Evennses, and now he was here she didn't know how to act. She thought of what

93

Desaunius had said: what did she know about love? "I didn't expect to see you again."

Krishani took a sharp breath and slid his hands into hers. "I never expected to meet you the first time," he whispered.

She tucked her hands under her arms. She looked at the falls, the weight of a thousand dreams of him pressing on her. She didn't know what he was feeling, if it was the same, or different, or if she was just a silly girl he had met a year and a half ago at a place he considered sacred.

"Why *did* we meet?" she asked.

Krishani looked uncomfortable. She wanted him to kiss her, but was afraid of how he might react if she made the first move.

"Because we did," he answered gently as her eyes met his. She relaxed at the answer. He took her hand in his and led her into the cave. He shrugged off his cloak and laid it on the grass.

Kaliel sat beside him and looked at the falls. She loved how close he was, but everything seemed different. The way he looked at her wasn't so conflicted anymore. Last time it was like she was the only one feeling nervous and scared. Now he looked the same.

"What did the witches do to you?" he asked after a long silence.

Kaliel glanced at him, his blue and green eyes still visible in the dark. They were intense, deeply penetrating her senses. "Um, one of them pricked me," she said, try to distract herself from the hypnotic trance she was slipping into.

Krishani carefully slid his hand into hers and placed their clasped hands on his knee. He looked at her with a small smile while she tried not to blush. "Where?"

She swallowed hard and tried not to choke on her own saliva. She coughed involuntarily and shook her head. "Um, the arm you're holding."

Krishani pushed the loose fabric of her sleeve up and ran his fingers along the inside of her forearm. His touch drove her crazy, the subtleness, the rush.

"You mean here?" he asked as he brought her arm to his lips and brushed them across the spot. She shivered. She should have reminded him he was a Brother of Amersil, but seeing him was so unexpected.

"Aye," she whispered, pulling her hand out of his grasp and shrugging the sleeve over her arm. "It feels fine now." She hugged her knees and rested her chin against them. She would marry the land, he would marry the land. There was nothing for her to hold onto. She had to believe the butterflies in her stomach, the shortness of breath and the clammy palms would go away.

"Sorry I scared you," he said.

Kaliel pressed her lips to her knees, hoping she could hold in her emotions. "I'm not afraid of you."

Silence hung between them for awhile. He shifted on the cloak, the black tunic he wore shifting with him. He stretched his legs out, and Kaliel looked at his shin-high boots and breeches. He stole a glance at her turtle shell. "What are you afraid of?"

Kaliel stood. "Happy endings." She didn't know how else to explain it. She had contemplated the parable so many times it was exhausting. It didn't matter which path she took—neither of them seemed very appealing. She let the mist soak her sleeves and stick to her skin. She heard Krishani behind her before he ran his hand down her back making shivers run up her spine. He stayed there, a foot away, and she wished he would move closer, envelope her in his arms. He wasn't supposed to talk to her. This had to be wrong. What would the brotherhood think?

"Happy endings?" he whispered. He sounded both unsure and nervous. "What do you mean?"

"What if someone comes?" She was worried Lord Istar would burst through the trees and find them in this compromising awkwardness. It seemed more taboo than practically drowning in the lake.

Krishani let out a breath. "Nobody ever comes here."

Kaliel closed her eyes. "*You* come here."

Krishani took a step forward and she could feel the heat radiating off him. "All the time."

She didn't answer, instead listening to the sound of the falls. Moonlight glinted off the flecks of water. She thought about the orb of ice he created for her. She hadn't been able to do anything close to that awesome.

"What are you thinking?" he asked again.

She closed her eyes and felt her energy shift; like it had the day she went to the Great Oak. Heat rushed through her as she leaned back, trying to feel him, but not trying to force it if it wasn't what he wanted.

It was clear to her he cared, but she was so worried about whether or not she should let him.

"My parable," she whispered.

He went rigid, his hand sliding down her upper forearm. "What did the Oak say to you?"

She shook her head. "Never mind, I have to figure it out. Both paths seem so dreary."

"You seem too sweet to have a bad parable."

She didn't want to talk about the nightmares of the Flames, the parable, the fact the Brotherhood would disapprove of him touching her. It felt so natural; the last few moons had been lonely without him. She couldn't explain what she felt, but she couldn't watch him marry the land and leave the island.

"But I do," she said. She drew her hands instinctively to her chest, her elbows digging into her ribs. He dropped his hand as she turned, and buried her face in his chest. He reluctantly ran his hands through her hair, letting them rest on the small of her back.

"I thought about you every day," he said as she pressed her cheek into his tunic.

She smiled against his shirt. "And I thought about you."

"Promise me something?" He wasn't holding her, not really, their bodies weren't pressed together and the inches between them made Kaliel feel cold.

"What?"

"You'll find a happy ending."

"What if I can't?"

He pulled back and brushed his thumb across her cheek. "Promise me you will." His eyes met hers and his jaw dropped. His hand paused, cupping her face in his palm. He held her gaze, her heart beating hard. Before she had time to answer, he pressed his lips against hers. She didn't expect him to do that and it was better than she imagined. She came to life under him, kissing him back with unyielding passion that made him pull away to catch his breath.

Kaliel's sadness drained away as he broke from her lips and then cupped her face with both hands and kissed her again, pressing the length of his body against her. His kisses made her feel light and giddy, like she could float into the sky. She slid her hands up his chest and looped them around his neck. There was swimming in the lake and losing her breath and then there was this. Being out of breath with him was like drowning in a sea of happiness. He could keep her prisoner forever and she'd never complain. He pulled away again, and wound his arms around her waist, trapping her against him. His lips found hers again, rough and inexperienced, but strong and satisfying.

She opened her mouth and his tongue grazed hers, warmth spreading from her heart to the rest of her body, making her tingle. She smiled against his lips.

"I missed you." She tried to steady her breathing.

Krishani shook his head and put his hands on either side of her face. "This is all I want. This and nothing else, ever." His mouth covered hers again. He pressed himself against her and she sighed. It felt like she had known him her entire life and even longer, if *longer* even existed.

Images appeared behind her eyelids—the shape of a boy and a girl wearing gaudy crowns on their heads. They were painted into parchment, but they were blurry. She was too elated by Krishani and his lips on hers to record the images, but they seemed familiar.

And then everything changed. Krishani pushed his lips against hers one last time and she felt the shift in her energy dissipate. It was as though all the joy evaporated, replaced by intense fear. She pushed him away and tried to understand the pounding in her heart that made her want to break in half.

Bloom the weed of temptation.

He looked confused and shocked. Without a word, she turned and fled towards the Elmare Castle.

12-INSOMNIA

The woman's face was full of fear, life pinned behind her eyes. Krishani stared into the colorless face; the drab grayness of the dirt below her stained a deep crimson red. It was the only thing coloring the gray world. Hooves dented the mud and Krishani floated out of the way as a man in a gray tunic and breeches approached the woman, kneeled at her side and ran his hand across her grayish-brown hair. Her eyes filled with recognition and relief as she put a hand to the faceless man's cheek. Their words were muffled as Krishani turned and stared at the dirt road studded with rocks.

Krishani heard the man whisper something he faintly recognized and turned back only to find the woman's eyes frozen, her body limp, dead. Smoke rose out of her form, wispy smoke that curled into the sky and dissipated near the clouds. Knots clenched in Krishani's gut as he stared at her. The man faced him, looking at him with a vacant expression.

"Who are you?" Krishani asked though his voice didn't sound like his own.

"I'm the Ferryman," the man responded, monotone. He looked at Krishani with something that seemed like pity, then mounted his horse and rode away, hooves clacking along the stones as he disappeared into the distance.

Krishani always wondered why he followed the same man in his dreams. It had been this way since the men had left him in Avristar, since he had woken up as nothing but a child in the thick forests of Amersil. All he remembered of the men was the color of their horses:

one white and two brown. They could belong to anyone, and be from anywhere. He glanced at the lifeless body of the woman, her eyes empty. The mysterious man usually closed their eyes. Krishani wondered what had pulled him away so urgently this time that he couldn't be bothered to complete the ritual. Krishani was so familiar with it, the dying bodies, the whispers, and the smoke. He had seen it countless times before.

A cold wind stung his face as he floated away from the woman, waiting for the dream to end. But it didn't. The dreams were never ever like this. He never lingered, there was always more to see, more bodies, more whispers, more smoke. He sighed and floated back towards the woman. She was older, probably nearing her final years. He glanced at the wound in her stomach, and for the first time realized it was no accident she had died. Someone had stabbed her; someone intended to end her life. He stood and sprinted down the path in the direction the man had gone. He desperately wanted to ask him the question burning in his mind, but as he ran he tripped over his own feet and went careening onto his head rolling down the hill.

Krishani stopped and opened his eyes. He was on the floor, face planted into the floorboards. He took a shaky breath and pulled himself up. He sat against the side of the bed and ran his hands through his hair. The grief began unraveling as he remembered where he was, and then it returned. Kaliel. Why couldn't he dream about her? He rubbed his eyes as the memory of their kiss flooded his senses. Why did she leave? He pressed his back against the bed and let out an exasperated sigh. He shouldn't have kissed her at all, and he shouldn't have felt the way he did, but he couldn't forget her.

He shook off the dream and carefully pushed himself onto the bed, only to bury his head in his hands again at the overwhelming stress. No matter what he wanted to believe, another person had died in the Lands of Men, and he was powerless to stop it from happening again and again.

• • •

"Insomnia," Istar stated as he paced around his study.

Krishani stood across from him in the lavishly decorated room. Istar was known for his collection of magical items, his study was filled with shelves and trunks and cabinets of them. In the center of the room was a solid oak desk, half-finished contraptions scattered across it. Istar stood in the corner of the room, his eyes focused on the items behind the glass of one of the cabinets.

Krishani grimaced. "Aye." Even though he had been dreaming it felt like he hadn't slept a wink. *Please don't ask about my dreams,* he thought.

Istar was acting weirder than usual and Krishani felt uncomfortable. He scanned the cabinet and then opened it, lifting out an oddly-shaped crystal. He turned towards Krishani and narrowed his eyes at him. "Describe your last meditation."

Krishani shifted foot-to-foot and tried to push away the thought of Kaliel and the woman from his dream. He thought for a long time then sunk into the words he had memorized. "It was dawn. I was in the forests to the west. I stood, and listened to the wind through the trees. It was a soothing sound, filled with calmness and peace. I felt as though the wind could carry me a thousand miles. At points I could feel myself floating from the ground. Is this enough?"

Istar frowned. "You will tell me when you do in fact lift off the ground. You were meant for more and yet the most you can accomplish is control."

"I still hold fear."

Istar softened. "Let go! Do not be afraid to let the power within you out. It is the only way to know your true potential."

"And if I destroy the land?"

Istar shot him a look. "You are in control of it. It does not have control of you. If your will is to destroy the land then you will." Istar placed the crystal back into the cabinet and closed it. He sauntered over to the shelf on the other side of the room and picked up a gargoyle egg. He turned back to Krishani and gave him a curious look. Krishani thought he wanted to ask a question, but he didn't.

"First task …"

"Aye, first tasks have been accomplished, you have control," Istar said. "Now you must let go of that control and gradually let your true potential loose. More meditation, less gallivanting in the country-side, and perhaps we will have you on focus training as well." He put the gargoyle egg away and tried a golden phoenix eye, holding up and staring through it. Nothing happened. He pulled his brows together in frustration as he marched towards his desk.

Krishani made an inward groan to the thought of focus training. He knew what Istar meant—focus training was a fancy term for mess hall duty, peeling thousands of potatoes, or spending an afternoon harvesting apples in the orchards. The point was to stay focused on a single task. *Less time gallivanting in the country-side will be no trouble if she won't see me.* "Aye, if you believe it will help."

Istar must have seen the disappointment in his eyes because he softened once again. He placed his hands on his desk and nodded. "Right then," he began, though he seemed to have lost his train of thought.

"Elder?"

Istar shook his head. "I have other affairs to attend to, please see Hernadette for your focus training assignment."

Krishani frowned and turned to leave, but then stopped. "If I may ask, what other affairs?"

Istar glared at him, smiling. "I have been called to attend an assembly at the Great Hall, nothing that would interest you. Perhaps you should spend some time in the library reading history as well."

Krishani ignored the comment about the library and beamed at the mention of the Great Hall. Adoron had told him a lot about it during his time in Amersil. Their brotherhood had a sworn oath to Tor, the High King. "Will Tor attend?"

"Aye, it is he who has called the assembly."

"Wow."

Istar shook his head. "It's none of your business, Krishani."

"Why have you been called?"

Istar sighed and stood upright. He glanced at the shelves full of magical items. "I have been called as an ambassador of Avristar. I am to state her position on the matters discussed."

"What will be discussed?" Istar shot him a glare and Krishani avoided his gaze. "If you are at liberty to answer, that is."

Istar took in a deep breath and stroked his beard. "Avristar has been charged with restoring the Lands of Men, you know that."

"Does that mean there's a war?" He wanted to know because of his dreams; it seemed there was no end to the deaths that plagued his nights.

Istar laughed. "You may be growing, but you are still quite naïve. War will always be, Krishani, whether it is on new lands or old, it will always exist."

Krishani thought about his comment. "Tor strives for peace, does he not? Why would war ensue? Can he not attain perfection?" He desperately wanted the dreams to end, but he couldn't even admit to Adoron that he suffered from them. Telling Istar would only cause more trouble. Istar would make him face the nightmares. He wanted to ignore them for as long as possible.

A shadow came across Istar's face. "Aye, however the pursuit of perfection is always that—a pursuit. Perfection will come in accepting that not all things can be perfect."

Krishani nodded. "Avristar is perfect." His thoughts wandered again to the vision of Kaliel at the waterfall, her snow-white hair framing her shy face. He coughed as tingles spread from his torso outward and clenched his muscles trying to control himself.

"Nay, Avristar is in peace, it isn't perfect," Istar said. "No land can attain true perfection."

Krishani nodded. Istar always said that. "What will you have me do while you're gone?"

Istar smiled. "You said you would do daily meditation, focus training and reading. That will suffice until I can challenge you upon my return."

Krishani sighed. The library contained countless volumes of history, tales of those that had gone before him; nothing that stood out significantly to his path. Not a single piece of literature had a shard of information he could relate to. "Are there any volumes you would suggest?"

Istar laughed. "It's only history, and it's ancient history at that. It's for your focus and development that you would read of the greatness of others. Studying history is a task meant to speed the awakening process. You would be so well to do it."

Krishani looked at the ground again. "Aye." He turned to leave, and heard Istar behind him.

"Ask Hernadette to prepare you Jessamine tea for your insomnia!"

13-Amethyst Eyes

Bloom the weed of temptation. Those words pounded in Kaliel's mind throughout the night. At one point they were so loud she threw off the covers and grasped her ears hoping to block out the sound and find some form of comfort. Why had her energy shifted at the sound of those words? She felt it, a familiar rushing of warmth and buzzing, like her whole body was a bolt of lightning. And it didn't just happen when Krishani was touching her either, but that didn't mean he didn't invoke other warm feelings within her.

Kaliel reached for the cord in the ceiling and pulled the ladder down. It was made of creaky wooden planks that made her step with caution. She climbed and poked her head through the opening. The tower room was small and dank, but it smelled of freshly-cut herbs; she was comforted by the scent. She pulled herself into the room and huddled on the wooden floor.

What am I meant for? she wondered, fearing she would always be plagued by the very real controversy of her parable. She tried to feel inside herself for it, but it had vanished again, just like the times in Evennses when the stars sang. She thought back to her home but it seemed a lifetime ago. She hadn't expected Krishani to be in Orlondir.

Temptation. The thought pushed at her. She hugged her knees again. Images. She had seen something. What about that? She closed her eyes and desperately tried to conjure them again. A parchment. It was blank in her mind. *Symbols, drawings, there was something.* She tried to force it, but vertigo set in and the tower swayed underneath her, like the currents of the lake were pushing and pulling the tower in every direction. *Stop!* she thought frantically as the movement made her nauseous. The crashing didn't stop. It turned into swirling and she felt like she was being sucked under by the tide. She held onto her knees and let her head sink between them. *Please,* she begged again.

You wished to find me?

Aye.

What do you want to know?

Who are you?

I'm you.

The voice faded as Kaliel was pushed by another current. She held her ears as a high-pitched ringing pierced her temples. She heard the door open from below, and scrambled to open her eyes. The person who entered said nothing, waiting. Kaliel saw the faint light of dawn billowing through the hole in the floor. She took a deep breath and tried to compose herself.

I don't understand, she thought as she descended the ladder.

"Good morrow," she said as she hopped off the last rung. She turned to look at the dark-haired maiden in front of her with black eyes and a content smile on her face. The woman didn't respond. When she motioned with her hand to follow, Kaliel frowned and reluctantly trudged along behind her.

The silent lady led Kaliel to the lower west wing towards a room she hadn't seen during the tour. The night before weighed on her as she thought of the kiss she had shared with Krishani. She fidgeted in her ivory maiden's gown as she shuffled along the plush carpets. The room was at the far end of the hallway, the door looking like it would lead to a dungeon. It had an iron handle and a small window in it with bars across it.

The lady that led her was from the Sisterhood of Araraema in the east of Avristar. Kaliel recognized the symbol on her gown. Kaliel assumed she was undergoing silence training. It wasn't something she was familiar with. The maiden stopped at the door and motioned towards it. Kaliel nodded, afraid to speak out loud in front of the woman. She frowned as the woman opened the door and ushered her in. Kaliel smelled sandalwood as she stepped into the dimly lit room.

"Greetings, Kaliel," Atara said. She stood in the center of the room clad in a rose-red linen gown and black robe, the hood pulled over her head to conceal her expression. The room, from what Kaliel could see, was a working room; dank with cobble-stone flooring, an empty wooden table on the left. In the corner was a cabinet with various items used by the older apprentices back when there had been older apprentices. To the right was a large, oddly-shaped mirror. It wasn't square; the edges zigzagged unevenly along the glass. The mirror was large enough to cover most of the wall. Kaliel stared at it for a moment, unsure of its place in the room.

"Greetings … Atara." She was still getting used to the name of her mentor and was nervous about the first lesson the lady would teach her. *Please don't ask me about my first night.*

"Your mind isn't focused. Did you sleep well?" Atara inspected Kaliel closely and then turned to the mirror.

She gulped. "Aye, it was pleasant."

Atara measured her response and Kaliel thought the lady knew it was a lie. "You cannot see in yourself what the Great Oak sees, and it is affecting you. I will show you this first so you may understand."

Kaliel nodded and stepped forward. She was apprehensive about this practice; she had never learned meditation in Evennses.

Atara put her hands on the girl's shoulders and led her to the spot in front of the mirror. She pulled out a small glass vile containing a yellow liquid and popped out the cork. "Drink this. It will help you relax."

"What is it?"

"Dandelion tonic. It will help quiet your mind so you can focus on what I am going to show you," Atara said.

Kaliel cautiously took the vile and downed the liquid. It tasted extremely sweet; she coughed involuntarily. "Now, look at yourself in the mirror."

Kaliel turned to the mirror, but there was nothing much to see. She was a couple inches taller, standing almost five feet now. The ivory maiden's gown hugged her chest and fanned out near her waist, hanging down to her knees. Her skin was a pasty white, soft and smooth like silk. Her eyes moved from the floor towards her face. Her green eyes stared back at her; they held insecurity. Her soft white hair flowed around her shoulders in curls and waves. She held her hands at her sides and noted nothing in the background of the mirror was unexpected. She saw Atara standing behind her, and the table on the opposite end of the wall, along with the soft glow from the torch resting on its post above it. She looked at Atara. "Am I doing this right?"

Atara nodded. "Continue looking into your eyes, and ask to see what others see."

I want to know what Krishani sees in me. She tried to push the thought of him away, but her heart began to thrum and her palms began to sweat as the thought of the Great Oak bitterly cut into her daydream. She looked at the mirror and swallowed hard, trying to stare into her eyes once again. *What does the Great Oak see in me?* She forced herself to focus.

Moments passed as she waited for something to happen, but she only felt more delirious from the drink. Her eyes unfocused and drifted towards the black pupils of her green irises. She wanted so badly to close them, to sit down, to sleep, but then a thick root presented itself from the bottom of the mirror, and on the right side a garden formed—Desaunius's garden. She recognized it and the trees, the sunlight shedding an unnaturally bright light on the flowers and plants.

Her eyes drifted from the brightness towards the other side of the mirror. It showed a different scene. The ground was charred black and the trees were limp and bereft of leaves. Kaliel noticed a figure standing in the shadows, and at first she assumed it was the reflection of Atara standing behind her, but as she stared at the mirror longer she noted the figure was larger than her elder.

Kaliel dismissed the visions in the background and moved her eyes to the center again, wanting to concentrate on them, but they were no longer her own. The white gown stayed, her hair still draped around her shoulders, her skin soft and white, but her eyes, they weren't her eyes. She stared back as fear and anxiety crept into her limbs. She blinked twice, but nothing changed. Her eyes shone a brilliant amethyst. She incredulously stared at herself as the eyes stared back at her, full of wisdom and strength she didn't know she possessed.

The affects of the dandelion tonic wore off and her head drooped towards the ground as fatigue set in. Her vision blurred as she looked at the bottom of the mirror. Her feet were surrounded by violet light, which seemed to extend from her body, but she was too weak to stay with the vision. Her eyelids drooped and her body went limp as Atara caught her by the arm, pulling her back to reality.

"There, there, careful now." Atara sucked in a breath as she helped Kaliel to a chair tucked into the corner beside the cabinet. Kaliel sat down hard, her head spinning, her thoughts muddled. "Take a moment before answering. Did you see?"

Kaliel shook her head. "There's something hiding in me." She didn't understand the amethyst eyes or the light that surrounded her form. It seemed so familiar, but she didn't know why.

Atara frowned. "Nay, it is you, your potential."

Kaliel shook her head again. "No, I'm the same."

Atara shot her a spurious frown. "I am certain the meditation worked. I saw you enter the trance. What did you see?"

"Myself, no different than I am now," Kaliel whispered. She was afraid of the affliction she had seen, the shadowy figure and the amethyst eyes. She assumed those things were hallucinations from the tonic.

Atara's expression turned hard and unreadable. "Very well then, the lesson is over. You should rest now."

Kaliel took her hand and carefully rose from the chair. She was spinning from the tonic, but Atara held onto her and led her back through the corridors towards her room.

"The background changed," Kaliel said when they were near the fountain.

Atara turned, surprised. "How so?"

"One side showed my elder's garden, the other side was … barren, dead? I don't know, it was too dark to see anything."

Atara grimaced. "Good, that is progress. You will sleep on it and discover more."

• • •

Istar moved quickly through the golden corridors of the Great Hall. He descended the golden stairway, entering into the lower levels. He found the docks for the boat, gargoyles were awaiting his return. He took a last look back at the golden stairs, and then nodded for the gargoyles to push off through the clear turquoise waters towards the mists. The boat moved slowly, the mists curling around them, and soon, it was as if the Great Hall vanished. All that was left was the dead open sea shrouded by fog.

Istar stood on the boat as it glided through the water. It was nearing nightfall on Avristar. The light of the sun faded into shades of pink, but none of that comforted him on his journey. *I must stop this.* Istar closed his eyes and remembered the old times, a time when the Valtanyana held power and reigned chaos on the Lands Across the Stars.

The boat docked in Nandaro and he began trekking through the forest to Mallorn the Kiirar's cottage. The Kiirars were the lorekeepers of Avristar, many of them eons old. Mallorn was a hermit, a former warrior in the Lands of Immortals. Whenever Istar returned from the Lands of Men, he would lend him a horse to return to the Elmare Castle. This was such an occasion. Istar came adorned in the finest garments and his anxiety was high. He had ignored the gargoyle's keep located at the docks. What once provided a homeland for over ten thousand gargoyles now housed a mere two hundred. Avristar believed in providing protection for the Lands of Men and thought herself bereft of any chance for war. Therefore the armies had been lent to those who could use them.

The forests waned as Istar saw the cottage atop the mound. A small barn was on the west side of the cabin. He approached from the east, taking care not to falter and step into the creek. Inside, the fire burned brightly, smoke escaping from the chimney.

"It has been a long time, old friend," Istar said. He heard Mallon shoot up from his tea, startled. He thought about the inside of the cabin, the fireplace, the books on the end table, on the shelves, on the desk, and on the kitchen counter. It was a mess, but an organized one.

"Ah, for an elven who lives alone you certainly know how to startle one!" Mallorn hollered as he opened the door. "Have you been to a celebration, my friend?"

Istar laughed, looking down at his clothes: a deep burgundy tunic lined in gold hung to his feet, a red velvet cape with a fur collar adorned his shoulders and he had his champion sword at his side. He shook his head as he entered.

Mallorn had served as a mentor to the Children of Avristar many years ago, but he preferred a life on his own, to understand the meaning of it. He spent most days rifling through books, correcting and perfecting the record of knowledge he held, learning history of other lands.

Mallorn went to the kitchen and poured Istar a cup of tea. "What has you returning so late?"

Istar frowned and took the tea. He perched on the wooden chair in the living room and stared at the fire. "An assembly at the Great Hall," he said.

Mallorn shook his head. "That cannot mean good things."

"No, the Lands of Men are not the only realms in need of aid any longer."

Mallorn looked shocked. "Istar, do you mean to say that the Avrigard quadrant has succumbed to corruption?"

He sipped his tea and nodded. "Aye, the lords seemed very agitated by it."

"They should be!" Mallorn shook his head and began gathering his reading materials. Istar knew he was searching for references or something, but he didn't know what good it would do. "The Lands of Immortals in Avrigard have not seen war since the Valtanayana—" Mallorn stopped, apparently noticing the mangled expression on Istar's face.

"Aye." It was the exact thoughts that had come to him during the assembly.

"Has Kemplan confirmed it?" Mallorn gave him a stern glance.

Istar shook his head. "Kemplan says they are sealed in Avrigost, no means of escape."

Mallorn let out a breath. "So Kemplan was at the assembly?"

"No, he didn't find it worth his time to leave the Great Library. He sent a Scrye."

Mallorn relaxed. "Aye, no reason for worry, then."

"Perhaps." He wasn't convinced.

"Be plain with me, Istar. What are you thinking?"

"Avristar would not survive a blow."

Mallorn sat back in his chair with a long hum. "Nay, I will not believe it. Until you have proof of his return, you shall disregard this. Treachery can build for a number of reasons."

Istar gave him a cold stare. "Any other you could propose?"

Mallorn paused; it looked like he was scanning his vast recesses of knowledge. "Nay."

"Then you understand why I am concerned."

"Aye."

Istar set the cup down and stood. "I should return."

Mallorn nodded and escorted him to the stables. "Take Rhina. She will get you home faster." Mallorn paused then added, "And, old friend, should you require an ear, I am but a lonely elven with no battle to fight."

"That I will remember," Istar replied as he mounted the horse. He bid Mallorn a farewell and took off into the forests of Nandaro.

• • •

Krishani sighed as he descended the stone stairway towards the pond below. Kaliel didn't show up. His feelings for her hadn't vanished, but the despair he felt was worse, so bad he wished he never sought her company in the first place. His eyes avoided the pond; he didn't want to look at anything familiar anymore. He hoped she would come to speak with him, to tell him the reason she fled. The possibility of her presence was all that brought him to the waterfall. He spent the last few hours sitting in the grass behind the falls, reliving their kiss.

However, the waiting caused so much sorrow he couldn't subject himself to the emptiness in his heart.

He trudged along the wide path that led back to the Elmare Castle, knowing that somehow, he would go to Kaliel and would ask her the question pressing on his temples.

Earlier that day he had gone to Hernadette in hopes the herbs would help him succumb to a deep sleep, but when night fell, he couldn't bring himself to relax, knowing that the only things he would dream about was Kaliel or death. The last thought made him shudder.

The castle came into view and Krishani breathed a sigh of grief as he neared it. She was somewhere within those walls, concealing a secret that had torn her away from him. *Why won't she try?* He continued up the path, entering through the main courtyard, but the beauty of it merely faded under the moon's light. Compared to Kaliel, everything else was pale and drab.

Krishani passed the archway, the Grand Hall in front of him. To the left was the corridor to the west, to the right the corridor to the east, his quarters. He paused a moment and drifted towards the path on the left. He assumed she would be sleeping, but he had to confront her. He trudged up the steps, feeling bricks attached to his feet. She didn't tell him which room was hers, but he could feel her. It was the same low pulse that made his body buzz with electricity, made him able to form the orb of ice. He paused a moment and took a shaky breath. There had to be a reason she left so abruptly, but would she tell him what it was? He continued down the corridor, passing by the darkened hallways that branched off it. Then he stopped, and stared down the length of one of the halls, feeling her pulse.

At the end was a small curved wooden door with iron doorknob. Krishani pressed his ear against the door. His eyes closed as a sense of relaxation overcame him. He heard her soft and slow breaths as she slept. The mere sound was enough to calm him. He knew this was dangerous, but he knew there was no one that made him feel the way she did. He stood there, lost in her breathing.

She stirred. The breathing becoming more alert and awake, but Krishani felt drunk with addiction. He stood frozen in his own dreamland, listening to her from beyond the room. He was so enthralled with the sounds he barely noticed she had come to the door and was listening carefully to his breathign on the other side.

· · ·

Kaliel swung the door open. "It's not yet morrow, is it?" she asked before she had opened her eyes. Once she did, she saw Krishani staring at her with an uncomfortable look on his face. She blanched.

"Kaliel," he began. He looked surprised and elated by her sudden appearance.

She found herself and tried to stop shaking. "You shouldn't be here."

Krishani gulped. The look on his face turned from openness to expressionless. He looked at the ground. "I came to ask why you ..." He didn't finish, but she understood what he was talking about.

Kaliel looked past him at one of the crystal torches on the wall, avoiding eye contact. She wanted to say something, but held back. She longed to reach out and fold herself into his embrace, tell him it would be okay. Whatever the Great Oak had said, it couldn't have known about him, about how she felt. It was so foreign it was silly to even consider it. Not even the elders would suspect it. She was elven like him; she shouldn't be able to fall in love. He shouldn't be able to either, but he couldn't help it. Even from where he stood she could hear his heartbeat, thumping with that irregularity she loved.

"I'm here for another reason," she said.

Krishani lingered, staring at her like a forlorn animal. "I—I'm sorry I disturbed you," he said, his voice hardened. Without another look he turned and fled down the hallway.

Kaliel watched him until he turned the corner and disappeared. She closed the door before he could look back, and sunk to the floor. He looked so broken and small, nothing like the tall poised Brothers of Amersil. She wondered if she had made the wrong decision, if the Great Oak was mistaken.

14-Fire Festival

There were no more nights like that and the moons came and went quickly until it was Samhain. Kaliel stepped lightly between apple trees in the orchard outside the courtyard. The castle walls were so difficult to get used to, and though six moons had passed, she felt lonely being cooped up within them. The only calming thought was that the kinfolk from Evennses would arrive soon for the Fire Festival. She spent time watching the servants prepare food and sparkling water, but when she tried to help, Melianna forced her out of the servants' hall and told her to go study. She didn't like the library much—it was musty and crowded, shelves of books reaching the ceiling and even more stacked on shelves. There was only a window sill to read on, nothing homey like a couch or even a bench. She tried not to go in there.

It was late afternoon, and the clear skies had turned to a pinkish orange. Kaliel smiled as she looked at the canopy and took in the scent of apples mixed with crisp of autumn air.

The trees in the orchard were perfectly aligned with one another. She ran her hand against the trunk of another one and tried to speak to it. The problem was, the trees in Orlondir didn't speak. The birds chirped and the squirrels chattered, but that didn't warm her heart as much as the words of the trees. She sighed and sat, resting her head on the trunk of the tree behind her.

"I know you'll never speak to me, but perhaps I could rest here."

A humming sound came from behind the tree and Kaliel sat straight and frowned. She had done everything she could to avoid

Krishani; how could she have been so foolish as to sit down at the very tree he was at? That was, if it was him, of course. She realized she hadn't felt his energy there—no—his energy had been segregated to the waterfall, and she hadn't dared tread that path for moons, no matter how much it pained her to stay away.

"I'll speak with you, Kaliel," a voice said. There was a *crunch* like someone was taking a bite out of an apple.

Kaliel would recognize that voice anywhere. "Pux!" She jumped to her feet and dashed around the tree only to find her childhood friend sitting precariously in a pile of pink apples. Some of them looked bruised as though they weren't really for eating. During Samhain, they always took the nearly rotten apples and made pies and apple sauce. Only Pux would be sitting there munching on them like it was late summer.

He raised his eyebrows. "Aye, would you like one?" He picked up an apple and extended it towards her. Its rosy pinkness made it seem artificial. She shook her head and pushed it away.

"When did you arrive?" She was bewildered but happy, the happiest she'd been since her first night in Orlondir.

Pux chomped on the apple like a horse. "Desaunius is hours away with the other kinfolk," he said between bites.

Kaliel frowned. "Then how did you—?"

He ruefully smiled, bits of apple stuck between his teeth.

She rolled her eyes. "Do they know your secret yet?"

He stood and dusted himself off. He was quite a bit taller than she remembered, but still a furry animal, even if his hair was combed. "Luenelle found out about a moon ago, and she still thinks I'm invalid." He looked at the pile of apples and for once when he focused on them he turned them red. He stepped away from the tree and began sauntering through the orchards, Kaliel on his heels.

"You can transport!" She hardly believed it. She adored Luenelle, but this was difficult even for her to digest.

"There's no point in using fancy terms for it. Grimand has been testing me. Despite Luenelle he believes I have some potential."

Kaliel beamed. "You do!" The past few moons seemed to fade away when she was with Pux, but she certainly didn't have romantic feelings for him. Her time with him was a childish escape from the seriousness surrounding her. Her lessons with Atara had proven that she had some skill with meditation, and some with seeing and hearing the voices of the land. None of it was new to her though, she failed at the same things too, like identifying herbs.

She glanced at the sky again and realized it was slightly pinkish. "Did you—?"

He followed her gaze to the sky and shrugged. "Aye." He leaned against another tree and reached into the branches towards an apple that hadn't fallen. It was dark red, badly bruised. He pulled it down and began tossing it between his hands. "Evennses hasn't been the same without you."

Kaliel turned and kicked the dirt. She had learned so much in the time she had come, and most of it frightened or hurt her. She took a deep breath and sat on the ground next to a tree. She tried to think of a way to describe it, but there were no words. No matter what she said, she knew Pux wouldn't understand.

He put the apple on the ground and stared at the sky again. "The orchards are pretty," he said like he was trying to make conversation. "Much better than that waterfall we found. Do you ever go back there?"

The land began to spin. Kaliel thought about the waterfall all the time. She couldn't go there. She sat in the grass stunned. Her mouth watered and she ripped up a patch of grass by her leg. Pux turned to face her, oblivious to her grief.

"You wouldn't understand," she said. Her whole body shook. She had never told Pux about Krishani and she was afraid of his opinion. He was her best friend, and a lot like a brother. She twisted her mouth in contempt as Pux seemed lost for words. She pushed herself up and started off away from him through the rows of apple trees.

"Kaliel!" he called after her. "You make no sense!" After a few long strides he pulled ahead of her. The trees around them were all the same, perfectly-lined rows and she felt like she was lost in a never-ending labyrinth.

She stopped in her tracks and looked at him. "I meant it. You wouldn't understand."

Pux shook his head. "Why do you do this to me?"

"Do what?"

"You share everything with Luenelle yet you shut me out from the important things."

Kaliel felt a pang in her heart. He was right. She turned and stared down the row of trees. She could see where the exit to the orchard was and she could try again to run, but she owed him an explanation at least. She hung her head, her white-slippered toes pointing towards one another. "I never told anyone in Evennses about him, not even Luenelle."

"Who?" Pux whispered.

Kaliel's heart beat erratically as she tried to find the words to describe her connection with—"Krishani." She stole a glance at Pux's questioning brown eyes and cringed. "I met him that time we found the waterfall."

His jaw dropped.

Kaliel looked at the exit again and something begged her to run. "He's here now. We met again when I came to Orlondir."

Pux had nothing to say.

"We kissed."

Pux walked away without saying a single word. He didn't give a huff or a cry or an indication of anything he was feeling. Kaliel desperately tried to keep up with him. She ran along, but no sooner than she started she tripped over her own feet and tumbled on the ground. She rolled onto her side and Pux stopped short, looking back at her.

"Love isn't something—" Pux began unsuccessfully. He closed the distance between them and assessed the damaged girl. She pushed herself up and avoided eye contact with him. Pux had an uneasy expression on his face. "You were never supposed to grow up." He stomped away and left her sitting in the grass, a new bruise forming on her knee where a scraggly root had made contact with it.

She watched him go. "I never meant to," she said even though he couldn't hear her.

• • •

Nothing happened after that first day. Krishani stood in the east wing balcony watching the ruckus below him, no sign of Kaliel. Even with the kinfolk wearing masks he'd still recognize her. He sighed as the bards played a happy tune, something the complete opposite of how he felt. The countless times he had almost encountered Kaliel … the waterfall.

He knew it was just as special to her as it was to him, but he couldn't be in the castle knowing she was just a hallway away. He had been drawn to it every night since he intuitively found her room, and the only comfortable place to be other than there was at the waterfall. He tried to create orbs of ice again, but it never worked. He didn't understand how he felt about her any more than he understood why she wouldn't talk to him, or even look at him. Her eyes had changed color, something that never happened on Avristar, and it seemed like she was completely oblivious to it. She had no idea just how different she was from everyone else. He wanted to be worried about her, but there was nothing to fear, nothing but marrying the land and leaving Avristar like the others.

Somehow her silence hurt more than all the summers he had spent ignoring girls and sparring with the kinfolk in the games. Even with all the dancing in the Grand Hall, some of them were out there, in the fields to the north, brandishing swords and armor and engaging in playful combat. Just because she wouldn't talk to him didn't mean he was going to go back to that.

The Brotherhood was so pompous about their winning streak, and because of the way he felt inside, he was too afraid he'd mess up and let one of them injure him. Losing wasn't something the Brotherhood easily forgave. He wasn't even sure they would forgive him for his continuing failure. Lord Istar had tried, but Krishani was no more focused than he had been two summers ago.

He stared at the marble floor and traced the outlines of perfectly adorned tables with little candle centerpieces and arrangements of utensils. There were kinfolk in elaborately decorated masks sitting at each table in the four corners, and in the center, senselessly dancing to the music. He didn't recognize them, but as his eyes idly traced the intricate patterns of the fountain in the center he caught a flash of Kaliel, a purple mask over her eyes. He scanned the room and there she was, barely in sight. The kinfolk she danced with pirouetted and skipped around her, and soon they were in full view. Krishani focused on her as she twirled and hopped to the joyful music.

She looked happy.

Unexpectedly, she glanced at the balcony and Krishani's chest clenched. *Did she see me?* The balconies were mostly cast in shadow. He sank towards the hallway wall in embarrassment. He had admired her from a distance for moons and wanted her to stay happy. For her to see him ... as he backed up he felt another person near him. He

119

pressed his back to the wall, but it was useless, he couldn't make himself invisible.

"Krishani!" a voice called from the hallway.

He tried to look into the Grand Hall again but Benir joined him and leaned against the balcony railing, blocking most of his view. Benir wore the familiar cloak which concealed most of his features. The only thing distinct about him was his blue eyes and shaggy blond hair. He had a gold mask in his left hand, looking like he didn't want to wear it.

"Greetings, Benir," Krishani said cordially. He bowed his head and tried to peek around him.

Benir raised an eyebrow and shifted to the right. "Greetings. I suppose life in Orlondir is different, nay?"

"Aye," *And agonizing,* he thought.

"Have you made the seed grow?"

Krishani sucked in a breath. The Brothers never answered a question that wasn't asked, and the way Benir looked, this was one of a long string of them. "Nay, I haven't been asked. Are you still being mentored by Sigurd?" He tried to make casual conversation, but he felt the energy from Kaliel drawing him in. Something in her was longing for him, and from the balcony it was all too apparent. He tried to push it away, pass off what he felt as wishful thinking …but she was just too hard to ignore.

"Nay, I'm with Adoron now," Benir said with a wink.

Krishani felt a pit in his stomach. Benir beamed. Adoron was the most respected elder in Amersil, and to fail him meant certain shame. He regained his thoughts and looked back at Benir and nodded. "Congratulations."

"Will you come down for the feast?"

More knots. "No, I would rather watch from up here." Krishani's stomach growled, giving away his hunger.

"Nay, that won't do. Come. The Brothers will be thrilled to hear about your adventures." He pushed off the balcony and moved towards the stairs. He looked back at Krishani expectantly. The boy sighed and trudged along beside him, pushing his black mask over his eyes.

He followed Benir into the Grand Hall. They passed the first few clusters of round tables and Krishani stopped in his tracks. Kaliel was with the kinfolk in the middle of the floor, spinning and giggling. Her laughter wafted through the air and he felt choked by her presence. The anxiety was too much. He turned to leave, but Benir had an arm on him.

"Come, they have a table near the servants' quarters." Benir went to lead them through the crowd again, but when he turned around he came face to face with an elven girl in a blue mask, edged with gold. She accidentally bumped into him and sheepishly looked up.

"I'm so sorry. Would you like to dance?" she asked.

Benir put up his hand to refuse and tried to go off in the direction of the Brotherhood. He looked behind him. Krishani still stood there without a word. Benir nodded his head at him, but Krishani refused to move an inch.

"Our friend Kaliel needs a partner. Perhaps you could step in?" the elven girl said. She was older, long brown hair and bright blue eyes. Krishani found her plain and unattractive, but with the mention of Kaliel's name, he realized the elven girl was from Evennses, probably from Kaliel's childhood. "Someone must save her from the younglings." She giggled, glanced in their direction and looked back at Benir, who was still motioning for Krishani to go.

The song ended, the bards stopped playing, and the girl stood there for a moment. Benir shook his head and took towards the Brotherhood, while Krishani looked ahead at the fountain, attempting to find the strength to move. He wanted to leave, but something told him to stay. The elven girl was pulled away by the other kinfolk as the bards struck up a slow tune.

Krishani tried to turn away, escape into the courtyards, but as the dance floor cleared, Kaliel came into view. She was a vision. She wore a deep purple gown that clung to her body and a purple mask edged with silver tear drops. She twirled with the last of the kinfolk and her white hair danced around her. She smiled and laughed, but when she saw him, she stopped, letting her hands drop from those of the kinfolk. She nodded for them to go to the tables and ran her hands down her dress, trying to smooth out imaginary wrinkles. As the song hit a sorrowful lull she stepped towards him.

"Krishani." She sounded surprised and confused.

Krishani searched the crowds beyond her for Benir. The scent of her was like freshly-cut herbs and grass and apples. *Beautiful,* he thought. Knots formed in his stomach as he longed to pull her into

121

his embrace. He knew she would protest. "I apologize. I didn't mean to interrupt."

"It's fine," she said. Her eyes had a pleading look to them, like she wanted something else but couldn't say it. Krishani thought she must have seen the Brotherhood arrive. They were intimidating with their full robes and ignorant attitudes.

Krishani let out a sigh. He knew how much it might hurt, but he couldn't take the tension any longer. He wanted to hold her closer, to smell her hair, and to feel her body pressed against his. "Would you...."

She stared at him, curious, her green eyes meeting his. They were cloudy and full of despair.

Krishani let out a nervous sigh as he cleared his throat and tried again. "Would you like to dance?"

She glanced over at the kinfolk at the tables. Krishani followed her gaze. One of the elvens had her hands full with them and none of them seemed to be paying attention to her. She took a deep breath.

"Okay."

He caught her hand and pulled her into his embrace, rocking back and forth to the song. At first she was inches from him, but as the song swelled he found himself against her tight, her head buried in his chest. It seemed so natural that everything but her faded away. Whatever the Brotherhood would say didn't matter. He hoped it was the same for her, that her kinfolk wouldn't notice her dancing. Krishani carefully moved his feet in a small circle as the song reached its apogee. The only question he wanted to ask pounded at the front of his mind.

Why?

"I'm afraid," she whispered as though he had spoken his thoughts aloud. Krishani wound his fingers through her hair, caressing her neck and sliding them down her back. He wanted the moment to last forever. The song neared its end, the notes dwindling. As the last notes were struck, he twirled her under his arm once and dropped her hand.

She took a wide step away from him. "Thank you," she said with a wan smile.

Krishani went to speak, but she turned and fled towards the lower west wing. He looked to his right, the elven girl staring at him with a fiery blaze. He passed it off and tried looking for the Brotherhood.

Benir had taken off in that direction, the Brotherhood's table on the other side of the fountain. He took a deep breath and moved towards the west wing, determined to face Kaliel in private.

15-THE CAVE BEHIND THE FALLS

Kaliel pulled off the mask, tracing the faint outlines of her splotchy cheeks and red eyes in the crystal water basin. She was in the lavatory, the only place close enough for her to be alone. She clutched either side of the basin and stared into her green eyes. Her heart thumped aberrantly, palms sweaty, an uncontrollable urge to melt into Krishani's embrace pulsing through her.

Stop it! she tried to command herself. *Temptation, temptation, temptation.* She recalled the nights she spent resisting the urge to end the silence between her and Krishani and allow herself to do what she wanted to do. She heard someone in the hallway behind the door. *Luenelle or Pux,* she assumed. One of them would come to tell her just how wrong this was, but she didn't need their scrutiny. She wiped her face and tried to find her strength. Someone entered the room and she stiffened. The earthy scent wafted through the air and she knew who it was. She turned and Krishani stood there, looking defeated and broken. She pressed her back against the basin and clutched it with both hands.

Her eyes hardened. "Why did you follow me? I wish to be alone." Her voice was high-pitched and shrill and she hadn't meant to sound so cruel. She cringed on the inside as his expression twisted into further anguish.

"Please, Kaliel," he whispered.

She wanted to press herself against him and feel his lips on her hair, on her temple, on her cheek, on her lips. She gulped and tried to control the emotions thrashing in her. It hurt so much to keep her distance and his plea was making it worse. "You shouldn't be here," she managed.

Krishani boldly stepped forward. She was terrified, and she knew it was written all over her expression. He loved her, that was clear, but she couldn't accept it, wouldn't accept it. "I can't do this," he said.

A tremor rippled through her. She fought for control, but the thing inside begged to come forward. *Please, let go.* She closed her eyes and felt them changing color, her aura pulsated and she wondered if he saw it. She bit her lip and her fingers ached as she gripped the basin harder.

"You can't be with me, the Brotherhood won't allow it," she muttered, trying to gain some ground, something to make him leave. She opened her eyes.

He took another step forward, and she tasted his earthiness on her tongue. Her hand slipped off the basin and she faltered, trying to find her balance.

Instead, his hand slid into hers and he pulled her to him, crushing her against his chest to steady her. His eyes were wide as she stared at him. And then he brushed his lips against hers. All her barriers fell. Wrapping her arms around his neck, she sank into his kiss with longing as tears slid down her cheeks.

His hands moved along her back as he pulled her away from the basin, trying to move to the music echoing through the walls. She broke off, and doubled over; clutching her torso as she sunk to her knees.

Krishani crouched next to her, his expression all compassion. "This is madness, I can't stop feeling what I feel." He brushed his finger down her face, wiping away another tear.

She buried her face in her hands. "I can't stop feeling it either."

Krishani slipped his hand into hers and pulled her up. He went to kiss her again, but she pulled away and moved towards the door.

"You will marry the land." The words barely came out. She covered her mouth and left the room.

• • •

Luenelle headed towards the powder room, determined to have a word with Kaliel about what she had seen on the dance floor.

"Where are you going?" Pux asked as she approached the west wing.

"Leave it," Luenelle snapped. She turned to face him. "This business does not concern you."

Pux playfully narrowed his eyes at her. "Business never concerns me. Come on, I need a dance partner."

She sighed as she realized everyone else was in good spirits and nobody seemed to have noticed the vibes between Kaliel and that boy from Amersil. She looked beyond Pux towards a group of younger kinfolk. "Eurida will dance. I can't at this moment."

Pux frowned. "Kaliel!"

Luenelle followed his gaze and noted the girl fleeing from the lavatory. She gave the feorn a hard look. The girl was fast as she neared the staircase and ran up the steps. Luenelle followed as she turned down the ninth hallway and closed the door behind her. She paused for a moment then knocked. No matter what her gut told her, she couldn't let this go.

"Leave me alone, I have nothing more to say," Kaliel said, her words choked with sobs.

Luenelle softened. "It's Luenelle. Will you speak to me?"

The door opened and Luenelle came inside, closing the door behind her.

"How are the kinfolk in Evennses?" Kaliel asked as she tried to hide her face.

Luenelle surveyed the room. "They're fine. I have been told I will be called soon."

"I wish I could go back there."

Luenelle gave her a stern look. "And pass up an opportunity to learn from the greatest elder on Avristar?"

Kaliel sighed and sat on the bed. She grabbed the journal on the end table and opened it.

Luenelle idly eavesdropped on the images Kaliel had sketched— two people with elaborate crowns and the sun shining down on them. It didn't make sense to her, but she didn't question what it meant to Kaliel.

"That isn't the reason I wish to return," Kaliel said.

"The elven boy you danced with tonight ..."

Kaliel looked at the floor. "Aye."

Luenelle paced, uncomfortable. "Love is a dangerous thing," she began, though she was at a loss for words herself.

"Love is meant to be when it is given by the land or the elders. Or so it has been in every story I have ever read."

"You're right about that. It still doesn't answer why you'd disobey the land so carelessly. You know what has happened to others who did." Luenelle crossed her arms.

"I don't understand what you mean."

"Desaunius." Luenelle sighed. "You spent more time with her than I did, didn't she tell you?"

Recognition dawned on Kaliel's face. "Yes, she is in solitude."

"Exactly, she wasn't given to him and look at where it led."

Kaliel seemed sick and Luenelle felt guilty for approaching her like this. "She said it wasn't like that on Tempia."

"It doesn't matter, history matters," she said like a true lorekeeper.

Kaliel furrowed her brow and twisted her hands in her lap. She looked agitated by something more than just the elven boy, but Luenelle was hesitant to pry.

"Who is he?"

"He's Lord Istar's apprentice and a member of the Brotherhood of Amersil."

"How does he feel about you?"

"I think he loves me." The look in her eyes was sincere, happy but forlorn. "He hates this as much as I do, but I'll resist it. I must obey the laws of the land. When Avristar is ready she'll allow me a mate." Kaliel spoke the words as though they were out of some history textbook in the library.

Luenelle felt uncertain and cautious at the same time. She nodded in approval. "You don't believe you'll marry the land?"

Kaliel looked at her as the other girl curled herself around the foot of the bed and sat down beside her. "Why would I?"

Luenelle knew it was a very real possibility, but the frivolous idea of settling down in one of the villages in Orlondir or Nandaro seemed more comforting.

"Desaunius is convinced you'll go to the Lands of Men. She hasn't said why."

Kaliel looked worse. Her forehead knitted in grief as she ran her hands along her torso. "My parable."

"Whatever do you mean?"

"Bloom the weed of temptation and expire the great garden of life. Bloom the flower of sacrifice and sustain the great garden in strife," Kaliel whispered.

Luenelle assessed the waif of a girl who looked like she had seen better days. What had happened to her since she left Evennses? She averted her gaze, looking at the window while sorting out her thoughts about the parable. She had only heard parables which were similar to her own and most were light and fluffy. However, Kaliel's parable carried a weight with it that perplexed her. She considered the words. Kaliel was so broken and she wanted to fix her. "So? Don't 'bloom the weed of temptation,' it's not hard is it?"

Kaliel looked at her, worry etched on her face, crossed with a certain peculiar confusion. "I don't know."

"You have misinterpreted the parable," Luenelle said. She stood with the eminence of an Avristar Elder and took towards the door. "I would be very careful about that elven boy. You don't want Avristar to get involved." She opened the door and left Kaliel to her thoughts.

• • •

Krishani stood in the lavatory, stunned by Kaliel's departure and her strong words. He reluctantly left the room that had grown stale and entered the Grand Hall. Most of the dancing had continued, but he noticed the elders were gone. He wondered if they had left to Mount Tirion to meet with the Gatekeeper. Istar, who had invited him to come for this portion of the festival, was also gone.

"Have the elders gone forth already?" he asked one of the kin from Araraema.

"Aye, and the festivities will continue for a while longer yet." The girl paused. "Would you care to dance?"

"No," Krishani spat. He brushed her off and wended his way through the empty tables and chairs, emerging in the courtyard. He smelled the crisp smoky scent of campfires, however, none of this mattered as he solemnly walked the path to the waterfall. He needed a place to be alone to think, to be, to wonder, and to find some glimmer of hope.

He tilted his chin towards the sky and looked at Mount Tirion. Istar would be disappointed with him for not attending, but he couldn't pass up the opportunity to be with Kaliel. He heard the rushing waters of the falls ahead of him and then shrieks of kinfolk. He frowned when he arrived. Around the edges of the pool were dozens of kinfolk milling about, stretching their legs into the water and darting in and out of the bushes on the other side. Krishani felt uneasy. This was his place, the kinfolk weren't supposed to be there.

Who told them of this place? he wondered as he scanned the kinfolk, hoping to find someone he knew. He recognized the elven girl on the other side with her arms crossed. She was eyeing the younger ones and seemed to be glaring at a feorn in particular. Krishani's mouth gaped as the feorn's eyes met his and he began to cross the forest brush to confront him. He didn't look happy.

"Are you the elven boy, Lord Istar's apprentice?" the feorn asked.

Krishani narrowed his eyes to slits and glanced over at the elven girl who was trying not to watch them. He realized this feorn must be one of Kaliel's kinfolk from Evennses. "Yes. And yourself?"

"Pux," he answered. He shifted, obviously nervous and looked back towards the elven girl for help, but she was still refusing to pay attention to their conversation.

"Who told you?" Krishani tried not to glower at him, but the feorn had trespassed.

"I found it long ago," Pux answered, an air of defiance in his tone. He seemed agitated about something, and Krishani assumed it had to do with Kaliel, but he couldn't be sure. He looked past Pux at the waterfall and shook his head.

"The waterfall is forbidden," he said. He so desperately wanted to retreat into the cave behind the falls and forget about the kinfolk defiling what he considered his secret.

"Aye, many things on Avristar are forbidden. Or so the elders have told me."

Krishani sighed. "Please leave." He shook his head as thoughts of Kaliel made him feel hollow. He moved towards the stone staircase and gave Pux a hard stare.

Pux smiled as though he had said something amusing. "Aye!" He looked at Luenelle and nodded. Glancing back at Krishani he tipped an imaginary hat to confirm their understanding. He bounded off through the forest, Luenelle and the kinfolk trailing behind him.

Krishani watched them go and sighed. It wasn't the same waterfall without Kaliel, seeing the kinfolk there made his insides tighten with anger. He doubted Kaliel would have told, but he wondered.

He stepped into the cave and continued until the darkness consumed him entirely. He ran through the memories of Kaliel—the times they had met at the waterfall, the kisses they had shared. So much had changed in less than two summers on Avristar. From the moment he saw her, he knew he wouldn't follow in the footsteps of the Brotherhood of Amersil. A life without a mate was no life for him, married to the land, a servant to the cycle of its life. Even if Kaliel chose to ignore him for a thousand years he would never fall out of love with her. That was something he barely understood, and something that scared him. He loved her, even if it was blind. He couldn't help himself. He heaved a sigh and opened his eyes only to find darkness. Moonlight illuminated the first few feet, but the rest faded into blackness.

A rock tumbled down the stony path and Krishani moved into a crouch. He expected to see the feorn again, and planned on having it out with him. He couldn't control how he felt; the feorn would have to understand. It was the same way the feorn couldn't help being hairy or smelly.

A silhouette crossed the mouth of the cave, blocking the falls with its form. Krishani froze; he would recognize her shape no matter how dark it was. She made it hard to concentrate. She moved into the cave and sat on the grass, pulling her knees to her chest.

He waited, but she stayed, her head buried in her knees. His heart swelled. She hadn't been to the waterfall since they kissed. He gulped and cautiously inched closer, waiting to hear what she had to say.

• • •

Kaliel's shoulders shook as she felt the sting of regret. She wanted to apologize to Krishani, tell him she felt something for him so profound that it was unimaginable. She was embarrassed at the depth of her feelings for him. He was just as good at avoiding her as she was of him. It would be easier to believe she was a silly girl that

131

disappointed him. She tilted her chin up and rested it on her knees, staring at the falls.

"I probably lost him," she whispered. "The Great Oak warned me about temptation and I stayed away for as long as I could." Somehow saying it made her feel better. Luenelle was wrong. Avristar was a utopian paradise. There was almost nothing to fear and she acted like her relationship with Krishani would make the trees rot from the inside out. She smiled and gave a short laugh at how impossible that seemed. Love wouldn't expire the great garden of life, so why would the tree scare her like that? She giggled and dropped her arms to her sides. She fell backward into the grass and traced the patterns of rock above her.

"I wonder if he still thinks about me?" she said, her voice echo off the walls. "I wonder if he hates me."

"I could never hate you, Kaliel," Krishani said from behind her.

Kaliel gasped, whipped around and moved to her feet with lightning speed. Her hand raked across his cheek with blinding force as she shrieked and jumped away from him. She brought her hands to her mouth as he removed his hood and rubbed the red welt growing on his cheek.

"Oh no!" she exclaimed, heat encompassing her body, embarrassment attempting to swallow her whole.

His eyes searched hers, intense, but in a way that made her melt. She laughed. "Will you ever stop scaring me?"

He closed the distance between them and pressed his lips against hers. She grabbed his cloak in her fists as his hands graced the small of her back and forced her against him. He led her to the ground and pressed her into the grass, his fingers trailing along her bare skin, his knee filling the space between her legs.

Breathless, she pushed his cloak off his shoulders, balling his tunic in her fists and forcing him away. He always moved too fast and she was never quite prepared for it. Being close to him made her feel more alive than ever. "I mean it. Will you stop scaring me?"

Krishani smirked. "Do you really want this?" He sat and rested his arms on his knees.

Kaliel narrowed her eyes, her lips twitching into a smile. "Only if you promise not to do that again."

"Can I kiss you again if I do?" He inched closer, his gaze knifing into her. He held his hand out and waited for her to take it. "Sorry I scared you."

She folded herself into his embrace, pressing her cheek against his cloak, feeling content at the earthiness of his scent. He traced idle patterns on her bare thigh. "Sorry I stayed away for so long."

He held her in his arms for a long while. "Why did you come tonight?"

She recalled the conversation with Luenelle and untangled herself from him. "I was given some advice from an old friend."

Krishani frowned. "Who?"

Kaliel smiled as she remembered home. "The House Master from Evennses. She warned me about where this could lead." She missed the days Luenelle passed out on the rocking chair in front of the hearth fire to keep her from going to the lake.

Krishani closed his eyes and ran his hands across them, rubbing them like he was stressed. "Do you ever do what you're told?"

Kaliel shrugged. "Not usually."

"And so you never wanted to avoid me?" His face flushed with concern and insecurity.

Kaliel took in a deep breath, the embarrassing truth circling around her lips. She sighed. There were so many ways to say it, but nothing that would make it sound less humiliating. "When I went on my journey to the Great Oak, I had a plan to sneak into Amersil to find you." She blushed as his expression registered fear. He laced his fingers through hers and shook his head.

"I was here by then," he muttered.

"Oh." Silence hung between them.

"I made a bolt of lightning strike down a three-thousand-year-old-tree in Amersil, because in the middle of a meditation I thought about your green eyes." A sheepish smile crept onto his face.

Her eyes widened. "Three thousand years?"

"All because of your green eyes." He pressed his lips against hers. He leaned back and she followed his lips, straddling him, pressing her hips into his groin, bracing herself on his shoulders.

"All I want is this, this and nothing else, ever."

Krishani grunted in agreement as her mouth came down on his.

16-HAWKLIN

I star impatiently tapped his foot on the cobblestone. It was already well past dawn, the skies above the courtyard a tangle of orange and pale yellow intermingled with light blue. Stars twinkled in the east, their white speckles melting away in the blue. He was irritated by the fact Krishani seemed to wake later and later each morning. Sometimes he wouldn't emerge from his room until Melianna had called him four, sometimes five, times. He couldn't tell what his apprentice was doing; he filled his schedule adequately with a mixture of chores and exercises Krishani could do on his own. The boy should have been progressing, especially now that he didn't have the Brothers to distract him. The Elmare Castle was empty except for Atara's apprentice and his daughters. Atara kept a close watch on the girl and when she wasn't seen in the castle, she was in the orchards. She never talked to anyone.

He pulled his arms into the sleeves of his beige cloak just as Krishani stumbled underneath the archway, still tying the laces to his shin-high boots. His hair was disheveled and there were faint shadows under his eyes. His belt was also crooked and his tunic was twisted to one side. As he hopped along the stone he managed to pull it all together, stood upright and smoothed out his garments.

"Apologies, Elder," he said as he passed the crystal statues and joined Istar on the sidewalk.

Istar didn't say anything; he briskly led the way towards the moat and the orchards. There was nothing he could say that he hadn't said to the boy before, from the way Krishani held himself to the way he tried hard and still managed to fail. Istar thought he had started slow with Krishani, taking training techniques from earlier summers and building up to the bigger things. It was no use though. Krishani reached a threshold and plateaued, always stopping himself before he let go. It was maddening and Istar planned to break that pattern.

They crossed the bridge and Istar quickened his pace down the wide dirt road that led south to Evennses. On the right were the orchards and on the left the hedges, perfectly cut so they were straight and square with turrets rising from them every few feet. Krishani shuffled along behind him. Istar frowned.

"Where are we going?" Krishani asked once they had passed the orchards and were heading into taller trees and thicker underbrushes. This was where the villages of Orlondir branched off from. Istar smelled the hearth fires in the air and heard the sounds of small animals as they flitted through the breaks in the trees. The villagers provided food for the Elmare castle, not that they needed much of it except during the Fire Festivals. Lord Istar and Lady Atara barely ever ate to begin with; being sovereigns of the land removed them from trivial things like that. Food had nothing to do with their essence; their sparks would last so long as Avristar was alive and well.

"Hawklin," Istar said. He looked over his shoulder but didn't stop walking. "It's one of the villages."

"Why are we going there?" Krishani asked.

Istar narrowed his eyes and turned his attention back to the path. "Hawklin is eldered by Falnir. He was injured in the Lands of Men years ago and came back to Avristar. He was a former champion of our land. What happened to him was unfortunate, but it doesn't stop him from teaching others what he knows." The point wasn't really who Falnir was; he didn't spar anymore, but he eldered one of the villages where inhabitants of Avristar were allowed to raise their own families. They weren't subjected to the same tradition as the Children of Avristar. Still, Istar always hoped that strong ambassadors came from the villages. The more presence Avristar had in the Lands of Men the better chances of success they would have for bringing them peace.

He grimaced as he thought about his last conversation with the Gatekeeper, the voice of Avristar herself. Tall evergreens shrouded the entire summit in shadows, nothing but the crystal clear night sky above. He had rubbed his hands together and sparked a fire, which was immediately a twist of white and blue. The voice of the Gatekeeper emerged from the fire, speaking on behalf of Avristar herself. Istar thought that with the pressing threat of the Valtanyana's return she would call the armies back to Avristar. Instead, she acted as though he was an insolent fool for believing in nothing but hearsay. He tried to plead with her, but she was firm and wouldn't allow the armies to return without due cause. She was powerful on her own. The Valtanyana had been defeated; there couldn't be much of their armies left.

Istar was vexed by Avristar's recklessness, but if she didn't believe there was a threat to overcome then he couldn't persuade her any further.

As he walked with Krishani, the boy became silent behind him, no doubt processing what Istar had told him about Falnir. He didn't want to tell Krishani what they'd be walking into. Falnir was known for having tournaments between the children during this time of year, and they went on for weeks. It provided some entertainment for the villagers as life was sometimes tedious.

He neared the thin path into the village, the one barely wide enough for a horse and cart, and turned down it, leading Krishani through the squishy black mud. His boots pounded across it evenly, the bottom of his cloak becoming soaked with dirt and leftovers of the morning's dew. It didn't take long to reach the village and there was already a crowd conglomerating around the hearth fire. Taller feorns were twisting wooden swords in their hands.

"What's going on?" Krishani asked. Istar went to move through the crowds, but Krishani dug his heels into the mud and crossed his arms. He had alarm in his blue and green eyes, his pale skin looking more sallow now that he was near the crowd.

Istar smirked. "Come, now, I told them they would get an audience with a member of the Brotherhood of Amersil." He turned back to the crowd, but the boy didn't move.

"Why would you tell them that?" Krishani asked, his voice being swallowed up by sounds of the crowd.

Istar knew what the villagers thought of the Brothers from Amersil: Avristar's best and finest children, meant for greatness. He had been searching for a way to motivate Krishani, to show him what he would become in the Lands of Men, how he would be respected.

137

He had no plans of making Krishani fall into the ranks; he wanted the boy to lead an army. He wanted Krishani to be a King's General, help him succeed in securing lands and ruling his people. If the boy was patient, if he could surrender his reservations force triumph. Istar wasn't a fool as to what Krishani's parable meant, but apparently the boy himself was.

Krishani shook his head and his expression turned livid. "You really think I'm anything like the Brothers?" He spat on the ground, and pulled his arms tighter across his chest.

Istar laughed, trying to keep the mood light. "You won't be beat." He went to push through the crowd again as Krishani dropped his arms.

"That isn't what I'm worried about," Krishani said as he reluctantly followed Istar through the villagers. It took only minutes to get through the crowd, Istar leading the way. He broke into the center of the village, a series of two-story cabins surrounding the large stone encampment that created the hearth. The cabins had triangle roofs and deep mahogany beams crisscrossed across the fronts to secure them. The craftsmanship was merely for aesthetics, but masterfully executed. Istar thought he could smell the faint scent of roasted hazelnuts, a common snack food.

He glanced at the villagers, then turned back to the hearth and caught sight of Falnir. His scraggly brown hair was speckled with gray and fell to his shoulders. He hunched forward, heavily leaning on one side of his body. He was a feorn, but disfigured, his right leg twisted. Falnir stood near the porch of the mess hall where the villagers all ate dinner together. None of the other cabins had a kitchen. It was easier to have one per village and for everyone to sup together. Istar noticed that Falnir was looking past him at Krishani. The boy's presence caused gasps to emit from the crowd.

"Is this him?" Falnir asked, nodding towards Krishani.

"Aye, I think he'll be quite the match for your boy," Istar said casually. He neared Falnir and firmly shook hands with him. Falnir smelled of tainted water and small game. It wasn't a pleasant combination.

"Wraynas is ready for him. I trained him myself," Falnir said. He gestured to a tall feorn inspecting his wooden sword bent over near the hearth fire.

Istar sized him up. "Very well, a fair fight. Is he your champion?"

"He's won every tournament for the past three summers."

Istar turned to Krishani, who looked ready to throw up. "Are you ready to test your skills in a crowd?"

"No," Krishani said, his eyes still blazing like he was going to cause Istar to catch fire.

Istar lowered his gaze and pulled Krishani towards him so their foreheads touched. "I will always do what I must to challenge you. You cannot forfeit the match." He pulled away and turned to Falnir. "Plus nobody is really keeping score," he added diplomatically, as though he had every confidence that Krishani would win.

Falnir laughed, a hint of nervousness lacing his chuckle. "Right, nothing to be worried about."

At that Istar held out his hand and waited while Krishani handed him his cloak and tightened his belt around his waist. Falnir passed the wooden sword to Istar, who then handed it to Krishani. It was lightweight; carved from the branch of a maple tree. Krishani swung it around in his right arm, getting a feel for it. He switched back and forth between his left and right hands, seeing which he preferred. Istar watched him with a scowl as Falnir limped into the middle of the village and neared the hearth fire. He whispered something to Wraynas and then pulled back, motioning for Krishani to approach.

Istar watched as Krishani moved forward, his face a mask of stone. Istar didn't feel guilty for the boy; he would face worse things in the Lands of Men, this was good practice for him. He shifted to the left to get a better view of the battle, and when he could see Krishani and Wraynas directly across from one another, he stopped.

Falnir moved to the other side of the hearth. "People of Hawklin! I would like to welcome Krishani of Amersil to our village." The people cheered and Falnir waited for it to die down.

Istar smirked; this would show Krishani to focus. It seemed an extreme way to force it, but he didn't know what else to do. Krishani was too lost in his daydreams to really pay attention.

"Lord Istar of Avristar has called a match between our finest warrior and his. I present to you Wraynas, winner of the Beltane Tournament!" The crowd went wild for Wraynas. Istar nodded to himself as he mentally sized up Krishani's opponent. This would be a good match.

139

Falnir didn't waste time. He called the match seconds later and limped away from hearth, keeping his eyes on the boys as they circled each other.

Wraynas was the first to land a blow to Krishani with the wooden sword. It tapped his shoulder and Krishani briefly fell to one knee. He scraped the ground and rubbed his fingers together, then was back on his feet, twisting around and avoiding the very forward advances Wraynas made towards him.

Eventually, Krishani's wooden sword met with Wraynas's and they moved across the dirt in a pattern of blows, each of them defending themselves with skill. Their sparring didn't get interesting until Wraynas shoved Krishani with his free hand and Krishani fell onto his back. Wraynas was on him in an instant, ready to end the match, but Krishani sprang to his feet, his expression colder, harder.

Istar was curious as to what he was doing. He wasn't striking Wraynas back; he was only defending himself and not letting go. He seemed focused, but he wasn't doing what Istar wanted him to do. He turned his eyes away from the sparring match for only a second and that was all it took.

Krishani didn't even touch Wraynas, but there was a loud crack followed by a rumbling under their feet. The sky darkened with clouds and Wraynas flew onto his back and coughed, blood pouring from his mouth and staining his vest and breeches. Krishani knelt in a ceremonial position, the tip of his wooden sword pointed to the ground. It smoked at the hilt. Krishani panted as the crowd screamed in horror.

Istar rushed to his apprentice. He needed to reach Krishani before the villagers realized what happened and attacked his pupil. He briefly glanced at Wraynas, who was passed out at the edge of the crowd. There was a group of younger maidens fawning all over him, not knowing what to do. Istar placed a hand on Krishani's shoulder and the boy looked at him, his cheeks stained with tears.

"What was that?" Istar spat.

Krishani's expression turned from sad to cold. He shrugged off Istar's hand and stood, throwing the sword on the ground like it was a deadly weapon. "I hurt him, didn't I?"

"You …" Istar's gaze moved towards the crowd around Wraynas. Falnir had managed to reach him and was parting the girls and kneeling at his side. "But why would you?"

Krishani looked down at his hands. They were red, but he wasn't harmed in any way. "I didn't mean to. I just let go."

Istar had never actually witnessed what happened when Krishani let go, and he felt punched in the stomach at having to see it there, in a group of villagers. He took Krishani by the elbow and began leading him towards the thin path back to the Elmare Castle. The clouds were darkening overhead and large droplets of water were beginning to splash onto the dirt.

Before Istar could pull Krishani through the crowd, Falnir glanced up and caught them fleeing. "Your boy is dangerous!" he shouted, clearly upset.

Istar glared at Krishani. "I'll send Hernadette to help Wraynas." He tried to be diplomatic, but he knew it was no use. Krishani had harmed their champion, and what was supposed to be a fun sparring match had almost turned into bloodshed.

Falnir nodded. "It is no fault of yours, my lord."

Istar only nodded, then pushed Krishani through the crowd and into the forests. He didn't say a word as he led the boy back to the Elmare castle, but he was afraid—afraid of what Krishani was and what he could do.

17-PARABLES

Kaliel carefully pushed the door shut, heard a soft click, and slid under the covers the way she had done so many nights before. Melianna would be around soon to wake her, or it would be the silent lady, whose name she didn't know yet.

She stretched and smiled to herself as she tried to grab a few moments of sleep. She settled into the pillows and began to drift off as she heard the familiar shuffling down the hallway. Soon there was a light tap on the door. She sighed. There were times when Krishani's body wasn't quite as comfortable as the sheets, and she wouldn't dare sneak a chance to spend the night with him in her wing of the castle.

She sat and yawned, stretching her arms out, feigning she had woken up from a fabulous dream. She slid on the slippers she had abandoned moments ago and shuffled across the floor. She opened the door and turned back towards the bureau to find a hair brush.

"Good morrow." Melianna poured into the room and stared at her attire. Kaliel wore a simple light blue nightgown and muddy slippers.

"Good morrow," she replied as she brushed out the knots in her hair. She looked at her green eyes in the mirror, and then looked past them to where Melianna stood behind her. The woman was expressionless as always. "What task awaits me today?" She was trying to be cheery, but in the past few moons Lady Atara had spent all her time testing her.

"I was asked to fetch you and show you how to make tea."

Kaliel groaned. She scrunched up her nose and worked out another painful knot in her long white hair. "Can we focus on something else?"

Melianna twisted her lips up in a smile, the first time she had ever seemed amused around Kaliel. "Atara mentioned you could try focus training."

Kaliel smiled, too; it was amusing. Both she and Melianna had witnessed Krishani in the kitchen, slaving away at a hundred pounds of potatoes during the last fire festival. Lady Atara had never been as strict as Lord Istar, but Kaliel had evaded the task of tea since she came to Orlondir over a year ago. She had seen sixteen summers, the coming of which she would look forward to spending with Krishani.

She put down the brush and turned to Melianna. "What kind of tea?"

Melianna corrected her posture and the smile faded from her lips. "Sarsaparilla." She didn't give Kaliel time to answer; she took towards the servants' quarters, checking every few seconds to be sure Kaliel had followed.

The only time Kaliel had heard of sarsaparilla was when Desaunius made reference to a flesh-eating disease that afflicted humans. She shuddered. Desaunius never made that tea because it was too dangerous, and they held to the belief that whatever would cure the ailment would also poison one without it.

Her breathing became heavy as she followed Melianna down the corridor. She had no words for the woman as they entered the servants' hall and headed towards the stairs that led to the kitchen.

It was a large room; in the center was a vast wooden island, with pots hanging from a rack attached to the ceiling. Cupboards and counters lined the walls to either side, and in the corner on the far left was a collection of burlap sacks. They were labeled in the native tongue of Avristar indicating different herbs, spices and cooking ingredients. Melianna wasted no time. She took out a pot, filled it up in the basin of fresh spring water, and hung it overtop the fire pit on the opposite end of the room. It was enclosed in stone, though most of the innards had been blackened by fire. Melianna took the flint stone and struck it, lighting the bed of hay and coals until a strong flame snaked through the pit.

Kaliel felt seasick as she glanced around the room, trying to wrack her brain for the knowledge it would take to be successful. She drew a blank; she didn't even know what Sarsaparilla looked like. She gulped. "I, I don't know how...."

Melianna let out a haughty breath and Kaliel pressed her lips together. Apparently Melianna didn't know how inept she was in the kitchen. She furrowed her brow. "Lady Atara asked me to show you how to make tea. I suppose that also meant you would be observing."

Kaliel looked at the floor, she felt so useless. Melianna didn't pay attention to her; she went to find the herbs to prepare the tea. Kaliel shifted her weight back and forth as she stared at the pot over the flames. *Beautiful,* she thought as she watched the fire licking the edges of coal.

"Sarsaparilla." Melianna slapped it down on the wooden table and skillfully cut the herb into pieces. She separated the root from the plant and discarded the leaves and stem. Melianna lined up a number of other herbs, of which Kaliel recognized jasmine. She mixed them together on the cutting board and continued chopping until they were finely diced. Kaliel noticed the water was already boiling. Melianna took a towel and removed the pot from the fire pit. In one motion she put the pot down and dumped the herbal concoction into it. Most of the herbs dissolved in the water as she stirred and what didn't dissolve she let steep.

"Sarsaparilla root carries the healing properties needed. The rest is garbage. Will cure the nastiest of ailments," Melianna said. She lifted the spoon to her nose to smell the brew, but she didn't taste it. She frowned at first and then relaxed, looking satisfied. "Smell."

Kaliel leaned forward as Melianna held out the spoon to her. She smelled the brew; it had a strong musky scent. She nodded even though she had never made the tea before. "What were the other herbs you put in the tea?"

Melianna sighed as she continued to stir. "Lemongrass, lavender, rosemary, sassafras, and jasmine."

Kaliel nodded. She wasn't sure what to say. She wanted Melianna to explain to her what the tea would do. Desaunius was always known for her back stories, but Melianna just stood there, tapping her foot on the ground as though something was making her nervous.

"Have I done something wrong?" Kaliel asked.

Melianna shook her head. "Nay." Kaliel noticed she was distrait. "My father hasn't returned from the Lands of Men, and he won't. This tea would cure him, but Avristar won't allow me to go to him."

Kaliel couldn't imagine what it would be like to be infected with such a disease. "I'm sorry," she whispered.

145

Melianna waved her hand in dismissal. "His ailment isn't severe," she assured. She took the pot from Kaliel and dumped it into the waste trough. Not even the animals would eat of that.

"Leprosy." Kaliel recalled the name Desaunius had given for that disease.

Melianna went rigid. She turned slowly from the trough and stared at her. "How did you know?"

"Desaunius told me once."

• • •

Atara sat on a bench in front of a stone table against the west side of the castle. Strewn across the table was a checkered board and pieces from a game she was fond of. It was something the adepts had brought her from the Lands of Men, fidchell. She had a cup of tea sitting beside it. Footsteps shuffled from around the corner and she sat straighter as Kaliel came into view, the traditional ivory maiden's gown hanging to her knees. She always had that shy look on her face like she wasn't sure she was in the right place, but Atara waved it off.

"I see Melianna gave you my message," she said.

Kaliel ran her hands along her dress. "Yes, she said you needed to speak to me about something?"

Atara nodded and motioned for her to sit at the other side of the table. The girl was much too short for the table, it seemed to swallow her up. She briefly glanced at Atara then swung her legs underneath her and perched on her knees so she was at eye level with her elder.

"I wanted to talk to you about the Lands of Men," Atara began. Kaliel turned whiter and Atara barreled on. "There is a lot of danger...." She wasn't sure how to explain that she didn't think Kaliel would survive in the Lands of Men unless she became stronger in her training, or without finding a better vocation. Atara had led her through various meditative and metaphysical exercises, had taught her lightly on the healing arts, both herbal and physical. She hadn't been able to count how many times Melianna had been used as a patient for Kaliel to practice on when it came to bandages and splinters. Still, Kaliel wasn't showing any formidable area of skill and it frustrated her that the girl seemed so normal. She almost thought she had been too hasty in calling her a Flame at all. It was as though even the Great Oak was wrong about her.

"I know," Kaliel said, interrupting her train of thought.

Atara looked up to see her curling her hair behind her ears. She clasped her hands together and buried them in her lap as she kept her eyes on the board-game. Atara moved forward and absentmindedly began setting up the pieces. "I think you need a lot more training before you go to the Lands of Men, that's all."

"Oh," Kaliel said.

Atara smiled and nodded at the board. "Have you played before?"

Kaliel shook her head. "We had other games in Evennses."

"This one is rather easy." She explained the simple rules of the game, how each piece had its own purposes and how they moved around on the board. They began playing and it was clear Kaliel was a beginner. After a few turns back and forth Atara looked at her. "You see how each of these pieces has its place and they all work together for a common goal?"

Kaliel nodded.

"Well, that's where you don't fit. You seem to have very broad skills, but nothing that you've mastered."

The girl averted her gaze. Atara thought about the merfolk and the way Kaliel could speak with them. It wasn't something other apprentices could do. The elder herself stayed away from the banks of the lake and the pond, knowing that only Istar had a way with convincing the merfolk to stay peaceful and, stay underwater. Istar said they were brash and wild, unwilling to listen to the tenets of Avristar. It was one of the only things different about Kaliel.

"I understand," the girl said, her voice low.

Atara moved another piece across the board and gracefully moved one of Kaliel's pieces out of the way. "What I mean to ask you, Kaliel, is if you know what the parable means?"

"It means I won't win," she said. Atara continued to stare at her, a blank expression on her face. She nodded for Kaliel to continue. "It doesn't matter what I do, something will be lost."

Atara swallowed hard as Kaliel slid another piece across the board and made it vulnerable. She frowned as she responded by moving one of her pieces to take the piece on the board. "There should be something else to it. Your part in it?"

Kaliel knocked over one of the pieces as her hand trembled. She stood it back up and pushed it onto one of the squares. "I don't know."

"You don't have that much longer to figure it out. What do you feel you are? A healer? A seer? I need to know what you think." She moved another of her pieces across the board to end the game. She knocked over Kaliel's last piece and waited for her to respond.

The girl pressed her palms against the edge of the stone table and went to stand. "I'm a failure," she whispered as she balled up her fists and stalked away from the courtyard.

Atara sat stunned as she watched the girl go. She didn't know how to help her anymore.

• • •

Kaliel sat in the cave, waiting for Krishani to arrive from his lesson. She idly watched the falls as she waited, letting the failure from earlier that day fade away. She would have thought longer on it, but there was a loud noise from outside of the cave and she jumped, startled.

She had that feeling of anticipation as Krishani came into the cave and fell into the grass beside her, bereft of his cloak and clad in a beige tunic and black breeches. He buried his face in the circle of his arms and moaned.

Kaliel turned and rubbed his back. It had been like this for moons. He had been forced into intense physical or mental labor and Istar had been relentless.

"I loathe Istar," he mumbled into the grass. He pushed himself onto his elbows and glanced at her.

She stared at him with a spurious look. "Making apples float?" she assumed, but she stifled a laugh. Istar was boisterous with his tasks, and they often involved what she thought was impossible.

"No, sparring in Hawklin," he grumbled, burying his face in his hands. She could tell he didn't want to relive the experience. There was a reason he avoided the sparring matches at the Fire Festivals, and he seemed more upset than usual. "Everything hurts."

He groaned, and pulled off his tunic. She tried not to react to his nakedness. He turned and leaned forward, and she carefully ran her fingers along the muscles in his back, smoothing them out and relaxing them. She shifted on the grass so she was behind him. Her hands flowed over his shoulders and pressed against his chest. He smiled and pulled her hand to his lips. "You taste funny," he whispered against her skin.

Kaliel frowned. "Sarsaparilla," she said, shaking her head. Krishani kept her hand in his and she pushed her cheek to his shoulder. She sighed. "It cures leprosy."

"Leprosy causes death," he said. He took a deep breath and slowly let it out.

Kaliel pulled away. "You shouldn't say that."

Krishani sighed. "It's not what you think."

She sat next to him, and pulled his arm away from his knees, entwining her fingers through his. "I know." He looked up, his mismatched eyes full of worry and regret. "Will you tell me about the nightmares yet?"

He shook his head and glanced at the waterfall. She felt elated by the slow pulse running through her at the feel of his skin on hers, but there was fear. After a long time he looked at her, smirking. "I promised I wouldn't scare you again."

Kaliel scoffed, her eyes narrowing, her lips pushed together to stifle a sad giggle. She knew he was only trying to protect her, but what he went through with Istar and all his nightmares made her afraid for him. There were some places she couldn't follow him.

"I wish they would go away," she said.

"Me, too."

She knew he was trying to push the memory of the nightmares out of his mind. When he was with her she didn't want him to care about Istar's trials or his sleepless nights. There was only her, and the way she made him feel.

He leaned against the cave wall. "Istar is pressuring me to learn more about my parable."

She averted her eyes. "Will you tell me what it is?" she whispered, feeling inadequate and insecure. He had been so tight-lipped about his parable, she worried it was bad.

Krishani stood and moved to the waterfall. He closed his eyes and let the words spill into the mist. "An apple tree knows not when the apple of its eye will fall, and must surrender its possession. Wither in desolate loneliness and bring the forests to their eternal slumber. Triumph in faithful patience and bring the forests to their endless summer."

Kaliel wrapped her arms around him. She pressed her cheek to his back. He turned and let his arms fall around her. "That tree will tear us apart," she squeaked, unable to hide her fear. Everything about the Great Oak made her loathe it.

"I won't surrender," Krishani whispered against her hair.

She nodded and clutched him tighter.

"Besides, I've been called to Amersil."

Kaliel frowned. "Why?"

Krishani held her against him and rested his chin on top of her head. "I'm attending an execution ceremony."

Kaliel tensed. "Don't go."

He chuckled, a familiar sound that made her flush with heat. "They're removing me from the Brotherhood."

"Because of me?"

"Nobody knows about you."

She pulled back and stared into his eyes, unable to deny the pulsating emotions that still raced through her at the sight of him.

"I'm an astounding failure to them," he whispered with a smile, tracing the outline of her jaw with his fingertips.

"Oh."

"This is a good thing. They'll remove me, and I'll go back to the Great Oak. It'll be forced to give me a new parable."

Kaliel's eyes lit up. "You mean?"

"I won't have to surrender."

She leaned forward and softly kissed his lips. A look of sheer longing came over him. He walked her back into the cave and led her to the ground, his body covering hers. His hand trailed down her dress and cupped her knee. She let out a soft moan and he pressed his lips to her collarbone. He hesitated, and she thought of him running his hand up her thigh. Before she could think, his teeth grazed her ear and he pushed his hand up her thigh. She let out a loud gasp and he pulled back and stared at her.

"I love you," he whispered, his eyes locking with hers.

"I love you, too."

He made a trail of kisses down her neck. "This and nothing else."

She smiled, the familiar words making her pulse sing with joy and longing. "Ever," she finished, her hands running down his back, holding his weight against her.

• • •

Shimma snickered as she gazed through the bushes at the waterfall. She had seen Kaliel and Krishani come and go from it frequently every day for the past few moons. It was no secret they were trespassing, and who knew what they were talking about inside the cave. She waited for them to emerge and, minutes later, Krishani descended the stone stairway, followed by Kaliel. He stopped, grabbed her hand and spun her around, his lips finding hers. Shimma felt the hairs on the back of her neck stand on end.

"Why are you lurking?" Kazza asked as she sidled up beside her. She followed her gaze and saw Kaliel and Krishani kissing against the stone by the waterfall. "That's disgusting."

"It's unfortunate," Shimma muttered.

"Why?"

"I hope she's still pure." She nervously chewed on her lip as the two broke apart and Kaliel laughed.

Kazza rolled her eyes. "They're acting like feorns. You really think Istar will allow them to remain together?"

"I don't think he knows." Shimma ducked further into the bushes as Krishani's gaze pierced the forest. He seemed to be the type who would be cautious enough to make sure he and Kaliel were alone, but Shimma was sly.

"That's interesting. I thought he knew everything that went on in Avristar," Kazza said.

"Apparently not." Shimma was disgruntled about their attempts to help Kuruny, their sister, all of which had failed because of Istar.

"You still want her blood for the ritual, don't you?"

Shimma shot her a foxy smile. "It's not want, it's *need.*" She turned her attention back to the lovebirds. "If that continues I won't get my chance."

Kazza shook her head as Krishani pulled Kaliel into his embrace again. "I have to stop watching this. I'll let Kuruny know. Maybe we can separate them somehow."

"Aye, with him around we'll never get near her."

"With him around you'll likely get hurt," Kazza said as she slunk into the forest brush, preparing to leave.

Shimma turned and crossed her arms, stepping away from her vantage point. "I'll wait until she's alone."

18-Dreams of Death

Kaliel sat in the orchard with her journal in hand, scribbling down thoughts from the day's lessons. Atara had been harsh, wanting to know what she could see in herself, but the truth was, she didn't see anything but Krishani.

She pressed her head against the back of the tree and sighed. *Please bring good news,* she thought. Krishani had left for Amersil, which made the castle walls seem even emptier. Hoping to ease her longing, she escaped to the orchard, but couldn't face the waterfall. It would be different without him there. She looked at the branches above her, limbs littered with green leaves and little green unripe apples. It was summertime on Avristar.

Evennses was a long ways away, and she hadn't seen Pux since he visited at Samhain moons ago. She felt guilty for the way it was left with him. She hoped he would understand one day, but knowing him he wouldn't. She wondered how he could be such a natural at things like alchemy and transporting. He had none of the knowledge she held, and yet he had the skills she only dreamed of possessing.

What is it that I can't see? Sometimes she felt like there was a block in her mind, something preventing her from progressing. She uncrossed her legs and looked at them. They were full of small blue bruises, which blended against the whitish pastels of her skin. Her slippers were muddy as always, and she bent her knees and pulled them off, leaving herself barefoot. She placed them beside her and looked at the trees. She felt deliriousness sinking in as she tried to find the unique part within herself, the thing that made her different. She used to feel it in Evennses—it was what made her awkward—but in Orlondir, there was nothing she affected.

Maybe it was Evennses and not me? A leaf from the tree began floating towards her. She focused on it, allowing her energy to mix with the leaf. It turned, and then paused in midair, and turned again. She traced the outline of its veins, and watched it turn in ninety-degree angles, obeying her, as it remained there suspended. A light breeze passed through the orchard and dislodged her concentration. She looked at her slippers and the leaf landed on her head. She reached up and pulled it out of her hair.

That was odd. Did you fall because I wanted you to fall?

"Nay, it stayed because you willed it so, Little Flame," a voice answered.

Kaliel jumped away from the tree and looked around behind it. "Pux?" she asked as she searched the area.

Nothing, only the sounds of the land met her ears. She heard a low hum-like laughter coming from somewhere. She cocked her to the side and stared at the tree. Her mouth dropped open with awe. She moved towards it carefully and placed her hand on it, allowing her energy to flow into it.

"Careful, I am not so old," the tree said.

She dropped her hand and twisted her toe in the ground. "You speak?"

"We all speak."

"To whom?"

"Each other."

Kaliel crouched in the grass and picked up her journal and slippers. "I apologize for my rudeness." She went to press her hand against the bark in thanks, remembering the peculiar flowers that grew at the trees' feet in Evennses, but she pulled her hand away, unsure if it would bloom the flower or the weed.

"Please, there has been no intrusion," the tree said.

Kaliel placed her hand on its bark and shared her energy with it. Nothing special happened.

"You carry doubt," the tree said.

She stopped, but left her hand on the bark. She nodded and bit her lip even though she knew the tree couldn't see the gesture.

"Relax."

She nodded again. She let her thoughts flow into the tree as she stared at the ground, expecting the little flower to sprout. Nothing happened.

"Close your eyes."

She sighed and obeyed; her body swaying back and forth as she sent the energy again. Her fingers slid across the bark as she swept around the tree in anticipation. She circled the tree once and her foot crushed something below her. She opened her eyes and smiled at first, then frowned. A small purple flower had sprouted from the ground, but she had stepped on it. The flower wilted, its stem cracked and petals smushed. She let go of the bark and grazed along the underside of the flower bulb. Her fingers curled around it as she knelt on the ground and closed her eyes again.

This time something happened. She felt the rush of energy cascading through her, growing stronger and stronger until—. When she opened her eyes it was as though she was holding the birthstone from the lake, the flower surrounded in violet light. The crack in the stem healed, and the flower bounded back to life. She fell away from the flower, exhausted by the process and elated by the peculiarity of it. She smiled as she looked at the branch-littered sky, nearing nightfall.

I'll show him when he returns, she thought as she drifted back to thoughts of Krishani.

"Goodnight," the tree said.

Kaliel pushed herself up, some energy regained, and whispered, 'Goodnight,' running a hand along its bark as she passed. She headed barefoot towards the courtyard. The moment she reached the moat her stomach leapt into her chest. Shimma stood there, her blonde hair waving in the wind, arms crossed. She leaned over the edge of the bridge, gazing into the moat below. Kaliel grimaced as her eyes glanced across the road, spotting a thin trail leading to the waterfall. She contemplated it, but stopped in her tracks when Shimma turned her attention to her.

"Talking to yourself?" Shimma assumed; her voice full of malice.

Kaliel felt her pulse race as she stood straight and tried not to show fear. She hadn't even told Krishani about how she used to talk to the trees in Evennses. There were some things about her childhood she wanted to leave behind her. "No," she said slowly, drawing out the vowel.

Shimma let out a snort and sauntered towards her. Kaliel backed away, tripping on her own feet and fought to keep her balance. "Stay away from me," she said, trying not to fall over.

Shimma scoffed. "I'm not here to hurt you."

"Then what do you want with me?"

"Nothing," Shimma said in a sing song voice as she turned and skipped back towards the moat. "I saw Krishani leave," she added as she hopped onto the bridge again.

Kaliel willed herself to move closer, to stifle her fear and pretend she wasn't afraid, but it was hard. The witches avoided her because she was either with Atara or Krishani, and Istar was always stalking the castle, keeping an eye on them. Since her first night in Orlondir they hadn't caused her any trouble. Sickness sloshed in her stomach as she worried about the unpredictability of Shimma. She stopped in her tracks and waited. Shimma said nothing, her body bent over the railing of the bridge, whispering incantations to the fishes. Moments went by in awkward silence before, finally, Shimma turned. "Do you ever wonder how it ends?"

Kaliel rubbed her toe in the ground. "How what ends?"

"Love," Shimma said, her eyes blazing with both glee and mischief.

Kaliel watched her, warning bells ringing in the back of her mind. She gritted her teeth and twisted her toe deeper into the mud. Shimma skipped towards her and stopped just a few feet away when Kaliel looked at her with her own fiery stare.

Shimma shot her a complacent look and laughed. "He will marry the land," she said as she turned on her heel and disappeared behind the gates.

Kaliel hung her head. She knew that, but she hoped that day would never come. She dragged herself across the moat and into the castle, willing herself to go to bed.

• • •

There was a girl screaming in the distance. Kaliel felt her stomach drop into her knees as she listened to it, like a succession of waves crashing over rocks. It was a constant pattern of silence then screaming, over and over. Kaliel waited in the lull of the silence and winced when another scream pierced the air. Everything around her was clad in awful blackness. She was too afraid of what she would see if she *could* see. She pawed around in the dark and found the wall next to her. She pressed her palm against it then her back, sliding down and hugging her knees to her chest, burying her face. The sounds reminded her of the witches.

Maybe their screams were interrupting her dreams? Maybe they were sick of avoiding her? Maybe they were going to steal her from her bed and flay her alive?

Kaliel curled into a tighter ball and tried to steady her breathing. There was nothing to be afraid of on Avristar. She tried to coach herself into calmness, but as another blood-curdling scream hit the air her insides shook and her stomach did flip-flops, threatening to heave its contents onto the floor.

Nothing but a dream, she told herself as she waited for the nightmare to end. She remembered crawling into her bed; remembered blowing out the candle. She remembered thinking about Krishani before drifting off to sleep.

"I'runya," a voice whispered.

This was different than the screams. The voice sounded strained and scratchy, as though it took all the effort in the lands to speak. Kaliel shuddered at the sound; it was as though the voice was addressing her, specifically.

"I'runya," *the Flame,* the voice whispered again.

Kaliel glanced up as a loud scratch ripped along the wall against her back. Torchlight flickered into the catacombs and she instinctively knew she wasn't dreaming of Avristar. There were tombs across from her, shadows dancing along the walls and sticky ooze underneath her. She trembled, squeezed her eyes shut, willing the images away, but when she opened them, nothing had changed. She glanced to the left and noticed a long corridor leading to what looked like metal bars.

"I'runya," *the Flame,* the voice whispered again. It was an exasperated voice, one that called out in desperation almost as if doing so was its last resort.

Kaliel buried her face in her knees, too afraid to move towards the voice, but she was sure it was calling to her. She tried again to wake up, but it was no use. The nightmare held her prisoner. She sighed, knots still pulling her stomach tighter. There was a torch above her.

She clawed against the wall, using it to brace her and pull herself up. She leaned against it, the fear forcing her to feel lightheaded and dizzy. She took the torch off the wall and carefully stepped towards the voice.

"Who are you?" she whispered as she waved the torch in front of her. The catacombs smelled like death and she scrunched up her nose at the awful stench. She passed an archway. The cell had flat iron bars that created a crisscross pattern, leaving a myriad of tiny squares. She could only see part of what was on the other side, but it made her gasp and fall into the muck. She landed on her back and dropped the torch beside her. It extinguished, casting her into darkness again.

"Vari'runya," *Protect the Flames.*

Kaliel sat stunned and paralyzed by what she saw. On the other side of the bars was a girl. She wore a beautiful mint green and purple dress, but her skin was covered in a reddish brown tinge, parasites eating away at her flesh. Her hair only covered her head in patches, her scalp showing the same sores as the rest of her. Shaking, Kaliel tried to stay focused on the words the girl was saying, but her mind was flying with the need for escape. She desperately needed to wake up.

Fingers curled around her leg and she fell back into the ooze, her body shaking as pain shot through her like a dagger being dragged along her skin. This was much worse than what the witches would ever do to her, much worse than the tragedies she had heard of in the Lands of Men. The pain was so real she bit her lip to stifle her own screams.

One escaped her lips and then another and another. She felt a shift in her energy as it rushed out of her, her aura shining a bright violet. The hand clamped to her leg like a shackle as the girl sidled up against the bars, her bright blue eyes staring back into Kaliel's violet enflamed ones.

"Vari'runya," the girl said again, her eyes piercing Kaliel's with a message that conveyed one thing—danger.

Kaliel panted and whimpered, silently begging to be free of the girl, the dream, the pain that coursed through her like fire. She pushed herself onto her elbows and watched the girl's body flop like a fish behind the bars. Her senses snapped to the staggering realization the girl was dying.

Kaliel clawed at herself, wanting to tear herself in half. After everything she had endured, this pain was ten times worse. She wanted to go back to when life was simple, when all she had to worry about was the creature at the bottom of the lake. The fingers gripped tighter, forcing her to lose her senses. There was nothing else in her mind but the pain, and how to rid herself of that pain. She kicked wildly, trying to shake off the hand. The pain intensified with each passing minute, leaving her helpless on the clammy dungeon floor. Eventually, she stopped fighting and shifted so she stared into the eyes of the girl.

"Vari'runya," *Protect the Flames,* the girl whispered. Her mouth didn't move, her vocal chords probably damaged by the parasites.

Kaliel nodded, trying to agree with whatever the girl wanted and begged for it to be over. "Why?" she forced out as her head spun with dizziness. She looked at the girl in earnest, hoping it would be over soon, but the girl seemed utterly deranged.

"Ro tulten lye," *He comes for us.* The girl's blue eyes darkened with fear as she released her grip on Kaliel's ankle.

The pain receded almost instantly and Kaliel shot up, coughing and pressing her chest. She choked as consciousness hit her and found herself sitting in her bed in the Elmare castle, crickets creaking outside her window, the sliver of the moon casting a faint light across her room. She breathed a sigh of relief and moved out from under the covers. Her hands slid down her legs until they rested on her ankle. Reddish bruises in the shape of a hand stained her leg. She poked at it and winced. It hurt like a deep burn.

Everything hurt.

Her muscles felt as heavy as lead, and her head swirled with dizziness. She pushed herself to the edge of the bed and slid on her slippers. As she stood, her knees knocked together. Her mind was still putting together the pieces of the dream, but the last words the dying girl said ran through her mind over and over. She shuddered as she pulled a shawl over her shoulders and opened the door. She leaned against the doorframe, her body weak. She forced herself down the hallway, wanting to reach the waterfall before day broke over the horizon. If there was anything that would make the pain fade it was the water.

She reached the end of the corridor with so much effort it was exhausting. She pulled herself towards the courtyard, and stumbled over her own feet, splaying out face first in the middle of the hallway, her cheek pressed against the soft crimson carpet. She closed her eyes for only a moment and felt herself sucked into oblivion.

She was tumbling down a hill, rolling over herself, hitting rocks jutting out of the land at awkward angles. She tried to find her balance, but the more she moved the worse it became. There was a thud and everything stopped. She rolled over and opened her eyes. Gray and white clouds gathered above her, an unmistakable sense of melancholy on the air. She tried to sit up, but everything hurt too much.

Kaliel glanced to her left and the boots of a shadowy figure approached her. He lifted her into his arms and began carrying her across the land. She couldn't see anything but the darkened hood of his cloak concealing his face, and the sky just beyond. She tensed in his cold arms, wondering where he was taking her. She wanted to scream, but when she tried, no sound escaped her lips. Her throat felt like it had been burned. She closed her eyes and listened to the steady beats of his footsteps. He stopped moments later and she saw an archway. A woman in white approached, shouting at them. She had a dagger poised high above her head. Kaliel felt too weak to fight, numbness weighing down her extremities which, gradually, encompassed most of her body.

There was commotion, and the feeling of flying, and then there were warmer arms surrounding her. A cold blade pressed against her cheek, ice blue eyes found hers, whispers of a foreign language, and then nothing. The sting of nothingness was the worst, darkness filling her body with prickling sand and turning her senses to mush.

She tried to move, but there was no feeling in her bones. She waited, paralyzed in the hall until her body jolted several times. Kaliel coughed as life rushed into her and stinging pain encompassed her. Her heart beat irregularly—one, one two, one and one. She instinctively curled into a ball as rushing waves of fire and ice washed over her, covering her in tremors of pain that pressed into her, making it impossible to stay awake.

She slid into the nothingness as her mind tried to comprehend what had happened. The girl was dead, and someone—or something, was coming for her.

19-THE EMERALD FLAME

Krishani hovered beside the white horse as its hooves scratched the gravel-studded ground. It followed the solemn processional through the wide forest path leading towards a cemetery. Krishani watched intently from his position. The man perched on the white horse had a blank expression on his face and trailed along behind the processional, giving quite enough distance that he looked associated, but might not be at all.

The people in black carrying the box trudged down a hill. The bare trees and evergreens parted on either side to give way to a large wrought iron gate. On the other side of the gate were tombstones. As they walked, the gate opened with an eerie creak. It was like the graveyard was expecting them.

The man on the white horse paused when he reached the gates. He stopped and stared into the cemetery while the four people wound along a narrow snaking path towards a plot in the distance.

Krishani stopped outside the gate. He tried to hover beyond it, but he couldn't. He stood there dumbfounded, his fingers curling around the bars, curiosity gripping him.

"You can't enter," the Ferryman on the horse said. He looked at him with such intensity that for a moment Krishani thought it was real and not a dream.

"Why not?"

"You'll get hurt."

"What will happen to them?" This was the first time the man had really spoken to him. He hoped it would continue; there was so much he was confused about.

"All of them will die."

"Why?"

"Family curse," he spoke solemnly. He bowed his head as the last of them passed through the mists in the graveyard and out of sight.

"Can you help them?" Krishani asked. They had seen each other many nights before. The Ferryman was always elusive, but Krishani had learned a lot from his actions. Nobody ever lived.

"I *have* helped them," the Ferryman said. He sounded perturbed. He turned the horse around and went to pound down the gravel road.

"How have you helped them?"

The horse entered a canter and Krishani floated behind them. The land here was so peculiar—hard, cold, and dry. Evergreens littered the forests, and the red cedars were bare this time of year. He hadn't noticed it before but frost covered the ground in a thick sheet.

The Ferryman didn't answer his question, simply staring ahead. A moment later, he heaved a sigh and stopped the horse in his tracks. He looked back at Krishani and shook his head. "You shouldn't be here. You're not ready to know about the Ferrymen." He whipped the reins hard and the horse erupted into a gallop, speeding away from Krishani too fast for the boy to follow.

Krishani stood there on the deserted gravel road for several moments until the surroundings began to swirl around him and he was sucked into darkness. He opened his eyes and found himself in the forests of Amersil.

What are the Ferrymen? he wondered. He smelled nascent red cedars and heaved a sigh of relief. He sat up, clucking a few times in the hopes that Rhina hadn't continued without him. He waited, and soon her glimmering white mane poked through two trees.

"Come, Rhina," Krishani said. He got to his feet and walked through the forest brush to the horse. He stroked her head and stepped backwards, coaxing her out from the trees. She came and Krishani mounted her. With a quick cluck to her ear, she trotted off towards the village where the Brotherhood lived.

• • •

Krishani took one last look behind him at the grove. Smoke from the fire twisted into the overcast sky, and the smoky scent covered the village. All the others had retreated to their homes. The execution ceremony was over. He couldn't tell a soul what it entailed even if he wanted to. The Brotherhood was a secret and he was lucky to know a tenth of its wonders.

He hung his head. What was done was done. There wasn't anything thing he could do to change the path. The ceremony had been ordered by Adoron, though Istar was a coward to admit it. Nineteen summers and he had experienced nothing but small triumphs. Everything magical about his life revolved around Kaliel, and without her there was no control, without her—he did nothing but ruin the land.

He took a step towards the Great Oak and paused. Anxiety crept into his heart. He hadn't expected this. He looked forward to hearing the words of the Great Oak, new words, better words, ones that would allow him a life with the girl he loved. He closed his eyes and took a deep breath, then began winding down the path. The red cedars in Amersil where he grew up were the same as those in Evennses, their wide trunks spreading through the soil below, their roots littering the path and creating an obstacle course. He saw better at night, and as each one came into view he stepped over them. There were too many fallen trees along the path and he sighed at his youthful destruction.

He thought about the seed, the second rite he had never passed. Adoron was his mentor then, and on the day of the full moon they set out. Adoron carried the seed with him. They reached a break in the trees where the sky could be seen through the canopy. The place was called Tolemny. Every apprentice before him had passed the task in the same clearing, the only difference was they had seen twelve summers, and Krishani had seen fourteen. He remembered the ordeal—it was catastrophic. He had raised his arms to the sky and called for rain. Buckets of rain fell from the sky, but as the pressure built, an invisible shield formed around the seed, and it alone remained dry. Adoron looked afraid when the storm lost control and lightning flashed.

Trees fell, one in particular having been in Avristar for a thousand years.

Even now, Krishani felt guilty at the thought of it as he climbed over the body of a younger fallen tree. He shared his guilt with the tree as he passed it, apologizing for his mistakes.

The three paths came into view, and he continued down the middle one. He knew all three paths led to the same tree, but he preferred the path with the least obstacles. The tree came into view, its thick roots protruding like giants out of the ground. He stared up at it and smiled. This was his moment. The Great Oak would reveal to him a new parable and he would know what his purpose was.

He approached confidently and the tree creaked in acknowledgement of his presence. He firmly placed his hand on the bark and shared his arrogance and relief to be visiting for a second time.

"I am never wrong," the tree said, seeming offended.

Krishani removed his hand, and noted that something sticky had transferred onto it.

"A tree knows not when the apple of its eye will fall and must surrender its possession. Wither in desolate loneliness and bring the forests to their eternal slumber. Triumph in faithful patience and bring the forests to their endless summer."

Krishani stood in shock at the words. They were the same as they had always been. His face twisted as anger bubbled up inside of him. "I will never surrender!" His voice echoed as it bounced off the trees surrounding the Great Oak. Without thinking, he approached the tree and pounded his fists on its bark, wanting it to change what it said.

The tree remained dormant.

"You vile, wretched tree. Say to me the truth!" He was so angry he couldn't believe what he was doing. He kicked the tree with the toe of his boots. The roots below him fluttered as though he was on the backside of a bird. He fell in the midst of them as they continued to flow around him.

"Surrender!" the tree howled at him. The volume was deafening. Birds flew from their nests into the sky; the squeals of small animals sounded as they ran to their holes, the other trees shook despite the lack of a breeze. Krishani trembled as he lay there in between the roots. They had grown cold and motionless. Angry tears slid down his face. He couldn't change the words. He could do nothing to escape his future.

He went to move, but darkness swept him under. It felt as though he was traveling through a tunnel. He saw the light at the end of it, but could do nothing to move faster or slower towards it. He drifted at some predetermined pace, noticing the nothingness around him.

The light grew until it encompassed him. He was sitting in a field. In front of him, an entire battalion of warriors in full armor stood in formation. His eyes widened as he realized he was in the way. A man wearing regal colors of purple and gold rode on a brown horse back and forth along the line, calling out orders.

Krishani scrambled to his feet and ran towards the trees. They seemed so far away. He took across the field as fast as he could, but his lungs ached for air and the field seemed to get longer and longer. Cannons exploded behind him. The battle was underway. He didn't want to look back only to see more death, more blood. He knew the man in purple and gold would be slain. *Why did he know?* He couldn't understand his foresight, but he refused to find out if he was right. He squeezed his eyes shut, hoping the trees would be closer when he opened them.

"You're intruding!" a voice shouted.

Krishani opened his eyes and came face to face with the same man on the white horse. "I—I don't want to be here." He looked at the man, who was inexplicably rendered faceless. When would he learn who he was? Krishani was desperate to get to the trees. Salvation rested there. He tried to look behind him, but he could smell the coppery blood and felt the souls rising up from the battlefield. He knew wispy smoke would careen into the air behind him, rising then disappearing into the atmosphere. His stomach churned as his knees grew weak and he slid into the grass.

"Your time as a Ferryman has not yet begun," the voice snapped. The white horse circled him and then took towards the battlefield.

Darkness swirled around Krishani again and the battlefield faded away. Helplessly, he followed the dream until another voice pierced his ears.

Krishani help me.

Kaliel.

• • •

Kaliel was in stasis. There was pain, but the kind that was numb, as if her entire body had been wrapped in ice. She knew it wasn't consciousness, it wasn't home. She cried. Death—if that's what this was—was too much for her. *Is this what it's like for Krishani?* she wondered as she recalled his nightmares. No, couldn't be. They were bad, but he didn't die in them.

She died with the girl. What was her name? Why did she know her? *Lotesse,* the familiar voice inside answered. She paused. *The Emerald Flame.*

The scenes changed rapidly. There was something on her head and a gold-framed mirror in front of her. The headdress had a feather on top of it, like the crown she had drawn on one of the figures in her journal. She stared at it; it seemed so out of place. She looked into her eyes: amethyst. A lavender and ivory nightgown fell to her ankles. Her delicate fingers went to touch the headdress. The moment they grazed along its base, it showered her in sand. With a cough, she blinked the granules from her eyes and looked at herself in the mirror again: green eyes.

The symbols on the parchment materialized in her mind but she couldn't make any sense of it. There was a boy with one hazel and one golden eye, wearing a headdress of snakes. Across from him was a girl with a headdress that had a feather at the top of it. The same one she had been wearing in the previous scene. Above them was a golden sun with rays of light shining towards their mouths. A chalice was in the girl's hand. She had a rough sketch of the same parchment in her journal but something was missing. Meaning.

She heard murmurs in the distance, voices she vaguely remembered. She tried to claw her way to them. The numbness thawed as she came to, feeling heaviness in her limbs, and prickles on her leg where Lotesse had grabbed her. She almost slipped back into unconsciousness, but her eyelids fluttered and she took a sharp breath.

She opened her eyes and was overwhelmed by the acuteness of her senses. Everything was so crisp. Someone had lit dragon's blood, she would recognize it anywhere. She smelled the faintness of nightshade near her bedside, wondered what use they had found for it, and furthermore noticed the distinct smell of star anise. She wrinkled her nose and found her hands; they were folded on her lap. She tried to push herself up, but her head swelled with dizziness and she fell back into the bed.

Atara entered. Kaliel didn't say a word even though her eyes were open. She stared at the trap door in the ceiling, letting out a sigh as Atara fiddled with a sachet of mixed herbs. She noted the ginseng and ginger root in the air.

Atara jumped; the satchel fell on the ground. "Kaliel?"

She moaned.

Atara rushed to her side and lifted her arm to check her vital signs. Kaliel stared into the elder's eyes and felt a slight bit of relief wash over her. Atara grabbed the cloth from the water bowl next to the bed, and lightly patted Kaliel's forehead with it.

"How are you feeling?"

Kaliel let out another long breath. She could handle the pain. She'd had enough bruises in her lifetime to understand that nothing but time would heal her.

"Who are the Flames?" she whispered.

Atara dipped the cloth in the bowl. She looked away when Kaliel spoke. The girl felt Atara's pulse quicken as she glanced back at her with compassion and wiped the girl's brow again. She watched as Atara opened and closed her mouth, seeming to choose her words carefully. Kaliel only felt more agitated the longer her elder took to answer.

"The precious jewels of the universe of course," Atara said.

Kaliel slid her hand into hers and gripped it tight. Fear made her tremble as tears spilled onto her cheeks.

"The Emerald Flame is dead," she whispered. Her hand fell limp in Atara's as the darkness closed around her.

20-The Amethyst Flame

He whipped the reins again but galloping was galloping and the horse couldn't move any faster. Rhina panted and as soon as Krishani spotted the light of the hearth fire in the center of town, he tugged back on the reins. Rhina slowed to a trot as they entered the village center. She bowed her head and lapped up some water from a puddle on the side of the thin dirt road. Krishani sighed and looked at the sky, big dark clouds covering the stars. He had been lucky Rhina was skilled in night travel and that this jaunt didn't seem to bother her so much as it tired her out.

The words had been clear—Kaliel needed help. His heart thumped wildly even as Rhina took her rest. Had it been another encounter with Kuruny? He detested Kuruny, always lurking around in places she shouldn't be, eavesdropping and trying to find reasons to perform her twisted form of magic. He avoided her and her sisters at all costs. Istar's attempts to purify them had proven unsuccessful.

He pulled Rhina's head out of the water, and clucked at her to begin moving again. The last thing he needed was to wake the folks in the village. He hoped it wasn't Hawklin. He didn't want to face the villagers about what he had done to Wraynas. The horse trotted carefully through the soggy dirt and once they broke into the forest Krishani urged her to a gallop.

She tried. On average it took half a day on horse to reach Orlondir. Krishani had been traveling for merely an evening, and yet he was nearing the apple orchards. Rhina slowed again as she zigzagged through the trees, avoiding low branches and fallen apples. The moat was a few paces away, and instead of forcing Rhina to move faster, Krishani hopped off her back and landed in the mud. His boots sloshed in the muck as he ran to the moat. He hit the main road, and then the bridge.

He pushed the large wooden doors to the courtyard open and crossed it in a few long strides. He was a mess when he reached the archway to the Grand Hall, but he had no time to think of that. He bounded up the stairs, taking two at a time, and clambered down the hallway until he reached Kaliel's door. He swung it open and froze.

She was asleep.

Melianna perched on a stool near the bureau, sleepily watching Kaliel and reading a book. She jumped when she saw Krishani and dropped the book on the floor. She almost knocked the candle over as she swayed on the stool. Seeming perturbed, put a finger to her lips and shushed him even though he hadn't said anything. She shot a glance over at Kaliel, who stirred.

Krishani's breath hitched as he realized his mistake, no doubt Melianna would tell Istar about this intrusion straight away. He realized he was soaking wet and with Melianna's disapproving gaze he removed his cloak and boots. He looked at her for some help, but she simply pointed to an empty place along the wall where he could pile his things. The rest of his clothing clung to his frame, making movement awkward with certain motions. He shot her another glance, apologetic, pleading. He wanted to know what happened, but he also wanted her to leave him alone with Kaliel.

He tried not to glower at Melianna as he viewed Kaliel from a distance, afraid to take another step forward. He would have preferred to take off all his clothes and slide under the covers next to her, but that would have been inappropriate.

"Why did you come?" Still glaring at him, Melianna whispered loud enough for him to hear. She bent over and picked up the book and placed it on the bureau next to her. She stood and walked towards him, stopping at the foot of the bed. Crossing her arms, she gave him an expression that told him to leave and she wouldn't tell Istar.

Krishani stood his ground, his concern for Kaliel strong enough that his heart wanted to explode from his chest. Melianna was merely an obstacle between a bull and a red cape; nothing could stop him from waking her.

"She needed me," he said. He inwardly cringed after he spoke. No matter how he worded it, his feelings for her were written all over his face.

"She needs rest. Have you any idea what she's been through?"

So it was that bad. His expression softened, losing all of its determination. He only wanted to see her well. He let his fists relax and ran his fingers through his hair. "I—" he began. "I've been away."

Melianna uncrossed her arms and stepped away from the bed. "She's been like this for almost a day. She awoke yesterday morning when Atara came to check on her. Whatever was said, she hasn't woken since."

Krishani ached with concern. He'd been following the Ferryman in a dream when it happened, and he heard no call until mere hours ago when he was slumbering under the Great Oak. The parable hadn't changed. He tried to push that out of his mind as Kaliel stirred. She mumbled something, and without regard to Melianna he stepped forward and crouched at the side of the bed. He noticed the water bowl on the end table, the strong smell of herbs rising from it.

He looked at Kaliel's face, eyes—pressed against her eyelids— darted back and forth. She seemed to tremble underneath the blankets. Hair was stuck to her forehead, a result of the water that had been patted across her brow more than a few times. Arms were drawn up to her chest, hands clasped together, resting against her heart. He heard her heartbeat from the distance between them, and he wanted so badly to wrap his arms around her.

She took a shaky breath and her eyelids fluttered. Krishani slid his hand between the two that were clasped and implored her with his eyes to wake up. He scanned the surface of her skin and hoped wherever she was she could find her way back to him. He squeezed tighter and it seemed as though Melianna had stepped into the hall.

"Krishani," Kaliel murmured. Her eyes slowly opened.

He smiled and shifted his weight. "I'm here." He leaned forward and kissed her forehead. He tasted the herbal concoction on his lips as he pulled away. Relief washed over him as he met her green eyes. They looked tired and worn, as though she had fought a war and barely survived.

She relaxed, unlocked her hands and tried to get comfortable, but didn't appear to find a position she liked. He wanted to help her more, smooth out the knots in her muscles the way she had done for him. She gulped and pushed herself up. Krishani sat on the bed next to her.

He wanted to wipe her brow again, she looked so wasted. Before he could do anything, she bowed her head and began sobbing. He inched closer and pulled her into his embrace. Despite the dampness of his shirt she melted into him.

"The Emerald Flame is dead," she whispered in his ear.

His eyes widened as he realized why she had called for him. He pulled back and placed his hands on her shoulders and forced her to look him in the eyes. "You dreamt of death?" he asked.

She only nodded.

He thought he was the only one to carry that burden.

"I felt every part of her pain." She whimpered as she pushed back into his arms.

He held her tight, but he was afraid. Her experience seemed ten times more extreme and powerful than his. He always watched others die. He never felt it himself, though he could feel the souls writhing out of the bodies, and he could tell when death was close at hand. He rubbed her back.

"Nothing can hurt you now," he said.

"Vari'Runya. Ro tulten lye," she whispered adamantly.

Krishani recognized the words. They might have been slightly different than the language he was used to, but they meant almost the same thing.

He shuddered, but more than that he was confused. He hadn't told her everything about the frequent dreams of The Ferryman, and she had never spoken of the Flames before. The fact they could be hunted them made him quiver.

Is that why I'm not ready? he thought as he contemplated the last vision he had. A fresh batch of tears spilled onto his shirt, warm, unlike the rest of his garments which had grown crisp and cold. He turned his attention back to Kaliel. "Why do you have to protect them?"

Kaliel shook as she took a deep breath. She was so fragile. He let go and she eased into the bed. She couldn't make eye contact with him, her stomach heaving in fits as she looked at the end table, worried and afraid.

"I'm the Amethyst Flame," she scarcely whispered.

And he comes for you, Krishani thought as the room spun around him. It had made sense from the beginning—the amethyst eyes, the aura—it was as though it was always there and yet, he wished it wasn't true.

• • •

"Why did you not come to me?" Istar stood in the hallway, his voice almost a whisper as he stared at Atara, his lady. She held a pitcher of fresh tea as she came from the kitchen, in the hopes that Kaliel was awake.

She squared her shoulders when she saw him and raised her head to meet his gaze. "She is my apprentice, and none of your concern." She took a bold step forward, like she wanted to dart past him, but his eyes only grew colder. He took a long stride towards her and gripped her elbow.

"She is a Flame!" he hissed.

Atara knew he was more concerned than angry, and that he could read her well. She feared he knew what she was planning to do—let the death go unnoticed, allow Kaliel to forget about Lotesse and the dream that almost killed her. She tried to shrug out of his grasp, but her eyes hit the floor at the harshness of his words. "She should not have to carry the burden."

"She has no choice."

Atara glared at him, curious. Istar glared back, and she knew he was doing his utmost to shield himself from being read by her. "Whatever do you mean?" She hung on each word as it passed her lips.

Istar let go and paced down the hallway towards Kaliel's door. "This is worse than you can imagine, Atara. The Valtanyana have returned!"

The clay pitcher slipped out of her hands and crashed to the floor. Body rigid, she barely noticed the shards and her soaked shoes. Her face flushed as she forced away the painful memories of the past.

She thought, if Kaliel remained innocent, even with the death of Lotesse, she could guide her down the right path, awaken the Flame in time—safely so it wouldn't destroy the girl it lived within.

"What?" she said, afraid of the answer.

"Crestaos."

Atara noticed the clay pieces below her and the need to do something made her bend down and pick them up off the floor. "He's trapped in Avrigost." She said it to comfort herself, but it was futile.

Istar continued pacing and put a hand to his forehead as if to smooth out the crease that had formed. He moved back towards the main hall, passing Atara. "Aye, however, the death of Lotesse ..."

Atara stood and turned to him. She gulped. "Nay, I cannot bear his wrath again." She tried to force away the tremors rumbling in her bones but memories of the First Era struck her. There was no running from the Valtanyana, they took what they wanted and destroyed what they couldn't take. Avristar had barely made it. She gained control of herself and took a step backwards. Istar gave her a hard stare.

He pounded his fist against the wall. "We must awaken her!"

Atara was sick to her stomach as she fought to gain control of herself. "She's not ready!"

"A Flame is dead."

Cold wrapped around her as the harshness of his words struck her. A tear slid down her face as flashes of the past pricked her mind's eye. Istar neared her and pulled her into his embrace. She knew he felt it too, everything she felt and thought; a dull hum in the back of his mind and present in his heart.

"The Kiirar will be able to help. Kaliel must focus," Istar said as he rubbed her back.

"Are you certain she will be safe?"

"Avristar is hidden. If the Flames are what he seeks, it is unlikely he will search here."

"Then we will do what we can to help her," Atara said, though her thoughts circled around something much worse, something she knew her husband didn't want to think about.

21-FERRYMEN

Hooves pounded the land, but Kaliel was surrounded by pitch black. She curiously followed the rhythm of the pounding, hearing ever so often the shouts of voices, speaking in a language she couldn't understand. Something orange glowed in front of her, small at first before growing into an orb. Kaliel shielded her eyes from its brightness.

"Tiki," a gruff voice called.

An outline of a hand shadowed the brightness. Kaliel watched as it drew the orb out of the small satchel they were being held in. She felt disoriented but content; Tiki wasn't afraid. Kaliel shrunk into the depths of the cloth as the horses stopped.

The satchel dropped to the ground and Kaliel stepped out onto wooden planks creating a porch. She was the same size as the little orb. Everything was black and white except for the orange glow of the orb. Kaliel looked up at the tall man standing on the porch with the orb in the palm of his hand. He took out a small boxy chamber and coaxed her into it. Tiki shone from inside, showering the porch in orange light.

Kaliel looked around. Beyond the porch, there was a row of mountains, stretches of lush black grasses and flowers. She turned her attention back to the glowing, orange orb.

"Who are you?" Kaliel asked.

"Tiki, The Carnelian Flame."

"Why are you here?"

"I was taken by him."

Kaliel felt nauseous as the mountains began to swell. The flowers whispered as she tried to understand the gravity of the situation. More than anything she wanted to be in her room on Avristar.

"You will die," she whispered to Tiki before she felt pulled through a vortex into nowhere. The fresh scent of herbs wafted through the air as her eyes fluttered open.

"Tiki," she mumbled as she viewed the hazy room around her. Lavender; that's what it was. The room was covered in a heavy cloud of lavender. It smelled like home. She pushed her hands into the bed and tried to sit up.

"I wouldn't advise that yet," Atara said. She stood at the bureau viewing Kaliel through the mirror. She had an incense stick in hand and she blew on it lightly, spreading smoke into the room. When she turned to face Kaliel it was no secret she had something important to say.

Kaliel slumped back into the pillows, but looked at the window and the sunlight shining through it. "How many days have passed?"

"Three," Atara answered gently. She crossed the room and Kaliel felt the woman's eyes raking over her features.

She felt very weak. "So many days lost, I must go back to my studies, I must—" She met Atara's gaze, and as if she wasn't white enough already, the woman became whiter. Atara was expressionless, compassionless, nothing sunny and happy or gentle and caring about her. Kaliel understood without the need for her to explain. "I can't return to my studies," she said flatly. The fits that had attacked her stomach earlier threatened to begin again. She fought against them.

Atara looked at the door. "Nay, you must go to the Kiirar."

Kaliel's eyes widened. *Being sent away again?* First Orlondir and now where? She knew The Kiirar were in Nandaro, to the North. She would have liked to go back to Evennses to play with Pux in the forests. Her thoughts drifted to Krishani, and all her time spent with him. "What about—" she began, though she knew she could never finish that sentence with what she was thinking. *Krishani?* Her mouth slightly opened, hoping for some words of comfort.

Atara turned, her arms crossed. "What about…?" She raised her eyebrows. "You will return in three moons. It won't take long."

Kaliel's head hurt. She thought back to the dream, to Tiki, to the man that had taken her. It didn't feel the same as Lotesse. It was softer;

he was gruff but she didn't feel pure corruption out of him. She looked at the window, ignoring Atara's comment. She couldn't bear to be from Krishani, but if the Kiirar could show her how to control her link to the Flames, then perhaps leaving wouldn't prove so bad.

"I won't be of much help even if you stayed. I have business to attend to regarding my adepts in the Lands of Men." Atara paced back and forth in front of the bed. She looked like she was afraid of something—war, tarnished lands, and the enemy that had killed Lotesse, maybe.

Kaliel knew what this could mean, but she didn't want to say it. Upset, she pulled the blankets off her. The rejection in Atara's voice was strong, and she had never felt like such a failure until that moment, when in a matter of seconds, the rest of her elder's life became more important than her. She threw her legs over the side of the bed and looked at Atara carefully before setting her feet on the floor.

"So the wretched Oak tells me sacrifice and I'm sent to you," Kaliel said, monotone. "So the Emerald Flame tells me protection, and you send me to the Kiirar." She stared at the embroidered rug on the floor and a tear splashed onto her foot. "All I want is to be normal."

Atara backed away towards the door. The expression on her face was mangled, as though she had figured it all out and wasn't willing to talk about it. Kaliel looked at her and realized what Atara *wasn't* saying. Kaliel was a Flame. She couldn't be normal even if she wanted to be. She never was normal to begin with. And her kind were being hunted, something she couldn't just ignore.

Atara reached for the door knob, her back to Kaliel. "Please do not see this as exile." She pulled the door open and retreated into the corridor.

• • •

Krishani aimlessly wandered through the corridors. He was looking for Istar; something told him that his elder knew more than he let on and he wanted to confront him about Kaliel. He turned the corner in the upper east wing and spotted the three witches pacing towards him. He groaned and tried to duck back the way he came, but Kuruny met his eyes, and there was no backing out. He stopped in his tracks as they approached and leaned against the balcony for air.

"You look horrible, Krishani," Shimma said as she sauntered along, hugging the rail of the balcony. She playfully twisted back and forth in the hopes of attracting his attention. Her blonde hair fell in waves over the railing and she tossed it over her shoulder and met his gaze.

Krishani stared at the chandelier and the empty floor below, the energy from the women making him feel nauseous. "Doesn't concern you, Shimma."

Kuruny stuck out her pouty lip and shot him a devious smiled. "Don't patronize him. Kaliel is sick." She had a singsong tone to her voice as though she enjoyed digging the knife deeper.

He curled his hand into a fist at the mention of Kaliel. She promised to stay away from them, and she had kept her promise, but Kuruny and her sisters were deceitful. "You know nothing," he spat. He turned around and made eye contact with Kuruny. Her eyes were shiny black orbs glistening against her pale skin and long black hair.

Kuruny stepped back. She looked like she was about to give up as Shimma and Kazza moved away, but as she turned she said, "All I want is this." The words wafted through the air like an insult, but what it really meant was his feelings for Kaliel were no secret. Kuruny looked at the ceiling. "Istar is in the stables. He's sending Kaliel somewhere." She turned the corner after her sisters.

Krishani followed her back the way he came. "What? Where? When did you hear this?"

She continued walking, not bothering to turn around. "Go ask him yourself," she said coldly.

Krishani stumbled away. *Send her away?* he wondered as he raced to the servants' quarters. He clambered down the stairwell and paused when he reached the hall. He took a few strides towards the archway that led to the stables. As Kuruny had said, Istar was standing in one of the stalls, fastening a saddle to his horse, Paladin. He paused and looked at Krishani, surprise crossing his wrinkled face.

"Our lesson isn't until tomorrow," he called, and Krishani recognized the attempt to make him leave.

Krishani crossed the distance between them and stopped at the opening to the stall. He tried to control his emotions, but he couldn't understand why Istar would interfere with Kaliel. "I wasn't aware you were leaving."

Istar studied his expression. "I'm not going far. I must speak with The Kiirar."

"Whom?" Krishani asked, feigning interest. There were dozens of Kiirar in Nandaro, 'Kiirar' being the official term for a 'lorekeeper.' His thoughts caved in around him, threatening to be set loose. He wanted to ask about Kaliel. He casually draped his arm over the railing and looked Istar directly in the eye.

"That is not your concern," Istar said.

Krishani's anger flared. "Everything to do with her concerns me."

Istar raised an eyebrow. "Tell me, why do you care so much about Kaliel?"

Krishani huffed, and looked at the ground. The secret was out, there was no turning back. His arm went limp as he realized what he had gotten himself into. He took a deep breath and looked at the hay. He couldn't bring himself to look at Istar.

"I love her."

Istar mounted the horse and went rigid. "Is that why you failed your tasks?"

He frowned, that wasn't the reaction he expected. "No," he answered slowly. He pushed off the stall and stepped towards an empty one on the opposite end of the stable. He thought back to the execution ceremony, the reason for his removal from the Brotherhood. They had done so on the grounds of his failure. However, it stung that Istar assumed his failure was due to her.

"She will be well protected," Istar said with a knowing look in his eyes.

Krishani worried he had known all along. He turned and shoved his hands into his pockets. "She was fine until I left."

"And what *did* the Great Oak have to say?"

"The same."

Istar frowned. He gripped the reins and moved towards the center of the stables. "Aye, that is peculiar."

Krishani paced back and forth, the tension rising. He was so angry with Istar, but he had to stay in control. "Please, allow her to stay. I'll help her."

Istar let out a laugh, but the boy was serious. Krishani stepped in front of the horse, his expression cold. Istar shook his head. "Nay, that will not do. She cannot be distracted."

Krishani hung his head. He had a point. His mind wandered back to her words, but he was too afraid to tell Istar that the foe was interested in her. Instead, he chose to ask one of the other questions burning in his gut. "Who are the Flames?"

Istar appeared caught off guard. Krishani almost smirked at the small victory. "An ancient race. They are one of a kind."

Krishani grinned. *No wonder it was impossible to ignore her.* He waited for Istar to continue.

"That is all you need to know."

He wasn't satisfied. He licked his lips and moved away from the horse. "And what is a Ferryman?" He looked at Istar, who seemed to turn to stone he was so still. Krishani gulped. That was a bad question.

"Where did you hear of Ferrymen?" The words bounced around the walls of the stable though Istar's lips didn't move.

Krishani's eyes widened as chills snaked up his spine. "The nightmares."

"The insomnia …" Istar came back to life and looked down at the boy. "How long have you been having these dreams?"

"Since I watched the men leave."

"What men?"

"The ones who brought me to Orlondir." He thought that sounded right but his memory was fuzzy. He closed his eyes and tried to remember, but all he saw were men. They dropped him somewhere, and then he was in Orlondir with Istar.

Istar frowned, confused and alarmed all at once. "Adoron brought you to Orlondir on foot."

"Oh."

"What have these dreams entailed?"

"Death. The Ferryman said it wasn't my time yet. What does that mean?"

Istar grimaced. "It means you're a Ferryman."

Krishani stumbled away from the horse towards the service hall. He had hoped it wasn't true, but Istar's words confirmed it.

"I will return soon. Until then, I advise you to spend some time in the library." He snapped the reins hard and sped out of the stables towards Nandaro.

• • •

"Ahdunie!" Mallorn called from the cabin. Istar and his horse Paladin approached from beyond the creek. Paladin bent down and was already lapping up water before Istar slid off his back. He hopped across the creek and looked at The Kiirar, a grave expression on his face.

"Greetings Mallorn," he grumbled.

"You do not come with good news, do you?" Mallorn asked. He paced towards the barn, preparing to take a walk with his old friend, but Istar stayed firmly planted on the grass.

"Nay. I know what the trouble in the Avrigard quadrant is," Istar said. He watched Paladin drinking from the stream and Mallorn followed his gaze.

"And?"

"A Flame is dead."

"Nay!" Mallorn gasped. He paced back and forth in the grass, unsure how to react. "How did you find out?"

Istar raised his head to gaze out at the forests. "Worse news yet. Kaliel, my lady's apprentice, witnessed the death." Istar took a sharp breath and let it out slowly.

Mallorn's eyes widened. "She is a Flame!"

"Aye." Istar grimaced. He passed Mallorn and rounded the left side of the cabin. On the other side was a patch of evergreens growing in a cluster to the right. The creek extended towards a crease between the forests, on one side the evergreens, and on the other the maple, cedar and birch trees of Nandaro.

"So the Valtanyana have returned. Have you received any word from Tor?" Mallorn asked.

Istar followed his gaze, but shook his head. "Tor is too busy dealing with The Daed in Avrigard."

Mallorn nodded. The Daed were known opposers of High King Tor. They were quiet, but if they figured out how to break into Avrigost and awaken the Valtanyana, there was no telling how many factions of them would crawl out of their holes, willing to serve their former masters. It was dangerous to even think about it. One of the Valtanyana alone would be enough to raise concern. Mallorn hoped that the Daed hadn't awakened all eleven of them. What it had taken to silence them in the First Era was unheard of, and if they stole the Flames.... Mallorn shuddered. "What does the Gatekeeper have to say?"

"I haven't spoken with the Gatekeeper, not since she denied me the first time."

Mallorn paused for a moment and then understood him, bemused by his alarm. "You did not know of this. Avristar did not warn you about the Flame being here, did she?" He was relatively new to the ways of the ancient land. He knew, however, that if the Gatekeeper, the very voice of Avristar, kept the knowledge from Istar, then that knowledge must possess some ancient secret.

Istar looked out at the horizon, the sun beginning its descent. "Nay, that knowledge was kept from me, but that does not worry me as much as my own apprentice worries me."

Mallorn frowned. "You have much on your hands, Istar."

Istar blinked. They could have been brothers with their similar features. "Krishani is The Ferryman."

Mallorn staggered back towards the front of the cabin. He passed the front door and turned the corner. Tucked away on the narrow side of the hill was a set of doors that led into a deep cellar concealed by the mound.

"I haven't time for a history lesson, Mallorn," Istar called after him.

Mallorn disappeared. He knew he was being less than hospitable, but that didn't matter right now. Istar followed him down the stairs. Mallorn shuffled through some scrolls he kept in the cellar, along with the rest of his library, mostly things he had brought back with him from Talanisdir, his homeland in the Lands of Immortals. He didn't want to think about what it had become after the Valtanyana. Istar joined him and he looked up from the scrolls. "A Ferryman and a Flame in the same place at the same time? You do have a dilemma on your hands."

"Aye, so I fear. I'm in need of a tutor for the girl. I will deal with the boy myself." Istar pursed his lips and waited for him to find what he was looking for.

Mallorn understood. "So that is why you came."

"Aye, Atara can't handle her. She is convinced the Valtanyana will attack."

"And what does Atara have to say of this?"

"Atara has agreed to it."

Mallorn ignored him and began shuffling through the racks of scrolls until he finally pulled apart the one he wanted. He made a small gasp of excitement as he pushed the scroll into Istar's hands. "The Tavesin family."

"Aye," Istar said slowly as he opened the scroll. On it was nothing but the family crest. He pulled his eyebrows together in confusion. "Will you take the girl or not?"

Mallorn laughed. "You think here? With a hermit? Oh, I do not know if that is such a good idea. I am rather harsh, Istar."

"That is exactly why I came to you."

"Train a Flame…." He pondered a moment and turned back to the stacks of scrolls lost inside the cubby holes of an old wine rack. "I once met the Azurite Flame, nice fellow, very intelligent." He stroked his beard as he peered through the diamond-shaped shelves.

Istar tapped his foot impatiently, rolling up the crest of the Tavesin family. He set it down on the work table and crossed his arms.

Mallorn smiled. "I would be pleased to meet her. I will try to train her. No promises." He gave Istar a stern look.

Istar sighed and climbed out of the cellar. He walked across the grass while Mallorn followed him.

"What was that about the Tavesin family?" Istar asked.

"Krishani is not a Child of Avristar. From what I know, Ferrymen only existed in twelve families in all the lands. The Tavesin family resides on Terra, he must be their successor." He moved towards the front door of the cabin while Istar mumbled something and descended the hill towards the creek, where Paladin waited.

"I will bring her by Samhain!" Istar shouted.

Mallorn nodded. "Ahdunie!" He lifted his hand and waved as his friend mounted Paladin and trotted into the forest.

22-GOODBYE

aliel stared at the packed bag against the door and dropped her arms to her side. She hung her head and paced in circles around the small room she had occupied since she had come to Orlondir a summer and a half ago. The Samhain Festival had just ended, and it was beautiful. Luenelle and Pux hadn't come to visit her this time, but that didn't matter. She had spent most of her time tucked away in the cave under the falls, waiting for trespassers and attempting not to giggle too loud to scare them away. The waterfall wasn't a secret anymore to the kinfolk in Evennses, even the sisters in Araraema seemed to know about it.

She glanced in the mirror and touched the bags under her eyes. Her limbs were weak, her stomach barely full of food, and her heart heavy. Of everything she had been afraid of becoming, a Flame was something she never expected. And the thought of Lotesse and the shadowy figure made her shake. She tried to avoid dreaming. Not only had she seen Lotesse, but there was Tiki, and that was something she couldn't begin to comprehend.

Atara was so cryptic with her answers. The Flames were the jewels of the universe—what did that mean? She felt more like a girl, a girl in love that was awkward and clumsy. What was out there that threatened to take it all away? She pulled her arms around her torso as a thick, sickening feeling crept into her gut. She wanted the fear to subside, but with Shimma's words and the ordeal pressing against her, it was hard not to melt into the floor.

There was a soft knock and her eyes moved to the door. She wasn't expecting anyone until tomorrow morning when Istar was to take her to The Kiirar. She didn't even know where he lived, but it wasn't in Evennses. Why couldn't she go to Desaunius? Her childhood elder was versed in the language of herbs and remedies. Kaliel was obviously beyond the helpful scope of teas and tonics. Atara had taught her meditation and second sight, but she was nowhere near reaching her potential in any of her studies.

Another soft knock pulled her out of her stupor. She delicately moved to the door, wincing at the stiffness of her muscles. There was pensive breathing on the other side and her heart quickened. She hadn't left the room for days, but Krishani was faithful with his visits. She opened the door, his back to it, his face tilted to the roof.

"Krishani?" Kaliel whispered, keeping her voice low.

His eyes fell on her and his expression warmed. He pulled his hands out from behind his back and plopped a rock into her palm. He said nothing as she backed away from the door and he came into the room, shutting the door behind him.

"What's this?" she asked.

His eyes lit up. "I brought it from the cave."

"Oh," she breathed, turning over the plain gray rock in her hands. It was nothing special, but to her it meant memories, something sentimental. In her life she had acquired very little. The birthstone from Evenness was probably the most amazing thing she owned.

She glanced at the bags against the wall and tucked the stone into the hole at the top. There were also tinctures, herb sachets and the birthstone tucked into the bag, things that would make the time pass quickly.

"So I can keep you near me." She smiled as Krishani shuffled back and forth. She knew he was trying so hard to contain himself. Her room was one of those places the maidens checked often, and she hated that he had to behave himself.

"I don't agree with Istar," he began, his eyes scanning the floor.

She knew if he looked at her it would be too hard to resist. There was a bed, it was soft; she tried not to think about it. She grimaced. "I think I have to go." It wasn't only Istar's judgment; it was the death of Lotesse, and the revelation she was a Flame pressing against her temples.

Krishani's eyes met hers. "I can't bear to see you this way. I wish he would reconsider."

She crossed her arms and paced towards the edge of the bed. She sat and closed her eyes. Standing made her chest heavy. "And what about when it happens again?"

Krishani groaned. She wanted to ignore the possibility of the Valtanyana. There was nothing in the lands that would endeavor to take her away from him. Lotesse had to be an accident. He moved towards her, stopping a foot away, making heat race through her limbs. "I want to be there when it happens again."

She reached for him, sliding her hand into his. "Stop blaming yourself."

"I should have been here."

"You came."

"I was late, the damage was done."

"It would have happened regardless."

"Not if you had been at the waterfall with me."

Kaliel ripped her hand out of his and wrapped her arms around her shoulders. "And then a Flame would be dead, and I wouldn't know what I am, and I wouldn't know something is coming for me, or anything else for that matter."

Krishani closed his eyes. Clearly he didn't want to fight with her.

She didn't want to fight either. She was all too aware that the frequencies of his nightmares were increasing. He avoided them by being with her. She was afraid how bad they would become when she was in some unknown place far from him. She stood, wrapped her arms around him, knowing he feared for her. "Why is everything so difficult?"

He closed his eyes and ran his hands through her hair. "I wish you could stay." He kissed her hair and tightened his arms around her. "Promise me you'll be careful."

"I should be safe in Avristar. Atara told me there's nothing to be afraid of."

"Except for nightmares."

"Aye," she whispered, not wanting to admit the nightmares were as bad as the possibility of an attack.

Krishani pulled away and cupped her face in his hands. He stared deep into her green eyes, leaned forward and placed a chaste kiss on her lips.

"This and nothing else," he whispered as he released her and turned to the door.

"Wait."

He turned; his eyes full of sorrow.

"Will you stay?"

Krishani frowned. "Won't they check on you?"

She glanced at the trap door. "Can you be quick?"

He moved closer. "I can try."

She took his hand in hers, running her fingers along his palm. "I don't want to have more nightmares tonight."

Krishani dropped his head and moved towards her, almost like he was a dead weight. She hated seeing him like this, the pale flickers of candlelight washing over his sullen features, outlining the angle of his jaw and tapering off into shadows in the crook of his neck.

She didn't say anything as his hands circled her waist, gripping her ivory dress firmly and pushing her onto the bed. She had been with him long enough to know instinctively what he wanted and yet, this was different. This was her bedroom in the castle, not the cave behind the falls. Without the cover of the falls and the coarse grass poking into her back she felt comfortable and nervous.

Krishani stood over her thoughtfully and she raised her face to study his contemplating eyes, one blue and one green. It was like he wasn't sure what to do with her next. She gulped as she waited for him to do what he had done so many times before, arching her neck towards him, meaning to wrap herself around him, but he took a step away from the bed, his fingers still locked in hers.

She gave him a puzzled look and he shook his head. "You're sure they won't come back?" He stole a glance at the closed door.

Kaliel sighed, and looked at the trap door. It was no secret this would be their last night together for awhile, until she had her abilities under control, until they knew what was hunting her, until she could protect the Flames the way Lotesse had told her to. She bit her lip and Krishani reached up and brushed his thumb across her cheek.

"We could hide in the tower," she said, her eyes finding the string that dangled from the ceiling. Krishani lifted the corner of his lips and before she knew it she was on her feet and he was pulling down the creaky stairs. He let her go first and she brushed past him, climbing the capricious rungs to the dank wooden floor.

She stood and reached towards the curvature of the turret just above her head. There was the faint slit of a window in the rock, moonlight filtering through it, casting a rectangular shape on the floor. She almost moved to the other side of the tower when hands found her waist and fingers locked together and she felt weightless as Krishani pulled her against him. Her stomach was filled with throngs of butterflies as he dropped his lips to her elongated ear and instead of saying anything he moved further south to the baby soft skin below her jaw. She gulped and tried to hold back the urges racing through her, she wanted him, she always wanted him in a way that was irrational and irresponsible. She closed her eyes as he rocked back and forth like they were dancing. Her hands covered his as he dropped them lower, one hand trailing to the fabric against her thigh, the other hovering somewhere above her naval. She took a sharp breath and Krishani stiffened, his lips moving from her shoulder to her ear.

"Do you want me to stop?" he whispered and she felt faint as he pressed himself against her harder. She curled her fingers against his hand, the one on her thigh. She wanted to drink him in like he was the crystal clear waters of the lake and drown in him like she had forgotten what it was like to breathe. She didn't have to say anything as his hand flowed in sync with hers, hitching up the hem of her dress and pressing his warm skin against her bare thigh. He pressed his other hand to her stomach harder and she felt heat spread through her.

"Don't move," he whispered. His forehead rested against her shoulder, his breathing ragged as she guided his hand between her legs. He slipped a finger inside her and she moaned, ecstasy trilling through her. Even in the cave he hadn't ventured to touch her like that, but desperation to escape her nightmares and his came to a climax. She belonged to him, and wasn't afraid of the things he wanted to do her.

23-The Kiirar

A falcon cawed high above the spruce and redwoods that stretched across Nandaro. Kaliel glanced at the sky; she stood next to Paladin. In her peripheral, Istar took the bags off the horse drawn cart. She heaved a sigh and glanced around. There was a creek darting around The Kiirar's cabin, which was situated on a mound.

"Ahdunie!" The Kiirar called from somewhere. He spoke in the traditional Avristar tongue, though that word—"Ahdunie"—was from an ancient dialect.

Kaliel peered past the horse towards the voice, the lorekeeper approaching from the barn. He wore a long gray robe, and sported shoulder-length grayish white hair. He had blue eyes. She was nervous; he looked strong and wise. More than anything, she was embarrassed she had to be there in the first place. She was old enough to control her abilities; being sent to the Kiirar was like hearing Desaunius's shameful tone telling her she didn't retain what she was taught. She turned to Istar.

"Greetings." Istar waved as Mallorn crossed the creek.

"You must be Kaliel."

"Aye," Istar said. He shot her a stern look, but she was more interested in the mud.

"I am Mallorn," the Kiirar tried. He extended his hand to her, but she kept her eyes downcast in the mud, twisting her toe into it. He pulled his hand back and rubbed it on his robes.

Kaliel thought being taught combat skills was useless; she would fall apart in a strong wind, let alone in battle. Mallorn glared at her, sizing her up, and she saw in his eyes he wasn't planning on wasting his time. He started back up the mound to the cabin.

Kaliel glanced at Istar's hard stare. "Please," she began; her voice cracking. She had no idea how to address such an ancient being. Desaunius forgave all her misgivings because she was only a child, but seventeen summers had passed and she would have to show her respect to Mallorn. She hoped her abilities would stop hurting soon and the enemies would be stopped so she could go home. Istar headed back to the cart.

"I need your help," she called after Mallorn. He didn't turn back.

"I hope you are prepared to work," Mallorn called as he entered the cabin.

Kaliel felt her stomach drop. She looked to Istar for comfort, but his expression was hard to read. He hadn't spoken much on the way there. She felt like a burden to him, and she couldn't shake the feeling there was something he wanted to tell her about Krishani.

"Right then. You'll be fine. Mallorn will help." He sounded awkward as he mounted the horse, shook his head and turned towards Orlondir.

"Farewell," she said though he probably couldn't hear her. She turned to the cabin, Mallorn stood in the doorway.

"Three moons, child, we cannot waste time." There was an edge to his words and she wondered why since she clearly wasn't tearing him away from prior engagements. His hand rested on the doorjamb until she crossed the creek. He dropped his arm and entered the cabin. "You can begin by bathing the horses," Mallorn said.

"Pardon me?" Kaliel asked, they had servants for that in Orlondir.

"I keep the horses for this part of Nandaro. They belong to my neighbors. Your first lesson is to bathe them."

She gulped. She supposed that since he was all alone, he had no one to help him. She stifled a sigh and headed out to the barn.

• • •

Hours later, she was soaking wet and her limbs were sore. She dragged the stool and bucket of water over to the last horse and briefly glanced at the name-plate. It read *Umber*, a name she could appreciate. This horse was unlike the others, grayish white with speckles across the tops of his hind legs. She stepped into the stall and put the stool down in the hay. His tail swished, but he was otherwise concerned with the mulch at his feet. The others had been something of the same, well-tamed and calm. She grabbed the small bucket and poured water over his back. Atara never had her do anything like this in Orlondir; it was always Krishani getting the laborious tasks. She watched water trickle down his backside and hopped off the stool. She'd been taking trips to and from the creek all afternoon.

When she came back, Umber was staring at her with one black eye and she jumped. The bucket swayed in her hands and water lapped up on her knees. She grumbled and stalked towards the stool, trying to ignore the prying eyes of the horse. Merfolk and trees were easy to talk to; she never thought about their voices. Horses and small animals were different. All afternoon none of them said anything to her. It made the idea of Nandaro and Mallorn dreary. She wanted to go back to Orlondir and huddle in her room in the Elmare Castle, wait for Krishani to find her and take off to the waterfall.

She pushed the bucked over Umber's mane and glanced at his eye, then scanned the hay , remembering the ordeal with Lotesse. There were more Flames out there; whoever was coming for them would never find Kaliel. Avristar was a stronghold, she was sure of it. Still, she wondered why Mallorn would have her bathe horses if he was trying to help her with her kinship as a Flame.

"Mallorn is a good master. You shouldn't be so hard on him."

Kaliel's heart thumped hard and wild at the melodic hum of the voice in her ears. She wobbled on the stool and fought for balance. Arms flailed, the bucket went flying and she landed in the hay on her back. Umber loomed over her, hooves padding the hay, stepping away from her to give her some room. She rubbed her temples and looked into his eye.

"So you *do* talk," she said.

"Why are you mad at Mallorn?"

She hadn't even realized how angry she was, but she recalled all the grumbling and sloppiness. She sat and pushed her back into the stall. "I'm not mad at him."

"Then why are you mad?"

She gritted her teeth. She wanted to be angry with Atara and Istar for sending her away from Orlondir. More Atara than Istar though, because the woman acted like she wasn't her problem now she knew she was a Flame. It seemed like her old mentor wiped her hands clean of her. Even Desaunius hadn't done that. She visited faithfully every Fire Festival and was always overflowing with wisdom. It was so disheartening to know the greatest elder on Avristar had given little thought to her during her hour of greatest need. She tried to piece together words to explain it to the horse, but nothing seemed to make sense. Her hands twisted in her lap and she pulled her lips into a frown.

"I don't think you would understand," she said.

Umber didn't say anything.

She pushed herself up and grabbed the bucket and crossed the sandy ground to the creek. She bent, scooping up another bucket of water. She tried to go back to barn, but when she turned around her head swelled with vertigo. She closed her eyes and saw brief flashes of light. Wisps of crimson red and rosy pink Flames clouded her mind. She knelt on the grass and let the nausea subside. It was like fire ripping through her insides. She let out short breaths trying to steady herself and pushed the images away.

Moments later she coughed and opened her eyes. She entered the barn, but the atrocious smell of manure hit her senses and she reeled back. Stifling her disgust, she made it to Umber's stall, and slopped more water on his back.

"That took a long time," he said.

She closed her eyes and the flashes of red and pink danced before her. She sucked in a sharp breath and watched as the water dripped onto the hay. "I'm here because something bad happened."

Umber didn't say anything, but she kept her gaze fixed on his black eye until he looked away. She sighed. So that was how it would be. She grabbed the stool by one of its three legs and stashed it in the cabinet near the barn's doors. She'd talk to Mallorn about the horse; maybe he could explain it to her. As she pushed the barn doors shut she came to a halt. Focus training. She laughed and let her hands fall off the doors. Mallorn was more like Istar than she thought.

She dragged herself up the hill and around to the front of the cabin. She smelled honeysuckle as she passed by the kitchen window and closed her eyes for a moment to take in the scent. She paused at the front door, unsure if she should knock, and when she was about to raise her hand the door swung open. Mallorn was smiling and holding a pot in his hand. Dinner was ready.

• • •

"Come, we must take a walk," Mallorn said after dinner.

Kaliel cringed. "Can't I rest before our second lesson?"

He laughed as he crossed the living room to the foyer. "Always train when you are at your worst." He winked at her, grabbed his staff and ducked out of the cabin.

She scrunched up her nose and followed him outside. He was already past the barn, zigzagging through trees, creating a path of his own. She stumbled down the hill and narrowly crossed the creek, her toe splashing in the water as her hands found the ground. She scrambled up and brushed off her dress, then tried to straighten out her hair. Where was he going? The rays of sunlight were dimming and they wouldn't be able to return before nightfall. She half-wanted to know where he expected her to sleep.

She reached the trees and ran her hand along one of them, feeling a shiver run up her spine. They were all alive out there, just like the ones in Evennses, only their trunks weren't yards wide and they weren't all red cedars. Some of them had nettles, and some had broad leaves with whitish-colored bark.

She spotted Mallorn and rushed to meet him. There were no roots scattered across the ground and she laughed as she almost tripped over her own foot. *Typical,* she thought as she mused at her clumsiness.

"You're slow," Mallorn said. He stopped in his tracks, having found a cluster of trees that grew in a circle. It was a small grouping, the clearing large enough for them to stand opposite one another. She entered the circle and stared at him. His features were hidden by the shadows growing around them.

"Isn't it late?" she asked. Nighttime was her time, the best time she found to speak with the trees.

"I do not sleep much." Mallorn glanced at the sky, as the last of the sun's light drifted over the horizon. He smelled the air then took his staff and slammed it against one of the trees, creating a wild cracking sound that echoed across the clearing.

Kaliel jumped and her stomach dove into her chest. "Ouch!" She gaped at him, bewildered. The tree he hit whined in pain. Why would he hit a tree?

"Our first mental lesson. You will—" He stopped short.

"That hurt the tree," Kaliel mumbled as she ran her hands along her dress.

He frowned. "You can hear the trees?"

She raised an eyebrow. "Atara didn't tell you?"

Mallorn stuck his staff into the ground and put his hand on his brow. "To be honest," he began as he twisted his hand around his staff, "nay."

She slightly smiled to herself, knowing if they hadn't told him all her secrets, she could probably keep some of them to herself. She closed her eyes and pushed her palm into the tree nearest to her. There were no magic words spoken to emit the words from the tree; she simply opened her heart and felt its words flowing through her.

"Beautiful night, Little Flame," the tree said.

Mallorn stared at it and her in wonder. "Only the Great Oak ..."

Kaliel shrugged. "They have spoken to me since I was born." She spread her fingers out on the bark and shared more of her energy, feeling it flow into the earth. She opened her eyes and smiled as a small, violet flower bloomed at the tree's base. It was too dark for Mallorn to witness it, so she bent down and plucked it from the ground. She held it out to him, twirling it between her fingers.

"And these grow whenever I speak to them. Perhaps you know why?"

Mallorn was nothing like Desaunius or Atara, who cowered or ignored her peculiarity. She learned from Pux early on that anything that made the Elders question themselves should be kept secret—but Mallorn wasn't an Elder, not technically. He was a Kiirar, a lorekeeper.

Mallorn stumbled back against the tree behind him. He stared at the petals of the violet flower as she spun it around between her fingers. His mouth dropped open. "I suppose you have already surpassed this lesson."

"Aye." Kaliel glanced at the dark green grass at her feet.

"Will you show me again?" he asked cautiously. He cleared his throat, attempting to seem regal.

Kaliel wondered why, but she felt relaxed enough around him and sensed he wasn't tainted like the others, worried about what her purpose might be. Her intuition told her he only wanted to help. She nodded and closed her eyes, pressing her hand firmly into the bark. She let her energy flow into it as her thoughts drifted back to Krishani. She wanted to show Krishani the flowers before the dream about Lotesse, before everything had to change again. She tried not to let her sadness mix with her contentment as the flower sprouted from the ground. When she opened her eyes she was caught off guard. Around the tree was a dotted line of violet flowers creating a half-moon.

Mallorn gawked at them as she stepped back. She was never boisterous about her gifts; they mostly frightened or shocked those who knew anything about her. He crouched by the tree and ran his fingers along the petals. "Brilliant." He stood and walked towards the cabin.

Kaliel knew she had surprised him. She trailed along after him, her thoughts a muddle of worry and excitement.

"Aye, our lesson is over," he said as they wended their way through the trees.

• • •

Kaliel's heart ached as she settled into the sheets and gazed at the small window of the bedroom. It was considerably smaller than both the rooms she had occupied in the past, barely big enough to fit a bed. While there was an end table with three drawers in it, there were no dressers for her to put away her clothes. She stashed her bags in the corner, hoping that not putting her things away meant she would be able to return to Krishani sooner.

She took a shaky breath and let it out. It wasn't only Krishani that she missed; it was everything hitting her hard, all the sudden changes in her life she had endured over the years. The fact she couldn't control the dreams, the fear of the unknown enemies, the way everyone looked at her—it was no secret Atara was afraid of her. Every lesson they shared together emitted some awkward emotional response from the elder and she fought hard not to confront her about it. Atara was clear she could guide, not give answers.

Kaliel sighed and rolled over onto her side, pulling her knees to her chest. Part of her envied Pux, he wasn't regarded with half as much scrutiny. She thought back to the days in Evennses when they spent hours running and laughing in the forests, when she escaped at night to swim with the merfolk. Those days were so far away. She wanted to turn back time. She wanted to be able to sit with Desaunius in her little cabin and talk about the Lands of Men. She squeezed her eyes shut as memories of the catacombs came back to her. She used to revel in the endless wonders of the Lands of Men, unsure of when she would be called to service. Instead, she trembled with fear at the words that she would never forget: *He comes for us.*

She tried to distract herself with images of the waterfall. She imagined Krishani's gaze on her and the warm feelings that invoked. She pictured his fingers trailing down her back, his lips nipping at her collar bone, her cheeks, and pointy ears. She felt the warmth of him surround her, the elation in her heart—then an ache in her chest intensified as reality set in. Three moons felt like forever. She hugged the blanket to her chest and closed her eyes.

• • •

The corridor was modern, with thick, elaborately-embroidered rugs, covering the floor. Wainscoting plated the bottom half of the walls, the top covered in creamy wallpaper dotted with dark red flowers and green leaves. On the walls, candles flickered inside glass bulbs, casting an eerie glow on the mahogany doorframes.

Kaliel stood at one end of the corridor, watching as tall, shadowy shapes billowed across the floor, smoke rising from the tips of their heavy black boots, the clank of metal sounding as they steadily swept across the carpets. They banged loudly on doors, opening each one in succession, peering in, then moving to the next. They were getting closer and closer to her, but she couldn't move, helplessly staring at their faceless hoods. She thought she had heard of their kind before— Daed, though she had never encountered any before.

A door swung open to her right and another shadowy figure emerged, a girl with long black hair and a silky pink dress stretched across his arms. Her glass-like face lolled to the side, and Kaliel noticed her rose-colored eyes. They looked pleading and hopeless. She stared at them, unable to remove her gaze, waiting for the faint sound of the girl's voice in the back of her mind, but it never came.

Instead, there was another bang on one of the doors, a flash and sizzle of fire, followed by alarmed screams and deep laughter. One of the shadowy figures removed their hood to reveal shoulder-length black hair and tattoos scattered across his face. The ink seemed to crawl along his skin like a series of snakes. He punched the doorframe, his fist moving like lightning towards something inside the room. He pulled back and there was a girl, identical to the other, same glass-like face, but crimson hair and bright, piercing red eyes. Her arms curled around the doorframe, pulling away. She was clad in a black and red gown, a black corset pulled across her torso. Her eyes shimmered like fire, but she remained still, sword tip poised at her gut. Her eyes were on the other sister and she went to cry out, but the hand that gripped her throat squeezed harder. Kaliel noticed metal scales covering the shadowy figure's fingers, skin and bone still visible around the elaborate armor. Quickly, they pulled the girl out into the hallway. She kicked and screamed, but they silenced her and her body went limp. The other shadowy figure followed them, carrying the other girl, his face a mask of darkness. Kaliel watched until they disappeared. The candles went out, covering her in smoke.

She didn't wake up as the dream faded away, however, she felt her eyes open, the scene around her completely changed.

Krishani's eyes were different; one shone gold, the other a rich brown. She traced the patterns in the irises, noting their intricate architecture. There was something about him she recognized, but all she could concentrate on were those eyes. A gold band wrapped around his forehead, a headdress attached to it, golden snakes hanging off it. It resembled a chandelier, aside from its obvious use as a crown. He had olive skin and a narrow nose. His mouth was drawn up in a bright smile and his warm hand was on her shoulder. Something begged her to look at the sun, but her eyes were locked to his. Nausea kicked in and her heart raced.

Something is wrong! she thought.

Kaliel tried to move, but his grip and his focus on her sharpened. His eyes pleaded with her, imploring her not to look up. She closed

201

her eyes; there was no way she could let it go. She felt the chalice in the other hand. She had drawn this scene over and over in her journal. She fought to lift her head to look at the sky.

"We have fulfilled our purpose." His voice was even and calm. She feared that he caused the reasons for her distress.

"What purpose?" she asked.

"The war is over," he said.

Why would that scare her? She fought to gain control of her emotions, but her knees buckled and heat rose up around her feet. It burned, sending pain shooting into her torso. She cried out and tried to pry her eyes open.

"Relax, my love. It will be over soon," he said.

"Krishani?"

"Nay, they call me the Ferryman."

"What?"

She tried to fight, but the fire was intense. It wrapped around her body, threatening to crush her insides with its intense heat. There was something else though, a barrier between herself and the heat, a shield. She felt the violet aura surrounding her. It spiked off the edges of her body in its own wisps of flames, protecting her from the final axe of destruction.

"And you are the Flame." There was no compassion in his voice.

The flames engulfed her face in their fury and she forced herself to look up. Smoke covered the sky. Flame-laced pieces of molten rock rained down on them. She gasped and tried to fight it, but with his hand on her shoulder, and his eyes on her, they seemed lost in their own world. She looked at him, his body engulfed in flames, only his mismatched eyes staring into hers through the waves of heat. "It's over." His smile faded as fire licked away his flesh.

"Kaliel!" A new voice. "Kaliel!"

Her eyes opened. She was drenched in sweat, her body trembling uncontrollably.

"What did you see?" Mallorn demanded.

She put a hand to her head, trying to shake away the stinging images. Her mouth moved, trying to form words, but her tongue was dry and her throat was scratchy. She longed for water—the *waters*. She needed to go to the lake. She pushed the covers aside, refusing to explain what she saw, anything to keep him from knowing her dark secrets.

202

"I can't stay here," she said as her feet found the floor.

Mallorn had his hand on her arm, but she wrenched it away and ran out of the cabin into the night. The moon waxed, half full. She took a deep breath and tasted the air. The pulsating waves of the waters lapped against the shore in the distance. She darted to the east, following the thin path leading through the scattered forests towards the lake. On her left were patches of evergreen trees and on the right the familiar young red cedars and birch trees. The ground below her moved from grass to mud, but thankfully it was dry. She traipsed along the land, desperate to get to the lake. It had been so long since her last visit.

She forced the images of the dream into the crevasses of her mind, refusing to listen to anything that could cause her pain. The Flame inside battered around like a banshee trying to overtake her. She fought to keep it suppressed. Her lungs burned as she ran; her mouth parched and sticky. There were no roots in her way, but she skipped along the ground as though they were there, an ingrained old habit.

The moist, fresh scent of water wafted through the air as she neared the shallow cliff. Her toes curled over the edge as she frantically searched for another way to the water. Stars swept across the sky, the half-moon brighter out in the open. She stumbled down the hill on the right as it sloped towards the lake. It curved around the cave and the sand, concealing the beach from the forest. Finally, she heard waves gently lapping against the oars of a boat.

She tumbled on the grass and glanced at the boat. It resembled a canoe, except the stern had a wooden figurine of a woman carved into it. The woman had pearls for eyes. She thought the woman was staring at her.

Ignoring it, she desperately shed her nightgown and moved to the ledge. There were moss and weeds along the edge of the island. She sighed and closed her eyes; the Flame encasing her in her dream wouldn't leave her mind. Without another thought, she took a few steps and plunged off the grassy ledge, straight into the deep water.

She pulled herself down, not bothering to call to the merfolk. They were never going to return. She kept her eyes closed as she felt the cool waters rush around her body, erasing any memories of fire, Flames, Ferrymen, the Great Oak, the foe. She held her breath as she traveled deeper and deeper. Her arms brushed along the prickly weeds floating through the waters. They scratched at her skin as she fought to free herself.

She sank deeper.

Pressure built as she turned and turned in the waters, trying to escape the weeds. She let out a few bubbles of air. She didn't have much time before all of it was gone. Her eyes opened as she tried to find her way to the surface. It was so dark she could barely tell which way to go until her body tumbled around and she caught sight of a glimmering light. She lay limp between the weeds, allowing them to float away from her, desperate to get to the surface. When they cleared, she kicked and pulled upwards.

Her head breeched the water and her eyes beheld the horizon in the distance. If she hadn't been so tired she would have paddled towards it. She thought of the boat, but remembered the foe. She turned to the shore.

Mallorn stood there with an exhausted look on his face. "Please, child, give me the chance to help," he said as he held her nightgown out to her.

Kaliel swam to the shore and nodded. He really wasn't like the others. She felt his compassion for her as she pulled herself out of the water. Mallorn turned as she grabbed the nightgown and slid it over her head.

• • •

Kaliel nestled into the big wooden chair in the living room of the Kiirar's cabin. Her body barely filled the chair, but she was content to feel drowned in it. She stared ahead at the cup in front of her, full of chamomile tea. Mallorn sat across the way, eyeing her carefully. He took a sip of tea and leaned forward, placing the cup on the stump between them.

"You know there are merfolk off the shores of Avristar," Mallorn began.

Kaliel glanced at him, her chest tightening. "Not anymore," she said softly as she turned her attention to the fireplace. She closed her eyes and tried to put the idea of fire out of her mind. The merfolk in Evennses were something she never talked about anymore. The last time she tried to go to the lake was the first time she bloomed the weed.

Mallorn frowned, seeming not to understand what she meant. "They came centuries ago, when Avristar was rebuilding. They are the protectors of the Avristar Stones that grow at the bottom of the lake."

Kaliel groaned. "Those stones belong to the merfolk." She thought about the nights she swam with them. That was long before the Great Oak sent her to Orlondir, long before she had been with Krishani.

"Istar has an agreement with them. They give us one stone for every kinfolk."

She grabbed her tea, took a long sip and fell back into the chair, staring into the fire again. This conversation was much more unnerving to her than he could imagine. "The merfolk are dangerous." Those were the same words of her elder Desaunius.

Mallorn sighed and put his tea on the stump. "That they are, which begs the question of why you would go diving into the lake at such a late hour?" He shot her a stern glance, his eyebrows pulled together in disappointment.

Kaliel sighed. "Old habit, I suppose. The water calms me."

"You've been in the lake before?"

She kept her gaze on the flames devouring the log and stifled a sigh. Her heart clenched from the images in her dream. She tried to push them away, but watching the fire made her think of Krishani covered in flames. "Aye, many times when I lived in Evennses."

"Did no one mention the lake is forbidden?"

"I've heard that." She glanced at him. He sat back in his chair and followed her gaze to the fire.

"Why did the dream make you go there tonight?"

Kaliel looked at the tea cups, closing her eyes she tried to imagine the forests, the merfolk that went away, and the stone she almost stole from them. "I was burning." She licked her lips, trying to moisten her mouth, but it was no use, it remained dry and scratchy.

"You are a Flame, flames burn."

The dream frightened her, but what Mallorn said was amusing at the very least. She glanced up to see him smiling and turned her attention to the stump between them. "Bloom the weed of temptation and expire the great garden of life."

"A parable? From the Great Oak?" he assumed.

Kaliel could almost hear what he wasn't saying. She was troubled and he wanted to help. He was also afraid he wouldn't be able to do it in the time allotted. Besides, in the end, all this came down to was more time away from Krishani. She didn't know if she could stand that.

"What does it have to do with the dream?" he asked.

"I don't know." *Krishani was burning,* she thought. If Istar hadn't told Mallorn about Krishani, she wasn't about to either. She wanted to pull away from The Kiirar's gaze. Something about him said he was trying to understand, that he wouldn't be as harsh as the other elders, but she was afraid of how he would react if he knew the entirety of the truth about her.

"Something makes you very different, Kaliel."

She scooted forward on the chair and took hold of her tea. She took another long sip, finishing it. She set it down and yawned, arms stretching above her head. "I think I should try to rest."

Mallorn shot her a stern glare. "Aye. We will continue this conversation later."

24-YOUR TIME NOW

The flame flickered and the man gripped the cot below him even tighter. The Ferryman Krishani followed in his dreams glanced at the flame, then back at the man on the cot. He was covered in blood, breathing in spurts, seizing from the pain.

The Ferryman bent his head as the candle flickered again, almost snuffing out. He heaved a sigh and took the man's hand. He gripped it and waited. Another tremor shot through the man's body. The Ferryman gripped tighter, the flame flickered again, and the man on the cot screamed.

Krishani floated by the man's feet. He watched the scene for too long, waiting for the man on the cot to die. It took forever. Krishani cringed as the man kicked and let out another agonizing roar. The Ferryman tried to sooth him using a language Krishani didn't know. He repeated the words over and over until the man went limp, wispy smoke rising from his body. Krishani watched it with wonder, and turned towards the Ferryman.

"And so you visit me again, young one," the Ferryman said. He grabbed a rag from the bottom of the cot and exited the tent into the wastelands outside, the ground wet and mucky. It was windy, shouts hitting the air from every direction. The Ferryman's boots squished with every step as he went to the next tent to find the next fatally-wounded warrior. Krishani floated along the ground, following the Ferryman.

"I don't know why I'm here," Krishani said. He would rather leave the man alone than watch him tend to the dead. The Ferryman stopped in the middle of the mucky field, and looked at him. It was nightfall; behind him a fire burned brightly in the distance, a village. He turned his thoughts to the smell of smoke and gazed towards the blaze far away.

"Oh, that. There's a war in these parts. You like death?" the Ferryman said. He looked at the ground and continued towards another tent.

Krishani knew the smoke wasn't caused by the fire alone. He smelled souls rising into the air, seeking to escape the mortal plane. He shuddered and continued to drift behind the Ferryman.

"Ignore those sounds. They'll corrupt your heart." The Ferryman ducked inside. A woman in armor lay on a cot, blood leaking out beneath her and onto the floor. Her blue eyes trembled, but her body lay still. Her hands piled on her stomach as if she were already at her funeral. The Ferryman gazed into her eyes and she relaxed. He whispered something to her in her native tongue and she grimaced, nodded. The Ferryman began muttering an incantation under his breath.

Krishani watched from the doorway and felt sick as the woman's body began to convulse. Despite trying to look away, he couldn't. He *had* to see what was happening.

The Ferryman's words spilled out of his mouth quicker, his voice louder. Krishani wanted to close his eyes, but they were glued open by the intensity of the vexatious energy around them. The woman was quiet, even though her body violently seized.

The Ferryman continued, and Krishani heard voices outside the tent. They were coming closer. He didn't need to look at them to know they were enemies coming to finish off the job. He knew from their cries they wanted to savor every last bit of bloodshed. He stiffened as the Ferryman raised his voice, almost screaming the words. And then the woman's hand dropped. Her body went limp and it smoked like all the others, thin wispy white smoke rising towards the roof. The Ferryman bent his head and recited what sounded like a blessing.

When he stood, he grimaced. "Don't let the work get to you. Marry the land, take the journey. You'll find similar sorry sites, I'm sure. You have to surrender everything you are for this work. But don't worry, you were born for it." He turned towards the back of the tent and lifted the side flap to escape the enemies on the opposite side. Krishani followed and trekked across the battlefield towards a lone tree in the distance.

"What is this work?" Krishani asked. His heart dropped at the word 'surrender.' All his life he had been told the same thing. Now the Ferryman said it, too. He listened to the commotion around, his heart thrumming. There was another person near death by the tree. He felt them squirming in agony, about to die.

The Ferryman laughed while Krishani looked at the muck on his feet. "The work of a Ferryman, the lands need them at all times. I thought I would always be one, except you've been following me, which means I'm probably going to die soon." He talked about death like it was a righteous part of living, like he wasn't afraid of it in the least. He walked towards a patch of trees on the field. The men who caused the bloodshed were close by.

"What do you mean I was born for it?" Krishani choked as he tried to ward off the sickness he felt.

The Ferryman continued without an answer. He reached a grassier patch of land, the mud from his boots smearing onto the emerald blades. A warrior was within the trees, spread on the ground, an arrow sticking out of his chest. He quickened his pace, knelt at the man's side, and whispered a few words in his ear. The warrior clasped his hands around the arrow protruding from his body. The Ferryman gently moved his hands away, replacing them with his own. He closed his eyes and pulled, blood gushing out of the wound.

Krishani staggered back, dizzy. He watched the wispy smoke curl around the branches. No matter how many times he saw death, it still left him shocked and frightened. He looked at the Ferryman, who recited a similar incantation as the one in the tent. When he was finished, he pulled the man's eyelids closed and looked at Krishani.

"You're a Ferryman." His tone was blunt, unwavering.

Krishani felt like he had been stabbed in the chest. "I'm a Child of Avristar."

The Ferryman ignored him, pulling a pocket knife from his breeches. He turned to the enemies. The Ferryman pierced one of them in the gut as the others continued running across the field. The man fell and then scrambled to his feet to flee. Krishani turned to see the Ferryman stagger and fall backwards. Blood poured from a wound on his side. Krishani drifted to him. Feeling a mix of confusion and anxiety, he dropped to his knees. His eyes surveyed the wound and the blood, the soul inside restless to escape the body. He trembled as he took the Ferryman's hand in his own and stared into his eyes.

"It's your time now," Krishani said.

"It's your time now," the Ferryman repeated. His head slumped into the grass, his eyes frozen. Krishani let out a sob as the wispy smoke began rising out of the Ferryman. He hung his head and recited a blessing from his childhood. Everything happened too fast; he was unprepared. Shaken with grief, he wanted to return home, stay on Avristar, but he knew the chances were slim.

He opened his eyes and saw sheets below him. He sat and glanced around the room, making sure none of the enemies had followed him. There was nothing but silence, no wispy smoke, no battle cries. He exhaled and tossed the blanket aside and buried his head in his hands.

The Ferryman is dead ... and I'm the next.

His body ached as he stood and paced the room. He felt flush with fear, resentment, and anger for the carelessness of the Ferryman. He put his hands behind his head and squeezed his eyes shut. This couldn't be happening. First Kaliel and now him? His life was unraveling before he had a chance to live it. He let out a long exhale and looked at the bed. He could try to rest and pretend it didn't happen, but he was afraid he would be brought back to the same place. He shook his head and fled into the corridors, moving quickly towards the orchards.

The moon hung above the trees, showering the apples in silvery moonlight. His heart thumped as fast as a rabbit as the depth of the dream hit him. He walked through the rows and rows of apple trees, stretching his fingers out to brush the leaves as he passed. He paused beside one of the trees and reached down to pick up an apple. He couldn't organize his thoughts enough to speak, so he stood there with the jumbled mess of words in his head. He glanced at the moon.

"It was only a dream." He tried to convince himself, but he knew it wasn't true. There had been so many of these dreams, each one following the same Ferryman, the same work. He barely understood the reason he was chosen, but he knew what the work entailed. He shuddered at the thought of it.

He hung his head and looked at the grassy path at his feet. An overwhelming feeling of helplessness washed over him as he reluctantly turned back to the castle. He looked at the widened path between the trees and saw a figure standing on the main road. She was a silhouette under the night sky, but Krishani knew who it was. He begrudgingly dragged himself towards her as she crossed her arms and waited.

• • •

"It's too late to be out, Lady," Krishani said.

Atara sighed. She had sensed his grief from her quarters and came to find out what the matter was. There had been plenty of other nights like this one since Kaliel had gone to Nandaro, but this was the first time she planned on confronting Krishani about it. Their relationship was something she didn't want to prevent. It was so easy to watch the feorns fall in love, easy to watch the fae play their games, but the elvens with their stoic attitude and attention to detail and duty? It wasn't forbidden as much as it was unheard of. She might have been arranged to marry Istar because of their sovereignty to the land, but the heart was complex. Krishani's connection to Kaliel went further than his physical form—she was in his soul. "Aye, too late," she said. "Why are you here?"

"Only a nightmare. I'm sorry to disturb you," he said.

Atara took a deep breath. "Istar says you have many of those. Tell me, what are they about?" She eyed the boy and felt guilty for sending Kaliel away. In the weeks the girl had been gone, Krishani had grown melancholy. She worried about him and the overwhelming grief leaking off his aura in bright flares.

Krishani shook his head and tried to step around her. "I watched someone die."

Atara shivered, partially from the cool air, and partially from the words of her partner's apprentice. She turned and watched him quicken his pace. "Stop," she called after him. There was something behind his eyes; a different sort of sorrow he had been struck with, like an arrow to his heart.

Krishani paused and clenched his fist. He turned around. "What will you have me say?"

"A dream is not always dream. Tell me what happened." She clasped her hands together and held them in front of her. She wanted to believe the corruption in the Lands of Men would come to an end, that the Valtanyana would be silenced before they could gain enough power to destroy entire realms. She wanted to believe in peace and she wanted to live in her dreamy fairytale life, a life that stretched centuries behind her, a life that hadn't seen war since the First Era.

Krishani looked at the moat and then back at the elder like he was contemplating his words. "I watched the Ferryman die."

Every part of him broke as he admitted it. He turned back to the moat. She froze. Another death. What Istar said was true—the Valtanyana were out there. She recalled her last conversation with Istar—the boy was a Ferryman. The dream was his calling. Compassion flooded her heart. "Oh child, I'm so sorry."

"I know," he whispered.

She knew what he wanted her to tell him—the same thing she had longed to tell Kaliel about Lotesse— tell them it was all a dream. There was nothing to worry about in the Lands of Men, nothing to be afraid of. But none of that was true. For now, Avristar was in peace, but for how much longer, she didn't know.

"You know what this will mean," she said. She thought back to Krishani's childhood and the rumors of his greatness. He was one of the chosen ones from the beginning. He had a purpose to fulfill.

"Kaliel …" Krishani took a step towards the moat, paused and met Atara's eyes. "Do you think there's a chance?" There was a weak sense of hope in his voice.

Atara sighed. "Nay, your destiny is greater than your love." She said the words because they were the truth, but the way he looked at her like it was poison washing over him made her wish she hadn't said it at all. He turned towards the castle and walked in silence.

25-HEED THE CALL

I could brew you a potion for your insomnia," Kuruny said. She leaned against the railing of the balcony opposite the corridor to Krishani's room.

Krishani glanced at her smug face and narrowed his eyes at her. "Leave me alone, Kuruny," he spat. He turned to the hall as she let out a short laugh.

"Is it your precious Kaliel? I could make you forget all about her."

Krishani clenched his fist and then released it. There was no point in bothering Kuruny with the details of his dream; she was always lurking in the castle, always looking for her moment. "You know nothing about love." His emotions battered around inside him, pain etching into his heart as he tried to stave off his grief.

Kuruny let out a snort. "Love isn't real." She pushed off the balcony and sauntered towards him. She looked like she wanted to reach out and touch him, make him bend to her will, but he hunched up, trying to shield himself from her. He said nothing, and she continued. "If love were real, my potions wouldn't make men forget their pain."

"I don't want to forget my pain." He moved down the corridor, tightening his fists and closed his eyes. Pain lit up every nerve in his body with sharp stings that turned to numbness. All he really wanted to do was escape to Nandaro, but it was so big and there was no guarantee he would find Kaliel before Istar found him. No chance he wouldn't be carted off to the Lands of Men before seeing her one last time. The sickness he felt at having to leave her made him want to rip himself in half.

Kuruny turned her nose up in apparent disgust. "You're so petulant. I offer my help, no strings attached, and you would rather stink up the castle with your grief." She crossed her arms and willed him to look back at her.

Krishani kept his eyes to the ground. There was darkness lurking inside him that threatened to lash out and attack her. He took a deep breath and tried to calm the beast within. "Your potions come with consequences."

"They didn't mind the consequences in the Lands of Men." She sounded like she would've liked to have stayed in the Lands of Men had they not cursed her for trying to help them.

Krishani perked up at the mention of the Lands of Men. His expression softened and he dared a glance at her. "What are they like?"

She laughed. "Some make you sleep, some make you happy, and some make you imagine things that aren't real."

He frowned. "Not the potions, the Lands of Men. What are they like?"

She grimaced, a twisted smile forming on her face. She let out a nervous laugh. "Why would it matter? Nobody is going there for a long time."

Krishani sighed. "That's no longer true." He looked at the cream carpet under his feet. It was awkward he was sharing anything with Kuruny.

She frowned. "It's corrupted with war and chaos. Not even I want to be there right now." He knew she left out the fact she didn't want to be on Avristar either. "Something very bad has happened to you," she said.

Krishani nodded, cautious. "I can't talk about it."

"The Lands of Men are full of betrayers and liars and scum of the land. Men who would rather kill you than help you. You're either on one side of the battle or on the other. Many of us barely escaped with our lives. It's self-destruction if you go."

Fear hit him as he processed her words. "I can't change that, I've been called." The words tore him apart inside as he spoke them.

Kuruny stared at him in disbelief. "You're barely trained to protect yourself. How will *you* help anyone?"

Krishani thought she was pondering how quickly he would die, and what he had done to make Avristar so angry she would send him to said death. Instead of continuing, she sized him up, baffled. He shrugged. "You care little, if anything, for me. Why this concerns you so greatly, I don't know."

"It's not you I'm worried about. The men turned on us without warning. This corruption … I'm afraid …" Krishani glared at her. "I worry it's reaching Avristar."

Krishani pounded his fist against the wall. He made a sound between a sob and a growl. "I have to leave her," he said quietly as he pounded the wall again. "I have to leave her and Avristar will do nothing to stop it." He paused to catch his breath, but his throat was sticky with tears. "Neither will Atara, neither will anyone. I have no choice but to leave and face my fate." He kicked the wall and sunk to his knees. "I doubt they will let me say goodbye."

Kuruny looked like she didn't know what to do or what to say. She was silent for several moments as he kneeled on the ground, shaking in agony. "You should get some rest." Her voice sounded ragged and hollow and he hoped she deeply regretted toying with him.

Krishani said nothing in response. He brought himself to his feet and dragged himself into his room.

• • •

Krishani stirred hours after Melianna's fourth call. He rose only to find himself wearing the same thing from the night before, and added only his cloak to the ensemble. He headed down the corridors towards Istar's quarters. Many people bustled through the castle just like any other day, everyone busy working or performing some task. Not feeling like talking to anybody, he tried to be invisible as he found Istar's study in the lower east corner of the castle.

He went to knock, but Istar opened the door and quickly ushered him in, mumbling something about his incredible tardiness. Krishani felt awkward as he stood in the common room, unsure if he should sit or continue standing. Istar moved about, but there was something unusual about the man. He seemed anxious and worried at the same time. He paced the floor, stopped and looked Krishani in the eye. "You weren't born on Avristar," he said.

Krishani gulped. He knew that already, but waited to hear more. Istar sighed and continued to pace back and forth. "Adoron found you in the forests of Amersil, like every other Child of Avristar, and we took you as one of our own ... but, you are not a Child of Avristar."

Krishani cringed. "Where am I from?"

Istar shook his head. "That's irrelevant."

He looked down, a bigger pit forming in his gut. "How did you know?"

Istar ignored the comment. "There is no mention of the Ferryman, his purpose, his kinship. Nothing exists in the Great Library."

He mustered a tiny smile. "Maybe it's all a dream and I'm not the Ferryman."

Istar furrowed his brow and continued pacing the floor. "Nay, you cannot ignore it." He shook his head, seeming deep in thought. "Perhaps the knowledge was hidden for a reason. Perhaps it was removed from the library for the safety of the Ferrymen." He scanned a shelf filled with crystal balls and pendulums.

Krishani felt sadness slide into him. Despite his earlier defiance, he hung his head. There would be consequences if he rebelled against Avristar herself. He hadn't thought about it before, betraying the land, but it wasn't something he was ready to do. Not without first trying to talk his way out of leaving. "I trust your judgment and that of Avristar. What will you have me do?"

Istar averted his attention to the matter at hand and sighed. Krishani knew the severity of the situation. "We will consult the Gatekeeper and you will heed the call." He put his hands on Krishani's shoulders and looked him deep in the eyes. "You have been chosen. There is no doubt the Ferryman is of great importance. One day you will return to Avristar." He made it sound as though the time away wouldn't cause never-ending agony.

Krishani's stomach churned as he thought of the Lands of Men. "Kuruny," Krishani began cautiously, knowing Istar would be displeased hearing about her. He knew what Kuruny and her sisters had been subjected to. He had a bitter taste in his mouth over the events forcing more kinfolk to return to Avristar indefinitely. With all his sorrow he hadn't thought about how much fuller the castle walls were becoming. "She told me the Lands of Men are dangerous."

Istar frowned, and then smiled lightly and chuckled a little. "You're the Ferryman. What I've taught you will prove to be your guide to the tasks that lay ahead of you."

Krishani let out a breath, and solemnly nodded. "Thank you," he said, though it felt forced. Even though he kept his head and kept her out of the conversation, Kaliel was the only thing he was really worried about. What would happen to her? To them? Istar was cold and Atara was clearly set against their relationship. It seemed so bleak.

Istar smiled. "Come, there is much to be done before we can consult the Gatekeeper."

26-Ruby and Quartz

Kaliel pinched the ribbon on her shoe and twisted it back and forth. Since returning from the lake, she had given Mallorn a chance, but their lessons hadn't helped much. Weeks passed and Winter Solstice approached, the longest night of the year. She tightly hugged her cloak to her shoulders as a gust of wind ripped through the trees. She sat on the mound, staring at the creek. The images of the dream wouldn't fade; they stuck to her memory like crusted tree sap, forever crystallized in amber. It was late afternoon, the sky covered in gorgeous shades of pink. She pushed her back into the grass and stared at the treetops, the sky and its beautiful shades of blue and magenta.

A smile tickled her lips as she thought of Pux. He added the pink to the sky. It was a familiar reminder of easier days. Her mind drifted to Orlondir, the waterfall, and her heart swelled with longing for Krishani. Lately, her thoughts of him were tainted by fear of the dream. It was so clear those eyes were his eyes, but why couldn't she remember? There was a life before this life, one that seemed so far away the only remnants of it were the sketches in her journal and that dream. She couldn't make sense of it; the end of the war, the warning of the Great Oak, the danger of the foe hunting her kind. She couldn't have been given a heavier burden in life, and all she had ever wanted was freedom.

There was movement behind her. She sat up and looked around as Mallorn approached with his staff.

"Another lesson, then." He dropped another staff on the ground and crossed the creek. She stood, grabbed the staff, brushed off her ivory dress and followed him into the forests. Mallorn used his walking stick to tap against the trees. Kaliel wondered what he was doing. He slowed to a stop and planted the walking stick firmly in the ground.

"I have organized a series of words, Kaliel. Every time I tap my stick against the trunk of the tree, I want you to tap into my mind and retrieve the word. Simple enough?" His eyes were stern.

She was uneasy. "Do you need to tap the tree?"

Mallorn smirked. "I will be gentle."

She nodded, and he turned around. She pulled a face, overwhelmed with the task. He walked a bit before he tapped a tree. She closed her eyes and moved with her mind, listening for his voice in her head. *Tree.* She was disappointed with the results.

"Tree," she said.

He laughed. "Right! See? It won't be hard."

The exercise continued for awhile, and parts of it lifted her spirits. They went through 'rabbit,' 'horse,' 'tea,' 'honey,' 'lake,' 'leaf,' and a few others before it came to an end. They were far from his cabin in a part of Nandaro she didn't recognize. She looked around. The grass was a dark green and the trees were slightly thicker. The smell of hazelnuts was distinct in the air.

Mallorn paused, nodding. "Good."

Kaliel was getting tired.

Mallorn swung his walking stick up to a diagonal position, holding it with both hands in front of his chest. He nodded at her to do the same.

"Now, we learn defense," he said.

Slowly, he moved his walking stick towards hers, and made cross-contact with it, lightly tapping the wood. Kaliel leaned back, allowing him to do it. She hadn't experimented with combat before and this made her uncomfortable.

"No," he shouted. He let out an exasperated sigh and shook his head.

Kaliel only widened her eyes, unsure how to act.

Mallorn pulled away and dropped the stick, then lunged out just a few steps from her, holding it diagonally across his midsection. "Copy my stance."

She took a step forward, not quite a lunge, and maneuvered the stick so it was diagonally across her chest, mirroring Mallorn. She felt like an idiot for not being able to follow his instructions, and there was the ever-pressing threat of other things on her mind. This seemed so frivolous since it wasn't like she'd master anything. She already knew fighting wasn't going to help her.

He cringed, but nodded. "Right. Just ... opposite of me." She frowned and switched directions. He smiled. "Fair enough. Taking this slower, then." He tried again as he lunged forward and tapped his stick against hers. "Step back and switch directions."

She followed him and gave him a crooked smile. She wanted to please at least one elder in her life.

"You have the movements, now you will protect your thoughts against my intrusions."

Kaliel sighed, ready to try defending herself. They slowly backed through the forest. Mallorn stayed quiet for a long time.

"Flower," he said with a stern look.

Kaliel frowned, growing determined to block him. The girls in the corridor, the shadowy shapes that took them, she had to be strong enough to resist them. She wouldn't be like the others and give up without a fight. She wouldn't have to face the enemies if she stayed on Avristar, if the Valtanyana never found her. Part of her knew hiding forever wasn't much of a plan, but it was all she had for the time being. His stick tapped against hers as she lunged backwards. She focused harder on shielding as Mallorn tried to penetrate her thoughts.

She didn't let him through.

"Very good," he said.

She only nodded. An owl hooted in the distance, a rabbit scuttled through the trees, which whined from the sharp winds clawing at their leaves. She cringed, her thoughts drifted to the dream of the Ferryman. She repeated the word Ferryman in her mind, over and over again, while Mallorn's expression remained. She glanced behind her to make sure she wouldn't step on anything. The barn was in the distance behind her and a bit of relief wash over her.

"Ferryman," Mallorn said as he tapped his staff against hers. His eyes met hers with awe as he stopped and stood straight, his body rigid.

Kaliel dropped the staff at his feet and raced to the barn. There were things she couldn't tell him—the whole of her parable and the dream about Krishani. Part of her was afraid he would look at her differently if he knew the truth. She was determined to steal what little innocence she had left. Giving him a chance to help her control her abilities was all she planned on doing. They had been through the tattered manuscripts a thousand times about the Flames, there was no information directly relating to the Amethyst Flame. Even though he was trying to help she didn't know more about what she was before she arrived. She reached the barn and ducked inside. The horses were asleep in their stalls. She stumbled over to Umber.

"Can you hear me?"

"As always," he said.

"Let me hide in your stall?"

"Why hide from Mallorn?"

She darted around the horse and slumped in the corner. "I messed up." She rested her head against the wood, tears rolling down her face as she fixed her gaze on the hooves. She didn't want to tell Mallorn she was in love with the Ferryman. Nobody knew about Krishani, he was a secret she'd never share.

"You cannot avoid him forever," Umber said.

"For now I can."

. . .

Kaliel dreamt of the lake. Her feet dangled over the ledge as she stared at the horizon. The waters were shrouded in a thick mist that curled around the surface of the shore, rising towards the hill she was on. She stretched out her arms and yawned, gazing at the sandy beach below. It was tan, littered with stray twigs and rocks. She got curious and leaned forward, wanting to see the beach up close. She would have to go down the hill and over the rocks if she wanted to stand on the beach. The gargoyle cave scared her away, the gangly creatures frightened her. Unlike the merfolk they didn't seem gentle at all. As she bent over, she sensed commotion in the cave. She perked up and watched as darkness fell across the lake, turning the waters black.

She frowned as a gargoyle emerged from the cave, scrambling on all fours towards the grass. It was one of the gargoyles that were said to protect Avristar. A boat pressed up against the shore, and Kaliel moved her gaze down the hill as people approached. She stiffened.

Krishani was there. Why was he there? She scrambled to her feet and clambered down the hill. She was careful to stay concealed as she watched the heads of the elders drifting through the trees. She darted between the spruces, trying to find him. Her hands clawed at branches as she got turned around, confusion welling up within her as a deep ache forced her to clutch her chest and crouch to the ground. Her knees hit the spruce needles in the grass followed by her hands.

She looked again; Krishani was pacing through the trees. She felt his anger, sadness and fear as she helplessly watched him go past.

Why are you leaving me? She desperately needed to know. Kaliel remembered the boats, the gargoyle. She scrambled through the forest brush, being careful not to make noise, to cry out. She reached the edge of the tree line and watched the crowd of elders, Lord Istar, Lady Atara, and others gathered around the boat. Krishani stepped into the boat. Kaliel raced to her feet and placed her hand on the side of a tree, trying to steady herself while attempting to comprehend what was happening.

Krishani turned and raised his head, his blue and green eyes staring into the crowd of elders. They looked pained in a way she couldn't understand. She stepped away from the tree, shock and anguish tightening in her gut. Her foot caught on itself and she tumbled down the hill towards the array of elders, landing on her hands and knees in front of them. They all looked at her with forlorn expressions, but none of them said a word.

She pushed herself up and looked at Krishani. He appeared so downtrodden, like he would rather crumble to dust than be on the boat. He wouldn't look at her.

"Are you leaving me?" she asked.

He hung his head as the gargoyle pushed the boat into the mists. The elders vanished and she cried out as she stood on the ledge, watching the boat drift away and out of sight.

"No." She gasped. Her eyes snapped open and she shook her head, noting she was back in the barn. It was a dream. Her heart pounded so loud she heard its pulse in her ears as she sputtered and attempted to breathe. She clawed at the walls as she fought to stand.

"Careful child. What troubles you?" Umber said.

"Krishani will leave me," she said.

"That cannot be." Umber grunted and scratched his hoof on the ground in apparent discomfort.

Kaliel felt the roughness of the wood under her frail hands as she pulled herself up and fell against the side of the horse. She felt so dizzy as the revelation hit her. She pressed her cheek into the fur and closed her eyes, trying to find her feet. Her hands pushed at the horse and she stumbled awkwardly through the barn and out into the forest. It was pitch black, the sky void of the moon. She wrapped her arms around her waist, trying to hold herself together. It was useless. All she could think of was Krishani's arms around her, his sweet nothings whispered in her ear, his lips on hers. She desperately wanted to be in his arms; no more Mallorn, no more lessons, no more dreams, no more Flames.

All I want is this and nothing else, she thought bitterly as she traipsed through the trees.

The border between Nandaro and Orlondir wasn't far. She needed to race against this twist of fate and find him before the unthinkable happened.

Dizziness swept her under as she fought to separate the shapes of the trees from shadows. She ran her fingers along the bark and turned and turned, winding through the spaces between the trunks. She tilted her head upward, tracing patterns of black leaves against midnight blue sky. She sighed as she continued to fight her way through the night. Desperation overwhelmed her as the longing for his warmth hit her again. She kneeled on the ground and let out a sob. Her limbs went weak as her elbows touched the ground and she buried her face between her hands. Tears spilled onto the grass. She was helpless and out of time.

There's nothing I can do, she thought as she pounded her fists on the ground. She rolled on her back, hands rubbing her stomach, begging for some kind of comfort to come. She saw the waterfall in her mind's eye, and heard Krishani's voice in her head. *I won't surrender.*

"He promised he never would," she whispered as the wind rustled the trees. She curled the blades of grass under her fingers and ripped them out of the soil. Her chest heaved in spurts of anxiety. She had no idea where she was anymore. Orlondir seemed too far away for her to travel on foot, and he would be gone before she could reach him.

"What troubles you, Little Flame?"

Kaliel jumped. She looked around, trying to place the voice. She stretched out her arms and felt for anything near her. There was a tree to her right. Her hand traced along the trunk and she realized it was older than the others. She dropped her hand and crawled over to the tree, aligning her spine with it. She let out an exasperated sigh. She longed to go back in time, to erase the words of the Great Oak, to stop the foe from seeking her, to live in bliss from her past, yet she knew none of that was possible.

"He's being forced to leave me," she said.

"Then it was not meant to be."

The words stung her heart. "But it was."

"And now it is no more."

The words crushed the last of her strength; darkness engulfed her in its cold embrace. Her eyes drooped shut and she slipped into the abyss.

Wansa.

The words were clear as crystal, but she couldn't understand them. She was … somewhere. Underground maybe … a crypt? Torches flickered on the walls and she felt the sticky ooze beneath her feet as she assessed her surroundings. Pain stabbed her stomach. She put pressure on the imaginary wound, but as she peered through the bars she saw a girl pressed up against the wall.

Corza.

More words in a language she didn't understand. Kaliel watched her with delirious attention. The girl's eyes were closed and her mouth moved, mumbling something. Kaliel moved towards the cage and curled her fingers through the spaces between the bars, pushing her face into the iron to get a better glimpse.

The girl's wrists were in shackles, her midnight-black hair matted against her face. Her eyes darted back and forth underneath their tan lids. Kaliel backed away from the bars and stumbled through the muck as she turned and tried to claw her way through the catacombs.

Behind her was a tunnel. She entered it and raced towards the end. There was something familiar about the place. She passed by the tombs and felt something holding her back. She pushed, but it was like she had hit an invisible wall. She stopped and stretched her arms out to the darkness but it pushed back. The hairs on the back of her neck stood on end as footsteps pounded the stairwell behind her.

She flushed with fear as she tried to stay calm and still. There was a splash behind her and her heart did a double jump. She clenched her fists together and gritted her teeth. She trembled to the bone and her mouth threatened to erupt in a succession of screams. She held her lips together and stifled the faint whines in the back of her throat. A sharp strike of flint sounded against the stone, and she cringed as she turned to witness the foe.

En guyen naha lin sanse.

Kaliel understood it this time, and the Flame inside of her struggled with all of its might to emerge. As she closed her eyes, it rushed out of her. She took a sharp breath as she looked at the people in the cell. There was a body on fire next to the girl now, flames smoking out of his form as the foul smell grew thicker.

The one with rosy pink eyes stared at her and the meaning of the words flooded her mind. *Run. Hide. He will take your soul.*

The Valtanyana didn't seek to kill the Flames, they sought to *possess* them. Kaliel felt sick as she fought to bring herself out of the dream, back to reality, back to the place where she could find Krishani, warn Mallorn, tell the elders everything she had seen. She tried to close her eyes, but she felt like they were fused open as the enemy crouched beside the girl and presented a tiny crystal clear orb. She watched as the pink essence from the girl's eyes flowed into the orb, turning it into milky pink vapors. He stood as the girl slumped to the side, dead.

Desperate, Kaliel tried to back away, but the enemy turned his gaze towards the darkened tunnel. His white-lightning eyes sparked, making contact with her amethyst enflamed ones until everything fell away into awful blackness.

27-Innocent Mistakes

There was a light tap on the door. Krishani raised his head, his face hidden behind his hands. He wanted to deny existence, move backwards in time, stop the Ferryman from dying in the first place. In the weeks since Kaliel left, the Elmare Castle had grown cold. He was a pawn in their games. Even Hernadette refused to make eye contact with him while she sorted out the herbs he would offer to the Gatekeeper.

Melianna, on the other hand, had been chirpy. As she measured him for the robes, she chattered on about the battles her father and his men fought in the Lands of Men. The conversations only made him more depressed that no matter what he wanted, not once had they bothered to mention Kaliel.

In addition, Kuruny was nowhere to be found. After that night he encountered her in the hallway, she had disappeared to some unknown place. He longed to speak with her more about the land she returned from so he could understand what he would face when he arrived.

That was the worst of it. The Ferryman followed death. It didn't matter where Krishani went—he would find death and it would find him. A thought he didn't want to relish.

Another knock on the door. He sighed and looked around his small room. There was nothing but what had been there since the day he arrived. He closed his eyes and tried to push away the sadness, the very urge to scream at Melianna. Profanities wouldn't help. He sighed. There was no way to stop this. *Sweet surrender,* he thought as he lifted his head towards the door that was already creaking open.

He stomped his foot on the floorboards as he stood and the door shut with a bang. He ran his hands down the robes. They were embroidered in gold and loosely hugged his form. He shuffled towards the door and placed his hand on the doorknob. As his fingers gripped it he had another thought race through his mind: The Valtanyana. When would he encounter them? He shook his head. That was fear he didn't need to carry. Corruption festered in every part of the Lands of Men. The Daed were crawling from every hole and crevasse they could find. Whoever sought Kaliel was much more dangerous than those he would encounter. He hoped she could evade the Valtanyana until he was strong enough to return to her.

"Krishani," a voice on the other side of the door said.

He turned the handle. Melianna stood in the hallway, appearing nervous and bothered. She took off down the corridor, swiftly leading him to where the Elders waited.

• • •

Kuruny watched from the shadows as the Elders gathered in the main hall. The spectacle made her sick. She had to get to Krishani somehow before the insanity continued. She peered around the corner up the grand staircase to the east wing and caught a glimpse of Melianna's satin blue slippers. She pressed her back against the stone wall.

The Elders arranged themselves in a line leading out to the courtyard. Kuruny recognized half of them, the others appointed during her extended absence. She glanced at the torch bearers. They were in twos, rounding the end of the processional. Lord Istar and Lady Atara were somewhere near the front in the midst of the courtyard. Kuruny was disgusted with her father. He wanted to keep her from the Lands of Men due to the hex, and yet refused to break it, and refused to allow her to join in the affairs of the land.

She scowled as she recalled the tasks she endured over the past few weeks. There was nothing she could say that would allow him to reconsider his decision, to consult with the Gatekeeper before sending his most prized apprentice to his death. And she was certain Krishani would die. She stifled a sigh as she recalled the fact she had barely escaped with her life. What would they do to someone like Krishani?

It wasn't as though his kinship wasn't clearly marked. Even that cloak couldn't hide the pointed ears, the mismatched eyes, or the pale white skin. All the men she had encountered were tanned, muscular and hairy. How they wouldn't see him as a demon was beyond her.

She turned her attention to the processional as she watched the torch bearers exit the main hall. Her heart leapt out of her chest as she realized they were truly going through with it. She peered around the corner. The castle was empty. She closed her eyes and took a deep breath. She tiptoed towards the archway as she slipped outside into the courtyard. She hid behind a bush and watched them cross the bridge. The processional turned left as she scrambled across the yard, careful to keep up, but careful to stay hidden. They began down the forbidden trail to the top of Tirion Mountain. No one ever ventured there save during the Fire Festivals, and even then, only a select few were given the honor of hearing the voice of Avristar.

The sky gave off the last rays of sunlight, as the midnight blue of the night and a blanket of stars crept across the horizon.

Kuruny's pulse quickened as she skipped over the bridge and watched them enter the forest path. She paused. She couldn't go walking a few steps behind them. The path curled, but if even one of those torch bearers looked behind them, they would spot her plain as day. She calculated the distance, and what it would cost her to forge a path through the trees. The processional trudged on and as Kuruny found herself lost in thought, it moved out of sight. She cringed and dove into the trees, doubting her options were any wider. She pushed branches out of the way as she clumsily traipsed over the forest brush. She had to move faster. Krishani was at the front and she was wasting time. She sighed and scrunched up her nose in disgust. Begrudgingly, she quickened her pace and soon flickers of more torchlight, and the bobbing heads of Elders. Each of them had their head down in meditation. She snickered to herself and hoped they felt ashamed of their decision.

There were more ahead of her as she flew through the trees. Her lungs ached from exertion. That was new, but then again she had never forced herself to run like that. She looked through the branches and saw Istar's long white hair. To his right was Atara, her auburn hair flowing behind her. Krishani shuffled along, the black hood of his robe pulled over his features to hide his fear. Her heart dropped.

There was little hope of getting a message to him. The path turned and she watched as Istar and the others flowed around the base of the mountain, moving to the gradual incline. She winced and tried to find a line of sight to Krishani. It was difficult; the brush was in the way and his head was bowed. She carefully moved through the vegetation and once again hated her options. She stopped and grabbed hold of a branch above her and shook it, hoping it would cause enough commotion for him to turn and look.

She felt like an idiot.

Sure enough the whole processional stopped and turned in her direction. She gasped and dropped the branch, crouching to the ground. She peeked at them, thinking maybe he'd catch sight of her. No one came to investigate the rustling. Istar turned back to the path. Krishani lingered, his gaze searching the trees. His eyes met hers though she figured it was just by chance given all the branches.

"Krishani," she telepathically projected.

His eyes widened as confusion and panic crossed his expression. She sighed and nestled herself into the brush below.

"I need to speak with you." She didn't bother to watch as the elders encouraged him to follow.

"What do you want, Kuruny?" His voice was a welcome change in her mind instead of her own panicked thoughts. She mused at both their competency as she assumed he was no good with the art of telepathy, but had proven her wrong.

"You're not going through with this are you?"

"I have no choice."

Kuruny sighed. He was too honorable to betray the land. He wouldn't try to escape. She didn't really care about him but she couldn't let Istar make such a mistake. Maybe it would be enough for the lord to reconsider his decision and then Krishani wouldn't be committing a crime. She had been worried about him since that night in the corridor. No matter what he thought of it, she feared for him, and if she could help, she would. She closed her eyes and tried to piece together her words so he would understand. Apparently the prospect of death didn't scare him, and that was peculiar. Why wouldn't he fight harder if he knew this would lead to his demise? She shook her head. Her own thoughts were muddled and she needed to be clear.

"It's an absolute choice." She shifted her weight in the grass. The remainder of the torch bearers had already passed her, rounding the mountain.

"I don't understand," Krishani said.

"If you leave, you'll never be with Kaliel again."

Kuruny sat back in the grass, stunned by her own revelation, but it was the only way she could explain it. There was no way he would ever be able to return to Kaliel and live by her side. His only hope was in denying his duty. She found her way through the trees to the path. Krishani didn't respond. She knew her words stung.

• • •

Krishani was agitated by the silent conversation. He stared at the ground as he tried to conceal its existence. The elders were known for their sharp abilities and he knew it was possible that Lady Atara could hear everything being said between him and Kuruny. He stuffed his hands into the sleeves of his robe and pushed his arms to his chest. The day had been bad enough without Kuruny's idle speculation and warnings about death in the Lands of Men. He already knew how much death he would encounter. Death wasn't the problem.

He shivered. Tremors raced through him as though an ice cold breeze had blown right at him. He took another step before nausea seeped in. Vertigo surrounded him as the word *never* clamored against his temples. He forced another step forward and tried to make it look natural, but he was breaking down. He had clung to Istar's empty promise of his return. Kuruny wouldn't lie; the Lands of Men betrayed her. She knew what kind of abhorrence he would face. If she went to such lengths to stop him, she must have good reason for it. And losing Kaliel forever was something he could never go through with.

"What do I do?" he asked, hoping Kuruny was still alert to his thoughts.

"Run."

He grimaced. He could do that, but he had no clue where to go. His sadness and pain had forced most of his abilities to go dormant. Even the art of sensing was difficult these days. He shuffled along, the sickness in him thrashing against his inner organs.

"Where is she?"

"With Mallorn, in Nandaro."

Krishani suddenly grew warm. How stupid could he have been? Istar left for Nandaro right before Kaliel had been taken away. Nandaro was a large province so finding her ... but there was one place he knew of. Istar talked a lot about Mallorn and his journeys in the Avrigard quadrant. Kaliel must have been with him this whole time. He smiled. There was nothing that could stop him from reaching her.

"Shimma is waiting for you in the stables," Kuruny said.

He set his plan in motion. He felt Adoron's eyes on his back as they neared the sharp turn towards the steep ascent. Istar and Atara turned in unison. He paused, and ran his hands along the sash that held his robes together. He loosened it, the robe sliding off his shoulders, revealing his tunic and breeches. His stomach lurched as he leapt through the forest and clambered down the side of the mountain, unsure where the ground was.

He heard the shouts from Istar and Adoron as he tumbled through ferns, fighting to find the ground. The trees grew thinner and he emerged in the rolling fields on the north side of the castle. He fell on his hands and knees, panting. He looked back towards the path; it was much higher than he had expected, and he had fallen most of the way. He pushed himself to his feet and continued racing across the hills towards the stables. It was exhilarating, the feeling of the wind whipping his face, his heart thumping faster than a rabbit's. He felt the rush of freedom and damnation at the same time, but at that moment all he could think about was Kaliel.

He rounded the castle and neared the stables. Shimma was standing outside with Rhina. Her hands grazed along the horse's side as she hummed a haunting melody. The music wafted through the air as Krishani felt his senses sharpen. He saw Shimma's face turn seasick as he approached her.

"Krishani!" she said.

He paused when he reached the mare, long enough to grab the reins and hop on its back. Shimma stepped away, but he looked at her, trying to gauge her twisted expression. He frowned and shook his head, too out of breath to speak.

"Something isn't right, she's not with Mallorn," Shimma said.

Krishani's eyes widened as he whipped the reins and sped off into the night.

• • •

Fear crippled Krishani as darkness closed in on him. Rhina was a skilled horse, but without the moon, the shadows in the forest deepened, making it impossible to see anything. He pulled the reins taut, leading Rhina back and forth through the labyrinth of trees, trying to feel Kaliel. This was bad. He wouldn't forgive himself if he didn't get to her in time and she had another episode. What was Mallorn doing to her? He heard nothing in the past three moons, no word of how Kaliel was. Istar avoided the subject, and kept giving him stronger herbs that made him pass out. Dreamless sleep was better than nightmare ridden sleep but it made him groggy and sluggish in the morning.

Rhina slowed as she stumbled over something and started taking cautious steps. Krishani gulped as nettles of a spruce scraped along his neck. He didn't know what to expect when he did find her, but chills raised the hairs on his forearm as he slumped forward, letting the horse pull him through the endless forest with its own intuition.

Prickles crawled into him, and deep guilt mushroomed across his chest. He pushed himself up, wrapping the reins around his hands and glancing around. Kaliel was near, and she was in pain, but not the same kind of pain he felt when the Emerald Flame died. This pain was a tearing, aching pain that came in successions. He squinted at the shadowy forms of trees, but everything else appeared in deep shades of gray. His heart quickened and he slipped off the horse, looping the reins around its neck. He treaded carefully across the dirt, forcing his senses to reach out and find her.

Urgency flooded him as he passed another copse of trees growing close together. Nandaro was a never ending forest with undefined paths. While his training as a Brother of Amersil made forging forest paths easy it didn't help him to find Kaliel. He sighed, his ears tuning in to the faint sounds in the forest. Grouses snickered as they passed, crickets creaked, and rabbits chattered. He tuned in deeper, hearing steady faint breaths. His stomach lurched as his hands slipped off the reins, a corner of the ivory dress appearing visible in the stark nighttime landscape.

He tripped over his own foot and came crashing onto his knees, his palms skidding in the dirt as he neared the girl. His eyes trailed over her ankle as he found his footing. "Kaliel?"

233

She didn't answer and the nausea returned. He took a deep breath, making out the shape of her body. Her knees curled towards her head, her back pressed against a thick red cedar. Her brow creased in worry, she looked terrified, even unconscious.

"Kaliel?"

She didn't move.

His heart jumped as he pressed himself against the tree and pulled her into his lap. Her steady breaths came in shallow spurts like she had fainted. He held her hands between his own; they were clammy. He ran a hand over her forehead. It was cold, damp. His fingers traced along her cheek, her stained with tears.

"Kaliel, come back to me," he whispered in her ear. He tried to stay calm, but panic settled in. He kissed her cheek, and pressed her face to his shoulder. "You can't leave me." He closed his eyes and tightened his grip on her, burying his cheek in her hair. He hadn't forgotten about her in the last three moons, and he didn't want it to be like this. Seeing her, he felt a surge of guilt and anger. He should have fought harder against Istar in the first place. He never should have let Kaliel go to Nandaro.

Moments passed in agonizing silence. Krishani listened to Kaliel's faint breaths flushing in and out of her fragile lungs. He wanted to kiss away all the pain. He ran his hand along her forearm and down her back to the base of her spine. He missed her in a way he couldn't comprehend until she was in his arms. She stirred and he stopped breathing, pressing his back against the tree as she came to life under him.

"Kaliel?"

She let out a groan, shifted her weight and lifted her head from his shoulder. Her emerald green eyes were bright even in the darkness. Krishani held his breath; he didn't want to scare her and risk her slapping him silly. He was relieved to see her alive, awake, and in his lap. She mumbled something incomprehensible and nestled into him, lighting his entire body up with fire.

"Kaliel," he whispered gently, trying to shake her back to reality. "I'm here."

She moved like lightning, her arms straight, palms digging into his shoulders as she stared at him, confusion, fear, and anger in her expression. He reached for her upper arms but she scooted off him and slumped onto her knees in the dirt, wiping her face with her hands the way she did when she was crying.

Krishani didn't want to see her like this.

"You left me," she said, her voice low and scratchy.

How did she know? he thought as the guilt lanced across his torso. He pushed himself to his knees and crawled to her, lacing his fingers through hers and trying to make her look at him. She tucked her chin in, avoiding him, her hands refusing to grip his. "I haven't left yet."

She shot him a look, her green eyes full of sorrow. "Why were you on the boat?"

He frowned. "What?"

She slid her hands out of his grip and stood, backing away. "I saw you on the boat."

Krishani hung his head. So Mallorn was helping her. In the time she had been gone her abilities had gotten sharper. He couldn't hide anything from her anymore. He raked a hand through his hair. "I have to go to the Lands of Men."

Her eyes widened. "Because of your parable?" She looked weak, like she might crumble if he said anything more about it. He neared her, trying to put his hand on her shoulder but she shrugged away, stalking through the forest. He jogged to Rhina, grabbed the reins and followed her.

"Kaliel, wait—"

She slowed down but didn't stop. Krishani followed her through the bushes, spindly leaves brushing along his shins. "Istar wouldn't let me ignore it anymore," he called after her.

She whirled, arms crossed, a fiery look in her eyes. "You mean the nightmares don't you?"

Krishani nodded, a lump in his throat. He couldn't tell her he was the Ferryman. It spelled so much disaster for him already he was afraid it would be the one thing that would shatter what he had with Kaliel forever. They reached a small clearing between the trees, thick ankle high grass below them. Kaliel stood beside a lanky cedar, the folds of her dress ruffling in the breeze. He wanted to make her forget all about what was happening, but he stood there, unsure if she'd let him touch her.

"You're the Ferryman." She sounded melancholy.

Krishani blanched. "How did you know?"

Kaliel sighed and it seemed like all her strength was failing, she pressed her palm to the tree to steady herself. "I had a dream … and in it we were burning. You called yourself the Ferryman, and you called me the Flame."

Krishani closed the distance between them, towering over her. He covered her hand with his own, pulling it away from the bark, his eyes imploring her to forgive him. "I watched the Ferryman die. It's my time now."

Kaliel shuddered and pressed herself against him, wrapping her arms around his waist. "It feels like I've already lost you."

He gripped her tighter, the feeling of her against him intoxicating. "I won't surrender."

"They'll force you to go."

"Come with me."

He arms dropped to her sides and she pulled out of the circle of his arms, striding across the meadow. Krishani followed her, unwilling to let her make this the end. What Kuruny said reverberated in the back of his mind. *If you take this path you'll never see Kaliel again.* He couldn't tell her this might be the last time he saw her. He couldn't let his destiny take over his life.

"What's wrong?" he asked as he took another careful step towards her.

She turned; her eyes full of the Flame's fire. Bright liquid amethyst shimmered in her irises, and her body sparked with the familiar white violet glow. "I saw him Krishani. I watched him kill the Ruby and Quartz Flames. If I go with you, he'll find me."

Krishani's stomach dropped. He could try to protect her but the Ferryman followed death. He'd be on a battlefield constantly. It was no place for a Flame. He put his hands on her shoulders, feeling a charge through his body. He pulled the strap of her dress over her shoulder slowly, gauging her reaction. She didn't move and he took another step towards her, cupping her face in his hand and sweeping his fingers down the nape of her neck. Her fingers curled around a handful of her dress as he ran his fingertips along her arm, lacing them together with hers.

She flushed a deep scarlet and the fire in her eyes faded, replaced by green. "What are you doing?" she whispered, uncomfortably fidgeting.

Krishani put his hands on either side of her face and forced her to look at him. "I'll protect you."

She let out an exasperated sigh. "You don't know what you're saying." She averted her gaze, and he felt her fear. He couldn't stand it, being this close to her, and so far from Orlondir, from any signs of life. It was the first time they were all alone, no threat of anyone interrupting them. He traced circles on her shoulder and she let out a shaky breath, clearly affected by what he was doing.

"I know I don't want a life without you, Kaliel."

She didn't look at him, and he brushed his thumb across her lower lip. "Then don't leave me," she barely whispered.

He didn't have to answer as she kissed his palm and he closed his eyes savoring the feeling of her touch. In a swift move he cupped her face and pressed his lips against her, forcing her mouth open, caressing her tongue with his. She gasped as he locked his hand around the back of her neck and held her to him, his hands making fast work of the buttons on her dress. It fell away from her chest and he cupped her breast as he walked her towards the edge of the meadow.

She let out a moan as he left a blazing trail of kisses down her neck. Her hands greedily explored his body. She had touched him everywhere before but this was different. She pulled at the hem of his tunic and he obliged, pulling it off and pressing himself against her.

"Krishani," she whispered, and he took it as a protest. He dropped his lips to her ear, nipping at the tips with his teeth.

"I don't want to stop."

He felt her smile against him as she dug her fingernails into his back and wrapped her legs around him. "I don't want you to stop." She affixed her hips against him as he pushed her against a tree, needing a moment to catch his breath. He kissed her shoulder as he shrugged off his breeches and buried himself inside her. She let out a cry, as he pressed his hips against her, rocking back and forth. Her body clamped around him, making it impossible for him to think straight. His body stiffened as she braced herself, her hands flat against his shoulder blades.

She let out another loud moan as he went deeper, and something happened he couldn't explain. She flared, bright wisps of white violet energy cascading off her body in sharp spikes. He lost control for a moment and swiveled, falling on top of her in the grass. He propped himself on his elbows, his eyes boring into her amethyst enflamed ones. She ran a hand down his chest, stopping at the baby hairs on his navel. Before she could say what he knew she was thinking he covered her mouth with his and pressed into her again, the exquisite feeling of being inside her making every bit of pain he felt evaporate.

He lost himself in the feel of her Flame as it circled them in its apogee of light and energy. He didn't know what was happening to her but he wanted more of it. She was like the sun, and when he moved against her, more of it exploded from her. He'd never experienced anything like this. His body contracted and he let out a groan, feeling completely spent. He feathered light kisses on her neck, her temple, cheek, corner of her lips and she claimed his lips one last time before the unnatural light faded and he lay beside her. She curled into him, letting out a breath as they fell into a deep sleep.

28-AVRED

Mallorn slept in his cabin, snoring, a tattered manuscript strewn across his chest. He snorted in a breath and wheezed out. Somewhere in the depths of his mind he travelled through a labyrinth of trees. These ones were whispering to him. He squinted into the fog and brushed his hand along the side of a trunk. The tree jostled. Ever since he had seen Kaliel make the trees speak he had been curious about what kinds of things they could have said to him all along. He anxiously paced through the forest; there was something he needed to see around one of the trees. He knew it was there and yet he couldn't reach it. He neared the sharp turn; the trees precariously placed at a ninety-degree angle, so precisely put it was as if they were pointing towards his destination.

With a huff, he turned the corner and peered down a vast forest corridor. It was a long ways to its end and there were no breaks in the trees, no way to deviate or take a shortcut. He wondered what he was supposed to find. It was right there beside his memory, whatever it was.

What was he supposed to see?

He took a few steps forward and faltered. A brilliant violet light erupted in the distance from behind the trees, casting them in shadows as it flooded through the forest. He put an arm to his face to shield his eyes. As the light grew, its edges reached for him, but he turned and fled. Seeing the darkness in front of him, he raced towards it, his body jolting with each pound of his foot against the ground. His feet hit the shadows and his body was encompassed by it.

The scene didn't change.

He stood in the forest, wondering why another dream wouldn't start. He knew where he was, but was confused by the light. He turned, expecting the light to illuminate the dark, but his mouth dropped open and he fell to his knees.

The horses neighed in the barn beside him and he smelled the familiar scent of the air in Nandaro. He saw the scattered trees in front of him as though he was sitting there on a summer night, taking in the beauty of the twilight. Everything was normal except for what was floating through the trees.

The shadowy figure carried Kaliel's lifeless body towards him as he knelt helplessly in the dirt. Mallorn made out the black mandarin style jacket and trousers of the foe, his bony fingers curled around the Flame's body like shackles. He let out a cry, as he realized the Valtanyana would take Kaliel. His mouth gaped open in anguish as Crestaos neared him, his face concealed by the vastness of his hooded cloak. All Mallorn could see were his eye-whites, crackling white lightning, like storms. Mallorn knew his name, though he would never dare to speak it.

Crestaos's steps carried with them utter precision. He walked with smugness in his posture, the sheer arrogance of his victory leaking off him. He passed Mallorn without a word, without a blow.

Mallorn couldn't lash out at the enemy, unable to stop him from taking the Flame.

"Kaliel!"

He shot up from the wooden chair, knocked the manuscript and teacup on the floor. He jumped to his feet. She was gone.

"No, not—" He shook his head and tried to breath. They hadn't actually taken her. Yet. He had time, but how much? Istar's fears were becoming reality, he could feel it; the danger was near.

Crestaos knew where she was.

· · ·

Sun kissed the treetops, showering Kaliel and Krishani in patches of sparkling light that danced along their forms. There were no nightmares last night; everything was seemingly perfect in their imperfect world. Wind rustled the leaves on the trees and Kaliel moaned as she heard birds chirping around her. She felt Krishani stir beside her and pushed herself off him. Her dress was in the grass beside her and she self-consciously grabbed it and pulled it over her head. She fumbled with the buttons in the back as she watched him, just as he began to wake up.

"Morning," she said.

Krishani opened his eyes and shielded his face from the sun. He grabbed his garments, dressing himself. This was nothing like the waterfall. The cave was concealed; no one ever went there. The forests were so open; anyone could go for a morning walk and happen upon them.

"Morning," he replied.

Kaliel hugged her knees and looked around the forest. She gritted her teeth as she thought about what might happen to them. She felt different, as though there was a buoy supporting her emotions, her strength. Everything was crisp and clear. She understood the songs of the birds, and sensed the presence of small game nearby. She turned to Krishani; he was even more amazing than he had been the night before. She was no longer afraid of him leaving her. That nightmare hadn't come true. She breathed a sigh of relief as he sat beside her and pressed his head into her shoulder.

"What are you thinking?" he said, his voice gravelly and low. It was so sexy.

She smiled and placed her hand on his thigh. It still sent shivers up her spine. She smiled at the familiar feeling, but it seemed even more vibrant than before. She swallowed hard, trying to stifle her desires. There were more pressing matters at hand.

"Home," she breathed. Not Orlondir; that had never been home to her. She wanted to return to Evennses, to live forever in the forests of her childhood. She wanted to show him the lake, and let him listen to the trees that spoke volumes to her. She wished he could meet Desaunius and the other kinfolk. They could sit in the meadow and trace the constellations. They could revel in simpler times and forget that the Lands of Men existed at all.

Krishani looked uneasy as he took her hand in his, lacing his fingers through hers. "I can't return."

Her eyes met his. She had something to say, but the expression on his face changed from concern to confusion.

"Your eyes are still amethyst."

Kaliel raised her eyebrows in amusement. She felt better when her eyes switched colors, when her aura glowed and the Flame inside fought its way to the surface. "I suppose they are. Maybe they'll stay that way." She let out a short laugh as Krishani leaned forward to taste her lips. Shamelessly, she pressed herself into him and he pulled away.

"We have no home," he said. He slumped into the grass as she lay down with her head in his lap.

Hope wasn't lost on her. If anything she felt like it had been restored. There was no boat, no mists, no lake, nothing that could take him away from her. "We'll find a home. Perhaps Desaunius—"

Krishani shook his head. "Desaunius was at the ceremony. She wills that I go."

She pushed herself up on her elbows and looked him in the eyes. She was at a loss for words, Desaunius only wanted happiness for her. This was the opposite of that. "Atara?"

Krishani shook his head again. "It was her order that I take the path."

Her head fell into his lap. "She knows you're the only thing that matters to me." Atara never confronted her about it, but she always stressed the importance of kinship. Kaliel never noticed until then how indifferent Atara was about her own relationship with Istar. Her dreamy presence was sometimes an annoyance, but it was her way of escaping the reality she lived in. She wondered what she really thought of the parable, and the potential for destruction. She rubbed her midsection while trying to find some comfort. Krishani ran his fingers through her hair idly.

"I won't leave," he said.

"They'll force you to."

She sat and tucked her knees to her chest, rocking back and forth. Krishani pulled her hair away from her neck and rubbed her shoulders. She felt his hot breath against the nape of her neck as his lips pressed against it, trying to pull her back into their reverie. He made a trail of kisses down her shoulder; the bittersweet mix of ecstasy and sorrow burned within her. She felt so different, as though she had crossed an invisible barrier and could never go back. Her thoughts drifted to the Great Oak, but with Krishani's hands on her it seemed frivolous. Nothing was ending. This was obviously not the temptation so forewarned about. She pushed away the images of the dream, the fire in the sky. That was so unlikely too. They were safe on Avristar. As long as they didn't leave, nothing bad could ever happen.

"Can we think of that later?" he said as his lips found her chin. He turned her face towards his and kissed her. She gave up and sank into him, knowing there was nothing sweeter than bliss.

"Mallorn," she murmured as his lips moved against hers. She recalled the last time she had seen him, the defense training, the word he drew from her mind. She eyed the grass. "He'll come looking for me."

Krishani kissed her ear. "Cross that bridge when we get there." He wrapped his arm around her torso and pulled her closer to him.

• • •

Mallorn busted the door open and hastily descended the hill towards the stables. Part of him hoped Kaliel fell asleep in the stacks of hay, but another part of him knew that wasn't true. His gray robes dragged along the grass, picking up the morning dew. Without thinking, he tightened the tassel-tipped cord around his waist.

He reached the stables, but there was no sign of Kaliel. The horses spoke to him with their neighs and he nodded. She looked so frightened the last time he saw her. He regretted the defense exercise. How she knew about the Ferryman was none of his business. He cared more about her carelessness, that rebellious spirit that rumbled under her fragility, it set her apart from every apprentice he had ever worked with. Unlike some of the untamable apprentices, Kaliel had a reason for everything she did, though some of those reasons were still shroud in mystery. She was ruled by passion and pressure, it seemed. And she was a Flame. That would always make her unique. Umber neighed and Mallorn turned to listen to the horse's laments.

"Who will leave her?" Umber asked.

"What do you mean?"

"She fell asleep here. When she awoke she said he would leave her. Then she took off into the forest."

Mallorn had only known her for three moons and she seemed melancholy the entire time. She hadn't said a word about anyone in her life.

He shook his head. No time for that; he needed to focus on where she was. He saddled up Umber, and exited through the back of the barn. They sped into a jaunt and Mallorn scanned the forest. There was something different about the energy reflected back at him, as though something else had happened. The light in his dream, it meant something, but he wasn't sure what.

Umber diligently weaved through the trees while Mallorn continued to scan. He felt Kaliel's energy, but when he went to approach her, Umber doubled back over paths they had trodden several times. Mallorn glanced at the sky and noticed the sun was near its midmorning point. That wasn't good. He needed to find her; they needed to be warned. The Valtanyana would strike without notice and they would bring the Daed and an army of creatures with them. Something Mallorn didn't want to think about, the battles in the First Era were always with the Valtanyana's beasts. He wondered what they could have access to now even though most of those races had been destroyed.

Umber seemed frustrated as the trees grew in uneven clusters. Mallorn pulled the reins to the right, leading the horse through a narrow pass between two maples. He scanned the path again. He needed to somehow break the pattern the horse was traveling. He made a sharp left, pulling through a gap between two clusters of trees. Umber broke through the invisible protective shield that housed Kaliel. Mallorn felt the hairs on the back of his neck stand on end.

Umber paused and wended around a cluster of trees that concealed a small meadow in the midst of the forest. As they turned the corner, Mallorn saw a pair of bodies nestled together in the grass. His mouth dropped open with shock as Kaliel looked up from beside someone else. Her eyes met his as the heat of embarrassment and guilt colored her cheeks.

"Kaliel," Mallorn snapped at her. He felt frozen on the horse. *Love?* Elvens didn't fall in love. They were logical creatures. He closed his eyes and recalled Crestaos carrying her away in his arms. He opened his eyes, anger hitting a boiling point as Kaliel ducked her head towards the one lying next to her. He heard the mumblings of a boy.

Mallorn slipped off the horse and stalked away from the scene, unable to witness another moment of their carelessness. His hand moved from his hip to his forehead to his hip again. He couldn't fathom this. Love wasn't forbidden on Avristar, but why had Istar failed to mention it? It should have been impossible for an elven, but Kaliel wasn't *only* elven. She was so much more—a Flame—which made it so much worse. He shook his head as he wondered what other pieces of the story he was missing.

He turned to see Kaliel standing beside Umber. She stroked the horse's mane as she stared at it in wonder, as though she was seeing the lands for the first time.

"You're angry." Her voice didn't waver as she spoke and it was directed more at the horse than at Mallorn.

He stared at her in disbelief. Something was different about her. He looked past her to see the boy standing in the grass. Mallorn couldn't deny the boy had an extraordinary presence, but he had no idea who he was, and the fact that he, too, was elven only made the anger sharpen its blade.

Kaliel glanced at the boy with tenderness. She turned her attention back to Mallorn, locking eyes with his. Mallorn noticed her eyes were amethyst.

The boy stepped through the grass and stood by her side. He seemed careful not to touch her while Mallorn gawked at them.

Mallorn felt the land spinning around him. She was only a child, and she was in danger. How could she act so cavalier? He tried to find his tongue. Every time he looked at her he saw her listless body, her fate stretched before her. It was as though the shadow of the enemy stood at her side instead of the boy, who was obviously very in love with her. Mallorn couldn't help it—the anger, the fear, the anguish made him lose control.

"Crestaos knows!" he hissed at her.

• • •

Kaliel recoiled, alarmed by his words. She never heard the name before, but she knew who Mallorn was talking about. She had seen his face, the sparking white eyes. Her stomach was a sea of nausea as she felt the Flame retreat.

She had never seen Mallorn like this. His eyes said it all: he was livid. He took a long stride towards her and grabbed her by the shoulders, pulling her away from the horse. His gaze knifed into her,

245

conveying the thoughts he couldn't speak out loud without wanting to shout.

Ro tulten lle. He comes for you, he told her.

No. Kaliel stiffened. Her body flushed with heat as she began to tremble. Normally, she would try to find the Flame; that would give her strength. She reached deep down, but the Flame fled o the hidden depths of her soul, and every part of her was afraid.

Avristar will fall. Mallorn dug his nails into her skin as he shared the images of the dream.

Her mind's eye taken over, Kaliel watched as the enemy floated through the forest, her lifeless body stretched across his arms. She gasped and tore away from Mallorn's grip, leaving red marks on her shoulders as she stumbled in the grass. Krishani caught her. His eyes scanned hers before she buried her face in his chest and wrapped her arms around him.

"What did you see?" Krishani asked, tilting her chin up to him.

"He will take me."

He wrapped his arms around her as his eyes shot towards Mallorn.

"Who are you?" Mallorn spat.

"Krishani of Amersil."

"The Ferryman?"

Kaliel felt Krishani stiffen at the words. So did she, but what he was didn't matter so much as what was coming for her.

Mallorn looked from Kaliel to Krishani and back again. "You renounced your duty?"

Kaliel heard Mallorn's thoughts. It was absurd to him. Boys were taught to obey the land first. Love was given when it was permitted by the land. She clutched Krishani's arm and tried to blot out the rest of Mallorn's rapid thought process. Umber let out a short neigh that seemed to have broken the Kiirar's concentration.

Krishani hung his head and pulled Kaliel closer to him. "You wouldn't understand."

She could still hear some of Mallorn's thoughts in her head. She turned to him and Krishani loosened his embrace. She wanted to explain it to the elder, but the words got lost in her throat. "I saw him on the boat," was all she managed to say.

Mallorn went back to pacing. She knew it was too hard for him to understand. Her heart broke a little bit. She kept her secrets from him because she didn't want him to act like the others. She almost told him about Krishani twice, but thought better of it. The way he was acting was worse than any reaction she expected out of Desaunius, Atara, even Luenelle. It was like the conversation she had in the orchard with Pux—love wasn't something she could explain to him. This proved that just like her best friend, he would never understand what she saw in Krishani and, worse, what Krishani saw in her.

"Two separate races, two separate destinies. Never have they loved, never have they been together. It is unheard of. It is an abomination." Anger punctuated every syllable. He was obviously referring to the Ferrymen and the Flames. They were solitary beings, ones that lived and worked alone, the Ferryman especially.

"The lake, the merfolk," Kaliel said. She moved from Krishani, giving him a look that said it was okay. She touched Mallorn's shoulder and the elder whipped around to face her. She took his hand in hers. His eyes were a cloud of confusion, his thoughts indecipherable. He nodded for her to continue. "I only went there to remember him."

She closed her eyes, trying to convey what she felt. Maybe since he could read her mind he would feel it and would understand. Along with her body gliding through the cool waters, she showed him the images she saw on the parchment, the headdress of the Ferryman and the Flame, the chalice she held in her hand. She was desperate to prove to him they were meant to be together, that somewhere in their past they had *already* been together.

Mallorn sunk to the grass. Kaliel knelt in front of him and stopped projecting her thoughts. She pulled her hands from his and watched his memories come back to him. She followed along as fuzzy images of the past whipped by her, a kind of large scroll rushing past that only she could see. Mallorn was stunned. Kaliel hung her head as she let the weight of the revelation hit her. The Valtanyana wreaked havoc in the First Era; they almost destroyed everything that was good about the lands. They were relentless and unstoppable. Her confidence began fading. She kept her eyes locked to his, but the nausea increased and she filled with an equal amount of fear.

Mallorn wiped his eyes and broke out of the reverie. "What happened last night?"

Kaliel felt Krishani's hand on her shoulder. He was only trying to protect her, but he hadn't seen what she had seen. He didn't know what she knew.

Mallorn slowly rose to his feet. "What happened?"

"I awakened," she whispered. The rest was self-explanatory. She hoped.

Krishani cleared his throat. "She's everything to me."

Mallorn glared at him and turned his attention back to Kaliel. "Don't you see what you've caused? Crestaos won't stop until every last living creature on Avristar is dead!"

The words sank into her bones, forcing every part of her to shake. There was nothing worse than that. She had seen it in Mallorn's memories. She knew it from the way the enemy had stared at her in her dreams, the way he took the other Flames like he was plucking flowers from a field. It was enough to make her faint. She felt the warmth of Krishani's arms around her shoulders, but she pushed him away. Tears rolled down her cheeks as she tried to fight the vertigo. She sunk to the ground and hugged her knees to her body as she rocked back and forth. "All he wants is me."

Krishani knelt beside her. He kissed her ear. "I'll die before he has that chance."

"Don't say that," Kaliel said.

"Avristar is so unprepared," Mallorn stated. He sighed and turned to the forest. Even the trees seemed fearful.

"How do we stop this?" Krishani asked.

Mallorn met his gaze. "Stop Crestaos?" He blinked. "I don't even know how he was stopped the first time."

Kaliel coughed. She stopped rocking back and forth. A calm came over her. She reached for Krishani and let him help her up. She was contemplating the same things Mallorn was, hearing his thoughts in the back of her mind. His thought process was incoherent, but clear enough she could pick out details here and there and compare them to stories Desaunius had told her as a child.

There was one story that came readily to mind. It was about Avred, another voice of the land. Her stomach curled in knots as her thoughts were interrupted by the vision of Crestaos carrying her listless body through the trees, to the boats. She never knew that would—or even could—be the alternative: if Krishani didn't go, she would be taken. She tried not to let guilt overcome her, but it was already there, nestling itself against her heart. She had been so selfish, allowing herself to feel something for him when it was obvious it would always come to this. She lost the train of thought with Mallorn, but she glanced at him and he gave a slight nod of his head.

"Awaken Avred," she said. Desaunius told her once about a time when Avristar fought against the Valtanyana, a time when Avristar wasn't the only voice of the land. When she saw Mallorn's mangled expression she knew she had it right. His expression was a cross of wonder and anguish, as though Avred was ominous all on his own.

He nodded slowly. "Aye," he whispered. "Aye, we can ask."

She closed her eyes and entwined her fingers through Krishani's. There was only one other way to make it right, and it was the one thing she never wanted to do. "You can't come with me," she told Krishani. "You have to go to the Lands of Men." She shook; her body unable to take the onslaught of grief that tore at every part of her.

"No, I won't leave your side," he said. His voice firm. His eyes pleaded with her as he repositioned himself on the grass. He tried to pull her to his chest, but she gave him a cold stare.

"There is only one way," Mallorn said, firm.

Kaliel glanced at him, imploring him not to say what he was thinking. The Ferryman's tasks were dreadful; Krishani would probably die. She hated she could hear the Kiirar's thoughts.

Krishani hung his head and nodded. "If it's what she wants."

"It is," she said. She looked at Mallorn for comfort, but there was no compassion coming from him. Her legs were shaky, and she held onto the reins of the horse for balance.

Krishani wrapped his arms around her and forced her to look into his eyes. "This is madness, Kaliel! Please, let me stay with you."

"Someone needs to warn the others," Mallorn said.

Kaliel knew Crestaos would attack full force, and Mallorn was afraid of what to expect.

"Go to Orlondir, warn Istar."

She was thankful that Mallorn was in agreement with her. "You have to warn them. Crestaos won't stop until…" The fear entered her voice again as she disentangled herself from his embrace and wrapped her arms around herself.

"There isn't much time," Mallorn said as he looked at the sky. The sun was pushing past noon and nightfall would fall early. It was Winter Solstice on Avristar, and instead of celebrations, they would be met with an attack, the first attack in centuries.

Krishani pulled her into his arms and placed his lips on her neck. "I'll come back for you, even if I have to kill him myself," he whispered in her ear.

Tremors of anguish washed through Kaliel as she tried to accept her choices. But there was this nagging sense that no matter what they did, the Valtanyana wouldn't be defeated. She closed her eyes and melted into his embrace, his breath hot against her neck. It wasn't comforting.

"Be careful," she said.

Krishani kissed her. "You mean everything to me."

Kaliel felt numb as she kissed him back, trying to control the flood of emotions overwhelming her. "You mean everything to me, too."

He let his arms drop and hung his head.

Rhina grazed a few feet away. Mallorn followed Krishani as he crossed the forest and pulled on the reins of the horse. "Tell Istar the truth," Mallorn said.

Krishani looked at him solemnly as he mounted the horse. He shot a forlorn glance at Kaliel. Mallorn took her hand and helped her mount Umber, then climbed on behind her. Her eyes met Krishani's one last time before Umber trotted through the forests.

"I love you," she mouthed.

"I love you, too," he mouthed back as he pulled the horse towards Orlondir, the last place she wanted him to be.

29-THE WAR

A girl stood in the meadow in Evennses. She was in a long beige dress, her brown hair flapping behind her like a flag, her blazing brown eyes alive and vibrant. Pux hopped off the last rung of the porch step and stopped in his tracks when he saw her. He went to take a step closer, but she noticed and stalked towards him.

"Where are the Elders?" she demanded, her voice full of alarm.

Pux didn't smile at her, but scoffed instead. "On lessons with other apprentices."

"Can you call them back?" Her eyes were wild, and beads of sweat ran down her neck towards her collarbone.

Pux thought for a moment and turned towards the porch. They had a horn, but it was in one of the locked cabinets and he wasn't even supposed to touch the hearth fire let alone the horn. "I don't think…"

"You're one of the older apprentices," the girl said suddenly. She flipped her hair over her shoulder and glared at him. "I need you to do it now."

Pux shrugged. He didn't like arguing with people and so he went into the common room. Strips of daylight caused a dreary glow in the dusty house. He turned to the cabinets along the wall. They kept the horn at the House of Kin for convenience, and because it was the meeting place if there was an emergency. He looked at the lock on the cabinet. It was a puzzle box lock, which required you to move the series of wooden panels into formation to open it. He hadn't tried before, but he was good at puzzle boxes. He narrowed his eyes and began sliding pieces into place. She sat as Pux finished with the lock. Inside was a large seashell, twice the size of his fist.

"Don't touch it," she said, jumping to her feet.

Pux glowered at her, but stepped away from the cabinet. There was no fun in not being able to touch something if he had picked a lock to get to that thing in the first place. Still, he held his hands up in surrender.

"I know how to use it," he said as she neared it.

She shook her head. "It isn't that. It just looks ... breakable."

Pux shrugged as she carefully lifted it out of the cabinet. Her delicate hands curved around the smooth shell as she turned and headed out the door. Pux followed and found her standing in front of the House of Kin, one end of the seashell poised at her lips. She glanced back at him.

"You can cover your ears if you like," she said.

Pux reluctantly placed his hands on his ears as she blew into the seashell and sent a loud crashing noise into the air. The sound reminded him of the merfolk and the stories Kaliel used to tell him about their calls. The noise was met with the familiar shrieks of birds, squirrels and other animals as they ducked for cover. She paused and then let out another loud wail, sending shivers up his spine. She turned back to him and the two marched into the House of Kin. She placed the seashell into the cabinet and sat down on the log.

Pux sat across from her, his arms crossed. "Who are you?"

"Melianna," the girl said with a chirpy tone. It sounded too happy, and her eyes betrayed her. They sat there staring at each other until Grimand shoved his way into the House of Kin.

"There's an emergency?" he asked. What's happened?"

Melianna hung her head. "A war is coming."

Pux clenched his fist the moment she said it and he was gone. He didn't know where he was transporting to this time, but all he could think about was Kaliel. It had been so hard not being able to see her every day, having to wonder about what was going on in Orlondir. That, and he was still angry with that elven boy for having anything to do with her. The confrontation at the waterfall was only the start of things he wanted to say to him. He felt scratchy fabric against his back as the twisting and tumbling through space and time stopped. He sat and looked around. He was in a tower room, a green embroidered rug stretching across the floor. There was a bed and a chest and a bureau, but it was otherwise empty. Kaliel's room? He frowned and got up, looking for something of hers. Finding nothing, he sighed. Maybe she wasn't in Orlondir anymore? Maybe they had sent her away? He cautiously opened the door and saw the familiar corridors to the Elmare Castle in front of him. He recognized the burgundy carpeting and grimaced. He was in the west wing, where the kinfolk of Evennses always stayed during the Fire Festivals.

Pux crept across the floor, keeping his eyes low in case anyone noticed him and thwarted his plans to sneak around. He reached the end of the corridor and glanced at the balconies that interrupted the thick, stone walls. They overlooked the Grand Hall. From where Pux stood he saw the shimmering crystals of the chandelier. He was momentarily distracted by it, but forced himself to turn his attention to the wider hallway. It was empty. He let out a breath of relief and then heard voices coming from the service hall. He quickened his pace towards them, hoping he could find another place to hide. When he was in the stairwell he paused and the hairs on the back of his neck stood on end.

"Hernadette, go to the catacombs. I need you to open the armory." The voice was thick and tense. Pux recognized it immediately as belonging to Istar.

"My lord?" a meek voice replied. It was Hernadette.

"Don't say anything to anyone, there is a war coming."

Pux felt like he was falling. One moment he was on the stairs and the next his face was planted into the stone of the service hall. His hair was ruffled and he was sore but he was otherwise unharmed. There was a surprised scream and a grumble that sounded far away, and he was hauled onto his feet.

Istar glared at him, his eyes full of icy blue storms. "Take this one with you. Get him to help you haul the chests up to the service hall." He didn't wait for Pux to respond. He abruptly turned on his heel and stormed off down the hallway.

Pux didn't know what to think. War hadn't touched Avristar in thousands of years. Suddenly he felt so small and helpless, and worse than that was that he hadn't found Kaliel. Where was she and was she safe? There was a hand on his arm and he flinched.

"Come on," Hernadette said.

Pux didn't say anything as she ushered him towards the catacombs.

. . .

Krishani sped across the rolling hills of Orlondir, his heart beating fast. His mind was clouded with a thousand thoughts, all of them fighting for space in his muddled mind. His strength faltered, threatening to throw him off the horse. Stabs of pain hit his gut with blinding force, causing him to wince. His eyes watered and tears flew into the wind. He snapped the reins and yelled at Rhina, encouraging her to go faster.

Krishani didn't relish the idea of facing Istar. He knew the depth of his elder's disappointment in him would be impossible to accept. He had betrayed Avristar and denied who he was. He should have known Istar would *never* understand love. He stifled the urge to vomit as he neared the stables.

He needed to believe there was a chance Avristar would survive. It was shielded by magic, protected by gargoyles at night, crawling with elders, and housed by the land itself. On Avristar the land was alive, its voice sending guidance to those who lived in her forests. From a purely strategic standpoint, it seemed like a stronghold.

But it would take more than strength to defeat the Valtanyana.

Krishani raked a hand through his hair as he tugged on Rhina's reins and led her into the stables. An eerie quiet that made him stop in his tracks. The Valtanyana would bring an army. He would hit Avristar with everything he had. His body fell limp as he realized he couldn't imagine the foe's arsenal. Would Avristar be strong enough to fight against him?

Krishani pulled Rhina into an empty stall and noticed a young feorn crouching in the corner, fiddling with a piece of metal. At first the shapes made no sense, but as he stared at them, realization hit. It was armor for the horses.

Istar knew about the attack.

The young feorn glanced at Krishani and fearfully dropped the metal at his feet before scuttling away. Krishani crossed the archway and stood in the bustling service hall. More piles of armor and weapons were strewn across the cobblestone floor. Chests drawn up from the catacombs of the Elmare Castle pressed against the walls. They had been cracked open.

Krishani's mouth hung open as kinfolk and servants fled past him, frantically fitting themselves and gathering weapons. It was something he never thought he would ever see on Avristar.

How did they know? he wondered. He knew what came next—anger.

He waited for a familiar face to find him and scold him for his treachery. He ran a hand through his hair and looked at his boots. No matter what, he had to tell them what happened, who they were fighting against.

It was probably better to leave out what they were fighting for. Mallorn's words circled to the fore of his mind: *Tell Istar the truth.* The truth was this was *his* fault. He was to blame for the attack that was coming. He wouldn't remind Istar they were fighting for the Flame. Anything about his love for Kaliel was bound to make him livid. As far as the rest of the inhabitants on Avristar were concerned, they were fighting for their home.

He closed his eyes, hoping Kaliel was okay. He had never heard of Avred, but the way Kaliel and Mallorn made it sound, it would make all the difference. He had confidence she would be safe, wherever she was going, whatever she was planning to do.

There was a familiar set of eyes on him. Krishani glanced up and saw Istar at the end of the hall, his eyes blazing with anger. Adorned in impressive armor and velvet, embroidered cloak with the emblem of Avristar sewn into the fabric. Krishani felt his knees weaken as Istar strode towards him and grabbed his elbow.

"Why did you return?" Istar hissed. His blue eyes were like ice as they bore into him.

Krishani slunk away and looked at the ground. He wanted to tell Istar it was unfair to send him away without saying goodbye, that if he was meant to be the Ferryman, he deserved a chance to make things right with Kaliel first. Everything between them had been left so incomplete. He never could have guessed that seeing her one last time would force the enemies to the shores of Avristar.

"You got what you wanted," Istar said. He gripped Krishani's elbow harder and pulled him up so he had no choice but to look at him.

"The Valtanyana are on their way," Krishani said, unable to quell the restless storm inside him.

Istar threw the elbow down and Krishani fell to his knees from the force. The elder paced in a small circle and faced him again. "You think we did not know? Show your elders more respect. We saw the beacon."

Krishani felt slapped, but it was a better feeling than the guilt threatening to swallow him in self-pity. He took a deep breath and stood, fresh resolve entering his bones. Since he caused the fray, he would do everything he could to change it, to bring peace back to Avristar. He clenched his fist and met Istar's gaze. "How can I help?"

Istar assessed him, grunted, then said, "Arm yourself and fall into the ranks with the others."

30-Village of the Shee

Kaliel pushed herself against Umber's mane as Mallorn coaxed the horse to speed through the trees with as much force as it could muster. Her heart beat in irregular spurts, her grief and sadness mixing into a muddle of thoughts. She knew there was only one thing that would make the foe retreat. She had to get there in time and ask for his help, Avred's help.

The forests thickened and moisture hung in the air. Kaliel took in a hot, humid breath; sputtered and wheezed at the awkward sensation of water in her lungs. She rubbed her torso, hoping to smooth out the pounding nerves racing through her limbs. She breathed in through her nose and exhaled loudly as she nestled into the horse's mane.

Sleep called to her as nightfall neared them. Even though her stomach was in knots she had a willful determination festering in her bones. She *would* stop the Valtanyana. She was unlike the other Flames; they were too aloof to heed the warnings, they were his pawns now. Kaliel refused to belong to him. She ran her hand along the horse's mane. There was only one person in the land she wanted to belong to, and he was fighting this battle as hard as she was.

"We're almost there," Mallorn said as Umber pulled through the vines and palm trees that lined the path. This was a part of Avristar Kaliel knew little about. All of the elders seemed averse to talking about what existed in the northwest corner of the island, as though the existence of Avred was a threat.

Umber followed the narrow path until it came to a dead end. The horse ambled forward and paused at a wall of vines and giant green leaves that stood in the way.

"Kaliel," Mallorn said.

She pushed up, disoriented from the thoughts clouding her mind. Part of her thought about Evennses, Desaunius and Pux, what they would be doing during the battle, but another part was focused on Krishani. Istar had never been lenient; she doubted he would start now. She opened her mouth to say something, but found herself awestruck by the heat emanating through the trees. It made her dizzy and sick. She slid off the horse and pushed the vines out of the way to reveal a small sandy beach winding to the left. The forests dropped away and the stars hung above her. She noticed the phoenix constellation in the sky above the village. She glanced at the lagoon that stretched to the far reaches of the tropical forest. It was shallow and smooth, the stars reflected on its surface.

She looked back at Mallorn. "What is Avred?" Desaunius never told her, but she was clear that in their darkest hour, he had been the only thing that pushed the Valtanyana back.

Mallorn creased his brow and hung his head. "He is the male spirit of the land."

Kaliel let her eyes whisper with hints of anger as she met his blue ones. "What *is* he?" she asked more earnestly, knowing the answer was something that scared all of the elders on Avristar.

Mallorn ran his hand along Umber's neck. "A volcano."

Kaliel gasped. Spasms raked over her flesh. She could face the enemy or face the volcano. She could hide and let Crestaos rip Avristar apart. She could let Krishani face him and die. She felt dizzy with grief. "Will he help?"

"The Shee will tell you that. I don't know."

She frowned. "Why not?"

Mallorn met her gaze. He tried to smooth out the wrinkles in his forehead. "The Shee speak for Avred, the way the Gatekeeper speaks for Avristar."

Kaliel rubbed her arms at the mention of the Gatekeeper. There was nothing she feared more than the voice of Avristar. Even the Valtanyana ran a close second. "I can't ask Avristar for help."

Mallorn didn't say anything.

"Will you speak to the Shee for me?"

He shook his head and took her hands in his. "They need to hear it from you."

Revelation came over her as he moved away and mounted the horse. She was all alone. This was something she would have to do, no one else. No help. No support. No anything.

"Then go to Orlondir!" she shouted, surprised by the tone and volume of her voice. It rose above the monotonous sounds that ran through the forests. Hot tears stung her cheeks and she wiped them away with her palms. She crossed her arms and glanced at the glade. "Make sure Krishani lives."

Mallorn sighed as he pulled Umber away from the village. He gave her a nod, a silent promise, and took off towards the Elmare Castle.

Kaliel dropped her arms at her sides, the weight of the tasks ahead pressing on her heavily. She dragged her feet across the sand and sunk into it. She felt the Shee peeking at her from their holes, her grief reflected in their eyes. She knew she should stop, but she feared they wouldn't help until they knew the extent of her burdens, and the dangerous enemy she didn't have the strength to face. She curled her arms around her chest, trying to hold herself together, and let her sobs echo throughout the village.

• • •

Krishani closed his eyes as the servant girl fitted the armor to his body. It was by no means a perfect fit; the chainmail underneath felt heavy and clammy against his skin. He frowned as she finished, and grabbed his helmet from her hands. He slammed it onto his head, and it didn't fit properly either, a little too big, but he could see through it regardless. He trudged over to the assortment of ancient weapons in a pile on the floor and picked a sword. It was a dull blade. He threw it down and tried again, hoping to find something better. He curled his fingers around a sword closer to the bottom. It was nothing special, but had a hilt that comfortably fit his hand, and a blade that was long and straight. It had an inscription that was nearly worn off the blade, but he couldn't read it.

Krishani nodded to the servant, this would do. He fell into the ranks lining up against the wall. They all looked scared. He was unsure what would happen. It was safe to assume the more experienced kinfolk would lead the battle. There were twelve of them that had returned from the Lands of Men, they would make up the cavalry. He had been so lost in Kaliel he barely noticed the castle gradually getting fuller by the day.

He had no idea what he might have to face. The fear that festered in his stomach created a pseudo sense of courage. He would fight with all the bravery he could muster. It was the least he could do for Kaliel. While he wanted to believe the Valtanyana would lose, Mallorn had been less than encouraging.

He closed his eyes as memories of countless nightmares flickered to the surface. This was no longer a dream. He couldn't simply wake up and shake it off and hope it never came again. They had known the enemy was hunting Kaliel's kind for moons. It seemed as though this battle was inevitable. If it hadn't been his defiance, something else would have made Crestaos find her.

She was that impossible to ignore.

His heart sank as he realized that even if Avristar made it through, there would be more battles in the Lands of Men he would have to fight, and the prospect of Kaliel being with him was unclear.

He wasn't ready to be the Ferryman. His training with Istar covered tournament-style sparring and defensive techniques, like blocking, shielding, protecting, and preventing. Nothing Istar taught him would aid him in battle, and this was the source of the fear that gripped him. Krishani watched while the others fell into ranks, lining up against the left side of the service hall. He closed his eyes as he awaited Istar's command.

"Where is she?" someone said to him.

Krishani looked up. He hadn't even bothered to see who was standing in the hallway with him, but his eyes focused on a feorn through the slits in the helmet. He scowled and looked away, not wanting to answer.

Pux rammed his hand into Krishani's shoulder, apparently trying to shake him up. The feorn looked confused and a little crazy.

"Where is she?" Pux demanded, raising his voice.

"She went to speak with Avred." Krishani dared a glance at the feorn, whose face had grown ashen. Pux stumbled backwards and stopped before he fell into a pile of swords.

"Why did she go there?" he asked, his voice floating through the air like a ghost. He steadied himself and looked around, but there was too much commotion to be concerned. Everyone was talking all at once.

Krishani didn't like how Pux reacted to that. The Brotherhood in Amersil never mentioned Avred. It was a story he was unfamiliar with, but it wasn't something he wanted to fight Mallorn about. He had to trust Kaliel knew what she was doing. "She's trying to help us," he spat back at the feorn. He clenched the sword tighter.

Pux neared him and fell against the stone wall. "I can't believe you let her go to him."

Krishani straightened. "I didn't have a choice. Mallorn sent her."

"Who's Mallorn?" Pux asked, shaking his head. "Desaunius would never let her ..." he trailed off into a coughing fit, and Krishani's muscles coiled at the mention of Kaliel's first mentor.

"Why wouldn't he help?"

"Avred is dangerous," Pux stuttered. The feorn doubled over and crouched to the floor.

Krishani followed even though, with the armor covering him, it was awkward and hard to do. Pux tried to curl himself into a ball. Krishani touched his shoulder and shook him.

"Why is Avred dangerous?" he shouted, but Pux trembled too much. He turned his head to the side and Krishani thought he saw the word form on his lips, no sound. Krishani stood abruptly. The word nestled in his mind caused more fear than the enemy that was threatening to destroy them.

Volcano.

He didn't have time to react or even time to leave as he breathed deeply and fell against the wall. He caught the panicked feorn boy out of the corner of his eye. It appeared to happen slowly: the boy running through the hallway, the screaming, and the way everyone around him reacted to it. He couldn't believe they had so little time to prepare. Half the kinfolk were barely armed; the other half still securing armor to their bodies.

The feorn was clear. "They're coming!"

Adrenaline rushed through him. He pushed the word out of his mind. Pux was delirious and invalid; he didn't need to listen to him. He watched as Istar and a group of men exited through the stables.

He stepped out of line and walked towards the opening, peeking around the corner. Istar mounted Paladin, while the others mounted the remaining horses.

Before he had time to react, Istar commanded the others to charge. The crowded hallways organized themselves and emerged in the rolling hills behind the Elmare Castle. Pux had gotten lost in the mess of kinfolk. Krishani didn't look back to find him.

It was impossible to fight from inside the castle, with no towers, no catapults, no cannons and, worst of all, no archers. They were stuck fighting a sword-and-shield battle against the enemy. Their only hope was that they were better endowed, and not outnumbered. It was possible; the lake forced them to come by boat, which meant they would come in successions.

Krishani followed the last of the kinfolk into the field. Istar and twelve others created a wall of horses while the rest of the kinfolk cowered behind them.

The sun abandoned them as night fell across the sky, stars shining in brilliant pinpricks of light. It was the longest night of the year, Winter Solstice. Cold winds whipped the land, but that was the coldest weather Avristar would allow. Snow had never fallen.

Istar called orders to the two hundred kinfolk gathered. Krishani was surprised by how many had come, but none of them were trained warriors. Maybe the ones perched on the horses were, but even their calm resolve seemed to be weakening. He craned his neck, agitated and restless, he knew the sooner he faced them, the sooner this would be over, and the sooner he could garner some sense of peace. The faint light of the stars glinted off the dark armor that covered the creatures, their skin as black as night. They reminded Krishani of the merfolk, without the fins. They scampered across the land in droves, emerging from the northeast corner of Avristar. "Hold!" Istar bellowed.

Krishani stiffened as he noticed the enemies searching the air for something. He smiled as he saw the wings of one of the gargoyles spread in the air, its claws taking one of the creatures across the field. It lifted the body and climbed into the sky. There was a whoosh as the creature crashed onto the field, dead.

More of them poured forth from the forest.

"Charge!" Istar called.

Fear welled up in Krishani's chest, but his feet broke into a run as the others rushed towards the battlefield.

The creatures didn't yield as they hit the wave of horses. They rushed past them and soon the field was interspersed with creatures, gargoyles and kinfolk.

Krishani raised his sword and wildly swung at first, not realizing how skilled they were at combat. He closed his eyes as he felt the sword connect with metal. He dropped his sword, the force startling him. Eyes open, he swerved out of the way as a gargoyle attacked the creature and picked up his sword again. The creatures were coming from every direction, injuring the kinfolk with ease.

He was glad Kaliel was somewhere else, even if Avred was a volcano. She wasn't strong enough to face the Valtanyana.

Krishani held his ground, gripping the sword in his right hand. He waited until the creature was closer, its lips snarling and his mouth foaming. Nothing like the merfolk and everything like a monster. Krishani thrust forward, the blade sinking through metal. Through the helmet, the midnight-black eyes of the creature widened as it fell. Krishani froze as he waited for the wispy smoke to rise out of the body. There was nothing, and before he could think, he pulled the sword out and continued striking down the creatures around him.

• • •

Empty boats floated along the shores of the waters. They were deserted the moment the battle began. Slow waves rocked them back and forth, water sloshing against wooden hulls. Another boat gracefully glided through the still waters. It hit the grass and slid into the earth.

Crestaos stood at the bow, his hooded cloak hiding his face in shadow. His arms were crossed across his chest as he floated from the boat onto solid land. As he stepped on the ground, the grass turned to ash. He grinned as he breathed in the sweet air of Avristar. The saccharine taste of it was like victory to him. He noted the weathered path to Orlondir, marred by the battle between the creatures and the gargoyles. His senses told him she wasn't there. He turned to the west, feeling her energy along a thin forest path leading into Nandaro. Crestaos smirked as he slithered through the forest, the trees rotting from the inside out as he passed.

31-Winter Solstice

They were unnaturally calm as Kaliel's chest heaved in desperation. Grains of sand stuck to her knees as her fingers curled around bits of damp sand, bringing it to the surface. She ran her hands along the dry grains on top and her sobbing ceased for a moment. All that remained was the sound of her heart pounding in her ears.

The Shee huddled near the edge of the beach, concealing themselves behind broad leaves. Her vision blurred as she gazed out at the glade. If it were more than three feet deep she would have poured herself into its depths, an attempt to calm her battered soul. The Shee were alarmed. She felt their response to her crushing sense of devastation, and their reluctance to help made her feel hopeless. She let out a deep breath and hung her head.

"Ahdunie," someone whispered.

Kaliel looked up, her eyes darting around the village. A small woman merely twelve inches tall shrouded in a silver silk cloth and shimmering silver wings moved towards her. It was the Kiirar of the Shee. She let out a breath and her body slumped into the sand.

"Please," Kaliel whispered. Her thoughts carried the extent of her request. She knew the elder Kiirar understood.

The ancient woman touched her arm and a buzz of energy rushed through her. "Nay child," she said. Her voice rang out like chimes, the words echoing in the air.

Kaliel shuddered. "Please, I need to awaken Avred." There was a gasp that moved through the forest like a gust of wind. Her stomach curled in knots.

"We will not honor your request."

Kaliel gaped at her. "Why not?"

"The volcano is dangerous." The woman moved to the sand and placed her tiny feet in it. They created miniature footsteps as she walked to the bushes where the others gathered.

"What about the battle?" Kaliel tried to control herself, but the emotions festering within her threatened to overload her body. She needed to change the outcome she had caused. She needed to stop the foe.

"Let the Gatekeeper take care of it," the woman said as she passed into the forest.

Kaliel felt sick. She couldn't speak with the Gatekeeper; she knew its answer would hurt her more than she could bear—exile. Since Krishani betrayed Avristar, she couldn't ask the land for help. Aguish built up, a slow ache that burned from the inside out. She squeezed her eyes shut as the woman walked away, her mind a haze of disorientation.

There were footsteps on the ground far away, a rumbling sensation moving through the land.

The battle had begun.

She clenched her fist, nervous. Krishani was in the middle of it.

Please stay alive, she thought.

The rolling hills of Orlondir stretched on without end. In her mind she was taking careful steps across the grass, rising and falling with the folds of the land. Her ivory dress fluttered in the wind, her hair whipped around her, covering her face in strands of white. She clasped her hands together and held them at her chest, her heart sputtering unevenly. She trembled as she found the rise of a hill and saw all the terrible things she had caused stretched before her. The clanging of swords against shields, the battle cries, the fallen bodies. She yelped and drew her arms closer to her chest, her eyes frantically searching the shapes of the kinfolk for Krishani.

Spotting him in the distance, she watched as he swung away from one of the black-skinned creatures and glanced briefly into the hills, his eyes wide with terror. She cringed as another one tackled him from behind and he hastily jabbed his sword into the creature's side.

A gurgle erupted from her throat as she choked on her tears. The vision was like her dreams, vivid and real, as though she was really standing on the hill watching it all. Nothing but grief poured through her. She had to convince the Kiirar to let her awaken Avred. There had to be something she could do to help. All of them were fighting for her. She recognized the kinfolk from Evennses. Even Pux was fighting.

When she opened her eyes she was laying on the sand at the edge of the lagoon. Nothing but quiet, crickets creaking, water lapping up against the shore. She watched a lily pad float across the surface, beautiful, benign. It was the last wisps of life, fleeting, fragile, nonexistent. She furrowed her brow in frustration and squeezed her eyes shut, the battlefield coming into view again, her astral form planted at the top of the hill.

She found Krishani in the midst of the fray, and she watched him fight. Even when her heart felt like it was going to explode, even when screams pierced the air, even when tears made her vision blurry. She watched because she couldn't help them, because she couldn't face what they were facing.

She flushed with heat as the Daed swept across the battlefield, their long flowing cloaks flapping in the wind. She recognized them. Flashes of the flames rolling across one of them crossed her mind. She pushed it away along with the rosy pink eyes of the Flame that was trapped in a little orb, a prisoner to the Valtanyana. As she watched, six of them surround the battlefield, intense apprehension filled her. One of them pulled out a thin blade and stalked towards Krishani.

"Krishani!" she yelped. Her eyes flew open. The wind rippled across the lagoon and rustled her hair. She braced herself, palms against the sand, heaving in and out, the revelation hitting her with full force.

"He'll die," she whispered, her voice hollow.

She glanced at the bushes, hoping the Shee knew what they were putting her through, hoping they heard what she said.

"He will die!" she screamed at them, her tone sharp, cutting.

The bushes rustled and the Kiirar emerged, the little woman keeping her distance as she hung at the edge of the beach. Her silver eyes bore into Kaliel's. "One death does not mean all will perish."

Kaliel growled. She had never heard anything more primitive erupt from her lips, but it escaped from her mouth in a giant roar. She wanted to tackle the Kiirar and force her to give up the secret to awakening Avred. She wanted to rip the trees from their roots and destroy the homes of the Shee. She had never been so angry in all her life. The Flame flooded to the surface, her aura erupting in a shower of amethyst flames that flared off her body like the sun. She felt a pseudo sense of strength and saw her reflection in the lagoon, her eyes a piercing violet.

"Wretched Kiirar!" she spat.

The Shee withdrew to their homes, cowering from the grandeur of her presence.

Kaliel pushed herself up and rested on her knees. She gazed at the water, trying to pull together the pieces of her heart. If she didn't awaken Avred, the enemy that craved to possess her would find her and take her, and everything would be lost. She felt sick at the thought of being his pawn.

"Ro tulten lye," she said quietly into the night. Unsure if the Kiirar heard it, she wanted them to understand her pain. Nothing happened. The night remained quiet. She sat there staring at the lagoon, waiting for Krishani to die. Her stomach dropped. Her body slumped as she hung her head and let the blackness engulf her.

• • •

Krishani was no expert with the enemy. He simply moved when he felt the need to move and thrust his sword when he had a good opportunity. The defensive training finally began to make sense. He could feel the creatures near him and knew when to dodge, duck, lunge and block. It was like a dance, and the more creatures that fell, the better he began to feel.

He closed his eyes and twisted around, his sword piercing the body of another one behind him. He pulled it out and then raised it straight above his head and thrust it into the back of one that was smothering a fallen comrade. Krishani kicked it in the side. His heart lunged as he looked at the face of the kinfolk. It was one of the brothers from Amersil. As hard as they were fighting, the creatures were stronger.

Vertigo set in as he gazed across the battlefield. More were coming from the northeast. The ground was already covered with bodies. He glanced down. Not only were the bodies of the enemy strewn around him, but the bodies of the kinfolk lay beside them. Wispy smoke rose from the kinfolks' bodies and twisted into the sky. Their numbers were dwindling; it would be dumb luck if they won. His eyes found the cavalry and his heart sunk. Only six of them were left.

Another creature rushed him and he listlessly raised his sword. He desperately wanted it to be over. The creature growled and his mind switched back to focusing on the battle. He clutched his sword and when the creature tried to land a blow, he ducked out of the way and stabbed it in the neck. Dark liquid poured out of the wound as the creature fell on the grass.

A horn sounded at the far edge of the field and everything stopped. The creatures scampered away, regrouping, forming a cluster near the opposite end of the field. There was a moan nearby and Krishani glanced around. He saw someone he didn't recognize laying in the grass, his arm covered in blood. He was panting and clutching his chest plate. Krishani offered him his hand and pulled the kinfolk to his feet.

"Thank you," the kinfolk mumbled as he stood and tried to regain himself. Krishani went to say something when a cold wind pulled his attention away.

The Daed emerged from the northeast with elegance, their cloaks sweeping across the land as their muscular forms towered above the creatures. Krishani panicked as he counted six of them. They spread to either side of the battlefield and removed their hoods, revealing elven features and haunting hate-filled eyes. There was no doubt by the way that they carried themselves that they were extremely skilled warriors. He watched as one with tattoos on his face and long dark hair approached Istar.

"Trunya," *the Flame,* one of the Daed hissed.

Istar roared in contempt and kicked him. The Daed was too quick. He slid away from Istar, laughing and turning from the battlefield.

The kinfolk had gathered on one side of the field and were tending to their wounds. Krishani stood with the lot of them and noticed Pux in the crowd, still alive. There was an eerie chill in the air as the Daed withdrew to the edges of the field. Istar rode towards the kinfolk, his mouth working like he was speaking but no sound came out. A shrill cry pierced the sky as the gargoyles overhead became restless. The creatures, seemingly under the hypnosis of the Daed, snapped back to life and the battle continued. Krishani noticed that both groups were quickly losing numbers, even the gargoyles were strewn across the land, licking their wounds.

Krishani raised his sword as the creatures bounded towards him and the kinfolk, the battlefield becoming a mess. This time his eyes followed the Daed with the tattoos on his face. Krishani felt like he was being watched, and as he kicked another of the black-skinned creatures away, the Daed with the tattooed face singled him out. Krishani twisted his sword into another of the creatures and froze. His eyes met with those of the tattooed warrior. Anger washed over him. Tonight, this Daed would die. He just didn't know who or what would kill him.

The Daed pulled out a thin sword and cocked his head to the side, a silent challenge. Krishani gulped and backed away, thinking of Wraynas. He was no match for this enemy. Even if he could focus on anything but Kaliel and her safety, there was no way he would live. His foot slipped on a body and he went careening to the ground. He landed on armor-covered carcasses and lost weapons. He yelped as his hand tread over something hard.

Krishani scrambled to his feet and turned away from the battlefield. There was no way he was strong enough to face a formidable enemy like The Daed. Again, he tripped and tumbled onto his hands and knees, his helmet falling on the ground. He glanced at the stables and relief washed over him. Atara and the other ladies approached the battlefield. He took a deep breath as the elders glided past him and began striking down enemies with their force.

Krishani went to stab another of the creatures when he saw someone riding from the northwest of Avristar. His eyes widened as Mallorn came into view. He ran towards him. Mallorn would know if Kaliel was safe.

"Mallorn!" Krishani shouted as he tried to bring his hand up to wave. His shoulder ached with stitches of pain that shot into the back of his head and made him dizzy. He swayed on his heels and tried to find his balance as the horse neared the battle. Mallorn had a grave expression on his face.

"How is Kaliel?" Krishani asked, forgetting all about the battle behind him, and the enemies that were winning.

Mallorn pressed his lips together. "She's fine, the Shee will help," he answered. "Are you wounded?"

Krishani shook his head. He closed his eyes and tried to force out the crippling feelings of uncertainty and fear weighing him down. It wasn't the blood on the battlefield, but what the Ferryman had said to him. *You will find similar sorry sites I'm sure.* This wasn't a dream. He felt the souls rising out of the bodies, their pain curling around him, forcing him to feel delirious and sick. He wanted to touch their foreheads, allow them safe passage to the Great Hall, but he knew he couldn't go back without endangering himself.

"Are you certain she's safe?" Krishani asked.

Mallorn nodded. "She's going to see Avred. Crestaos won't find her."

Krishani wanted to throw himself into the battle, but the word on Pux's lips stopped him. "Avred isn't a volcano, is he?"

A shadow crossed Mallorn's face, but it was gone as fast as it had appeared. "Avred won't let Crestaos take her."

Krishani nodded, strength flowing into him. He gripped his sword with all the force he could muster and held it aloft. "Then we will end them," he said. It was a promise.

He got his second wind as Mallorn grimaced and followed him into battle.

32-WEED OF TEMPTATION

ittle Flame.

The slithering voice of Crestaos hit her senses with striking magnitude. Kaliel opened her eyes to find herself hovering in the grove near Mallorn's cabin. There was an unnatural chill in the air and she rubbed the tops of her arms with her palms. The grove was where she awakened, where she gave in to the desire racing through her, where she said goodbye to Krishani. She didn't know why she would be having a vision of being there instead of envisioning the battle.

The hairs on the back of her neck stood on end as someone drifted through the trees. As she stumbled to her feet, Crestaos himself moved into the grove, the grass turning to ash. He was impossibly tall, his clothes confused her, long jacket with silver cufflinks and a wide hood covered his features. He had straight, black pants covering what looked like rough leather boots. She cried out as the last memory of Krishani was forever replaced by the image of his silent and unnatural destruction.

I see you.

His voice was like poison as it wafted through the air. She felt like her astral body glowed, showing the fear streaked across her expression. She could never hide how she felt. She glanced at his shadowy form, she could see him and he could see her. He said nothing as he floated towards the Village of the Shee.

Stop! she said, putting as much strength behind the thought as she was able. She fell on her knees and brought her hands to her heart.

Hot pain curled around her as the energy of the enemy pressed against her, crushing her.

Her eyes snapped open and she found herself kneeling on the beach at the glade. She glanced at the bushes; the Kiirar Shee stood there, a worried expression on her face. Kaliel realized she had screamed "Stop!" into the night air. Shivers ran through her as she looked into the small woman's silver eyes.

"He's almost here," Kaliel said.

The Kiirar nodded, understanding. She ducked into the brush and moved deep into the rainforest. Kaliel waited, her body slumped forward as the spasms of pain shot through her. The agony was getting worse as Crestaos neared her. She didn't know how long she could take the feeling of knives stabbing her insides. She coughed involuntarily and tasted blood in her mouth. She spat it on the white sand and winced.

The Kiirar emerged from the brush carrying a dagger half the size of her body. She flew towards the girl and laid it beside her. "The pure one must shed their blood and tears for the mountain to have mercy."

Kaliel didn't think she could feel worse. Yet the quiet chimes of the Kiirar made her scream as the pain lashed at her heart. This pain wasn't caused by the enemy on his way, or because Krishani would die, this pain was caused by the parable she could never escape. *Bloom the weed of temptation and expire the great garden of life.* Liquid caught in her throat and she choked on it.

"I'm the weed," she whispered in disbelief. She pressed her hands into the sand and poured her energy into it. Whispers of the Shee flooded the village as she forced out more energy. Her lungs burst in exasperation, stitches of pain lacing themselves through her. She opened her eyes in frustration and cried at the sight before her. The lagoon was covered in a thick bed of weeds, hundreds of them littering the surface of the water. She growled like a feral animal and pulled her hands out of the sand. She ran her fingers through her hair and clamped around clumps of it as she fought against the madness that threatened to consume her. There was nothing she could do but wait for Crestaos to find her. Nothing she could do to stop them from killing Krishani. Everyone would die, and she would be the Valtanyana's pawn. She fell to the sand and her aura faded.

Numbness washed over Kaliel as she waited. The jolts of pain had become a comforting feeling like the waves of the lake as they lapped against the shore. Sleep was inevitable. Between the onslaughts of pain she felt false comfort. Bitter self-hatred filled her with hopelessness and regret. It was as though Crestaos had already won.

The trees rustled loudly and her eyes shot open. She pushed herself to her knees and gawked at the shivering bushes. It wasn't the enemy. There was a whimper from beyond the trees. She crawled across the beach to investigate the sound. Her hands pushed through the brush and found the ball of fur huddled in the bushes shaking uncontrollably.

"Pux!" she gasped. She tried to stifle the pain and reached for him, pulling him towards her. He was hurt; she smelled blood covering him. She found his hand and yanked him through the brush. He tumbled onto the sand, shaking his head back and forth and swiping at the air. He opened his eyes when he realized he wasn't on the battlefield. He looked relieved.

"Kaliel." His eyes were full of tears. "I—" He grabbed his stomach, covering up the wound that stained the sand a deep crimson. Falling on his knees he looked like he was going to pitch forward. "There were so many of them! I didn't know what to do. I thought of you. I wanted to see you." He was plainly delirious, shocked.

Kaliel gulped, another shock of pain rippling through her as Crestaos drew nearer to them. She couldn't let Pux face him.

"Your side." She knelt over him, running her hands just above his body, unsure where she should touch him. But this wound ... it was so deep he wouldn't survive. Finally, she pushed her hands into the blood, feeling flesh and liquid between her fingers. She hoped she could stop the bleeding.

Pux cried out. Then, barely managing the words, "You were the only one I wanted to see before I died."

Tears stung her eyes as she looked at him. "Me too. It's been so long since I saw you." She pressed her hands harder into the wound as his eyes rolled into the back of his head. Heart pounding, bile licked at her throat as she resisted the urge to vomit. She thought back to the flower, the one she had ran her hands under, and covered in the light

275

of the Flame. It had bounced back to life at her touch. She needed Pux to live. He was never meant to face any of this and yet he was being so strong. She desperately focused within, begging the Flame to erupt. She squeezed her eyes shut and it consumed her.

When she opened her eyes, violet-colored light flowed around her hands, healing the wound on his side. She smiled briefly to herself. "You won't die." She focused harder and the energy intensified, pulling skin together, searing the wound shut. The blood on her hands dried, remaining crusted against her palms. She carefully looked at Pux. He was the same, only with shadows dancing across his face.

"Why are your eyes that color?" he asked when he came to his senses.

Kaliel frowned, she knew what he meant. They must have turned amethyst during the healing. "I'm the Amethyst Flame." She bowed her head and looked away from him, unsure of his reaction.

"They came because of you."

Kaliel moved towards the dagger lying in the sand. She wanted to plunge it into herself to stop the pain. The way he said it made her heart crushed in a way worse than heartache.

She pushed herself onto her knees. "I know."

Pux rubbed his shoulders. "Krishani ..."

She gritted her teeth. Why would he want to berate her about her relationship now? She narrowed her eyes. "Is he safe?"

Pux nodded. "He was fighting when I disappeared from battle. He hasn't got a scratch on him."

She breathed a sigh of relief, but the thought of a sword in his chest still made her shake. She wondered how much time he had left. Hugging her knees to her chest and closing her eyes she remembered when she caught Krishani's attention behind the waterfall, when he saved her from falling in the pond. Every memory stung her heart.

This is what I want, this and nothing else, ever. Krishani's voice soothed her senses. She closed her eyes as a fresh wave of tears streamed down her face. She needed Pux to leave before Crestaos found her, before he got what he wanted.

"You love him more than anything, don't you?" Pux asked.

She nodded. "I do."

Pux had grown; he seemed much wiser than the boy she once knew. "He loves you more than you know."

"I can't help him."

She heard him draw closer.

"I think I understand it, Kaliel. I would do anything to know you were safe and happy. Even if I wasn't sure it would help, I would still do it. Is that what love is?"

Kaliel nodded, ever since she had seen him at Samhain a year ago she thought he would never accept her feelings for Krishani ... but he did. She wiped away the tears and glanced at the dagger on the sand. Pux picked it up and folded it into her hand. He pulled her to her feet and wrapped his arms around her.

"I know he's almost here," he whispered. His looks and mannerisms betrayed, he was much smarter than she gave him credit for. She trembled as she tried to find the words to tell him what was coming for her. No words would explain it. She simply tightened her arms around him. "Run. Hide. He will take your soul," Pux whispered.

The same words the Quartz Flame spoke.

Her mouth fell open. She let her arms fall to her sides as he pulled away.

"I have to go." She glanced behind her at the forest, a thin path wound through the trees, leading to the mountain.

Pux stepped backwards towards the brush. "I'll make sure it's me and not him." He disappeared into thin air.

Without a second thought, she gripped the dagger and fled towards Avred. She hoped it wasn't too late.

• • •

Krishani was lost in the rhythmic dance of the battle, his sword twisting through armor and flesh, bodies dropping. More creatures poured from the northeast, and as the night drew on, it seemed like the battle would never end. Half of the kinfolk were dead, only four of the cavalry remained. Istar and the elders fought with a magnitude that paled in comparison to the vengeful nature of the cloaked beings.

One thing pricked at the corner of his mind, something he hadn't seen yet—where was the foe that was coming for Kaliel?

Krishani spun and kicked one of the creatures in the chest. The force caused him to fall back into a pile of bodies, and as his head collided with hard armor, truth hitting him.

She couldn't hide from Crestaos.

He scrambled to his feet and scanned the battlefield. Mallorn fought atop Umber, the horse dodging blows and loudly neighing over the screams.

Krishani broke into a sprint and leapt into the air, knocking Mallorn clear off Umber's back. He wrestled to his feet as Mallorn shot him a bewildered look.

"You're mad!" Mallorn shouted.

Krishani had no time to respond. He grabbed the reins of the flailing horse and swung onto its back, racing towards the Village of the Shee.

The battle was nothing but a distraction.

Crestaos knew where she was.

33-Awakening

B ranches whipped Kaliel's face as she ran, her lungs aching for air. Her throat felt as though it was on fire as she fought through the forest. Her foot snagged on a root and she hit the ground hard, a prickly bush cutting into her skin as the dirt seeped between her fingers.

Kaliel winced, but overall she felt better the farther she went. She had no idea how long it would take to reach the mouth of the volcano. With the foe on her heels she wasn't sure of time in general. She paused, her hands and knees still pressed into the soil, the dagger firmly pressed against the inside of her right palm.

She took a shaky breath and found her feet. She stood, vertigo sweeping into her as she clawed her way through the vines. The path was overgrown; nobody had used it in thousands of years. Kaliel slowed as she pushed vines and bushes out of her way, trying to reach the volcano and escape Crestaos. She shut her eyes to avoid being whipped in the face by branches and continued darting through the trees. The battle flashed before her, images of her kinfolk, her elders and Krishani caught in the fray. She gritted her teeth as she spotted Pux. He darted out of the way and injured more than executed the enemies. Her gaze snapped to Krishani. He kicked one of the creatures in the chest. She shuddered and opened her eyes, breathing heavily.

Please live, she thought.

The mountain wasn't as steep as she thought it would be. She quickened her pace, pulling herself through the brush that covered most of the mountain in foliage. A new wave of fear and uncertainty surged into her. Crestaos was near; there was no way to avoid him. Her only hope was to awaken Avred and that idea brought scarier thoughts to her mind. What if she was unable to do it? She was the weed. A wave of sickness washed over her as the stabbing pain in her gut resumed. She slowed down, climbing. The trees were a thick mess of moist forest as she trudged on. The path twisted and curved, the mouth of the volcano evading her. Time dragged on as the air thinned.

She gasped and closed her eyes, slipping into a vision. The trees around her disappeared and Crestaos emerged from the brush on the east side of the Village of the Shee. Sand blackened, water sizzled, weeds faded to sickly brown. Her body shook as she watched him desecrate the village. Her knees hit the ground and she clenched her stomach and screamed.

"Stop!"

Crestaos glanced at her astral form hovering near the glade.

"Not until you belong to me," Crestaos said.

Kaliel heard the obsession in his voice. She forced her eyes open. She tried to climb, but every step was a struggle. She plodded up the mountain, desperate to evade the enemy long enough to awaken Avred. There was nothing to stop her muscles from giving out on her, but more importantly there was no way she could allow herself to get so lost on the mountain she would succumb to his wrath. She would find some way out of it; somehow she would help everyone, no matter what it took.

Pux, she missed him already. She never thought it would come to this, his carefree days in Evennses stripped away. Everyone's death would be her fault if she didn't do something. She pulled her eyebrows together and tried not to think of the kinfolk that were already dead. Pux was fighting hard. He could transport, he didn't need to be there. But she knew he wouldn't stop, not until the enemies left and she was safe. He was everything to her in the years she lived in Evennses, a hidden genius. She reveled in the days they spent together in the forests, collecting herbs and playing hide and go seek.

She hit the ground unexpectedly, her face smashing into the mud. A burst of stars danced across her vision then faded. She pushed herself to her knees and rubbed her face. It hurt, but she welcomed it. New pain made the old pain feel less painful.

She closed her eyes and thought back to the first time she met Krishani. She had kept the ice orb until it melted away, something about him she would never forget. He might have been harsh back then, but he knew her better than anyone. He wouldn't stop until Crestaos was dead.

She grimaced as she wrapped her arms around herself and attempted to stop the searing pain in her chest from exploding. She wouldn't get to see how beautiful her life with Krishani would have been. He was always there for her when she least expected it, even when she didn't want him to be. He had comforted her fears about the Great Oak. He wouldn't leave her, and because of it, the Valtanyana were threatening to take her. She gulped. They didn't even want to discuss it. She wasn't a person to them. She was a *thing*. A spasm ripped through her and she winced. She was nothing more than a pawn in their plans. She stood; her knees wobbling as she stepped forward and pushed away the branches. The trees were finally getting shorter.

She pushed strands of hair out of her face as she continued up the mountain. An icy wind blew through the trees and she rubbed her arms. The temperature had dropped considerably. Despite the chill, she thought she was running a fever. Her insides were on fire. She limped forward, ready to collapse.

She broke through the tree line only to reveal a stony incline to the mouth of the volcano. Her eyes moved to the clear sky above, stars gathering together in clusters, providing natural light. She exhaled deeply as she realized it was almost over. She would awaken Avred and save Avristar. The thought made her feel better. The mountain would know what to do. She fell on her knees, scraping against the rock. She winced; the pain wasn't as bad as before, but blood trickled down her knee from a shallow gash. Her stomach heaved involuntarily as she vomited on the rocks. She wiped her mouth with the back of her hand and pushed herself to her feet, carrying her broken body to the top of the plateau, the gaping hole of the volcano.

She remembered the dagger pressed to her right hand. She opened her fingers revealing deep indents in her palm. Taking the dagger with her left hand she summoned the last of her strength. She closed her eyes and heard the song the bards played the evening she danced with

Krishani. Six moons had passed without a single glance at him. She felt the softness of his shirt as her cheek pressed into it. She turned in his arms as the music swelled. It hit the last note and she twirled under his arm before letting his hand drop. She wanted to stay in his embrace forever, but the words of the Great Oak were so adamant.

Temptation.

Kaliel moved the blade to her right hand and sliced into it, drops of blood mixing with her tears as they fell into the chamber of the mountain. She couldn't be the weed of temptation, not when so much rested on this end.

"Awaken, Avred, awaken," she choked.

She closed her eyes in expectation, some sort of sign that it worked, but as moments passed and nothing happened she panicked. The comfort of the mountain faded, the dam broke, and all the emotion and pain being held back flogged her. She hunched forward and fell on her side, her left arm curling around her waist in an attempt to grasp her chest. Her right hand trailed to the edge of the crevasse to prevent her from falling inside the fracture. She felt cold as the land became a dizzy mess of utter silence.

This and nothing else, ever.

Krishani's words reverberated in her mind as she rolled onto her back and looked at the stars. She tried to be optimistic; a few more moments and the mountain would awaken. It would speak to her; it would help her defeat Crestaos. She closed her eyes and tried to calm herself.

Please, Kaliel, Krishani said.

She smiled to herself as her hands gripped the ledge of the water bowl in the lavatory. Her strength faltered, her hand slipped. He caught her and pulled her to him, his lips pressing against hers. She wondered why she gave him such a hard time, why she had spent so long hurting him. Her stomach heaved as she tried to find some words of comfort, but the memories were distorted and messy.

The scene changed and she pressed her back up against the trees at the dead end of the path to the lake in Evennses, breathing a sigh of relief. She tried to imagine the feeling of the cool waters touching her skin as she swam deeper into the lake. The elated feeling it gave her to swim with the merfolk was long gone.

On the mountaintop, she shivered as the wind blew across her skin. She blinked and looked at the stars one last time, the memories of her life flashing before her. It was over; the war would never end, not until Avristar was a wasteland. She pressed her hands to her stomach. Her eyes were dry and scratchy, tears crusted to her skin, eyes fused open. Dehydrated and weak, the searing pain became a mere thought in the back of her mind as it ravaged her insides. There was nothing left to fight against. Even the mere presence of Crestaos made her writhe in agony.

You were the last person I wanted to see before I died.

The thought of Pux crossed her mind as she slid deeper into delirium. She wanted to see all of them alive. She wanted to marry Krishani in the presence of her elders and have them celebrate their union, their rightful union. There was something wrong about her, like she was never meant to be alive in the first place. Life was backwards; an endless monotony of confusion and worry. She was never normal or innocent or invisible. She couldn't have a life that wasn't plagued by disaster if she wanted it. Something would always crave to possess her.

Avred seemed far away, like it had pulled deeper into itself, proof it would remain dormant, deaf to the quiet pleading in her heart, deaf to her desperation.

She fell back into the reverie and her hands brushed along the thin protective trees surrounding the Great Oak. It almost killed her to imagine that part of the forest, to walk amidst its unwilling trees. She stumbled over roots snaking across the path and fell on her hands and knees. Tears escaped her eyes as a frightened cry moved past her lips. Her heart was thumping hard. She didn't want to hear the tree's words again, never again. She pressed her hands to her ears and shook herself away from the tree, trying to drown out its voice with the loudness of her whimpering.

Bloom the weed of temptation and expire the great garden of life.

She lost control, words weaving through her like a poison, twisting, carving out her insides. *Temptation, weed, bloom the weed, expire the garden, weed of temptation, expire the garden, the weed, the weed, the weed.*

"Little flame," Crestaos hissed as he broke through the tree line.

The sound pulled Kaliel back to reality. Her eyes shot open and fixed on the canopy above her. She dug her fingers into the rocks, cursing the mountain for not helping her, cursing herself for being the weed. Her heart thumped unsteadily as she shook against the force of silent lacerations. The last of her courage collapsed. She ran her hands along her stomach as the torture of his nearness threatened to throw her into a coma. Her head fell to the side, her eyes cast across his deathly form.

He lurched towards her, a grin creeping across his face. His piercing white eyes shocked her with their lightning. Even clad in a black jacket, the intensity of his presence leaked off him. Pleasure, obsession, victory—all cascaded off his broad shoulders, his long arms, bony hands, and towering figure.

Kaliel was caught in the devastation of his evident strength, a force she couldn't fight if she tried. Mallorn was right—he would take her.

She fought to scream, but the sound caught in her throat and she choked on it. There was only one thing worse than becoming the Valtanyana's pawn, one thing that hurt more than any of the other things she had felt—Krishani. Instead of him leaving her, she was leaving him. He would be devastated.

Bloom the flower of sacrifice and sustain the great garden in strife.

The Flame burst forth, showering the night in amethyst spires. Her eyes met with the crackling white lightning of Crestaos. She was deathly afraid of him, but the final words of the Great Oak were her salvation.

The force of the Flame exploded out of her, pressing itself through the void of her body. Her heart emitted a sonic boom then stopped beating altogether. The girl gaped as she fought for air and clawed at the ground.

Crestaos towered over her, his palm poised and ready to pull the Flame into an orb, ready to take her.

She smiled at him. Drawing her hands to her chest, she lunged towards the frature in the mountain. The only thing left was the serenity of death. She closed her eyes as life slipped away, a voice sounding in the back of her mind. It was so familiar, so soft, so sure. It was something she would never forget.

This is what I want, this and nothing else, ever.

• • •

Death was the only place Crestaos couldn't follow her. He thundered a cry of anguish as his hand swept across the bare rock. He leaned forward and peered into the mouth of the mountain, but she was gone. His eyes met with the blazing fires of Avred, molten lava quickening as it entered the chamber, furiously threatening to erupt. He stumbled away, cursing under his breath as he retreated. Defeat.

• • •

Kaliel fell, heat wearing away her body, pressing in. She would have screamed if she wasn't out of breath. Flames rolled across her ivory dress, threads catching fire, flame spreading, engulfing her. Regret lanced through her, forcing the fire on the inside to intensify.

She was a thing—a girl—the lines blurred between the two.

She was a thing trying to be a girl.

There were two fires—one that surrounded her and threatened to devour her body in its wrath, and another on the inside, threatening to explode. She was ripping to shreds, splitting apart, filling with fire. Heat consumed her, crawling across her pale white skin. Angry red welts melted into black, crusted skin, pulling away from the bone.

And bone turned to ash.

She didn't scream. Tears evaporated, salt sticking to her lips as sour liquid trickled across her tongue and she gagged at the taste. She gasped as heat flushed into her lungs. It touched the fire on the inside and the reaction made her panic.

All she had left was the Flame.

Blinding white-hot amethyst flames started somewhere near her heart and spread until they encompassed what was left of her body. Violet flames burned her from the inside out, boiling her blood and dissolving her flesh.

The girl she used to be couldn't fight anymore. It pained her to admit the truth and to be unable to stop it. She always felt it on the inside, and she denied it. She was a *girl*, not a weed, not a flower, not a Flame. She clung to the idea of everything that made her corporeal: curls of snow-white hair, a heart beating in her chest, breath flushing in and out of her lungs. She didn't have those things anymore. She felt … nothing.

Remnants of her body hit the magma. The liquid rocks devoured her limbs, leaving the girl she used to be far behind. Two fires became one, amethyst flames snaking through the river of lava, melding, shifting, sizzling with intensity and pressure. She couldn't feel pain anymore. Instead, the Flame took over, replacing everything that was normal about her with everything that was destructive.

She was still conscious, but she didn't want to be. She couldn't speak, couldn't scream, couldn't dance or swim or kiss or hold or feel. The Amethyst Flame was a weapon. Unleashed she could possess, burn, compress, engulf, erupt.

The only thing that kept her from becoming Crestaos's pawn was the way Krishani looked at her. She wanted to be a girl because of him. She was strong enough to fight against the Valtanyana because of him.

She never thought she would have to destroy herself to escape. The lava quickened into the hollow tunnel and she felt the increasing surge. What she was now was much more powerful than what she had been in the body of a girl. She was the lava, she was the rock, she was the Flame.

The only thing she wasn't was the only thing she ever wanted to be.

His.

34-EXPLOSIONS AND SNOW

H ooves pounded as Krishani raced across Orlondir. Umber faltered under him as he traveled over the rolling hills. Everyone was dying around him, and he knew he should have turned back to help, but there was nothing if Kaliel wasn't safe. He deeply regretted ever leaving her side. He should have fled to the village with her. He should have stayed with her like he wanted to. He should have been there to fight off the enemy stalking her. Had she faced him yet? He closed his eyes. It wasn't too late, he tried to convince himself. Not yet.

He whipped the reins, trying to steady the horse, but Umber's frustrated panting got louder. Krishani spotted a gaping hole between the trees in the distance. He steered Umber towards the break, knowing Kaliel was there … somewhere. He could feel her lack of hope. It was as though she knew she would lose.

Someone pulled up beside him on the right, riding with force and agility. The white horse flew alongside him, matching his speed. He caught a flash of the royal cloak that flapped in the wind like a kite. It was Lord Istar. He glanced at him briefly. Paladin charged forward, threatening to overtake him.

Krishani narrowed his eyes and kicked Umber hard, begging the horse to move faster. His worst fears had been realized. Crestaos would find Kaliel, he would take her. He couldn't let that happen. If it wasn't for the rush of adrenaline, the battle and the determination in his heart, he would have collapsed long ago. He pushed away the feelings of dread that gathered in his stomach and pooled in his heart as he broke through the trees. He gritted his teeth as he pushed Umber along the wide path. The horse stumbled as he galloped. Umber expertly jumped over a log but slowed down right after and tried to find his footing. As Krishani whipped the reins in desperation, Istar flew past him and stopped, blocking the way.

"You cannot take this path!" Istar shouted.

"Kaliel needs me!" Krishani screamed as Umber slowed to a stop. He pulled on the reins and tried to pass him, but Paladin was too quick. The stallion raised its front legs and punched at the air. Umber copied the other horse, their hooves threatening to collide. Umber let out a startled neigh as he fell on all fours, fatigued.

"You cannot go to her!" Istar said. He glared at Krishani and the boy knew what he meant. He wanted Krishani to go to the Lands of Men and forget her. Istar's eyes shifted across the forest, but it was quiet around them. The battle cries from Orlondir could barely be heard in the distance.

"The Valtanyana will take her," Krishani said. He seriously needed to be with her, to see her amethyst-filled eyes and snow-white hair. He needed to stop Crestaos. Jolts of pain raced through his body as the enemy neared her, threatened her, hunted her.

"She is not your concern."

"She's ..." All his strength faded. "Please ..."

There was nothing his elder could say that would make him turn from the mountain. If the Valtanyana reached her, if they took her, he would never forgive himself.

"You will be reunited when the danger has passed," Istar said quietly.

"No ... I won't," Krishani said. He didn't care about Istar's oaths; the Lord was already the enemy. He pushed himself up. The adrenaline had worn off, but his determination had been restored with a sorrow he never thought he would have to face. He yanked on the reins and snapped them against the horse's hide forcing Umber to attention. The horse tried to push against Paladin, but Istar stared him down and Umber yelped and rose into the air, throwing Krishani from his back.

The sound of his body hitting the ground echoed through his bones, then a deafening explosion shook every fiber of his being. Molten rock and lava shot into the sky as Krishani got to his knees and watched, dumbfounded.

Then he understood.

"Kaliel!" he howled. He hunched over, the force of her death hitting him like a battering ram. Without warning, he slipped into the blackness, his will giving way to the pain engulfing his body.

Surrender. His thoughts blinded him as he slipped deeper into the abyss.

• • •

It felt like time stopped as the mountain exploded. Istar watched with disbelief, the sky filling with a dark cloud of smoke and ash. The sound echoed throughout Avristar as the mountain took its vengeance.

Avred, he thought with fear and confusion. He turned to Krishani, who was unconscious. Panic engulfed him as he thought of nothing but survival. Kaliel was dead and Krishani was slipping away from the land. He slid off Paladin and rushed to the boy's side, throwing him over the horse. He mounted and kicked Paladin into action. They sped through the forests with precision, dodging fallen trees and branches as the path behind them disappeared in the aftermath.

They broke through trees and slowed to a trot. Snowflakes trickled to the ground like tiny white flags. Dawn seeped over the horizon, but a black storm cloud hung above the land. Paladin shivered as the eruption dissipated. Istar pushed the horse to a trot, hooves crunching the snow.

Shock rippled through Istar as the battlefield came into view. The enemies were gone, the field left a cemetery. Atara knelt, her face buried in her hands, weeping. A thousand thoughts clouded his mind as he neared the Lady of Avristar, but one rose above the others.

Krishani had destroyed Avristar.

SURRENDER

THE FERRYMEN + THE FLAME

BOOK ONE

ALTERNATE ENDING

34-Alternate Ending

They came and went, came and went, from her little glassy chamber. Kaliel watched them, the people in the silvery white coats, their tawny hair caught in buns or shaved close the nape of their necks. They didn't know she could see them, feel them, hear them.

They didn't know.

She felt heavy, her limbs like boulders, her head a dead weight. She had been lying on the linoleum floor for what seemed like forever, the faint glow of crystals creating an artificial light above her. It brightened and dimmed, casting a pale rosy glow over everything.

The sound of feet shuffling made her aware. Her amethyst enflamed eyes shot open and caught the ceiling. One of them loomed into her peripheral vision, their face a blurry mask of shapes and colors blending together. She simpered trying to make them understand, trying to make them stop but they didn't. Something clamped over her arm and it was followed by a slight pinch as a needle slid into her skin. Her stomach heaved involuntarily as they depressed the plunger. Her vision went blurry, her chest crushed, and everything moved in clockwise circles. She trembled involuntarily and tried to scream but she had no voice. Tears escaped the corners of her eyes and slid down her temples, getting lost in her thick white curls of hair. They left the room, the glass door sliding shut and plunged her into the nothingness again. The eerie glowing light, the deadness of her heavy muscles, vertigo taking over her every sense, she couldn't fight it if she tried. All she remembered was his white lightning eyes. Her elder Mallorn on Avristar called him Crestaos, one of the dangerous members of the Valtanyana. His eyes crackled like electrical storms before he drew her into his arms, his bony hands wrapping around her soft flesh like metal shackles. He floated through the forests, past the cabin on the mound belonging to Mallorn. He reached the wooden boats at the edge of the island and dumped her unceremoniously into one of them. They glided away from the shores of her home without a whisper. She tried to cry out, she tried to fight, she tried to escape. She tried to alert the merfolk, but they had long since left the shores of Avristar. Nobody came to her rescue, not even the boy she loved, Krishani of Amersil.

Her heart felt like shattered glass when it came to him. It ached in a succession of beats, forever poisoning her limbs with drought. Her mouth like parchment, her shoulders cold, her heart on fire. The flame inside of her retreated to some unknown place and her eyes became their usual shining emerald.

She went for one last attempt at escape and that was when his bony hand wrapped itself around her forearm, the white lightning crackling as Crestaos's eyes bore into hers. All it took was one more look at him, and Kaliel felt darkness wrap around her like a carpet being pulled out from underneath her. Her strength crashed as she descended into an abyss, unable to move, unable to speak, unable to do anything to rescue herself.

She woke up in the glass chamber, and for days and weeks and maybe moons, she laid there, spread eagle on the floor in her ivory maiden's gown. She spent the better part of her entrapment thinking about Krishani. Was he dead? Was he captured? Did the Daed kill him the way she had seen in her vision? Was he looking for her? Did he leave Avristar? Did the elders force him to the ugly fate of being the Ferryman? Was she ever going to see him again?

The questions went unanswered. Her lips were like rubber, she babbled like an infant when attempting to form coherent sentences, her words slurring together, her lips betraying her. She whimpered and gasped, growled and guffawed but nothing changed the way they treated her. They poked and prodded her until she was bruised and sometimes bloody and then they left.

Injections were the worst. They burned from the inside out forcing an internal struggle in her paralytic state. She couldn't do anything but let the pain run its course, let it burn out to her extremities until she passed out. Longing for Krishani was trumped by the idea of hanging onto consciousness long enough to fight whatever it was they were doing to her.

Kaliel waited for the injection to take effect. She waited, her thoughts swirling, her mind braying for mercy. And then the glass door slid open again and the stench of him hit her nostrils. She didn't need to think about it anymore, he smelled like the burnt tips of fabric combined with the hint of lavender. She thought it was disgusting.

"Little flame," he breathed.

She had heard that voice before, in her mind when she was begging him to stop. He wouldn't stop until she belonged to him. She felt like she had been thrown into the lake in the middle of winter, water stinging her skin as his footsteps paced around her. She felt him kneel at the crown of her head. His hand pressed into her shoulder and shocks ran through her body forcing her to seize involuntarily. Kaliel tasted foam in her mouth as she shook with violent force, the electricity running through her like a wild current. She heard something pop and his hand released her. She slumped, an ache mushrooming through her back.

"I was expecting more from you little flame," he mused as his footsteps recanted.

Kaliel tried to reach out with her hands, she tried to protest, but she couldn't do anything if he was going to leave her there. His hand smacked the interior wall playfully and her eyes widened. The orderlies rushed into the room, one under each of her shoulders, pulling her to her feet. Her knees buckled as her feet bent against the concrete floor. Hands pressed violently into her torso, forcing her to stay upright. Kaliel ran her eyes over Crestaos's form. He was in black polished shoes, black trousers and a mandarin style jacket with silver buttons running down the left hand side. The cuffs were tapered with those same little buds of silver. His face was the product of dismay. Sallow skin spotted with tiny translucent red spots dotted his face. His nose was jagged and long, his cheeks droopy and his eyes sunken into their sockets. He had a high forehead and slicked back stringy white hair. There was a smirk on his colorless lips, and when he spoke, Kaliel noticed his black teeth and tongue. She cringed at the unseemliness of it and avoided his eyes.

"I don't want to hurt you anymore," he said, dead pan.

Kaliel still couldn't find her feet; blighted in her paralytic state, unable to give him a reaction other than the one in her eyes, her shining violet colored eyes. The injections forced the flame to the forefront of her mind. It forced her aura to spark with the faint white violet color Crestaos was addicted to. She hung her head, not wanting to hear lies, not wanting to know what he wanted to do with her, what that mouth wanted to do with her. She would rather crawl out of her body than let him touch her.

Crestaos snapped his fingers and like a marionette on strings, Kaliel snapped to attention. Her body stiffened like a board and there were aches everywhere. Her feet found the ground, and the orderlies eased up on her torso. "Follow me," he said, turning from the door, his shiny shoes clacking on the concrete.

Kaliel was still paralyzed, she couldn't stride forward, nor would she want to if she had control of her body. The orderlies moved her stiff as a board body down the corridor after Crestaos, lights and shadows collecting in strips on the bare concrete. She couldn't glance up to see where the light was coming from, and part of her didn't care. She knew she was far from home, a prisoner in the lands of the Valtanyana, somewhere in the Avristyr quadrant, the Lands of Beasts. Her heart thrummed in her chest, threatening to push her into overdrive, but she tried to keep her calm. This was different than the days of cowardice torture, of neglect, of idle experiments. She wasn't sure what this was.

They carried her until they stopped, Crestaos perched on a ledge, and she was terrified. He looked over his shoulder at her and moved out of the way so she could see what he was looking at. The orderlies pushed her onto the balcony and then she saw it. Kaliel gaped, letting her eyes wash over the rushing rapids, the red rocks, the cages of rabid animals. Crestaos snapped his fingers again and Kaliel pitched forward, the paralysis wearing off in an instant. She fell on her hands and knees and retched. She wiped her mouth with her back of her hand and glanced up at Crestaos.

"Why are you doing this?" she asked; her voice hoarse and raspy.

He sneered and put a hand on the railing. There was movement, rocks sliding out of the way, and people emerging on the ledge of the battlefield. Kaliel pulled herself to her feet and peered over the ledge. Faces she didn't recognize stood shocked. She scanned each of them, looking for something familiar until her eyes found them. Her whole body shook with tremors as she traced the contours of his face, the high cheek bones, the elongated ears, and the full lips, the hairy exterior, the wolf-like feet. She let out a blood curdling scream and fought to throw herself over the balcony. She didn't care if she landed in the molten rock or if she died from the fall.

"Krishani!" she screamed as the orderlies pulled at her arms and legs, an impossibly strong force clamping her back in place. Her head wobbled back and forth as she tried to comprehend. She couldn't believe it. He took Krishani, he took Pux, too. Who else had Crestaos killed? Who else had he imprisoned? Who had lasted long enough to face the battlefield?

Crestaos lowered his lips to her ear and she could smell the rot on his blackened teeth. "I want you to kill them."

Kaliel straightened her back instinctively. Her mouth went dry, her mind blanked, her heart slammed against her ribcage as she thought of the idea of killing her best friend and the only boy she ever loved. She couldn't do it, she wouldn't do it. She would rather destroy herself than destroy the only things she ever loved. She knew what Crestaos wanted her to do, let the Flame loose, let it encompass her until it crushed her. He wanted her to burn everything the way she had in the First Era. He wanted to watch her do it again and again and again. She bit back tears and whined against the pain as Crestaos placed his hand on her shoulder and familiar shockwaves rippled through her.

"I can't," she whispered breathlessly as she stared at the edge of the balcony, unable to see the others gathered below.

Crestaos lifted his hand off her shoulder and pressed his back into the railing of the balcony. He crossed his arms. "You have no choice. You're mine now."

JUSTICE

THE FERRYMEN + THE FLAME

BOOK TWO

SPECIAL PREVIEW

0-THE GREAT LIBRARY

T he truth hurt.

The book hit the floor with a thud and Kemplan leapt out of his large leather chair at the sound. His pipe slipped from his fingers and fell to the floor as he turned in the direction of the sound, exploring the corridor. Another book hit the floor and the old librarian jumped. Only he and the Scryes were allowed to tamper with the books. Even in that capacity the Scryes were only allowed to touch books they had been told to touch. He straightened his back, pulling his vest taut over his round chest. He was going to yell at whoever it was when another stack of books hit the floor. He inhaled sharply and narrowed his eyes as he headed to the nearest row of shelves and peered down its length. It was empty, but his ears perked up when he heard a faint snarl. He quickly rounded the shelves and stopped dead in his tracks, heels digging into the wooden planks.

Tor stood surrounded by a pile of books. His back turned, a cloak concealing the shiny gray scales trailing up and down his humanoid form. He muttered an incantation and held his hands out over the books.

Kemplan gasped as a spark hit the paper, bursting the pile into flames. "No!"

Tor turned, his gray, scaly face contorted in malice. His hood fell around his shoulders, showing off shallow horns, spiked ears, and scaly head. Claws for hands clenched at his sides, and in a swift move he drew Kemplan from the pile of burning books to the wall above the fireplace, catching his throat in the vice grip of his hand.

"What did you do with it?" Tor seethed.

Kemplan struggled to catch his breath as cold reptilian fingers with talon-like hooks dug into his thin flesh. A drop of blood oozed from a wound on his neck; he coughed. "The books ..."

"Forget them. What did you do with the parchment?"

Kemplan's eyes widened at the mention of it. He had forgotten all about the loose page that had fallen from the highest shelves, the one he had thrown so carelessly into the fire. He was bound by the laws of the Great Hall and the law stated he wasn't allowed to destroy anything unless it was by Tor's command. He hadn't even thought of it when he saw the images of the Ferryman and the Flame. He thought it was something that had long been destroyed. He stopped kicking and stared into Tor's gold, lightning-filled eyes. They were like their own self-contained storms, irises spiking with jagged black lines every few seconds.

A growl rumbled in Tor's throat, low and ominous.

"I burned ... it," Kemplan said, barely.

"They found it," Tor said.

Kemplan tore his gaze away from the livid eyes and fought for air. A second later he hit the floor. He coughed and curled into a ball. He didn't want Tor to say their names. He thought the memories of them were long forgotten. It had taken forever to erase them from the Great Library.

"The Valtanyana know," Tor said as he stepped away from Kemplan. He tore into the leather chair with his left hand, thick, clean claw marks marring the soft leather.

Kemplan winced at the destruction. "I never meant to," he began, but his voice was nothing more than a faint whisper.

Tor turned, clenching and unclenching his fist. Kemplan was afraid of what he would do next. When Tor was angry it was hard to stop him from destroying things. "No one can know about the Flames. Erase them from the Great Library and they will fade from existence." He sounded calmer until he opened his fist and a wind storm blew through the library, pulling books off the shelves.

Kemplan pushed himself to his feet, hair blowing back from the gale force of the hurricane wind. Pages flapped around him as he fought to comprehend what was happening. The Great Library contained every book ever written in any land, secret and shared, finished and unfinished, plus the literature of the Scryes, the Great Hall's personal writers. Kemplan watched the maelstrom of books as it swirled into the skies of the library in a tornado of parchment and leather. He held his breath until it was over, wind dying down. Piles of books were strewn across the crowded corridors, tables turned over, chairs knocked down.

Tor snapped his fingers and a controlled blue blaze lit the books, turning each one to ash as the flames ate away the pages.

Kemplan's heart dropped. "What will you do about the Valtanyana?"

Tor glared at him and bowed his head in defeat. It was Kemplan's fault the Valtanyana had the original copy of the prophecy, the very thing that explained without confusion what the Ferryman and the Flame were meant for. He thought about the distant past, the way Tor had defeated the Valtanyana and locked them away. It scared him to know so much and to be able to do so little about it. He could never measure up to Tor's greatness, the choices he had to make, the things he had to sacrifice. He glanced up to find Tor looking reserved and pensive.

"Their fate lies with the Ferryman," Tor said.

THE FERRYMAN + THE FLAME GUIDE

Timelines

First Era (Circa, 250 million years ago - 65 million years ago)

The Lands Across the Stars were in their birth and growth stages, the Valtanyana was forming and gaining more and more power. The Flames were created by Toraque (Tor) of Avrigost, the final member of the Valtanyana. Aria, The Amethyst Flame and the other eight Flames fought against the Valtanyana and won, locking them away in Avrigost.

Second Era (Circa, 65 million years ago – 5000BCE):

Toraque (Tor) of Avrigost takes over as the High King of the Lands of Peace, ruling a Golden Age. Factions of Daed warriors rise up to oppose High King Tor, but without the rest of the Valtanyana backing them, they are nearly powerless. High King Tor gives Aria, The Amethyst Flame and the other eight Flames new lives. Aria is reborn as Kaliel of Evennses.

People

Kemplan (kemm-plan)

The Great Librarian

Kaliel of Evennses (kal-ee-elle)
Aria, The Amethyst Flame from the First Era. She's been reborn as a Child of Avristar, a second chance after all of the destruction in the First Era

Krishani of Amersil (krish-aw-nee of am-er-sill)
Kallow, The Ferryman from the First Era. He's been reborn and sent to Avristar by his ancestors the Tavesin Family from Terra (Earth), the Lands of Men

Pux of Evennses (puhx of evan-sess)
A feorn (half man, half wolf) considered invalid, but in fact is a hidden genius

Adoron of Amersil (a-door-on of am-er-sill)
Child of Avristar, has lived on Avristar all his life. Krishani's first elder

Luenelle of Evennses (Loo-en-elle)
House Master at the House of Kin, Evennses.

Desaunius of Evennses (Dess-aw-nee-us)
High King Tor's former betrothed, originally from Tempia, fled to Avristar due to the wars with the Valtanyana. Kaliel's first mentor.

The Great Oak
Located at the border of Amersil and Evennses, this tree provides guidance to all kinfolk from Evennses and Amersil. Could be considered a Spirit of the Land.

Benir of Amersil (ben-eer of am-er-sill)
Member of the Brotherhood of Amersil, loyal to High King Tor. Krishani's friend

Zulnas of Amersil (zool-nas of am-er-sill)
Member of the Brotherhood of Amersil, loyal to High King Tor.

Lord Istar, Sovereign of Avristar (iss-tar)
Appointed in the First Era, is married to both Avristar herself and Lady Atara. Krishani's second elder.

Lady Atara, Sovereign of Avristar (at-are-ah)
Appointed in the First Era, married to both Avristar herself and Lord Istar. Kaliel's second mentor.

Grimand
Elder in Evennses, Pux's mentor

Sigurd of Amersil (cig-erd of am-er-sill)
One of the Elders in Amersil. Benir's mentor.

Melianna of Handele (Mel-ee-anna)
Daughter of General Handele, leader of the Armies of Avristar. Lady Atara's servant.

Shimma, Daughter of Lord Istar of Avristar (shim-ma)
Witch, half human, half elven. Istar's youngest daughter, grew up in Avristar, escaped to Nimphalls, Lands of Men, returned due to the unrest in those lands.

Kuruny, Daughter of Lord Istar of Avristar (Koo-roo-nee)
Witch, half human, half elven. Istar's daughter, grew up in Avristar, escaped to Nimphalls, Lands of Men, returned due to the hex placed upon her by the humans.

Kazza, Daughter of Lord Istar of Avristar (kaz-za)
Witch, half human, half elven. Istar's eldest daughter, grew up in Avristar, escaped to Nimphalls, Lands of Men, returned due to the growing unrest in those lands.

Hernadette of Avristar (hern-ah-dett)
Lives in the Royal City of Orlondir, feorn, servant, one of the oldest Children of Avristar.

Mallorn the Kiirar (Kee-rawr)
Fled to Avristar from Talanisdir, Lands of Immortals due to the wars with the Valtanyana. Kaliel's last mentor.

Wraynas of Orlondir (Ray-ness)
Feorn. Son of Falnir of Amersil, lives in Hawklin, Orlondir, Isle of Avristar.

Falnir of Orlondir (Fall-near)
Feorn. Wraynas's Father, former Champion in the Armies of Avristar.

The Gatekeeper
The voice of Avristar herself

Davlin Tavesin, The Ferryman of Terra (dahv-lynn)
Krishani's predecessor

Avristar
Has been around since before the First Era, a living, breathing island. She is often known as the Female Spirit of the Land. In Celtic lore she is called the Dan, Bredan, or Dana.

Avred
Has been around since before the First Era, a living, breathing land mass. He is often known as the Male Spirit of the Land. In Celtic lore he is called the Dan, Bredan, or Dana.

Kiirar of the Shee (kee-rawr)
Nameless, lives in the Village of the Shee, speaks on behalf of Avred the Male Spirit of the Land.

Ferrymen / Valkyries
Children from twelve chosen families appointed to keep the Vultures/Wraiths at bay and send souls to the Great Hall. All chosen boys are Ferryman, all chosen girls are Valkyries.

The Valtanyana (The Powers That Be)
A brethren of eleven powerful kings and queens whose only goal is to gain absolute power over the Lands Across the Stars

Crestaos (cress-tae-oss)
Former ruler of Draconis, Lands of Immortals and Lord of the Valtanyana

The Daed
A group of anarchists from the Lands of Men, Lands of Immortals and Lands of Beasts. The loyal followers of the Valtanyana.

The Flames

A collection of nine weapons created to defeat the Valtanyana. Also known as the hand-crafted jewels of the universe, each of them is one of a kind.

Lotesse, Emerald Flame of Innocence (low-tess)

In the First Era she was a seashell, reborn on Nazole in Lands of Immortals, speaks all languages, versed in healing.

Kaliel, Amethyst Flame of the Apocalypse (kal-ee-elle)

In the First Era she was a girl, reborn on Avristar, versed in psychic, healing and transmutation.

Tiki, Carnelian Flame of Healing (tee-kee)

In the First Era she was a lantern, reborn on Terra, Lands of Men, she can absorb darkness, and is versed in healing.

Clamose, Azurite Flame of Knowledge (clam-oh-se)

In the First Era he was a crown, reborn on Nimphalls, Lands of Men, absorbs knowledge through touch, empathic.

Cossisea, The Ruby Flame of War (caws-iss-see-ah)

In the First Era she was a sword, reborn on Zanandir, Lands of Immortals, telekinetic, versed in combat.

Shezeel, The Quartz Flame of Magic (sheh- zeal)

In the First Era she was a wand, reborn on Zanandir, Lands of Immortals, mind control, possession abilities.

Places

Lands Across the Stars (See Map)

The Great Hall

Center of the Universe, often thought of as a hollowed out planet. The Great Library takes up a large part of The Great Hall. Home to High King Tor of the Lands of Peace.

Lands of Peace

All Lands Across the Stars who have pledged allegiance to High King Tor and who benefit from his generosity and protection.

Lands Across the Stars
The Universe (usually meaning planets that are scattered across the sky.)

Lands of Men /Avristar
Home to Humans, Earth is over there somewhere too.

Terra (tara)
Earth, circa 7000BCE

Amaltheia (am-al-thee-ah)
The Obsidian Flame lives here.

Nimphalls (nimb-falls)
Shimma, Kuruny and Kazza lived here.

Arathia (air-ah-thee-ah)
The Armies of Avristar have been here for years, fighting against factions of Daed Warriors.

Matakasha (mat-ah-kash-ah)
One of the seven Lands of Men of the Lands Across the Stars.

Ronannon (rown-an-non)
One of the seven Lands of Men of the Lands Across the Stars.

Seventia (sev-en-sha)
One of the seven Lands of Men of the Lands Across the Stars.

Lands of Immortals /Avrigard
Home to Elvens, Fae, Draconians and other creatures who live for a long time.

Lands of Beasts /Avristyr
Home to demons and nasty creatures.

Angrenoth, The Lands of Beasts (ang-wren-awth)
Home to Mithronians, Goblins, and stronghold of Crestaos, Lord of the Valtanyana

Land of the Dead /Avrigost
That place nobody ever talks about. It used to be known as Land of Kings.

Isle of Avristar (see map)

Orlondir (Oar-lawn-deer)
Royal City, located in the center of the Isle of Avristar.

Elmare Castle (elle-marr-ee)
Located in Orlondir, it's where Fire Festivals happen, and where the Lord and Lady live.

Mount Tirion (teer-ee-on)
Located to the East of Elmare Castle, it is where the Gatekeeper lives and where Avristar herself can be summoned.

The Waterfall
Located at the border of Orlondir and Araraema, it's an unnamed river that leads to the lake surrounding Avristar.

Amersil (am-er-sill)
Located in the West, this is where the handpicked Brothers of Amersil are trained.

Araraema (air-rah-ray-ma)
Located in the East, this is where the handpicked Sisters of Araraema are trained.

Evennses (evan-sess)
Located in the South, this is where the rest of the kinfolk are trained.

House of Kin
Located in Evennses, it is where the kinfolk live while being trained.

Desaunius's Cottage
Located in Evennses, this is her home.

The Lake
Less of a lake and more of a sea, it's endless until someone activates the mists that allow the kinfolk to travel to other lands (like the Lands of Men)

Tolemny (toll-emm-nee)
A sacred site

Beonwyn (bay-on-win)
A sacred tree

Larna (lar-na)
A meadow Krishani burned

Yerbia (yer-bee-ah)
A grove Krishani flooded

Nandaro (nan-daw-row)
Located in the North, it is host to villages of Centaurs, Kiirar, Shee, Feorns, and others who are considered permanent residents of Avristar. They often stay to their own affairs.

Village of the Shee
Located in Nandaro, it is very close to Avred.

Hawklin (hawk-lynn)
One of the towns in the province of Orlondir

Gargoyle's Keep
Located in Nandaro, these are the Northeast shores, where the boats go to and from Avristar. They are often manned by a gargoyle, and most travel at night when gargoyles aren't stone.

Mallorn's Cabin
Located in Nandaro, very close to the Northeast Shores.

The Orchards
Endless rows of apple trees on the southwest side of Elmare Castle

The Tower
A secret place above Kaliel's room at the Elmare Castle

The Catacombs under Elmare Castle
Where they keep the weapons and armor they haven't used in thousands of years

Words on Avristar

Lands
The World (usually meaning a single planet)

Moons
Months

Summers
Years

Kinfolk
People, children

Samhain (sow-ann)
Fire festival held before the beginning of Winter

Beltane (bell-tayne)
Fire festival held before the beginning of Summer

Kiirar (kee-rawr)
Lorekeeper

Ahdunie (ah-done-ee)
Greetings, farewell

Traditions on Avristar

Marry the Land
Literal, meaning to marry Avristar, the Female Spirit of the Land. This is a tradition that occurs around a kinfolk's twenty fifth summer. It ensures the kinfolk protection, signifies adulthood and loyalty to their home.

Journey to the Great Oak
A journey all kinfolk take around their fifteenth summer to learn their destiny. Half the battle is decoding the parables the Great Oak speaks in.

Fire Festival
A festival held at the Elmare Castle in the Royal City of Orlondir during Samhain and Beltane. The idea is that they light bonfires, hold games, a feast, and bless the land.

Children of Avristar
Literal, meaning Children born in thickets of grass, hollows of trees or beds of flowers.

Birthstones
Gifts from the Merfolk for each of the Kinfolk

Creatures on Avristar

Merfolk
Webbed hands and feet, mohawk fins, black skin, gills

Kraken
Giant octopi that live in the deep waters surrounding Avristar

Shee
Six to twelve inches tall, glittery, wings, pale

Centaurs
Part human, part horse

Gargoyles
Bat-like wings, smushed faces, turn to stone in daylight

Umber
The horse Kaliel befriends

The Shee
Six to twelve inches tall, glittery, wings, pale skinned

Drow
Black skinned Elvens, also known as "creatures" simply because my characters didn't know what the technical term for them was.

Constellations seen from Avristar

Phoenix
South part of the sky

Eagle
Northeast part of the sky

Griffin
Intertwined with the wing of the phoenix

Common Destinies for Kinfolk of Avristar

Landkeeper
Kinfolk that will tend to the harvest

Weaver
Kinfolk that will assist and upkeep Avristar's magic

Messenger
Kinfolk that will deliver messages to those in the Lands Across the Stars

Seer
Kinfolk that will divine prophecies, omens and fortunes

Healer
Kinfolk that will be proficient in the healing arts

Lorekeeper
Kinfolk that will keep track of history, laws and lore

Elder
Kinfolk that will train other Kinfolk

Uncommon Destinies for Kinfolk of Avristar

Judge
Kinfolk who will be judges in the Lands of Men

Warrior
Kinfolk who will join the Armies of Avristar

Catalyst
Kinfolk who will bring change to the Lands Across the Stars

Peacemaker
Kinfolk who will bring peace to the Lands Across the Stars

Troublemaker
Kinfolk who will bring mischief to the Lands Across the Stars

Destroyer
Kinfolk who will bring destruction to the Lands Across the Stars

ABOUT THE AUTHOR

 Rhiannon is a booksmith from the North, telling her fantastical tales to unsuspecting folk on mountains, in valleys and mostly in cities around the world. She holds a PhD in Metaphysical Science and Parapsychology, which is to say she happens to know a lot about what goes bump in the night. When she's not writing she's singing karaoke, burning dinner, and hiding her superhero identity. She'd like to own a unicorn one day, as long as it doesn't eat her. You'll find her sipping iced cappuccino despite her allergy to coffee at yafantasyauthor.com

OTHER WORDFIRE TITLES

Be sure to check out the growing list of other great WordFire Press titles at:

www.wordfirepress.com

13754113R00201

Made in the USA
San Bernardino, CA
04 August 2014